BEULAH

Peake Road Press
6316 Peake Road
Macon, Georgia 31210-3960
1-800-747-3016
©2018 by John McKee Sloan
All rights reserved.

Library of Congress Cataloging-in-Publication Data

Names: Sloan, John McKee, 1955- author.
Title: Beulah : a novel / by John McKee Sloan.
Description: Macon, GA : Peake Road Press, [2017]
Identifiers: LCCN 2017050273 | ISBN 9780991574469 (softcover : acid-free
paper)
Subjects: LCSH: Clergy--Fiction. | GSAFD: Christian fiction.
Classification: LCC PS3619.L6274 B48 2018 | DDC 813/.6--dc23
LC record available at https://lccn.loc.gov/2017050273

Kee Sloan

Beulah

A Sequel to *Jabbok*

For McKee and Mary Nell,
who make our lives full and whole

Acknowledgments

I have a lot to be thankful for, and so many people to thank. It's probably best if I don't start naming names; I might overlook somebody you know—I might even forget you! But I do want to thank you, those of you who pick up this book wondering what it might be, and those of you who read my first book and are hoping for something like it.

Since *Jabbok* was released in 2014, people have been asking me how much of the story is true and how much of it is fiction. The story in this book is set in places I've known, with characters based on people in my life. Sometimes the places or people are exaggerated or minimized or blended together. JoJo is an amalgamation of many campers I've loved and learned from in Special Sessions in Mississippi and Alabama. I actually did meet a man sitting on the steps of the parish I was serving who told me he was John the Baptist and wanted to preach in that parish to prepare the way of the Lord.

Beulah is completely based on Tina Brown Sloan, my wife of thirty years and the great love of my life. We met at a summer camp session in Mississippi; she was unsure about being there with a group of exuberant high school kids and a goofy Episcopal priest; we played horseshoes and fell in love. I have a lot to be thankful for, and I certainly want to thank her.

I want to thank all of the parishes I have served, as curate, vicar, priest, chaplain, rector, and now as bishop. Thank you for your support, for your patience, for all of the laughter and tears, and for everything I've learned from you, whether I liked it at the time or not.

I will never write a systematic theology; I could never put together a Summa of the Christian faith. But I can tell stories, and I've been grateful that people have listened to them and read them for a long time now. It's in stories that the writers of the Scriptures point to the glory of God, and in stories that our Lord Jesus invited his followers and friends to see the true nature of God and the potential for humanity.

I hope you find a glimpse of God in this story. If you're looking for something to make you laugh, I hope you'll find it here and laugh out loud as you did when you were a child. If you're looking for something that touches you and brings you to tears, I hope there's something like that in here somewhere and you cry like a baby. If you're looking for something to challenge you or make you angry, I expect you'll find a spot or two in here that will satisfy you there as well. And whether you laugh or cry or nod or shake your head, I hope you'll find something true.

Contents

PRELUDE

After graduating from Becket Seminary right on schedule, with stories to tell and the emotional scars to remind me of them, I was ordained a deacon in the Episcopal Church in May 1981 and a priest in May 1982. With my hard-earned and long-awaited diploma awarding me a master's degree in divinity and my ordination certificates in hand, I still didn't know everything I needed to know, but at least I had enough sense and self-awareness to realize it. I've been learning ever since.

I've never been a particularly good student when the learning had to do with books and lectures and tests, but I've had hundreds of other teachers share their wisdom with me through their lives and stories. One of the best teachers for the first part of my life was the Rev. Jacob J. Jefferson, who taught me the value and challenge of being faithful, how to think honestly, and why it's worth the effort to live in hope. His classroom was down in the woods where he caught catfish, bream, and my imagination, and in his letters to me when I was in college and seminary and he was in prison.

This is the story of my continuing education, in different class-rooms, with three new teachers: JoJo McCain, John Cahill, and especially and most wonderfully, Beulah Grace Bayer.

1

THAT WONDERFUL AND
SCARED MYSTERY

"Excuse me, Father. Could you tell me where young Buddy is?" I recognized the woman asking the question as someone from my childhood there at Holy Trinity; she was shorter and more frail than I'd remembered, and her hair was thinner and bluer than it was when she'd been my first grade teacher. Now she'd come to see me ordained a deacon in the Episcopal Church. I wondered which part of this experience struck me with the most force: that she didn't recognize me, that she called me "Father," or that she was wondering where young Buddy was. Right at that moment it was an existential question of sorts; I was beginning to wonder where that kid was, too.

"Miss Nicholson, it's me," I answered. "I'm Buddy Hinton."

"Oh," she replied, "you're the Hintons' younger boy?"

"Yes, ma'am."

"I know your mama's proud."

"Yes, ma'am, I hope so."

And Mama was, standing across the room with my father and both my sisters, beaming and being congratulated by friends and relatives. I figured they must have been relieved to think I was going to turn out okay after all. I'm sure I'd given them cause to wonder from time to time over my twenty-five years to that point.

Miss Nicholson patted my wrist and said, "Well, just don't go changing everything in the church to suit you."

"No, ma'am. I won't."

"It's not your church, you know."

"Yes, ma'am."

She tottered off toward my parents, and I watched my father lean down to receive her congratulations.

I was standing in the parish hall of Holy Trinity Episcopal Church in Vicksburg, Mississippi, where I'd played as a child, practiced with the choir when I was in high school, and sat through Sunday school classes and youth group programs too many and often too boring to remember.

The minutes were passing, but they were taking their time about it. In only twenty minutes the service would begin, the service in which the Bishop of Mississippi would make me a deacon in the Episcopal Church. It was a beautiful morning in May 1981—a good day, it seemed, to be outside, a good day to be doing something else. It was also the first time I'd ever worn an Anglican clerical collar. The rector of the parish had to show me how to work the buttons, and I was reminded yet again that I was not ready for this, not by a long stretch.

Watching Miss Nicholson talking to my parents, I wondered if she was remembering the day she rapped my knuckles with a wooden ruler for coloring on my desk. Twenty years later, here she was at my ordination, calling me "Father." I didn't know if I was ready to be ordained, or to serve as a deacon, but I was definitely sure I wasn't ready to be called "Father." Just eight years out of high school, standing in a big room crowded with memories and relatives, I found lots of reminders of young Buddy Hinton, but like Miss Nicholson I was having trouble recognizing him at the moment.

I'd finished my classes in seminary, done well enough on all the papers and tests, and worked my way through a poor showing in the dreaded General Ordination Examinations. I'd even negotiated my way through a two-week unexcused absence in the spring of my senior year when I took my old friend Jake to his home to die. The bishop and the dean of the seminary had apparently agreed that

God's Church had survived worse than that through the years, and now I was set to be ordained, a week before graduating from Becket Seminary in South Carolina.

My brother, Lee, was married now; I watched him and his wife herd their energetic toddler toward the rest of the family, joining an impressive array of cousins, aunts and uncles, and my mother's mother from Alabama. My grandfather hadn't been able to come because of his health, but he sent me a message of encouragement and congratulations.

I looked the part of the young cleric, wearing the bright new white alb and rope cincture my liturgy professor had recommended I buy; my mother was cradling the red damask silk stole that she had assembled from a kit she ordered from the liturgical supply catalog and would put over my left shoulder as an outward and visible sign of the diaconate. Dad had taken me to get a suit (the first actual suit I'd ever owned), I'd gotten a haircut that was way too short for me and not nearly short enough for him, and I'd even polished my shoes and put on a shirt as black as midnight. All in all, I looked like somebody you might ordain as a deacon, but . . . .

Well, "but" is a big word.

I wasn't ready. I wasn't smart enough. I didn't know what to say. I'd only preached fifteen or twenty times in my whole life, and wasn't sure any of the sermons were much good. I didn't feel holy in any way. I had questions, fears, and doubts. I wondered if any of the stuff the Church said about God and Jesus was really true. I didn't feel like I wanted to bother anybody else about all this, but I was scared that I wasn't adequate for the job I would be ordained into. To be honest, I wasn't sure if I would ever be ready, at least within my own head.

My friend Ellis Stennis had been an ordained deacon for almost a year now, and in two weeks, he'd be ordained as a priest. He'd taken me out for a drink or two earlier in the week and commiserated with me, understanding my crisis of confidence. He was trying to be helpful, but what I got out of it was this: "You just have to fake it 'til you make it."

And that was the thing: I didn't want to fake it. I didn't want to spend my life blowing smoke at mirrors. If this wasn't true, if it wasn't real, I didn't want anything to do with it. Surely I could do something else for a living; I just had to find something I'd be qualified to do.

The night before the ordination, I'd looked at the service in the Book of Common Prayer to get more familiar with it, to do what I could to ensure that I'd stand in the right place at the right time. I'd read through the ordination service in seminary, but it was hypothetical then, and the night before my ordination it became suddenly and terrifyingly real.

There's a wonderful prayer that concludes the Litany for Ordinations, which includes this petition: "Look favorably on your whole Church, that wonderful and sacred mystery . . . ." The night before I was ordained a deacon, with a cold wave of panic approaching in my emotional forecast along with the hope of reassuring myself through some degree of familiarity with the service, my lying eyes read "that wonderful and *scared* mystery."

My Freudian slip came to mind as I stood in the parish hall, waiting for the service to begin. I wondered wildly whether I could just slip away, retrieve my good hound dog Jabbok, get into my old Mercury Comet, and drive away. But it would turn my mother's pride into shame, Dad would shake his head as if his worst suspicions had been verified, and everybody would be disappointed. Of course I couldn't just drive away. But could I fake being a deacon?

There was a mild commotion in the parish hall as my old friend Neal rolled in. Neal had been my camper at Camp Bratton-Green ten years before, when I'd served as a counselor at a summer camp session for people with mental and physical disabilities. Neal is a compassionate friend I'd been looking forward to seeing. Because of his cerebral palsy, he spends most of his time in a wheelchair.

A path seemed to clear between the two of us, and I walked through the parish hall to hug him and kneel beside his chair. His brother put his tattered cardboard communication board in his lap, and Neal used his right little finger to spell out "proud." I put my face on his shoulder and waited a moment for him to get his arm up and to pat me on the back. It was exactly what I needed, right when I needed it the most.

I led Neal and his brother to the place I'd saved for them just behind the pews reserved for my family. By the time I got back to the parish hall, the rector of the parish was lining up the procession. I was to come in behind the presenters: my parents and siblings and my old friend Trey. We were just ahead of my friend Ellis, the deacon carrying the Gospel Book, who was followed by the preacher, one of the small handful of professors I'd liked in seminary, and, last, the Bishop of Mississippi.

We processed in, and I sat in the front pew between Mom and Dad, just as I had as a child. Miss Mabel and Cornelius Jones were there on the front pew with us, friends of the Rev. Jake Jefferson, who I knew was watching from his place of honor in the Communion of Saints. Across the center aisle I exchanged glances with Trey's wife, Anne, and his parents the Reverend and Mrs. Swayze from the First Baptist Church of Riggsville. Mrs. Swayze looked graceful and comfortable, as I suppose she would anywhere; the Reverend gave the impression of a combatant behind enemy lines, ready for hostilities to break out at any moment. That's sort of how he would look anywhere, too, I realized.

I was presented to the bishop, who sat in his chair at the top of the steps leading into the chancel, and he asked me the questions from the Book of Common Prayer, which also provided me with my responses. All I had to do was to read my lines. But (there's that big word again), being who I am and how I am, I couldn't help thinking about what I was saying, even if my answers had been written centuries before.

The first question the bishop asks of the person being ordained either as a deacon or a priest is, "Will you be loyal to the doctrine, discipline, and worship of Christ as this Church has received them? And will you, in accordance with the canons of this Church, obey your bishop and other ministers who may have authority over you and your work?" The answer at both ordinations is, "I am willing and ready to do so; and I solemnly declare that I do believe the Holy Scriptures of the Old and New Testaments to be the Word of God, and to contain all things necessary to salvation; and I do solemnly engage to conform to the doctrine, discipline, and worship of the Episcopal Church."

That was the exchange of question and answer that my family and the bishop and everyone there heard; the bishop said his lines and I said mine. The question they didn't hear was me wondering what I really meant when I said that the Holy Scriptures are the Word of God. Surely I didn't mean that the Bible was dictated by God and was therefore perfectly plain to be read without critical thinking. I also wondered what I meant when I said that the Scripture contained all things necessary to salvation, as if there wasn't also plenty to learn in God's world among God's people.

I decided to choose to believe what the Prayer Book said, even if I didn't know what it all meant. I answered the question the way I was supposed to, and then I signed a document attesting the same thing; the rector of the parish and Ellis joined my parents, signing as my presenters. I justified me to myself—surely I'd figure out what I meant later.

We sat for the readings, and Trey read the lesson from the first chapter of the Prophet Jeremiah:

> Now the word of the LORD came to me saying, "Before I formed you in the womb I knew you, and before you were born I consecrated you; I appointed you a prophet to the nations." Then I said, "Ah, Lord GOD! Truly I do not know how to speak, for I am only a boy." But the LORD said to me, "Do not say, 'I am only a boy'; for you shall go to all to whom I send you, and you shall speak whatever I command you. Do not be afraid of them, for I am with you to deliver you, says the LORD." Then the LORD put out his hand and touched my mouth; and the LORD said to me, "Now I have put my words in your mouth."

The other readings were read, and the sermon was given: boring but benign, which I assumed was about as good as you could hope for in a situation like this, especially if you invite a professor to preach. After the sermon and the Creed, there were more questions and answers, again scripted in the prayer book.

As you get on an airplane, check into the hospital for a procedure, or buckle yourself into a roller coaster car (I'm told), there's a moment when you have to realize that you are no longer in control of your own life, and all you can do is hope and trust.

I experienced such a moment that morning during the part of the service called The Examination, after the bishop described the work of the deacon as a ministry of servanthood—"At all times, your life and teaching are to show Christ's people that in serving the helpless they are serving Christ himself"—and then said, "My brother, do you believe that you are truly called by God and his Church to the life and work of a deacon?"

Do I believe I am truly called? Do I believe I am called by God to spend my whole life serving others? This was not a question obscured by theological nuance, to be worked out later; this was a simple yes or no question: Is this what I believe I'm supposed to do with my life?

I said, "I believe I am so called," and from that moment on I have no longer been in control of my own life. Since then, all I've ever been able to do is hope and trust.

I answered all the questions just like I was supposed to, and finally the bishop laid his hands on me and said, "Therefore, Father, through Jesus Christ your Son, give your Holy Spirit to Buddy; fill him with grace and power, and make him a deacon in your Church."

And then, all of a sudden, *presto change-o*, nothing happened. I was still just me—I checked—still with the same set of hopes and fears and doubts. The primary difference was that people I'd known my whole life now assumed that I had access to the answers.

The bishop's next line was to ask the Lord to make me "modest and humble." I felt like in this, at least, I had a shot; I've always known I had a lot to be humble about.

The best part of the whole service came when my mother put the red stole over my shoulder, kissed me on the cheek, and whispered, "We're proud of you, sweetheart."

As the bishop and I gave each person a wafer of bread during Communion, the congregation mumbled through "What Wondrous Love Is This," a hymn new to the Episcopal Church—the song my friend Jake used to whistle or hum. I looked up to see Miss Mabel and Cornelius singing strongly, beaming at the connection.

After the bread and wine, after the blessing and the last hymn ("Christ Is Made the Sure Foundation"), I gave the dismissal: "Let us go forth into the world, rejoicing in the power of the Spirit." Even then, I thought, "What a concept: let us go into the world rejoicing!"

2

ESOTERIC THEOLOGY, EXISTENTIAL CONCERNS, AND GHERKINS

The next day was Sunday, and I served as the deacon there at Holy Trinity for the principal service of the day. That afternoon I packed up everything I owned, including a 29-gallon aquarium and three cardboard boxes of comic books, told my parents I'd call them later, and my good dog Jabbok and I drove up the Natchez Trace to Tombigbee, Mississippi, where the bishop had placed me to serve as deacon-in-charge of St. Thomas Episcopal Church, the little mission of the Diocese there. It was tiny, just a couple of handfuls of members, but the bishop was convinced that the area was going to grow rapidly because of its proximity to Memphis. And in fact the little town of Tombigbee did grow exponentially, but did so about ten years after I left.

It was getting close to midnight by the time we arrived at the vicarage, the small house owned by the congregation. Jabbok seemed unusually fretful and eager to get out, so I opened her door and she raced around to the back of the house, barking and whining at the same time. I followed her to find out what was going on, and saw what she'd already smelled: three goats, the largest and most menacing one facing her down through the gate of a cyclone fence.

I found Jabbok's leash in the car and dragged her away from the belligerent livestock so we wouldn't wake our new neighbors before we'd even met them. I didn't really know what to do about goats, and it made me wonder whether I had the right address. Nobody said there would be goats. The key was in the mailbox where the senior warden said it would be, though, so I unlocked the door and went in. The house was more than adequate; it would be years before I learned to say that the appliances were dated or the linoleum needed to be replaced. I was just happy to have a home, goats and all.

I kept Jabbok in the house as I brought in what I would need for the night. It was late and I was tired; we would have to worry about the goats the next day. Mom had put sheets and towels in a box with a pillow and a quilt. The sheets didn't fit the bed provided, but it was more than good enough.

In the morning, Joe (the senior warden) and his wife, Molly, came by to welcome me to Tombigbee and St. Thomas. They didn't know anything about the goats, either, but they knew that Jack Martin, a member of the congregation who lived around the corner, kept goats. My telephone wasn't connected yet, so we couldn't call him, but they felt safe in assuming that these had to be some of Jack's goats. They were still in the backyard, issuing their own goaty sounds and smells, just as confrontational and bellicose as they'd been the night before, but it was comforting to know that they belonged to somebody I was going to know.

It didn't take long to unpack all my worldly goods, especially since I'd left my seminary books at Becket to be picked up when I went back for graduation in a few days. I walked to the church, less than half a mile away, and opened the unlocked door.

It smelled like a place that was only used for about an hour once a week. The pews were old and needed polish or stain or something. Every pew had three or four hand-me-down prayer books—not the recently approved 1979 books, but the well-used and well-loved 1928 books. The bishop had made the church purchase the new prayer books as a condition of getting their very own clergy person; the new books were still safely in their boxes stacked in the tiny sacristy. The Altar Guild had no doubt been working around them and tripping over them for months anticipating my arrival. I wondered if somebody had resented me every time she stubbed her toe.

I would be expected to introduce the congregation to the new Book of Common Prayer, and I realized it was probably safe to assume that they already didn't like it since the boxes were still taped shut.

In the little closet of the cluttered office crammed to the ceiling with old, useless church debris, I found another hand-me-down: an ancient hand-cranked mimeograph machine. It looked like it hadn't been used since the attack on Pearl Harbor. Part of my seminary work study involved using a mimeograph machine to crank out materials for the professors; the remarkable thing about this machine was that it had obviously not been used for years, and that the cylinder was turned by hand rather than by a motor. I knew how to make a stencil, where to add the ink, and how to crank out the copies. It was nice, in the face of all the things I didn't know how to do, to find something I actually—if somewhat accidentally—understood. This one had long been immobilized with age, but I decided to take it home and tinker with it a little, just to see what might happen.

I started lugging it back to the house, wishing I'd brought the car. About halfway there I saw an old green Chevy pickup truck puttering toward me, trailing a fog of burning oil, with three familiar-looking goats in the back. The driver stopped and asked me if I was the new preacher. I told him I was and asked if he was Jack Martin the Goat Man. He laughed and said he was, and then he asked if I needed any help. I started to put the mimeograph machine in the back with the goats, but Jack said they'd probably try to eat it, so I put it on the front seat between us instead and we rattled back to the vicarage.

Jack Martin and his family lived across from the church, around the corner from the vicarage. He'd dropped out of high school to work on the railroad so he could help his mother pay the bills after his father died; his wife, Milla, was a nurse at a big hospital in Memphis. He was a scrapper from start to finish, fiercely loyal to his family, St. Thomas, and Ole Miss. He had worked hard in a variety of jobs for almost all his life and had a knack for mechanical things; he and I and a can of Three-in-One oil got the mimeograph up and cranking in a couple of hours.

Milla came to check on her husband and wound up inviting me to dinner, where I met their two teenage children. It was the first of many invitations for me there, as they took pity on my complete lack of any identifiable domestic skills. Without those good people I would have survived on the only things I knew how to cook: spaghetti with sauce from a jar, hot dogs, grilled cheese sandwiches, and scrambled eggs. I probably wouldn't have starved, but it was a lot more fun this way.

Having dinner with the Martin family, I learned a critically important thing about the ministry of a priest—it's all about relationships. Theology is important, liturgy is important, sermons are important, but if the people like you, if you listen to them talk about their aches and pains, if they know you really care about them, all that other stuff seems to work itself out. Administration and organization are good things, but it's always—always—all about relationships.

My first Sunday at St. Thomas was still a couple of weeks away, but my work there had already begun. We had fried catfish, hush puppies, and French fries, with several extra-cold Budweiser beers in long-neck bottles. The Martin family made me feel like part of their family, and it seemed like I was a little less lost in the big world. For the first time, I thought I might be okay after all.

The following Friday I took Jabbok to stay with the Martins and drove back to Becket's School of Theology for my graduation. It was good to see some of my classmates again, and good to know that this was the last time I would likely ever see some of the others.

A retired bishop from somewhere in Florida gave the baccalaureate address. I remember thinking he was entirely too serious about all of this, preaching joylessly for well over thirty minutes about the impending doom and strife that awaited us in an ineffectual Church seduced by a culture going to hell in a handbasket, without ever cracking even the hint of a smile. I leaned over to my classmate and friend Danny, who would be ordained a deacon the next weekend, and told him about my accidental reading of end of the Litany: "that wonderful and scared mystery." He said, "Definitely scared, but it's not sounding so wonderful." He asked me how it was to be a deacon and I told him about my ordination and moving to Tombigbee, and about finding goats in my backyard, and having catfish with Milla and Jack and their children. He nodded appreciatively and whispered, "That's the church, not some dried-up, angry, bitter old man." I said, "Amen."

During the reception after the service, Professor Sprague came to talk to me as I stood by the punch bowl, and the people who'd been standing there subtly backed away to watch the encounter from a distance.

In my senior year at the seminary, Jake Jefferson, an old friend of mine, had come to visit. He'd just been released from prison because he was dying, but before he'd gone to prison he had been a tent preacher. He had befriended me when I was a little boy, and he'd taught me a lot about faith and hope along the way. In the course of his visit to Becket, he wrangled an invitation to address Professor Sprague's class, and most of the seminary came to hear it. In his sweet, honest way, Jake gave his last sermon, without talking down to anyone or making us feel stupid. Dr. Sprague felt like Jake was trying to upstage him and demanded an apology from me. I refused, and after I'd left the school to take Jake to the Resting Place in Mississippi to die, Dr. Sprague had been forced to leave before the end of the semester to receive counseling in Arizona. He was still officially on leave from the seminary, but he'd been allowed to come back for the graduation, and now he was at the reception looking as haughty as ever. I told myself there was nothing he could do to me now; I was ordained and graduated. This particular alligator had lost his teeth. He didn't extend his hand, and neither did I; I just waited for him to speak to me. After a long moment, he inclined his head and whispered, "I am told I owe you an apology."

I didn't want his apology. I didn't want to punch him in the mouth, either, though I'd enjoyed imagining it more than a few times in the last several months. Quietly, trying to keep it between the two of us, I said, "I don't need an apology. I don't want anything from you."

"Nevertheless," he murmured, "I have been instructed to apologize, so"—he took a deep breath, steeling himself to do something unpleasant, before speaking more loudly than necessary for the benefit of those still paying attention—"I do apologize, Mr. Hinton, for my treatment of you and your friend who came to visit." I didn't say anything, but stared at him blankly, as he continued, "And I wish you both well."

It felt like a slap in my face. Surely he knew that Jake had died; could it be that he hadn't heard? Or was he turning the knife he'd stabbed me with, trying to force me to relive the pain by making me tell him? I've never been prone to violence, but I am a large person; it occurred to me that I could probably reach back and knock the ever-living crap out of this old bastard and completely get away with it. Most of the people standing around, students and faculty, would've cheered. And Sprague deserved it, not just for bullying Jake and me but for intimidating and harassing students for as long as he'd been there.

I stood up straight and stepped closer to him. He shrank away, obviously scared of what I might do. I laughed—I hadn't planned to, but it just came out and it felt good—and declared for those around, "I hope your counseling will help you." I put my cup of punch on the table and walked away. Later that afternoon, after I'd said my goodbyes to the people I thought I would miss, with the Mercury Comet chock full of books and boxes of notes and papers, I left Sprague to his academic swamp and prayed that the next class would fare better than I had.

Back in Tombigbee, I worked for two or three days making stencils for a service bulletin, typing in the day's readings and prayers, and carefully trying to make the service of Morning Prayer from the Rite I traditional service in the new prayer book look like the service from the old prayer book. I used a sermon I'd written in seminary; I don't think it particularly fit in with the lessons, but I'd gotten a good grade on it and I felt like I needed to play it safe.

There were twenty-four people in church that first morning, including me. I was disappointed, but Joe and Jack were excited; they hadn't seen that many people there at one time for years. Jack told me, "That's pretty nearly everybody in the whole congregation, except for Edgar and Nance. Edgar's in the hospital, ain't doing real good."

"But the records show there are ninety-three people on the books!" I protested.

Jack said, with all innocence, "Yeah, but some of them folks is dead or gone." Joe was a little more diplomatic, but he told the same disturbing truth: "Well, I guess some folks that died just never got taken off the records, or the families who've moved away. That's about everybody, though—what you saw this morning."

They didn't know the service we'd used was from the new prayer book, and I didn't tell them. The whole service was printed and folded into a mimeographed pamphlet, and they could sort of follow along in their old books they loved so well. We used the booklet I'd made for months, until I confessed that it was from the new Book of Common Prayer, and by that time most of them had decided I was okay and that it didn't matter anymore. It's all about relationships.

The day after my first service, I was tinkering around the vicarage, trying to look like I had something to do. I'd spent the morning getting the telephone connected and making sure the gas was working. I'd already read the lessons for the next Sunday and started writing a new sermon. I'd cleaned up some of the goat residue from the backyard, and I was thinking I'd have to borrow a lawnmower to cut the grass and try to recycle some of the goat byproducts into fertilizer, when a car pulled into the driveway.

The driver sat crying in her car for a while until I went out and tapped lightly on her window. She said, "I'm sorry to bother you, Father, but my husband has just died, and I need to talk to you about the funeral." It was Nance Suggs, and her husband, Edgar, had died the night before.

There is no right thing to say in response to someone telling you that someone they love has died. Nothing you can say will make it any better. All that junk about God calling him home or her living all the days the Lord gave her is just baloney invented by somebody who felt they ought to have something to say. Death is a part of life that we don't like, but it's still a part of life. It almost never comes when we think we want it to; it's always too soon or too late.

The best thing I'd ever heard was said to me when my father's mother died. I was in seminary in South Carolina, and by the time I could get back to West Mississippi it was the afternoon before the funeral. One of the patient women who'd taught all four of the Hinton children Sunday school greeted me when I came into the funeral home, hugging me and saying, "I just want to say *Hallelujah* for your grandmother!" At the time I thought it seemed insensitive or odd, but I'd had a lot of time to think about it since, and I came to believe it's about the best thing I could ever say to a grieving person.

I told Mrs. Suggs, "I am so sorry about your husband. I know it's a painful time for you and your family. But I also want to say *Hallelujah* for him. He's not suffering anymore, and he is with our Lord now."

Then I added, "It's times like this that we have to decide whether we believe all the stuff we say in church, about hope and resurrection."

She seemed a little startled, but she thought about it for a moment before gathering herself enough to reply, "Thank you, Father."

I'd have a pickup full of nickels if I had a one for every time I've invited somebody to call me Buddy instead of "Father," but if you took a nickel away for every time they kept calling me "Father" anyway, I'd probably be broke all the same. I appreciate the respect for the ordained person, but if it is all about relationships, and I really think it is, then putting clergy up on pedestals and behaving as if they're on a higher level can only get in the way.

"Just call me Buddy, Mrs. Suggs."

I invited her in and got her a glass of water, all the hospitality I was able to offer her. We talked about when the funeral could be, and which readings and hymns she wanted. She wanted to wait until their son and his children could get there from Houston, and I assured her that would be fine.

She had some business affairs to tend to, so I gave her my brand-new telephone number and asked her to call if I could do anything to help.

The next morning she called to tell me that her son and grandchildren would be arriving that afternoon, flying in from Texas. She wanted something but was hesitant to tell me. So I asked, "Do you need me to pick them up at the airport?"

She answered, "No, Father." There was a deep breath on the other end of the line, and then she said, "I need you to take Carrie and Walt to see their grandfather."

I had not imagined anything like this. I wondered how old the children were and whether it would be a good idea to take them to see the body of their dead grandfather; I wondered why the children's parents or grandmother weren't doing this. Then, while I was wondering how I could manage it and whether I should ask any of those questions, she answered some of them. "Their father is getting a divorce, poor little things, and his wife is a mean-spirited shrew even when she's happy, which is almost never. She announced last night that she can't possibly be here for her children, now when they need her the most. And my poor Eddie is a total wreck. He can't face Edgar's corpse all laid out right now."

I felt awkward about viewing the body. I was twenty-five years old, and the only two dead people I'd ever seen were my father's mother, whose casket was closed, and my friend Jake, who didn't have a casket at all. Something about meeting someone after he'd died made this especially awkward for me, and I was worried that my clumsy apprehension would add to what was already shaping up to be an unhappy moment for the grandchildren of the deceased.

We arranged a time that afternoon for me to come and get the children at the house. When I got there, I met nine-year-old Carrie and six-year-old Walt. I also met their father, Eddie, a chubby computer programmer with no discernible social skills, whose pale, clammy hand trembled when he held it out for me to shake.

Mrs. Suggs told me that the children's mother, who couldn't be bothered to be there, was quite insistent that the children see their grandfather. She was apparently insistent about all of her views and opinions and felt very strongly that her children should face reality squarely, rather than be "shielded by the fiction or fairy tales" concerning death. According to their mother, Mr. Suggs had not passed on or gone to heaven, he was dead, and they needed to see his lifeless body to know the truth of it. By the time I met them, it had become important to Carrie and Walt, too, not because they wanted to see their grandfather's body, but because they were generally desperate to do what their mother wanted them to do. Mrs. Suggs told me she would go to the funeral home with us but that she herself could not go in to see her husband. "I don't want to remember him like that," she whispered.

So we drove to the funeral home and went in. Mrs. Suggs sat in the lobby and I said to the children, "Are you ready?" They both looked at their grandmother, and at each other, and I bent low to tell them, "You don't have to do this."

"No," answered Carrie firmly. "Let's go."

The sign, one of those black racks with white movable plastic letters, directed us to the parlor where we'd find Mr. Suggs and the reality of death waiting for us. We walked down the hall, all three of us nervous and scared.

In seminary I'd had several sessions in my Pastoral Theology class that dealt with dying and grief. It was almost all I knew about death, and I was terribly aware that it wasn't sufficient for the moment. Still, it was all I had to work with. I was trying to remember what the professor said and what the page in the textbook looked like when we came into the parlor and saw the casket.

We walked over to it, and I saw Mr. Suggs. I'd never met him in life, and I didn't know what he was supposed to look like, but I was relieved that he at least looked like a person. I don't know what I'd expected, but I was glad that he just looked like a guy, laid out in his best suit, as if he might take a deep breath and sit up at any moment. I looked a little more closely and saw that he had a lot of makeup on, that he really looked more like a mannequin or an escapee from a wax museum. It seemed to me, as it has seemed every time I've seen a corpse since, that there was something missing. I reached into the coffin, made the sign of the Cross on his forehead with my thumb, and said, "The Lord bless you and keep you and make his face shine upon you."

Into my already crowded mind, filled with my own insecurities, esoteric theology, and existential concerns, another issue demanded some attention: the casket was too high for the children to see into it.

They looked up at me and I asked Carrie, "Can I pick you up so you can see in?" She nodded, some of her earlier resolve fraying at the edges, and I picked her up and put her on my hip. When she saw her grandfather, she gasped and stiffened a little. We stood there for a long moment until she whispered, "Okay, put me down."

I did, and I asked Walt if he wanted me to pick him up, too. As I was lifting him, Carrie announced, "It's okay, Walt. That's not really Grandpa."

My first thought was that I'd taken these poor kids into the wrong room. But no, there were only two parlors; we'd passed Parlor A to get to this one and it had been empty, and the sign by the door of Parlor B had assured any and all that this was Mr. Walter Edgar Suggs, when he'd been born and when he'd died. This was Mr. Suggs, no denying it.

I figured this had to be the denial of death we'd talked about in seminary. I was trying to remember the five stages of grief from class: denial, anger, trying to make deals with God, and . . . those other two. Well, hang on, I knew them all for the test. Suddenly, Carrie, trying to reassure her younger brother, told me and Walt everything any of us need to know about death and grief and hope: "That's just his body. Grandpa's up in heaven with Jesus."

Mr. Suggs's funeral went well, although the funeral home people were somewhat confused about who's in charge when the funeral is at a church, but we worked it out. Eddie's wife, Laura, made an entrance just before the service, apparently as drawn to family drama as a June bug is to front porch lights. She gathered her "poor darlings" to her as if she was saving the day, but there was no crisis for her to avert. Mrs. Suggs the senior was polite but cool to Mrs. Suggs the junior, who was condescendingly aware that she was in rural Mississippi, clearly not where she thought she belonged. I agreed with her about that; anybody can visit, but it takes some grace to belong in the Deep South.

The weeks and months that followed were happy days for me. I learned a lot about my new role and about people's expectations of clergy. Some days I walked around the town, not strategically but out of curiosity and boredom. People wanted to meet me, to welcome me to town; some people wanted to argue a religious point or ask me about something they'd read or heard, but most of them just wanted to know who I was.

A woman named Rita Knutson started coming to church with a friend. She told me she'd grown up in Philadelphia in the Catholic Church; she and her husband, Carl, had moved to Millington, Tennessee, with the Navy and found their way to Tombigbee after he'd retired. She said she'd tried to go to church on base but it had never been what she wanted, and that her husband never went to church at all except for funerals.

"Not even for weddings?"

"Well, our son's wedding a few years ago was in the base chapel. Carl went and griped the whole time. I'm hoping our daughter will elope, or marry a Buddhist." She said the last with a twinkle in her eye, inviting me to think she might be joking.

A few weeks after I met her, she invited me to their home on a Thursday night for supper and Scrabble. They had a niece, she said, whom they'd like me to meet. I was limited in what I knew how to cook, even though I'd added macaroni and cheese from a box to my repertoire. I was always glad for an invitation to eat out, even if it came with an arranged meeting with a young lady, which I regarded with a mix of dread and excitement.

Captain Knutson met me at the door, his crew cut and upright bearing making him look as if he'd just stepped off the bridge of a ship under his command even though he'd been retired for almost a decade. He asked if I would have a drink and I asked for a beer. He laughed and said, "I thought you people only drank Scotch or something." I'd never had Scotch, but it didn't seem like the time to mention it. He introduced me to his niece Julia, who was pretty in a giggly sort of way, one of those girls who made a point of not knowing much about anything and wanted to be sure everybody knew it.

We sat down at their table and had a salad first, and when Rita brought the spaghetti the Captain cut his into tiny half-inch pieces. Rita saw me watching the operation and informed me that Carl loves spaghetti, and they had it once a week. He said, "If I was in charge of this house, these noodles would all be reduced to manageable size before they're boiled." His wife, I noted, didn't cut hers at all, instead preferring to twirl them on her fork as I did. Julia giggled and announced that she wasn't sure how she should eat spaghetti, and Rita suggested that she could cut it just once or twice, sort of as a compromise.

After supper we played Scrabble. I did all right in the first game but lost. As it turns out, the Captain and Mrs. Knutson were both accomplished players. Rita played in Scrabble tournaments and had her own Scrabble dictionary. I didn't realize until the second game that they were intensely competitive. By sheer dumb luck I was able to use all seven of my tiles to make the word "gherkins," using an E Julia had carelessly placed between the two triple word score tiles on the lower left-hand side, and a blank tile for the N. The Captain was dubious, but Rita was delighted, informing us that this was very rare and was called a "triple-triple." The appropriate way to score such an event was to count up the letter values, including the double letter score for the K, and multiply that times nine, then add fifty more for using all seven tiles, which totaled 230 points on one word.

It was a moment that became legend, at least in that house. After that, we played Scrabble almost every Thursday night, and every time I went over, before the spaghetti was served Carl and I had a beer and a little dill pickle—a gherkin. Julia came back for my second visit there, but she stopped after that; Scrabble was clearly not her strong suit, and apparently she wasn't interested enough in me to endure the game week after week. Years later she married a dentist in Germantown, and I was honored to perform the ceremony.

On those Thursday nights, we always had spaghetti; Carl always told us that if he was in charge of the house it would be cut before it was boiled; we laughed every time. I asked about his service in the Navy, and he told me that most of his time was spent as an instructor, both of naval history and strategy. Rita asked about St. Thomas and about the Episcopal Church. We actually talked about that quite a bit, and I realized it was mostly for Carl's benefit. He stayed on the sidelines in these conversations, but it seemed like he was listening intently, in spite of himself.

One week the conversation touched on the plans for my ordination to the priesthood that spring. I told them I would be ordained a priest in May, and that the service would be there at little St. Thomas. The consequence was that, as a priest, I could offer the sacrament of the Eucharist; I told them I was looking forward to that. Carl pronounced that he didn't think Rita should be receiving Communion in the Episcopal Church anyway, because she was still on the books at the Catholic Church. I told him I didn't care about that, and I didn't think God cared, either. Rita asked about becoming an Episcopalian, and I told her she would have to be received. Since she'd already been confirmed by a bishop in the Roman Church, our bishop could receive her confirmation when he came to visit. She asked if there were classes or something, and I told her we could have some conversations about it if she wanted to. Carl proclaimed that he would not be interested in that, and before he could build and fortify his defenses, I told him that was fine—he didn't have to. I didn't recognize the look he gave me then; much later I understood that he had lived most of his life doing what he was told to do, and the freedom *not* to do a thing meant he was also free to do it if he wanted. It was a pivotal moment for him, one that I didn't even see.

One Thursday night in December Captain Carl suggested that he wanted to make a gift to the church. I told him that any donation would be most welcome, assuming he had an eye on the end of the fiscal year and wanted to make a charitable contribution for his taxes. Instead he took me into their large well-ordered attic and showed me an old electric organ that had belonged to his sister, who'd played for a Methodist church in Ohio where he'd grown up. He said he couldn't bear the idea of the organ being sold or given away when she'd died a few years before, so he'd brought it down to Mississippi after her funeral. Neither he nor Rita played the organ, he said, and they had discussed it and wanted it to go to the church.

The next day, Jack Martin brought his trusty green Chevy pickup truck, and we carefully loaded the electric organ into its bed, unloading it at St. Thomas. There were a couple of fuses to replace, but Jack knew an electrician who did well with that sort of thing, and it was up and running within the week.

On Christmas Eve of 1981, we had thirty-three people in church for the midnight service, the largest congregation since the difficulties with the ordination of women and the new Book of Common Prayer had ripped the Episcopal Church into quarrelsome factions. When Milla's sister, who played the piano but had warned me repeatedly that she wasn't any good on an organ, played "Silent Night," the night indeed became holy, and familiar words were new: "Glories stream from heaven afar, Heavenly hosts sing Alleluia, Christ the Savior is born! Christ the Savior is born."

You're a Good Kid

One Sunday morning in February, as I looked out at the little congregation scattered in the pews listening to me read the passage from the Gospel of Mark, I realized I'd written the wrong sermon. It wasn't a bad sermon. I felt like it would probably have earned a B in seminary, but it wasn't what I wanted to say. The faces in the pews were anticipating being bored; it's what they had learned to expect from preachers through the years, and another pretentiously academic mind-numbing sermon from me probably wouldn't hurt anything at all.

Even worse than them expecting to be bored, I was expecting to bore them. Surely if the preacher is bored with the sermon, the congregation doesn't stand a chance. I'd been preaching at St. Thomas for about eight months, and things were going well, but I was already getting tired of being boring.

The passage from Mark was the reading appointed in the Lectionary for the Fifth Sunday after the Epiphany: Mark 1:29-39. Just after the story of the calling of the first disciples, St. Mark tells about Jesus going to Simon's home in Capernaum, where Simon's mother-in-law was sick with a fever. After Jesus healed her, apparently word got out that there was a healer at Simon's house, because the rest of the town came to visit, with all their aches and pains. As Mark wrote it, "the whole city was gathered around the door. And he cured many who were sick with various diseases, and cast out many demons . . . ."

Then, Mark wrote, "In the morning, while it was still very dark, he got up and went out to a deserted place, and there he prayed." The sermon I'd written was about taking time away to be quiet, to pray. Actually, that's something most of us need to pay attention to more than we do. But I didn't think the people in the pews were likely to pay much attention. They all had lives to live, bills to pay. They were living in the real world, and I was getting ready to preach another seminary sermon that might have looked good on paper but had nothing to do with any of them or their lives.

As I read the words from Mark to the congregation that morning, it was as if I'd never seen or heard them before. When the friends found Jesus, they told him, "Everyone is searching for you." I could imagine they wanted Jesus to come back and start healing people again. It had to be good for business: Jesus of Nazareth's Magical Healing and Works of Power Tour. They could increase their membership; they could take up a collection; they could become a force to be reckoned with; they could make a difference in the world!

But Jesus replied, "Let us go on to the neighboring towns, so that I may proclaim the message there also; for that is what I came out to do." And I wondered, even as I read the words, what was this message that was so important, more important than healing people and casting out demons? Surely the healing had to be the most important thing to the people who were lining up at Simon's mother-in-law's door. But for Jesus, the message was the most important thing in the world. So what was the message?

For well over thirty years now, I've wondered why the people in the pews are actually there. My own experience doesn't provide an answer. I went to church as a child because my parents made us go, pure and simple. Then, as I grew up, I found a place to belong in the church and eventually a vocation. But all those people who come to church, who put money in the plate, why are they really there? Do people come to church to get their tickets punched, to earn enough credits to outweigh their demerits, because they feel like it's their duty or because the Lord God will "get them" somehow if they skip? Does any of that line up with the message Jesus came to bring? Some parts of God's Church seem to have been successful by reducing the message of Jesus to that terrible Christmas song: "You better watch out, you better not cry, you better not pout, I'm telling you why." Jesus is coming back, and he's ticked. But that can't really be the message.

So what's the message? What's the point? What are we supposed to be talking about? Surely it's not the mission of the Church to scare people into salvation or to threaten them with doom and gloom. How could that be good news? And surely the purpose of the Church cannot be the survival of the Church so that all the effort is just to be sure the membership and donations are increasing. What is this message that Jesus walked away from sick and hurting people to bring?

I felt like it was time for me to stop trying to make Bs for a class I was no longer taking and consider what the people in the pews needed to hear, something that mattered to their real lives. So I told them a story. I wasn't trying to be avant-garde. It wasn't a strategy; it's just how I talk. As it is with many of the best parts of my life, I stumbled into it by accident. For the first time, and completely against what we'd been taught in seminary, I abandoned my notes, stepped out of the pulpit, and told the congregation the story of Mr. Flowers's mailbox.

When I was growing up south of Vicksburg, Mississippi, my family lived on a long stretch of road at the top of a ridge between two gullies. The boys in the neighborhood seemed to gravitate to our yard; sometimes we played baseball or football, and more often we played some variation of war with whatever we could pick up and throw at each other: acorns, dirt clods, or sweet-gum balls.

Purvis and Durant Calhoun lived down the road about a half a mile and had an uncle who was in the Air Force. His job took him all over the world; from time to time he would come home for a visit and bring his nephews presents from exotic lands. Once it was a newspaper from Egypt, which was interesting for as long as it took us to realize it didn't make any sense at all. Another time it was coins from England, which had an even shorter moment of interest. Then there was the Samurai sword from Japan, which of course intensely held everybody's attention until their mother snatched it away before somebody got hurt. We never saw it again, but the gleaming danger of it lingered long in our imaginations.

In the summer of 1963, as important events were swirling beyond our awareness or interest, Uncle Jimmy brought his nephews a small paper bag full of M-80s. M-80s are remarkable in many ways, not least being that they were legal at the time and were for some incalculable reason made available to a bunch of boneheaded little boys. It might have been safer to let us play with the Samurai sword.

An M-80 is like a firecracker but a good bit larger and considerably more powerful. It's about an inch and a half long, with a thick waterproof fuse coming out of the middle. I'll never know how they got past Mrs. Calhoun; by the time the brothers showed the rest of us, there were sixteen or seventeen left. They'd already used seven or eight for "experimental purposes."

The gang of boys in the neighborhood was made up of the Calhoun brothers; my brother, Lee; Lewis, who lived next door; and me. That summer I was seven years old; Lee, Purvis, and Lewis were all eleven, and Durant was nine. None of us were friends, especially, but we were the boys available to play with. Actually, Lewis and I could have been friends, but it was hard because he was four years older, and that seemed significant when we were kids.

Purvis and Durant were proud to have something that none of the rest of us could have ever gotten, and they delighted in showing off the destructive power of the M-80s. They told us that M-80s would explode underwater, but it was hard to believe, so they showed us by throwing one into Tadpole Creek at the bottom of the gully behind our house. It was satisfying to all of us to see water exploding out of the creek. I worried about the tadpoles and crawfish I knew were living there, but some things I had to keep to myself.

After that, we were looking for new experiments, painfully aware that each explosion left us with one less M-80. Durant wanted to use the explosives to blow the top off something. We tried to blow the lid off our big tin garbage can but were disappointed to hear a muffled *whump* that left the lid securely attached.

We duct-taped an M-80 to a plastic army man, who died a gruesome, disfiguring death. It was too much explosive for one little bazooka man; a major explosive like that deserved a more challenging victim. So we convinced Lewis to ask his younger sister Lucille if he could borrow one of her Barbie dolls, but apparently all of our sisters had been expecting something like this, and they wouldn't let us borrow one, even for a minute.

We went back to the tin garbage can, using two M-80s with their fuses twisted together. This time the *whump* was significantly louder, but the top stayed on. With only a few of the implements of destruction remaining, we rode our bicycles into the Vicksburg National Military Park. The place boasts cannons and artillery pieces of all shapes and sizes, and for a little while we could imagine what it must have been like exactly one hundred years before when Vicksburg was besieged and the cannons thundered in earnest.

Finally, only two M-80s were left, and we had much discussion about how to use them. We all agreed that they should explode together, go out with a bang, so to speak. But what would the target be? Nobody ever listened to Lewis, but he always had opinions: he wanted to tape several plastic army men around the two remaining explosives. Lee wanted to take them down to the big bayou to see if the explosion would stun some of the big catfish he suspected were living at the bottom. Purvis was working on a plan to find a cat or a stray dog and tape the M-80s to its tail, so there was some urgency in finding an alternative before he could work all that out. And Durant had given up on the tin garbage can, but he had not given up on his primary goal of blowing the top off of something, blowing something open. At just the right moment, he suggested, "Maybe something smaller, like a mailbox."

That caught everybody's imagination. We quickly agreed that it should not be *our* mailbox or Lewis's mailbox, but there was Mr. Flowers's mailbox across the street, just sitting there minding its own business, inviting, defenseless.

This was the moment Lewis chose to tell us all that it is a federal crime to tamper with the US mail. We were all accustomed to disregarding whatever Lewis had to say, but about this he was insistent: "We could go to jail!" We paused a moment, but even then we knew it was too late; the plot had reached full momentum and could not be stopped. And anyway, the likeliest alternate might involve the maiming of an unlucky stray.

The plan came together quickly after that. I, being the youngest, was relegated to opening and closing the mailbox door. Lee would light the fuses that would be twisted together, and Purvis and Durant would toss the M-80s into the box. Lewis, for his part, announced that he was going home and that he was *going to tell.* We ignored him, and I suppose he must've gone home; for years I wondered if he ever did *tell.*

On the count of three, I opened the mailbox door. I noticed that there was something in there, but the plan was in motion and could not be stopped. Lee had already lit the fuses; Purvis and Durant were inserting the explosives. Too late, I realized that my hands were closest to the lit incendiaries. I slammed the door shut and ran behind the other boys. I didn't actually see the explosion, but I can still hear it in my mind's ear. I turned around in time to see scraps of smoldering paper floating down—some blossoming small flames around the edges.

When some of the smoke began to clear, the reality of what we'd done hit us all, hit us hard. The mailbox door had not only been opened but also mostly torn off its hinges. One side of the mailbox was no longer attached to the bottom. Most frighteningly, yesterday's mail was smoldering in Mr. Flowers's yard. Without a word, we agreed to follow the example of little boys throughout history when they have found themselves in trouble—we ran for it.

It was a summer weekday; Dad and Mr. Flowers were both at work. I spent the afternoon fretting and speculating about the possibilities of what could happen next, none of them pleasant; my brother Lee spent the afternoon trying to convince me that "They can't prove a thing." But everybody knew the boys had been terrorizing the neighborhood with a small paper bag full of danger and destruction. There was no way out.

We waited for Dad to come home, as minutes crawled and hours dragged. Finally we saw Mr. Flowers drive up, stop in his driveway, and look at the wreckage of his mailbox. We could see little fragments of yesterday's mail all around, and Mr. Flowers shaking his head. It looked like a buffalo had sat on his mailbox. A few minutes later we saw Dad driving down the road in our black 1959 Pontiac Catalina, and we watched from behind the azaleas in front of our house as he stopped on the side of the road to talk to Mr. Flowers. When he was mad, Dad clenched his jaw; we could see it clenching and unclenching from across the road, a sure indication of uncomfortable moments in our near future.

Lee grabbed my arm and made me look at him. "They can't prove a thing!"

I was about to cry, anticipating the punishment on its way. "But they know, Lee—everybody knows! We're gonna get it for sure this time!"

Lee was adamant. "Just tell him you don't know anything about it. Tell him we were down in the woods all day. He can't prove anything."

Dad came straight to the backyard, where he found us angelically pitching a baseball back and forth. He unclenched his jaw long enough to say, "Lee, Buddy, come over here." Lee stood up and trotted over to where our father was seething. I had to admire how unconcerned my brother looked, for all intents and purposes a young man without a care in the world. He said, "Hey, Dad. How was work?"

Dad disregarded Lee's question and asked the one that needed to be answered. "Do either of you know what happened to Mr. Flowers's mailbox?" Lee had a care now: he seemed very concerned that something must have happened to good ol' Mr. Flowers's mailbox. "No, Dad. What happened?" I was amazed and more than a little envious at how smoothly he lied. Dad answered, "It looks like it was blown up."

I thought, "Well, that's it. He knows. 'It was *blown up*.' And we all know who blew it up!"

But Lee was cool. "Aw, man—that's terrible!" I nodded in agreement.

Dad looked at us, his jaws clenched so hard I wondered how he'd ever talk or eat again. He knew we were lying. But maybe Lee was right; *he can't prove a thing!* Dad asked, "Do either of you know anything about this?"

Lee answered quickly, "No, sir." Dad looked at me, and I shook my head. There was a terrible pause, and Dad concluded, "All right. You two can go sit in your room until you see if you can remember something."

Dad and Mr. Flowers both worked at the Waterways Experiment Station, both of them employees of the US Corps of Engineers. They both got off work at 4:30 and were home by a quarter to five. Supper wouldn't be until 6:00, so we had some time to remember. I had time for anxiety and dread; Lee had time to coordinate our story and arrange the lies he was going to tell.

"Buddy, listen—we were down in the woods all day, just you and me. We went to the pond, understand? Everybody knows it takes a long time to get to the pond, right? We couldn't possibly have had anything to do with Mr. Flowers's mailbox, right? We went to the pond today, to see if we could catch any fish."

It was a reasonable story. We had gone to the pond many times before. It was a long way away, almost a full day of walking there and back, with a couple of hours to fish or swim or throw sweet-gum balls at the turtles. We'd been to the pond lots of times. We just hadn't gone today; I was wishing we had.

"But we would've told Mom that we were going. We didn't tell Mom."

"But we can *tell* Dad we told her we were going. You know she forgets sometimes. We'll tell Dad we told Mom that we were going to the pond, and that she just forgot. *They can't prove a thing!*"

I wasn't convinced, but I kept it to myself. I was the youngest of a bunch of boys who fought and bickered for entertainment, and the third of four children; I kept a lot of things to myself.

Supper was an uncomfortable affair, with few words spoken but a lot of meaningful looks shared. Our sisters were delighted that we'd gotten caught doing something wrong. They didn't say anything, but their eyes sparkled at the prospect of somebody else being in trouble.

After supper, Lee and I were sent back to our room and given some time to dread the next conversation with our father. When he came in, he sat on the lower bunk and we sat on the floor facing him. He asked us if there was anything we wanted to say, and Lee persisted, "Look, Dad, we didn't have anything to do with blowing up Mr. Flowers's mailbox. We went down to the pond, and we were there all day. You can ask Mom—she'll tell you. We told her this morning we were going to the pond." Oh, he was smooth.

Dad replied, "I did ask her. She told me that you and the Calhoun boys were shooting off M-80s. Now Mr. Flowers's mailbox has been destroyed. How would you like to explain that?"

There was a pause, and I was sure that Lee would have to confess, but instead he startled us, proposing, "Maybe it was struck by lightning!"

Sometimes I wonder if a father's most difficult task in raising his children is just keeping a straight face.

Dad countered, "There wasn't a cloud in the sky all day."

But Lee was determined. "Then I can't explain it."

And there it was—the only possible explanations were a highly improbable meteorological marvel or that we had blown up Mr. Flowers's mailbox, and we weren't willing to admit to that. It was a standoff. Our father knew what had happened, but *he couldn't prove a thing!*

Dad stood up, clenched his jaw, and shook his head. You could feel the sadness in his voice when he said, "I'm very disappointed with you boys." Then he left the room and closed the door, leaving us to our deceit and stinking with disappointment.

Mr. Flowers had taken Dad and Lee and me fishing a few times and had just bought a bigger johnboat, a wide, flat-bottomed, aluminum fishing boat almost twenty feet long. He and Dad had been planning an all-night fishing trip in Stump Lake, and Mr. Flowers had invited Lee and me to come along. We'd gone once before, jug fishing with fifteen or twenty Clorox bottles rigged up with nylon string and big hooks baited with chicken necks and livers to catch big catfish; staying up all night and listening to the two men was a lot of fun. But now, after the Great Mailbox Explosion of 1963, the trip was in jeopardy. Nobody mentioned it, and I wasn't going to ask about it, but it seemed impossible that we would still go after this incident.

The next day, I told my brother I was going to go apologize to Mr. Flowers. He hissed, "They can't prove a thing!" And he was probably right. Maybe they never could have proven anything. The thing was, though, that I knew my part in destroying the mailbox. I knew, and it didn't feel right. It didn't feel right to lie to Dad, it didn't feel right to get away with something like that, and it sure didn't feel right to go fishing on Mr. Flowers's new boat. I repeated, "I'm going over there to apologize."

So that afternoon, after Mr. Flowers got home from work, I gathered my courage and walked across the road. I stepped onto the Flowerses' stoop and reached up to ring the doorbell. *They can't prove a thing!* What did I think I was going to say? "We blew up your mailbox"? How can you say something like that out loud? What would Purvis and Durant do if I *told*? I backed off the stoop and ran back home.

Then I realized I couldn't go back in my own home; deceit and disappointment wouldn't let me through the door. I stood there in the middle of the road for a second or two, and then, before I had time to think about it anymore, before I could talk myself out of it again, I ran back across the street, up onto the Flowerses' stoop, and rang the doorbell.

It took a moment or two for Mr. Flowers to answer. I had time to think about running back home, but then he opened the door and looked down on me. He was a tall man with a white crew cut. He talked to me through the screen door. "Yes?"

I just blurted it out, without trying to say it right. "Mr. Flowers, I blew up your mailbox!"

The look he gave me I later learned was one of compassion. He opened the screen door and leaned down a little to say, "I know." Then, with his huge right hand he tousled the half-inch of hair on my head and said, "You're a good kid."

That's the story I told for the sermon on the Fifth Sunday after Epiphany. The people in the pews didn't know what to make of it, but they enjoyed hearing something more real than me trying to talk like a professor.

I ended the sermon by saying, "I think that's the message Jesus brought, and brings still. I think it's a large part of the good news of the love of God that Jesus came to proclaim to the neighboring towns—so important that he left the lame and sick waiting for him in Capernaum. 'You're a good kid.' God knows we are broken, selfish, cowardly, lazy people. *He knows.* And God loves us anyway. It's not about being caught or getting away with anything; it's about accepting the love of God.

"The whole point of sin isn't that we get demerits. The point is that it messes up our relationship with our Father God."

I told the congregation that I'd had to wash Mr. Flowers's Studebaker and our Pontiac every Saturday for the rest of the summer. Lee had to weed their garden and ours every week. We did go jug fishing that Friday night and caught some large catfish. Mr. Flowers had gotten a new watch with little dots of radium by the numerals and on the second hand; we watched it go round and round. We saw shooting stars, and Mr. Flowers told us that meteorites hit the planet all the time. We watched bats darting through the twilight, and the highlight of the evening was when a bat attacked Dad's lit cigar and knocked it out of his hand into the dark water.

But Lee, unrepentant and unconfessed, sat in the back of the boat, miserably wishing he could be anywhere else.

I was amazed by the reaction to that sermon. Somewhere in the middle of telling the story, I realized that the people in the pews were listening, really listening, to find out what was going to happen. I had caught their imagination, and it was a powerful moment. The church was completely quiet except for my voice, and I realized I'd been listening to myself talk. It was like magic.

At the end of the sermon, after I made the point about the compelling message of Christ being about the love of God, I reached down and tousled the acolyte's hair and asserted, "You're a good kid." And then, completely full of myself, I put my hand on the head of an insurance salesman in his sixties on the front pew and disheveled his hair, too. "You're a good kid."

After the service, in the Enjoyed Your Sermon line, Miss Ellen, the matriarch of one of the two principal families that made up most of the congregation, shook my hand with her right hand, and then with her left she took off her little pillbox hat and bowed her head. I didn't know what to do until she looked up with tears in her eyes and beseeched, "I want to be a good kid, too." I carefully ruffled her perm, just a little, and assured her that she was.

4

Ex Opere Operato

St. Thomas Tombigbee has a small nave, with very little capacity for any sort of extra space for gathering except its tiny kitchen, and on the day I was ordained a priest, we squeezed almost two hundred people in there: shoulder to shoulder, knee to knee, cheek to jowl. The members of St. Thomas didn't take up much space; most of the pews and the chairs we had borrowed from the Methodists down the road were occupied by members of my family and other people from around the Diocese.

Milla's sister Early (short for Earline) had gotten better on the piano, but she would have felt much more confident with the Broadman Hymnal of her Baptist Church. Even so, we found a few numbers she could play and we all made the best of it. She did learn a simple hymn for the occasion—"I Sing a Song of the Saints of God," a favorite hymn from my childhood that contains this line about everyday saints: "And one was a soldier, and one was a priest, And one was slain by a fierce wild beast." I was never meant to be a soldier, and I was going to do everything I could to avoid fierce wild beasts, but I was about to be ordained a priest; I felt like I was becoming part of the hymn.

The rector of my home parish in Vicksburg preached the sermon. I don't remember much of what he said, but I do remember him saying that part of the job is to love people. "Love them all," he preached, "saints and sinners alike. The Lord can determine which is which; that's not your job. Your job is just to love them. Love is the great gift you have been given, and the great gift you have to give. Your obligation as a priest in God's church, and your very great privilege, is to love." I wrote it down in the service bulletin so I wouldn't forget. And I haven't.

After the service, various people pitched in and moved all the pews out to the yard; some went to their homes to get the goodies they'd cooked for the reception; and others set the tables we'd borrowed from the Presbyterian church. Jack's nephew Larry Wayne played in a bluegrass band ("The Pelahatchie Pickers"), and what they lacked in musical skill they made up for with an infectious love for their music. When they played the Mother Maybelle Carter version of "Will the Circle Be Unbroken," they were surprised that so many of us knew it; we all formed an impromptu circle and sang along. Even when we didn't know all the words, we belted out the chorus:

> Will the circle be unbroken
> By and by, Lord, by and by?
> There's a better home awaiting
> In the sky, Lord, in the sky.

Later that afternoon most everybody went home. I stayed to help clean up the mess—I've always been glad to find a job that I'm actually qualified to do, and I can sweep up with the best of them. Jack and Milla had offered to bring some barbecue by for my family, most of whom were staying the night so they could be part of the congregation when I celebrated my first Eucharist the next day. Close to suppertime they brought two big aluminum foil trays of meat, another of baked beans, and an extra-large sweet potato casserole, Milla's specialty. I asked Jack why there was so much meat, and he murmured, "One of the trays is pork. I didn't know if your folks'd eat goat."

I asked him if it was one of the three goats that appeared in the backyard when I moved into the vicarage; I thought I saw a mischievous sparkle in his eye when he assured me that it wasn't, but I might have imagined it. The pork was really good, and there was plenty of it; some of the family joined me in politely trying the goat, but only Jack could actually say he preferred it.

The next morning I woke up well before my alarm went off. I went through the service from the Book of Common Prayer, trying to remember the various hand motions, practicing my lines. Years before, when I told my parents that I wanted to be priest, Mom only said, "Oh, Buddy," but Dad had cautioned, "You have to be good to be a priest." Now, on the morning I would start my priesthood, I knew that I was not in any way good enough, and that I never would be. How could such an imperfect person serve the perfect God?

Then I remembered one of the measly handful of odd things I could recall from seminary, the principle of *ex opere operato*. The idea is that the efficacy of the Sacraments does not depend on the holiness or worthiness of the priest. I remembered taking some comfort in the idea as a seminarian, that many of those who had gone before me through the history of the Church had probably been just as flawed and scared as I was. Now I was grateful to recall it, again comforted by the generations of unworthy clergy who'd preceded me. I wondered if the bishop had ever felt anything like this, but I knew I would never be able to ask.

I'd thought that the profound moment for me would be the *epiclesis*—the moment of asking the Spirit of God to bless the bread and wine of the Eucharist—but it wasn't. The moment that touched me the most was giving the bread to my parents, my brother, and my sisters. My emotions rose up into my throat, choking off my voice, so all I could do was blink the tears out of my eyes, put the bread into their upstretched hands, and nod.

After we'd all shared the bread and wine, after my young niece had put her hand in the chalice and I'd cleaned up the holy mess of wine on the floor, after all the ablutions of the paten and chalice were completed, after the post-Communion prayer, once I thought I was back on stable emotional ground again, it was time for the blessing. The line is right there in the prayer book, and I had practiced it until I was pretty sure I wouldn't have to read it: "The peace of God, which passeth all understanding, keep your hearts and minds in the knowledge and love of God, and of his Son Jesus Christ our Lord; and the blessing of God Almighty, the Father, the Son, and the Holy Ghost, be amongst you, and remain with you always."

I raised my right hand, just like I'd been taught in seminary, to make the sign of the Cross and say the words, but I couldn't speak. It was a desperate moment, needing to say something and being too emotional to utter a sound. I saw my mother nod her patience to me, swallowed once, and then again, and finally said the blessing.

I didn't know I'd asked God's blessing on all of us rather than on the congregation until my brother told me I'd messed it up a little: I'd said "amongst us" instead of "amongst you." I think I'd been concerned about saying the word "amongst" out loud.

My sister said she preferred my wording, and I did, too. I didn't like the distance it created when the blessing was aimed at the people in the pews, as if I didn't need to be blessed as well; it felt better to ask God to bless us all alike. That's the way I've said it ever since.

I learned a lot at St. Thomas, Tombigbee, about the faith, about the Episcopal Church, about myself. I learned that most people didn't really think I'd always have to have the right thing to say, that nobody expected me to have all the answers. I learned that not all Episcopalians are nice people, and that some Baptists and Methodists are okay after all.

It would make for a better story if I could tell you that after my ordination, the church was crowded every Sunday and hundreds of people's lives were changed. But this is a story about a real life and a real ministry—it wasn't and they weren't.

But I did love those people there, and it felt like they loved me, too. It is an incredible honor to serve God's Church as a member of the clergy in any denomination. It was a good time in my life, there at St. Thomas Episcopal Church in Tombigbee, Mississippi. There's a lot of me that thinks maybe I should have stayed there, a small parish in a small town where I knew everybody—knew where they lived, knew all the folks in town and their mothers and most of their dogs.

A few days after Easter in 1983, I got a call from Mary Downs, secretary to the Bishop of Mississippi. Every time I ever talked to her, she sounded like she was inviting me to a funeral. "Buddy," she intoned, "the bishop would like to see you."

I had tried to stay away from the bishop as a general rule. It's not that I didn't like him; in fact, I thought he was a really nice guy. But he was The Boss. My first thought was, "Somebody must've made a complaint! I'm in trouble! Why would the bishop want to see *me*? What have I done?" I tried, without much success I'm sure, to play it cool. My voice quavered, but only a little, when I answered, "Yes, ma'am."

She continued, "How is next Thursday for you?" What I wanted to say was that it was eight days away, and *what does he want with me anyway*? But I replied, "That would be fine."

She asked, "When can you come?"

I responded, "Thursday."

She was patient with me. "What time next Thursday would be good for you, Buddy?"

The truth was that any time was just as good as any other. I didn't have anything planned that far ahead except Scrabble with the Knutsons, and no matter what time the appointment was, I would have to drive to Jackson, a little more than two hours away. She put me on his calendar for one o'clock in the afternoon; I hung up the phone and started fretting. Bishops are scary for some priests, especially young priests.

So I made myself miserable for a week, worrying. The only thing I could think of that might have landed me in trouble was something I'd said in a sermon a few weeks before.

I was still learning about preaching without notes, that while the rush of not knowing what you're going to say next gives you a great deal of focus for that particular moment, sometimes you say things you wouldn't have said if you'd had another moment to think about it.

What I'd said was something like, "Fundamentalism is a virus in the Body of Christ." At least that's what the woman who said she was insulted by it claimed I said. Another problem with preaching without notes is that later, you don't really know what words actually came out, and you have to rely on other people's accounts of it. The woman had joined the parish just before I'd gotten there, and she was trying to hang on, but apparently I wasn't making it easy. Her parents were still in the church she'd grown up in, still fundamentalists to their core. She insisted she'd taken offense at having her parents referred to as an ailment, and she threatened to write a letter to the bishop.

So when Thursday came, I forced myself into my old 1971 Mercury Comet and dragged myself down to Jackson. I went into the Diocesan Office and told Mrs. Downs I was there. "Please go right in, Buddy," she said in a mournful tone. "He's waiting for you." I'm fairly sure it was my imagination, but it sounded like she was asking a defendant to stand to hear the verdict.

The bishop must have seen that I was as nervous as a cat on a caffeine high, and he walked across the room and gave me a warm handshake. It was not at all the sort of greeting I imagined you'd use when you were about to chew somebody out.

"Buddy, are you okay?"

"Yes sir, I think so."

"You *think* so?"

"Well, yes sir. I hope so, anyway. But really, it depends on why you wanted to see me and what you're going to say."

He laughed—a full, rich chuckle that was relief down to my toes. "You think you're in trouble, Buddy?"

"I hope not."

"No, Buddy. I wanted to ask you a couple of questions, and I thought it would be better if I asked them in person. That's all."

"Oh. Okay. Okay, good."

"First, I want to ask you to direct the second special session at camp next summer."

I was dumbfounded. I had been hoping that I could direct one of the summer camp sessions for people with mental and physical disabilities one day, but the priests who directed them for years seemed firmly entrenched there. And besides, I was much too young. It was something I'd assumed would be out there for me someday when I was ready.

When I didn't say anything, the bishop asked, "Would you be willing to do that?"

"Yes sir, I'd love to, but what about Ray?" Ray had directed the second session for years; I'd been on his adult staff for the last two. He was a friend, but I knew he had a long, difficult history with the bishop; Ray was something of a lone wolf.

The bishop had steel in his eyes when he answered, "He won't be available this summer. Or ever again, for that matter. I'm afraid that's all I can tell you."

As it turned out, I found out much later, Ray's wife had caught him having an affair with a soprano in the parish choir, and the bishop had sent him to Texas for two weeks of psychological and professional evaluation. We never saw him or the soprano again, though years later I heard that they'd been married and divorced, that he was doing well selling life insurance in Fort Worth and was a deacon in a humongous Methodist church out there.

I answered, "I'd love to. I don't really know how to direct a summer camp, but I can probably figure it out."

He was assuring. "Sure you can. You've got a good heart for it, and that's what matters. But you'll need to get busy to get your adult staff together." He had directed camp sessions for years before being elected bishop, and knew all about this. "You don't have much time, and a lot of the regulars might already be signed up for other sessions. Find a good nurse, that's the most important thing."

"Yes sir. Thank you very much."

"The other thing is more sensitive, and it might not be something you want to talk about. In fact it might not be any of my business."

"Oh." I felt myself getting nervous again. "All right."

"Miss Nora"—he always called his wife Miss Nora—"is concerned about your personal life, and I told her I'd talk to you about it."

"My . . . personal life?"

"Yes. As nature abhors a vacuum, so women of a certain age just can't stand seeing a young man unattached. She wants to know if you're seeing anyone." I must have looked blank, so he continued. "Are you dating anyone?"

Well, this was awkward. In fact, I wasn't dating anyone, and I hadn't had any sort of serious romantic relationship since a girl named

Tiffy had dumped me when I was in seminary. I'd pretended my heart was broken at the time, but since then more reasonable parts of me had suggested that I should actually be relieved: I could never have afforded the life she wanted to live.

The unspoken irony was that when I had worked at camp for three summers, I'd had several camp girlfriends; the bishop, who was then a priest, had directed several of those sessions and had commented to me more than once about these casual romances. Sure enough, it did cause me some discomfort when three of the previous summer's girlfriends all came to be counselors at the same session. As I was trying to get through the process to go to seminary, I had worried that one of the bishop's concerns in sending me might be the lingering idea that I was some sort of playboy. Now he was asking me about my love life and whether I had a girlfriend. The truth was my only option: "No sir."

"Well, you don't have to hurry, you're still young—what are you, twenty-eight, twenty-nine?"

"Twenty-seven."

"Ah, well. You've got lots of time. But it's not good for priests to be alone. It can be a lonely job, you know."

I hadn't been ordained long, but it was long enough to hear the truth in what he was saying. It's an odd thing. Sometimes people want you to be around, need you to be around, because you're a priest; and other times people don't want you to be around, and certainly don't need you, because you're a priest. But once you're a priest, you're never ever not a priest, except among other priests. I wouldn't trade it for anything, but it's an odd life, an odd sort of loneliness.

"Yes sir."

"Well. I appreciate your dedication to your parish and to your ministry. But you need to remember that you have to be healthy to be of any service to anyone. Okay?"

"Yes sir." We talked about the parish for a little while after that, and then I asked about the upcoming General Convention of the Episcopal Church. Every three years, the whole Episcopal Church in the United States and in several other nations has a church-wide convention, and it seemed to me that it was mostly a gathering of people whose passions and causes were terribly important to them, but not always what I generally thought was or should be important in the Church.

That year, one of the raging issues was a resolution dealing with what was becoming in other denominations of God's Church a strident insistence that Creation be understood as a seven-day event. The memorable language was that the convention "affirm its belief in the glorious ability of God to create in any manner, and in this affirmation reject the rigid dogmatism of the 'Creationist' movement." I remember that because I thought it was funny that we were giving God permission to create however God thought was best.

It was a good chat, and I was starting to be a little more comfortable with the bishop. After a while, Miss Mary knocked gently on the door and pronounced in funereal tones that his two o'clock appointment was waiting. I stood and we shook hands; as I was leaving, the bishop said, "Oh, and Buddy . . . ."

"Yes sir?"

"Be careful what you say in a sermon. Some folks really are listening, even when it looks like they're not."

"Yes sir."

"A virus in the body of Christ—that's a good line, though."

I thought about telling him that I might have not really said that, or at least that I didn't remember saying it, but he was right: it was a good line.

"Yes sir."

5

Things that Change Your Life

When I was fifteen years old my friend Clif, whose father was the priest of the Episcopal parish my family attended, signed up to be a counselor at the diocesan summer camp, Camp Bratton-Green, and he wanted me to come, too. My brother and both my sisters had gone as campers, but I'd never wanted to go, even though Mom and Dad had tried to get me to: I was skinny as a pencil, awkward, sensitive and shy, and I had never been away from home for more than one night without some member of my family. As you might imagine, I've worked on myself for years and have successfully overcome being thin.

Clif tried to talk me into it by telling me there would be singing and softball and a swimming pool, but I was not convinced. He told me there would be pretty girls there, which scared me even more. Then he said if I went to camp for a week, I wouldn't have to cut the grass, and that, I thought, was a compelling argument. It's funny the things that change your life.

So I filled out an application to be a counselor for a session of third and fourth graders, and was surprised to be accepted. I was also surprised to learn that my friend Clif had been accepted to a different session, earlier in the summer. When he came back from camp, two weeks before my session was to begin, he told me about all the fun I was going to have. He talked about the skits and the songs and an imaginative, energetic program. And he told me about the permanent staff, a group of college kids who were hired to serve all summer. Clif said they were the Coolest of the Cool, that I would really like them. But I knew, being awkward, goofy, and shy, that it would be safer and easier for me to hang out with the third and fourth graders.

The day the training session was to begin, my dad drove me to camp. It turned out that we arrived a couple of hours early. Dad offered to stay but needed to leave, and having my father wait with me seemed clearly uncool, so I asked him to let me out at the administration building, which Clif had told me was one of the few air-conditioned buildings at camp. I waved to my dad to let him know I was okay, opened the door, and went in.

And right then and there, I was faced with what I was dreading the most: the permanent staff, the Coolest of the Cool. There were four of them, three guys and a girl sitting around a table playing cards. One of them looked at me with eyes I'd seen in the news—Charles Manson eyes. Another looked like Scooby Doo's friend Shaggy, with long red hair and a scraggly beard. The girl had long, straight, dark hair that looked like it hadn't been washed in a few days; she seemed quite intent on making sure that everybody knew she was In a Bad Mood. The fourth seemed like the most normal of the four, with a twinkle in his eye and an infectious smile. But it seemed like there was something wrong with his hair.

I knew the moment was coming when I would have to say something, something that wouldn't reveal how scared I was or how inadequate I felt. There was a soft drink machine, and I sort of tried to blend into it so they wouldn't have to notice me anymore. They all looked up, saw a tall, thin, awkward, goofy, shy kid trying to merge with a Coke machine, and it looked like they were going to go back to their card game, which would have been fine with me, but then the guy with the crooked hair smiled and asked me my name.

I hoped my voice wouldn't crack as I said "Buddy."

He cleared his throat, and the Girl in a Bad Mood groaned, and he sang a limerick for me. I didn't know what a limerick was, but I recognized the traditional Mexican tune from the Frito Bandito commercials.

There once was a young man named Buddy
Who jumped in the lake and got muddy
He wiped off his feet
And he combed his hair neat
'Til he looked like an old fuddy-duddy!

The guy that looked like Shaggy leaned back in his chair and joined in the chorus:

Ay-yi-yi-yi! In Spain they do it for chili
So sing me another verse that's worse than the other verse
And waltz me around by the willie!

Then Shaggy started on another limerick—"There once was an old man named Dave, who kept . . ."—but the Girl in a Bad Mood stopped him just in time. Apparently there are thousands of limericks that are not appropriate in this book, or anywhere for that matter.

Then the guy with something wrong with his hair asked me if I knew how to play spades. Well, of course I knew how to play spades; everybody knew how to play spades, but the other three at the table grumbled. You can play spades with five players, but it's not nearly as much fun as playing with four, so you can play with a partner and keep score. I didn't want to be the cause of grumbling among the Coolest of the Cool, so I said, "No."

Scooby, Manson, and Bad Mood relaxed, but Limerick didn't give up on me. He told me to have a seat and said they'd teach me how to play. He threw his cards in the middle of the table, then took Shaggy's cards out of his hand and threw them in, too. Manson looked at me with those piercing eyes and threw his cards in with complete resignation, and Bad Mood stayed true to her form and said, "Aw, c'mon, Bill!"

Limerick, aka Bill, pulled up a fifth chair, sat me down, and taught me how to play a game I already knew how to play. In the course of the conversations I pieced together that Bill had lost a bet and shaved his head a few nights before. Earlier that day he'd gotten a woman's wig out of the costume closet to cover the fresh sunburn on his scalp. By the time the rest of the staff arrived, I was comfortable with them. More than that, for the first time in my life, I was cool—even if it was only Cool by Association. It's funny the things that will change your life.

For the rest of that day and half of the next, the staff for that session got to know each other, learned some songs, planned some activities and programs, and generally did what we could to get ready for the session. The campers came and I spent a week looking after sixteen extra-silly eight- and nine-year-olds. I loved the songs and the games and the pool, and the pretty girls were nice to me even though they were all a little older than I was; I kept a respectful distance, which seemed fine with them. But most of all, and for the first time in my life, I was okay, just like I was. It was okay for me to be Buddy Hinton—not my father's son or Lee's kid brother. It was okay to be me. In truth, it was the beginning of the process of finding out who I was and who I was going to be. There is deep magic in belonging to a community.

Toward the end of that session, some of the other counselors started talking about another session coming up, a session for adults with mental and physical disabilities. They needed more counselors, they said, especially guys. As they talked about the session and the campers who would be coming, they told stories. If they told stories about how sweet and loving and wonderful these campers were, I don't remember them now. The stories I remember were about people who were scary and difficult and nasty.

They told about a man in a wheelchair who had one weak arm and one incredibly strong arm, and if you got too close he'd reach out and grab you! They told about a camper who had been standing next to someone who'd caught a fish in the lake, and in the excitement of the moment, he took the fish and bit it right through the dorsal fin, on the back, so that the tail was flapping in his mouth, bit it so hard it broke the skin of the fish. They had to remove fish scales from the guy's mouth!

I listened to the stories in fascinated horror until some of those same counselors turned to me and asked what I would be doing in a couple of weeks, and whether I might sign up to be a counselor for the special session. I remember sarcastically thinking, "Yeah, right. Sign me up for that!"

But then one of the lifeguards on the permanent staff took me aside. And behold, she was Fair to Look Upon. She was a real live college girl, and she told me I was doing a great job as a counselor. When she invited me to come and be a counselor at the special session, I found that I was powerless before her. I was surprised to hear myself agreeing to come back in a couple of weeks. It's funny the things that will change your life.

When I got home, I told my parents I'd had a great time and had signed up to go back to camp in a couple of weeks. When they found out I'd signed up for a special session for people with disabilities, they were concerned. I was a sensitive kid, and they were worried that I wouldn't be able to do it. My father especially thought it was a bad idea and that I'd never make it through the whole session. But I was fifteen and just beginning to think I should have some sense of independence; Dad telling me I wouldn't be able to do it made me all the more determined to do it, just to prove him wrong.

He took me back to camp a couple of weeks later, giving me plenty of chances to come to my senses along the way. It was good to be back, and good to see that members of the permanent staff were glad to see me. Still, before that first special session I was scared to death.

By the time Ray the session director had gone through all the training and planning, he'd talked about Down Syndrome, epilepsy, cerebral palsy, spina bifida, and various other disabilities. The word among the experienced counselors was that if one of us were assigned to two or three campers, those campers would be relatively high functioning and not much trouble. The campers who were difficult or needed experienced care and attention were assigned to someone who'd been there before, and the most challenging were one-on-one assignments.

It was my first time, and I was probably a little too young to be there. The old hands assured me that I would be given easy campers.

The night before the campers arrived, we came together for Ray to hand out the assignments. It had been clouding up all afternoon, and by the time we came together after supper the wind was blowing hard. It rained, there was lightning and thunder, and the lights went out, adding to the drama of the moment. Ray met us in the rec hall, a big, screened-in-porch kind of building, holding a candle he'd appropriated from the chapel. The wind gusted through the screens, threatening to put out the candle and leave us all in the gloom. Ray called out each counselor's name, listed the campers that person was assigned, and gave the counselor the applications. By the time he worked his way down to my name, it felt like he'd been up there doing that for about a week. There was lightning, there was thunder; it could not have been any more terrifying if Mr. Hitchcock himself been directing the scene.

Finally, he called me and read the name of the camper I had been given, a young man named Neal: one camper. One camper. My imagination remembers a clap of thunder right at that moment, but I might have embroidered the memory a little. He handed me the application form.

Neal was seventeen years old, difficult to understand, needed help eating and in the bathroom. If you ever want to see a fifteen-year-old boy tense up, tell him he's going to be spending a week with someone who needs help in the bathroom. One of the other guys told me I'd have to pick him up and put him on the bed, in the chair, or on the commode. I was frantically trying to figure out what "help in the bathroom" might mean.

Right at that moment, more than anything else, I wanted to go home. But that would mean Dad was right. My sense of independent self-awareness, which had just started to take root, felt like it was about to be washed away.

One of the members of the permanent staff, a roguish special education major named Harry, saw my distress and asked me who I got. I couldn't look at him; I was afraid I was going to cry. I whispered, "I got a guy in a wheelchair." He looked at my application and said, "Naw, man, you got a lot more than that. Neal's been here for the last couple of years. He's a great camper; he's at least as smart as me, maybe as smart as you. He'll take good care of you."

I was dubious, but Harry said, "Tell you what, Buddy-boy—this time tomorrow night, if you still want to go home, I'll take you myself."

Harry convinced me to stay, and he was right: Neal took good care of me. He taught me how to steer his wheelchair, and after a couple of days I could tell what he was saying when most other people could not. All the girls on staff loved Neal and gave him and me much more time than they would have ever given me on my own. They would come over and flirt with Neal, and I would lean into it and just breathe it in a little.

After a while I relaxed and joined the wonderful and unique community forming around me. There were about sixty campers, maybe thirty counselors, and about fifteen adults: nurses, priests, and other old people—each of us with our own set of gifts and disabilities. The guy with an arm as big as your leg was not there, but the guy that bit the fish was. He was exceedingly energetic and easily excited, but he was also a pretty good guy. That week was an odd gumbo of the human condition, with a wide variety of different zesty spices, but after we simmered in the July heat for four or five days, we melted and blended together into a strong, delicious dish. Neal taught me that every person with disabilities was a person first (which, looking back, I'm ashamed to say I had to be taught); he taught me about dignity and respect. And I learned something I'm afraid some people never learn: there are no disposable people.

On the last full afternoon of the session, it was storming again, and again we were all in the rec hall. I was sitting with Neal, watching everybody else as they tried to play dodge ball in a crowd or do the Hokey Pokey (as if that's what it's all about), or just enjoyed hanging out. At some point Neal needed ice for his cup, and I stood up to get it. I looked and saw the whole camp together, and I realized that it wasn't worth the effort to separate everybody into all the categories we sort people into, all the types and labels. In that incredible, enchanted moment, everybody there looked and smelled and sounded just about the same. We became us, all of us celebrating the love of God in this remarkable community. Right then and there I thought, "This is the kingdom of God."

That's pretty heady stuff for a fifteen-year-old kid. If you could line up all the days of my life and point to two or three moments that have the most to do with shaping and forming me, this would certainly be one of them, that magical stormy afternoon when I first saw the kingdom of God, immersed in the most wonderful, diverse, unique, peculiar, frustrating, and loving community I'd ever been a part of.

I returned to camp the next summer, and the next, all through high school and college. For three years I was a member of the permanent staff, the Coolest of the Cool. When I came back from seminary in 1981, I was invited to be on the adult staff, which I was glad to do for two years. And now, two years later, the Bishop of Mississippi had invited me to direct the second special session.

The first time I directed a special session I wanted to do it right, which as an Episcopalian meant Doing Things the Way We've Always Done Them. The session had started in 1968 as the only session for people with disabilities in Mississippi that would welcome both black and white campers. The first directors had set it up so that all the campers would be assigned to activity groups, and they made an elaborate schedule so that each day all the campers and their counselors would go to the activities with their groups—the same schedule every day so the campers wouldn't be confused.

Everybody was required to wear a name tag. The campers' name tags had the camper's first name on one side and their counselor and cabin on the other. The staff's name tags were a little different in that their name appeared on both sides, and each of us wrote "Miss Ruby" or "Mr. Oliver" on it so the campers would remember what to call us.

That's how it was in 1971 when I first went to the special session, and that's how it was in 1981 when I came back from seminary. It was the Way It Had Always Been, the way it was supposed to be. I still have my name tag from that first week: "Mr. Buddy" in big red letters on a three-by-five square of thin plywood. I made my camper's name tag, too, and wrote "Neal" on it.

For the camp session I directed in 1983, I convinced a wonderful woman named Brenda, a member of the parish I was serving, to come to camp as the nurse. The bishop was right—the nurse was critical, and I was lucky to get the right person from the start. Then I put together an adult staff that included a couple of people I'd been counselors with along with rascally Harry, who now worked at a center for people with disabilities.

And I asked my old friend Neal to come, to be in charge of schedules and time, and to be sure that someone would ring the bell to let us know when an activity period ended or when a meal was going to be served.

I wanted to do it right, the way it had always been done. So before the campers came, we got it all set up, made sure the activity groups had equal numbers of campers and counselors arranged by their abilities and disabilities, made an elaborate schedule for the groups, and made name tags for everybody: "Mr. Bob," "Miss Kathy" for staff; "Susan," "Kevin" for campers. I wanted to carry on the great traditions, keep everything the way it had always been.

The week went well, as far as I remember; it's hard to keep those people from having a good time. As the campers and counselors were leaving at the end of the week, my friend Harry came to talk to me. I asked him how he thought it had gone and was surprised when he told me he was disappointed.

He asked me if I was serious about treating people with dignity and respect, or if that just something "you church people" want to talk about. I asked him what he meant, and he told me that if we were going to treat people with dignity, we'd ask them what they want to do instead of making all the decisions for them. He told me we needed to do away with the activity groups and let the campers do what they want to do. I said, "But what if all they want to do is swim in the pool every activity period?" and he said very loudly, "THEN LET THEM!"

I told him camp would be complete bedlam. I told him that's not the way we've always done it. I told him it would confuse the campers. He told me I was more interested in maintaining control over people than respecting them. And while I was still working out some way to defend myself and camp and the church from this unfair, unwarranted attack, Harry poked my chest with his finger so that it touched my name tag right on the "Mr.," and asked me why the staff was "Mr." and "Miss" but the campers were not.

I started to tell him what I had been told when I was fifteen, that it was so there wouldn't be any confusion about who was on staff, but before it got from my brain to my mouth I realized that was stupid; it's not really hard to tell who's a camper and who's on staff if you need to, and then I wondered why we would ever really need to. So I fell back on the tried and true Episcopal bureaucratic position and mumbled something about tradition. Harry said, "You are trapped by your traditions."

Well, he was right, and it was time to change. So the next year I told the staff that we were going to try something a little different. I called it "Plan B" and assured them that we were going to give it a try, and if we didn't like it we could go back to Plan A, the way we'd always done it. I told them I wanted all the name tags to use just first names—no "Mr." or "Miss"—and during the activity periods I wanted the campers to choose what they wanted to do. The staff, especially the ones who'd done it before, rebelled in unison and told me it was going to be chaos, it would be confusing, it went against our tradition, and I was going to ruin special session. One of the know-it-all counselors who'd been there for the last two summers and thought he knew everything asked, "What if the campers just want to go to the pool every time they have a chance?" I smiled and said, "Then let them."

There was indeed a good bit of confusion, and I think this is when we started saying "Embrace the Chaos," which became an unofficial motto of special sessions from then on. It probably made the counselors' job a little more difficult, especially if they had more than one camper who didn't always want to do the same thing when activities were offered. But they worked out systems for making switches and covering for each other, and the campers got to do what they wanted to do. More important, they got to choose for themselves. After the first year, nobody missed the name tag distinctions; actually, we started to take pride in blurring the lines to make it more difficult to tell the difference between campers and staff, and "just treat people like people."

That second year, I was taught another valuable lesson and learned some of the most important words a faithful person can ever say.

At the heart of things, the special session is summer camp, and most of the activities are the same as you might expect from any summer camp, although sometimes at a different pace. We start and end each day with chapel; we have boating, games, music, arts and crafts, canteen time, and a variety of programs at night, including the talent show and the big dance.

One of my favorite moments at special session comes at the end of the day, after the evening program, after chapel, when it's time for milk and cookies and going back to the cabins for a restful night. As the director, it's my job to make the announcements and reminders, and in this moment I routinely say that we've had a full day, that I'm sure they're all tired, and that we're going to have all sorts of fun the next day. "Now it's time for milk and cookies," I say. "Remember to take your medicine, and I'll see you all in the morning. Good night, good night."

That's a great moment for me, when I say "Good night, good night" and step back a little, glad to be out of the center of attention, glad to watch all the campers and counselors find each other and move toward the dining hall for milk and cookies on their way to bed. We would have a staff meeting after the campers were asleep or at least peaceful, but that was a little while off, so in that glorious moment I usually had nothing to do but watch the whole community disperse.

In that moment, in my second year to direct the session and in the first year of Plan B, as we ended the day in the A-frame chapel, Glenn Turner walked toward me purposefully, looking like a man with something to say. He was a good camper, fairly self-sufficient but with some cognitive disorders and learning disabilities that resulted in his not really being as smart as he appeared to be. He was competitive and athletic, a perennial star on our softball field.

I said, "Hey, Slugger. Whaddya need?"

The closer he got, the more his resolve seemed to fade. Whatever he had to ask was important to him, and he was afraid to ask it. I said, "Glenn? You okay?"

He straightened up a little and said, "Mr. Buddy, I want to go back behind the chapel and smooch with my girl."

I have to admit I was not expecting that; I'd never heard anything of the sort at camp. But, I thought, surely a priest in the Episcopal Church could not give permission for two people with mental challenges to go off and make out behind the chapel. I said, "No, Glenn, I'm sorry. This is a church camp. We don't do that kind of thing here."

Without missing a beat he said, "The counselors do."

Apparently some of the counselors in his cabin had been smooching behind the chapel and had shared some of the details with their friends. And in truth, I'd been a counselor, too, and knew firsthand that behind the chapel was a prime place to smooch. But now I was the director; surely I couldn't give my permission for campers to make out.

"No, Glenn. I'm sorry, but I can't let you do that. It's against the rules." Actually, there were no rules about campers smooching, but just then I thought we ought to regulate that sort of thing. Then Glenn looked at me—not as a camper to control but as a man, and all of a sudden this wasn't about summer camp; this was about being a person. He said, "Mr. Buddy, I'm thirty-one years old. I don't want no damn milk and cookies."

Now it was me losing my resolve, and all I had to back me up were imaginary rules and nonexistent regulations I was trying to invent on the spot. But still, but still . . .

"No, Glenn. I'm sorry."

He gave in then, and I watched him walk back to the young lady with whom he was trying to smooch. Her name was Jaylene, and she was full of fire and pepper and hormones gone wild—actually a lot of fun to be around until she was upset about something. I felt for Glenn then, having to explain his failure to get my permission. I was reading their body language, which was not subtle: as he told her they couldn't go behind the chapel, his shoulders slumped in defeat and disappointment, and she became more and more animated, insisting that he come back and try again.

Sure enough, he walked toward me once more, this time a man on a hopeless mission. I realized that his whole life had been bound by other people's rules, invisible reasons why he couldn't do what other people could.

I readied myself for round two, reminding myself that I had obligations to the camping program and the Diocese of Mississippi. So I wasn't prepared for the lesson I was about to learn.

He came up to me with tears in his eyes, looked up at me, and said, "Mr. Buddy, you could be wrong."

Of course I had known that in theory, and at the ripe old age of twenty-seven, after a little more than two years of ordination, I had already lived long enough to see that it had been true, several times. It just sounded different coming from him. It sounded more powerful, because somewhere under all those rules and The Way We've Always Done It, I knew he was right. Not only was it possible for me to be wrong; it sounded like Glenn was giving me *permission* to be wrong, and permission to admit it. If the purpose of the camp session was to treat people with dignity and respect, as we'd always said it was, why shouldn't Glenn Turner be allowed to go behind the chapel and smooch with his girl?

I said, "All right, Glenn, you and Jaylene have ten minutes. Keep all your clothes on." He said, "Yes, sir!" and as he turned to go tell Jaylene, I caught the sleeve of his shirt and pulled him to me. "But Glenn—gentlemen don't tell the other guys about smooching, all right? Just let 'em wonder."

He gave me a big, beautiful smile and went straight to Jaylene; I watched as they slipped out one of the side doors of the chapel. As I looked to find their counselors to tell them what was going on, I saw my old friend Harry, who'd been watching the whole thing. He nodded his approval. I could be wrong, but sometimes, if I get enough chances, sometimes I get it right.

6

New and Contrite Hearts

That fall I accepted a call to the Church of the Holy Incarnation in West Branch, Mississippi. I hated to leave my friends in Tombigbee, but they understood that this was an opportunity I needed to pursue. My last Sunday there was very emotional, for me and for the congregation; even Captain Knutson, who'd started coming with his wife and been confirmed the previous spring, had to wipe away a tear or two as he gave me a big jar of gherkins with a bow taped to the top. "For the road," he huffed. As I shook his hand, he pulled me into what was almost an embrace, to whisper in my ear, "And thank you, Buddy . . . thank you."

Once again I loaded up everything I owned; this time it took not only the old Comet but also Jack's considerably older pickup pulling the trailer he used for his lawn mowers to load it all up. I'd collected a rich hodgepodge of home furnishings, mostly rescued out of various parishioners' attics. Jabbok had the whole back seat to herself.

The last stop before leaving Tombigbee was Jack and Milla's for hugs and goodbyes, liberally seasoned with assurances that they'd come visit and that I would call them. When Jack said, "Well, all right then" for the third time, it was clearly time for us to be on our way. Milla gave me a smothering hug and kissed my cheek, and then, as I was almost through the door she remembered: "Oh, wait! I made something for you, oughta last a couple of days while you're moving in." In a big glass casserole dish, she'd made a huge banana pudding; it must have weighed ten pounds. I wondered aloud, "How will I ever eat all this?" and Jack laughed. "One spoon at a time," he said.

It was about an hour and a half drive to West Branch, through pastures dotted with serene cows and the occasional field whose soybeans had just been picked. It was Sunday afternoon; Jabbok and I were off on another adventure, and I was content to trust that the gracious God of all I could see and all that was beyond me was guiding me where I was supposed to go.

We got to the rectory at about four that afternoon. Jabbok was glad to get out of the car, and I took her to her new fenced-in backyard, larger and flatter but with a disappointing lack of goats. There were two large pecan trees that held the promise of squirrels, which I imagined was even better from Jabbok's point of view. By the time I got back, Jack had started unloading the trailer, putting the little table with four wildly mismatched chairs into the carport. We wrestled the incredibly heavy sleeper sofa through the carport and into the house, and when Jack said, "Where do you want it?" I pointed to a likely wall in the little den, hoping I'd never have to move it again.

The ancient chest of drawers with the names of children I'd never known carved into the sides, the aquarium, boxes of books—comic books, books from seminary, and other books—were all unloaded and brought in. Then, after everything was under the roof and well before it was where it was going to end up, it was time for Jack to head back home.

It was awkward in a distinctly manly way—two friends feeling the emotions of the moment but unwilling and unable to express them, at the same time both funny and pathetic. Finally I stepped toward him and gathered him in a big hug, and he hugged me right back, hard. I said, "Thanks, Jack. Thanks for everything."

I watched him back the trailer and old Chevy truck out of my new driveway, and he was off in a cloud of oil smoke.

It was starting over in some ways: meeting people, building relationships, connecting the utilities, and unpacking all the household goods. It took a while to figure out how we did things there at Holy Incarnation, which was different from how we'd done them at St. Thomas in Tombigbee or in my home parish, but still just as unchangeably The Way It's Always Been Done. I'd known some of the young people of the parish from summer camp, and they came over to help unpack boxes and share some pizza.

The cycle of the church year continued: Advent, Christmas, Epiphany, Lent, Easter, Pentecost. For the first cycle I wanted to do everything the way the people of the parish were comfortable doing it; I'd heard tales of young priests who came into a parish trying to change everything in their first year, to line up with How It's Supposed to Be according to their seminary professors or a book on liturgy, and remembered the wisdom of Miss Nicholson the day I was ordained a deacon: "Well, just don't go changing everything in the church to suit you." I spent the first year learning how we do it at the Church of the Holy Incarnation. Later, if something really had to be changed, I would have built up some trust. It's all about relationships.

The first Sunday I was there, I noticed an older woman with her hair in a bun who sat in the back of the church and left during the final hymn. She was there the next Sunday and the one after that, and I asked one of the Altar Guild ladies who she was. "Oh, that's Emma Donne. She's kind of shy but as sweet as she can be." She went on to tell me that Emma had never missed a Sunday at church and that she worked at Bilson's, a department store downtown.

The following Tuesday I went to visit her at Bilson's, but I didn't see her. I asked one of the workers if she knew Emma Donne, and she seemed surprised that somebody might be asking for her, but told me she worked in the business office and pointed me in the right direction. Emma was sitting at a desk piled with bills and receipts, writing checks and punching the keys of an old hand-crank adding machine. When she saw me, she looked flustered, checked her bun, and said, "Oh, Father Buddy! How nice to see you!" but I wondered whether it really was all that nice for her.

I said, "Hi, Miss Emma. I don't mean to bother you, but I just wanted to meet you. I've seen you several times, but you always slip out before I can say hello." She didn't say anything, so I continued, "How long have you worked here?"

I could see that she was doing the calculations in her mind for a moment, and she said, "Fifty-seven years."

"Good heavens! Fifty-seven years?"

She did the figures again in her head, checking her math before nodding. "I started working here when I was seventeen, and that's fifty-seven years ago, in nineteen and twenty-six."

Her father had been killed in the First World War, she said, and she'd dropped out of high school to work at Bilson's to help her mother raise her younger sister, Elaine. Then the Great Depression had hit, and hit Mississippi hard, and she'd never had the chance to go back to school. Her mother had died in 1964, and she'd lived with her sister until she died in 1976. She walked to work five days a week and had never had or needed a car or a license to drive, she said, because it was only two more blocks to the church, and the grocery store was on her way home. When I asked if she had any family living, she smiled a little and said, "Just my cats—Fred and Ginger." I started to tell her that it was nice to have company, but she continued, "And Lucy and Ethel . . . and Laurel and Hardy." I waited a moment, just in case there might be a Groucho, a Chico, and a Harpo, but apparently six cats was all she needed, maybe all anybody needs.

After that visit, Emma was much friendlier when I saw her at church, in her own way. She still didn't stay through the end of the service, but she smiled at me from the back of the church during the sermon. From time to time when I gave her the bread of the Eucharist, she made a point of putting her hand over mine; I wondered if it was the only real human contact she had in her whole life. A few weeks later I was walking downtown and happened to see her coming out of the store. She asked me where I bought my clothes. I told her I'd been going to a Big and Tall Men's shop in Memphis, and she said she could order whatever I needed through Bilson's, from a distributor in New York City, at a discount.

I continued to meet the best people in irregular ways. After I'd been in West Branch for three or four months, I got a call at the office from a woman who told me she was a member of the parish, though she hadn't been there for a while, and that she needed to talk to a priest, that she had just been to the doctor's office and had been crying all afternoon. I told her I'd be glad to talk to her and that she could come to the church whenever she wanted to. She said she really needed to talk to me now and that she couldn't leave the house; she was hoping I could come and talk to her there.

I told her we could meet at the diner, that I'd buy her a cup of coffee, and she repeated that she had been crying all afternoon, which was apparently why she couldn't leave the house. I was still working that out when she pleaded, "Father, *please.*"

She gave me the address, and I drove up to a nice house with a well-kept lawn and a basketball goal by the driveway. I walked up the little path to ring the doorbell. The woman who answered it almost immediately was also well kept; she looked like the kind of woman who played tennis at the country club three times a week and skimped on the salad dressing after the match. She looked at me appraisingly before asking with just a touch of incredulity, "You're the priest?"

I thought the collar might have given me away, but I answered, "Yes, ma'am. I'm Buddy Hinton. We spoke on the phone."

She was clearly disappointed; I realized she'd been looking for someone else, someone older and probably more respectable. But desperate times call for desperate measures. She invited me in and said, "How long have you been a priest?"

"About three and a half years." Then I noticed that there were two little piles of pieces of colorful baseball caps on either side of the parquet entranceway—the bills of the caps on the left and the rest of them on the right. I didn't want to ask; I thought maybe she assembled baseball caps in her home.

We stood there awkwardly for a moment, until she said, "I thought I was calling Father Reed." Edward Reed had been my predecessor there at the Church of the Holy Incarnation. I said, "He moved to Sewanee to work on his doctorate."

She said, "Oh." Then she invited me into the den and asked if I'd like a cup of coffee. I declined, and she asked me if I was married, and it seemed like her disappointment was confirmed when I told her I was not, as if that somehow added to her troubles. Then I said, somewhat awkwardly, "I don't think you told me your name when we talked on the phone."

"Phyllis . . . Phyllis Rust."

"Thank you. And I'm Buddy Hinton. Please call me Buddy."

"Thank you . . . Father. You can call me Phyllis."

"Okay, Phyllis. How can I help you?"

Relieved of her obligation of hospitality, she took up the burden of whatever had been upsetting her, but apparently didn't know how to start talking about it.

"You said on the phone that you've been to the doctor," I prompted.

She nodded but couldn't say anything, so I offered, "And the doctor gave you some upsetting news."

She nodded again, and, seemingly encouraged that I'd made this much progress all by myself, waited for me to guess what she'd been told. I said, "Are you seriously ill?"

She shook her head and waited to see if I would guess again, but I didn't, and after a while she mumbled something I didn't understand. I said, as gently as I could since it seemed I was asking her to repeat something upsetting and apparently shameful, "I'm sorry, Phyllis, but I didn't hear what you said."

She sank into herself, part of her collapsing as she repeated, "I have genital herpes."

What I said was "Oh," which never hurts anybody, but what I thought was "Why does she feel the need to tell a priest about this?" She didn't say anything else but sat quietly weeping on her sofa, and the silence dragged for a while before I said, "I'm sorry to hear that." She continued to cry, and I continued to wonder why I was there and what I was supposed to say—something a priest would say—until I ventured, "What kind of treatment is there for that?"

The look in her eyes told me I'd missed the whole point, but all I could do was keep missing it until she sobbed, "Rusty and I started dating in high school." That was a clue, I knew, but it still didn't explain what was going on, and she continued, "I've never . . . been with . . . never had any other . . . ."

The pieces came crashing together then, and the puzzle started taking shape. Her husband—I guess if your last name was Rust it was nearly inevitable that you'd be called Rusty in high school—was the only man she'd ever had sex with, and now she had contracted a sexually transmitted disease. The only possible conclusion was that he had had an affair with someone with genital herpes. I wasn't there because of a medical crisis; it was a marital crisis.

Oh.

I didn't know what to say, so I didn't say anything for a while, and after that strategy was clearly not going to move us along, I said, "Phyllis, what do you want?"

She quickly replied, "I want to be so mad I could spit in his face!"

I said, "Yes ma'am. I think that's probably appropriate. But you don't need me for that."

Another long silence, with me sitting in a pretty but uncomfortable chair clearly meant for someone who skimps on their salad dressing after two sets of tennis at the country club and not for someone who's had to order his clothes from a Big and Tall men's distributor in New York City, I hazarded, "You have grounds for divorce, if you want out of the marriage."

Now she looked up with the pain full in her eyes as if I'd slapped her. "No, I do not want a divorce! Can't I just be good and mad for a while? Is that too much to ask?"

Well, the wound was completely open now. I answered, "No ma'am, that's not too much. No one could blame you for being mad. But what are you going to do about it? That's why you wanted to talk to a priest, right? If all you wanted was to be angry, you wouldn't need me. You'd be talking to one of your friends right now, right?"

She was quiet for a while, and, hoping to get her to talk, I pressed on. "Do you want to stay married to him?"

She hesitated, and admitted, "Yes."

"Why?"

"Because we have two children—our son is about your age; it would be devastating to them."

"Not enough."

"What?"

"That not enough of a reason to stay with him. Your children don't want you to be miserable."

"Are you telling me I should divorce my husband?"

"No. I'm telling you that staying with him because of the children is not a sufficient reason. Why do you want to stay married to Rusty?"

"It would be a scandal for our whole family."

"Yes ma'am, probably so. But that's still not enough."

"What do you want me to say?"

"Do you love him?"

"He betrayed me! He cheated on me! He lied to me!"

"Yes ma'am." I took a breath and let it out slowly. "Do you love him?"

She was silent again, and I wondered if she would just sit there until I said something. This time I decided to sit there to see what would happen. The silence stretched out, past uncomfortable and on toward unnerving, and finally she said, "Yes."

Much later I realized that was the turning point in our conversation, in their marriage, and in her life.

"You love him?"

"Yes."

"And you want to be married to him?"

"Yes. Yes, I love him, but I'm still mad as hell!"

"Okay, I understand that." I started talking about forgiveness, stacking what sounded to me like worn-out old saws and sayings on top of empty aphorisms and clichés, and just as I was about to get into the impressive-sounding and equally vacant maxims and adages, Rusty came through the front door, paused between the piles of baseball cap parts, and said, "What the hell is this?"

He burst into the den to find his wife talking to a young priest he'd never met, and looking at me he stammered, "Sorry," but I wasn't sure if he was apologizing because he'd given his wife genital herpes or because he'd had an affair or because he'd cussed in front of a priest. Either way, it seemed like a good time for me to leave, and I stood up and whispered to Phyllis, "I'll talk to you later."

But Phyllis grabbed my hand and said, "Please stay." I stood frozen between good sense and the request of a woman in pain, and in a few seconds the man stepped across the den and held out his hand, saying, "I'm Walter Rust. My friends call me Rusty."

"Hi, Rusty. I'm Buddy Hinton, the new priest at the Church of the Holy Incarnation. My friends call me Buddy."

We all sat down, and, piece by piece, the rest of the puzzle came together. Rusty worked for Holiday Inn as an upper-level accountant of some sort, and his job involved a lot of travel. He was a big baseball fan, and through the years he had visited every Major League city and gone to a game, bringing home a cap from every stadium—his prized collection, now carefully dissected at the hand of a woman who was so mad she could spit in his face.

He'd gone to St. Louis some months ago. There was a bar on the same block as the Holiday Inn and the waitress was young and pretty and friendly and it had been a long difficult day and he was feeling lonely and he'd had one or two or maybe three more drinks than he should have and one thing led to another and later he realized that he had herpes and he loved his wife so much and he didn't know how to tell her about the herpes and he'd never wanted to hurt her in any way but now he had and he was so, so sorry, so very sorry.

We all fell into a silence then, the calm after the storm, until I felt like I needed to say something. "Rusty, what do you want?"

"I want this to go away!" Then to his wife he said, "I am so sorry. Please forgive me!"

I thought I was going to have to go back through all the worn-out, empty, and impressive-sounding stuff about forgiveness I'd been slogging around in before he'd arrived, but the realization crashed into me that the important thing was not for me to have something to say but for them to have something to hear.

I said to Rusty, "Do you want to be married to Phyllis?"

He snapped, "Of course I do! What do you think I—"

"Do you love her?"

"Yes."

"Do you trust her?"

"Of course. She'd never given me any cause to—"

"Yes sir. She wants to stay in the marriage too—she told me—because she loves you, too, although I hope you'll understand it's probably hard for her to feel it just now."

His face showed his relief, but before he could get too comfortable I continued, "The problem is that you *have* given her cause not to trust you."

He was crying now, and so was she. I was feeling a little teary myself. He moaned, "I'm sorry, I'm so sorry."

I felt some sympathy for him and wanted to help him, wanted to help both of them, but what came out next was, "That's not going to be enough."

Then I kept talking, and I had that strange and wonderful sense of listening to myself talk that I'd had in sermons sometimes, like I didn't know what I was going to say until I said it. "Trust is the issue here. You can stay together, you can say you're married, you can claim to love the other person, but if you can't trust each other, it's all just pretend. If both of you can't trust the other, this marriage is dead. No matter what people say, trust can't be earned; it can only be given. And the only way to rebuild broken trust is through forgiveness."

Turning to Rusty, I continued, "You won't ever be able apologize enough that the one who's been hurt has to forgive you. You can only be forgiven out of the loving goodness of the other, when the other chooses to forgive you. It's like one of those suspension bridges, boards held up by ropes or cables, lined up to swing over a canyon or a stream. Rusty, you've kicked out some of the boards of your marriage, and you can't replace them. They can only be replaced by Phyllis."

She said, "That's not fair!"

"No ma'am," I said, "it's not. But it's true. This won't be over, won't ever be healed, until you forgive Rusty, and he can't do anything to earn it. It's not fair, but it's all on you, Phyllis—a choice you have to make."

Rusty said, "I'll do anything!"

"Yes sir. I know. But there's nothing you can really do. You can apologize a thousand times a day, and you probably should. But it all depends on Phyllis and her love for you."

We talked for a while, but it seemed clear that I'd said everything I knew to say, and that they had some talking they needed to do without me hovering around, so when I stood up to leave again, Phyllis didn't stop me.

They were in church the following Sunday, sitting together but looking a little forced, nothing that anybody else would have noticed. After the service, in the Enjoyed Your Sermon line, Phyllis hugged me, which was a surprise, and when I asked her how it was going she whispered, "Well, I don't feel like I want to slap him anymore."

I replied, "That's good," before she continued, "Or touch him at all, in any way."

He shook my hand and told me he'd enjoyed the sermon. I said, "You okay?" and he answered, "Just fine," leaving me to wonder if he was lying or oblivious.

A week or so later I was alone in the church about half an hour before the Ash Wednesday evening service, making sure the ashes were ready and things were generally the way they're supposed to be and that I knew what I was doing—a never-ending struggle—when I realized I wasn't alone at all. Rusty Rust was in the middle of the nave, looking at me as I stood by the altar.

I called out, "Hey," but he didn't answer. Something in the way he didn't answer led me to realize that he wasn't just early for the service, and I walked down to where he was. He had been crying. I didn't say anything but opened my arms in greeting, which he stepped into as an embrace, sobbing.

Most men don't like to cry, especially in front of another man. But sometimes you just need to, macho be damned. This was one of those times, and Rusty stood there and wept for what seemed like a long time. After a while Elnora and Wadsworth Mills came in and looked at us, wondering what was going on. I called out, "Hi, Elnora; hi, Worth. Rusty was just helping me get set up here." Then I said, "Rusty, let's go look in the sacristy."

When we got there, I said, "Are you okay? What's going on?"

He lamented, "Oh, Father, it's just terrible! I've messed up everything, and all I can do is tell her how sorry I am . . ."

He stopped, and I prompted, "And?"

"And she says she forgives me . . ."

"Do you think she really has forgiven you?"

"Well, yeah, but . . ."

"But?"

"But I don't feel it, Father. I just don't really feel forgiven."

"The hard part is that you have to forgive yourself to feel like you're forgiven," I said. Then I told him I'd had a friend who'd spent some time in prison, who told me about some of the other inmates who couldn't forgive themselves for what they'd done. "Jake said they would have to let it go, or drag it around with them for the rest of their lives. He said it was just prideful to hold on to something God has let go of."

Rusty stood there in the sacristy, surrounded by all the trappings of the Eucharist: brass and silver, silk and linen, cartons of bread and gallon jugs of port wine, and wondered what it might mean to just let go of his guilt and shame.

I put my hand on his shoulder and said, "Look, Rusty, you messed up. There's no getting around that. You messed up. I've messed up, too—everybody messes up. Yours is more dramatic than some, and with more serious and definite consequences. You hurt somebody you love. But you love her, and she loves you; you've apologized, and she's chosen to forgive you. It's over; you can let it go. Let her forgive you, Rusty."

Other people had come in, and it was time for the service to start. He nodded, and stepped out of the sacristy trying to look like he was supposed to have been in there the whole time.

The Liturgy for Ash Wednesday starts without any procession or music—just a prayer: "Almighty and everlasting God, you hate nothing you have made and forgive the sins of all who are penitent: Create and make in us new and contrite hearts, that we, worthily lamenting our sins and acknowledging our wickedness, may obtain of you, the God of all mercy, perfect remission and forgiveness; through Jesus Christ our Lord, who lives and reigns with you and the Holy Spirit, one God, for ever and ever."

Somewhere in the middle of that I looked up to see Rusty, sitting wretched and alone in the agony of having hurt Phyllis and the dread of having damaged his marriage, and willed him to hear what we were saying, and in so willing, I heard the prayer as I'd never heard it before, even as I said it. God really doesn't hate any of us ever, but forgives us freely, wants us to be forgiven. And still we hold on to whatever wicked, stupid, cowardly, selfish thing we've done, as if it's precious to us, as if that's who we are. Jake was so right: it's prideful for us to hold on to something God has let go of.

The problem is not that we're wicked but that we're too proud to let ourselves be forgiven. Maybe that's just another flavor of wicked.

Two or three Sundays later, Phyllis and Rusty were in church, and the change I saw in them was striking. They were easy in each other's company. Trust had been restored; the suspension bridge had been repaired. Our worship, still in the season of Lent, was penitential, but I was much heartened by the idea that these two got it, understood forgiveness in a beautiful way.

After the service Rusty took me aside to say, "Thank you, Father."

I said, "I'm so glad it's getting better. Y'all have done some hard work."

Phyllis said to her husband, happily holding his hand, "Tell him the three things, Rusty."

He said, "Every day we say three things. The first one is 'I love you,' which I'm always glad to say. The second is 'I apologize,' which I have an opportunity to say at least once a day—"

"And I do, too," she interjected.

"—which leads to the third thing, which is 'I forgive you.'"

"Not 'That's okay,'" Phyllis put in, "or 'Don't worry about it,' or 'No sweat,' but '*I forgive you.*'"

"And then," Rusty concluded, "once it's forgiven, it's gone. The person who is forgiven can't hold on to it, and the person doing the forgiving can't pick it up and use it later." He beamed. "It's gone."

She nodded. "It's gone."

Amazing.

1

BURNING LOVE

It was a glorious Easter that year, as I luxuriated in a new understanding of the depth and breadth of forgiveness. Easter Sunday was also the last Sunday that Miss Emma was able come to church.

For many years before I got there Emma had never missed a Sunday service, but when I saw her that Easter morning she didn't look like she felt well, and she didn't come up for Communion. I took the bread and wine to the back of the church, knowing that she would be horrified to have any attention directed at her in any way, and made a point of bending down to talk to her briefly after she had received the elements.

"Are you okay?"

"I'm fine, I'm just fine. My legs are a little tired, I think, so I didn't want to walk up there. I was afraid I might need some help up the steps. But I'm fine. Don't make a fuss about me."

But she wasn't fine. The next Sunday, she was not in church. On Monday morning I went to Bilson's and found out that she'd called in sick. She didn't have a telephone, so I walked to her house and knocked on the door. When she came to the door in her housecoat and slippers, I could see that she was failing. I told her I was going to go and get my car to take her to the hospital, that she should get some things together. She protested, of course, but I drew on whatever authority she thought I had and told her she had to go, and she believed me.

By the time I got back, she was in a dress and sensible shoes, feeding her cats and loving each one of them individually. I was in a hurry to get her to the hospital, but knew better than to rush this moment. It took her a few minutes to find Ethel, who she explained was always the shy one, but she did, and picked her up to give her a squeeze and a kiss.

She was in the hospital for three weeks. I went to see her almost every day, and every time I went she told me I didn't have to come see her, that I had more important things to do. I assured her every time that I did not. She also told me not to tell anyone at the church, and I told her I was going to anyway; in fact, I pointedly invited several of the ladies to pay her a visit. I took her Communion on Sunday afternoons.

The last Sunday afternoon I saw her, she was in and out of consciousness, and I wondered if she could hear me praying until I saw her lips moving with me as I said the Lord's Prayer, words she'd cherished her whole life. She couldn't take the Communion bread, so I ate two pieces, one for me and one for her. I sat there for a while, and when it came time to leave I bent down and kissed her on the forehead, and she perked up enough to motion me over. I put my ear down next to her mouth so I could hear, and she said something I really wanted to hear but didn't understand.

I thought, "Man, I missed her last words." She cleared her throat and said quietly but clearly, "It's Graduation Day." The nurse called late that night and told me that she'd died in her sleep: Graduation Day.

A few days later I had to decide how many bulletins to print for Miss Emma's funeral. I ran off fifty, thinking it's always better to have too many, to have some left over. She was very sweet, but she was very shy; she didn't join groups, and she didn't stay after church for receptions or lunches. I didn't know how many people would know her.

So I was shocked when I put on all my vestments and came to the back of the church to find the place packed! The church was so filled with people that ushers were setting up chairs in the aisles—people from the parish and people from the town, people she'd known for fifty or sixty or seventy years. I had not realized how many people she had touched in her life, or loved, or ordered clothes for, or brought casseroles to, or listened to, all in her own quiet, shy way. I went back to the copy machine and ran off another hundred copies, and we ran out again.

Miss Emma Donne was shy and beloved, a quiet saint. I think everybody in the church that morning was surprised to see so many of us there, to see how many people were connected to her, a web of relationships we had never seen until we all came together.

Sometimes people come to a funeral just to sign the guest book, some of them leaving before the service even starts, as if there's some credit gained by signing the book. Some people stay for the service but don't really follow along, don't sing the hymns or open the prayer books, not allowing themselves to be taken in. Often people will come to a funeral in the funeral home or the church and skip the graveside service. For Miss Emma, it seemed to me that everybody who was there was really there, following the service and singing the hymns, and that almost all of us went to the cemetery. It was as if we had all too late discovered what a treasure she was, and now we didn't want to let her go.

The summer following Miss Emma's passing was the first year that Bobbo McCain and his brother JoJo first came to camp, two African-American brothers from Mayersville, Mississippi, a little town in the Delta north of Vicksburg, the county seat of Issaquena County. They had never been away from their mother before and were almost never separated from each other while they were at camp. Bobbo was thirty-seven, three years older than his brother, and was a natural entertainer who loved to be the center of attention. He had a big personality: loud, colorful, and flamboyant.

JoJo was at the other end of that spectrum; even though he was an extra-large man, you'd only notice him because he was with Bobbo. He was easily six feet three or four, but mostly he was Bobbo's biggest fan. Their applications indicated that they both had mental disabilities, but JoJo seemed to look after Bobbo, whose attention was always on the audience.

Bobbo loved show business and adored all the stars of stage and screen. He brought a paper bag filled magazines about celebrities and Hollywood stars and would talk about their various rises and falls at great length. He especially loved *The Wizard of Oz* and could sing the Cowardly Lion's soliloquy in full, his voice quavering when he sang, "If I-I-I were ki-i-ing of the forest!"

We put them both with the same counselor, a sixteen-year-old kid from Natchez, back for his second year. His name was Nathan, but we all called him Nat, mostly so we could say "Nat from Natchez." Nat figured out pretty quickly that Bobbo was going to be a star at camp. Bobbo drew pictures of various celebrities, although they all looked vaguely like Walter Matthau, and showed Nat from Natchez his movie star magazines, which the counselor looked at with great patience, even when it was the third or fourth time through. And JoJo was along for the ride.

When Nat told Bobbo he would receive an award at the end of the session, Bobbo decided it must be sort of like the Academy Awards, and they worked out a plan for Bobbo to give out his own awards. They were all camp-themed. Nat from Natchez received Best Leading Man at the Pool. When another counselor in the same cabin won Best Supporting Actor in the Dining Hall, it was Nat from Natchez who insisted the counselor should make an acceptance speech, and so a new camp tradition was born.

Nat from Natchez was the one who'd written out the awards, and on each envelope wrote "The Camp Bratton-Green Acamedy Awards," a happy misspelling that caught on. That first year it was just for the other guys in his cabin, but by the second year it grew so that anybody could receive an award; I still have my "Best Fishing Camp Director" award.

The biggest problem with Bobbo was that he never wanted the show to end, even when it was time to go to bed. Not only did he not want to waste his own time by going to sleep, but he didn't want any of his fans to go to bed, either. He could not be quiet, would not be still. He would sing and laugh and pretend to fart, or sing and laugh and actually fart, until the whole cabin was desperate to go to sleep, and even then he'd keep on and on. And on.

After the first night of this, I suggested to Nat from Natchez that he'd have to sit with Bobbo outside the cabin until he got sleepy. Bobbo spent the night throwing sticks and pinecones on the roof of his cabin and howling like a wolf. After the second sleepless night, the whole cabin was walking around like zombies, and I asked Nurse Brenda if she could help us out.

Bobbo didn't have anything prescribed, and there hadn't been any mention of hyperactivity in his application. She told me that she had an over-the-counter antihistamine that might be effective; I asked her what an antihistamine was, and she said it was used for several things, including insect bites and coughs, but that it often had what in this situation might be the happy side effect of making people drowsy. She assured me that in any case it would do him no harm.

That night, after milk and cookies, she asked Bobbo if he had any bug bites. Of course he did, and he wouldn't have been able to resist the extra attention to admit it if he hadn't. She told him that she wanted to give him an antihistamine so he wouldn't itch so much, and she noticed that the itching caused by his sudden realization that he had bites all over his body was now very nearly debilitating.

Unfortunately, the antihistamine was not as effective as we had hoped, and it was another long night for Nat from Natchez and the rest of the cabin, this time with the added drama of trying to make sure Bobbo didn't scratch himself bloody. But it did give Nurse Brenda an idea.

In the canteen, she told me, we had packages of Spree, a small round colorful hard candy with a tart taste. They weren't selling all that well, but Nurse Brenda thought she had a use for them. She educated me about placebos, usually sugar pills that were given to help people think they were getting some sort of medicine, often as a control in medical research. She said we didn't have any sugar pills, but she was wondering if the Spree candy might be used as placebos for Bobbo. I thought it was a silly idea, but the only other alternative was to send Bobbo home. He couldn't keep going like this, and neither could the rest of his cabin.

So that night after milk and cookies, I came up to the administration building to help Nurse Brenda dispense all the medications. We had worked out our script, and we knew our lines.

When Bobbo, JoJo, and Nat from Natchez came to get their medicines, Brenda said, "All right, Bobbo. Tonight you need to sleep so you can sing your song in the talent show tomorrow night."

Bobbo nodded dubiously.

I said, "You're singing an Elvis song, right? I bet you're a great Elvis! You got the Elvis moves?"

He nodded again, more sure of himself here.

Brenda said, "So I'm going to give you a placebo to help you sleep, okay? It's a pill."

He hesitated, and I filled in the moment: "Are you singing 'Jailhouse Rock,' or 'Hound Dog?'"

Bobbo was suspicious and mumbled, "Hunka hunka."

That puzzled us, until JoJo stepped in and murmured, "Hunka hunka burnin' love." I think this was the first time I ever heard him speak; Bobbo had always talked more than enough for both of them.

I said, "Oh man—I love that song!"

Back on track now, Brenda continued, "So you need to get some rest tonight. Now, I just don't know . . ."

Bobbo said, "Don't know what?"

Brenda knew she had him now. She brought out ten or twelve Sprees in a sandwich bag, all of them either yellow or red. She looked at me and said, "Should I give him the 250 milligram placebo, or the 500 red?" She pointed to the yellow Sprees at the mention of 250 milligrams and the reds at 500.

I said, "Oh, I don't know, Brenda. Those 500s are pretty powerful. We better give him a 250."

She thought about it for a moment and went on. "Well, I suppose so. We want to be sure he gets enough rest, though."

Now JoJo, who hadn't been getting much sleep either, said, "Better give 'im the 500, preacher."

I said, "You think so?"

JoJo looked at me, and I could have sworn he winked, but I couldn't be sure; I might have just imagined it. He said, "Bobbo, you better take the strong one."

Bobbo took the red Spree with a gulp of water and was dramatically, miraculously almost asleep on his feet before he could get out of the administration building. Nat from Natchez told me later that he and JoJo almost had to carry him to the cabin.

The cabin was quiet that night, giggles and farts replaced by Bobbo's unpleasant but constant snoring, actually a huge improvement. And the next night, after a rousing talent show rendition of "Burning Love," Bobbo came to the administration building to get his medicine and asked Nurse Brenda for a yellow pill this time.

When the campers were all packed up and waiting for their drivers to come and take them home, JoJo left Bobbo's side long enough to find me. "We have had us a time, ain't we?"

I said, "Yes sir."

He said, "You comin' back next year, preacher?"

I repeated, "Yes sir," and added, "How about you?"

"Yes sir. Bobbo too." He paused a minute, thinking, and continued, "Y'know, he don't normally have no trouble sleepin'."

I laughed, not sure where we were going with this. "He did this week, though, didn't he?"

"Yes sir. I think he was just all excited up 'bout bein' here and all. He just loves being here, and y'all was so good to him, to both of us. He loved it so much he just didn't want to miss nothin'."

I tried for a moment to form a joke about it, to tell JoJo that it was like the Elvis song about the love that was burning him up, but I couldn't put it together quickly enough before JoJo continued, "The people back home don't pay him much mind, but it's like y'all just eat him up. It was smart for y'all to give him them candy pills, though. I don't think them other mens in the cabin could've took much more of him at night."

I said, "Well, don't tell him they're just candy, all right?"

He said, "Aw, *Lord* no! He thinks they's something just for him, and ain't nobody else gets 'em. I call 'em 'Bobbo's seebos,' and they's special, just for him."

And every night at camp after that, for the rest of his life, Bobbo would come and ask for a yellow seebo before bed. Those red ones were just too strong.

A Cause for Wonder

Some weeks passed, and life went on with the small accomplishments and frustrations you might expect in the life of a priest in a small parish. The summer neared its end as it always does: too soon for school children and in a blaze of heat and humidity.

One rainy afternoon in late summer, the mail included an envelope from Mississippi State Penitentiary, Parchman, Mississippi. Just seeing the envelope took me back to college and seminary, when I'd wait for letters from my dear friend Jake Jefferson, who'd spent some time in prison there.

This one was from his friend Cornelius, who worked in the prison kitchen and lived with his wife, Mabel, in nearby Riggsville. The letter was carefully written on a piece of typing paper with a fountain pen, the print both cramped and smudged. It was hard to read, and hard to take.

21 August 1983
Dear Buddy,

I hope you are doing all right, now that you is a preacher over in West Branch. Mabel sends her love, too. She and me are just fine, so that's okay. The boys are doing real good. Benjamin is married out in Houston Texas with a good job. Abraham is still here in Riggsville working at the prison but he is close to home so that is good too. I am writing this letter cause Eugene Jefferson asked me. I hope you remember Eugene, the big man who loved Preacher Jake but also listened to Eddie Walker too much. He wanted me to write you and let you know that all of his courtroom time is done now, and that the prison is going to put him to death in the gas chamber on October 7. They will put him to death for murder right after midnight on that day. There isn't no more appeals and the lawyer says there isn't nothing he can do any more than what he already has. Eugene says he just wanted you to know but said you don't have to come but I think he would love to see you before he passes. He has done many things to feel guilty about and I believe he wants to face the Lord with a clear mind and heart. He believes that there is a heaven and a hell and he is pretty sure that he will not be going to heaven. He usually listens to Mabel pretty good but he will not listen to her about this. He is sure he will be going to hell on October 7. Buddy I hope that you can come before they kill him that day. Mabel says she would like to see you, too.

Sincerely,
Cornelius Jones

I'd encountered Eugene Jefferson twice, first when I went to visit Jake in the prison and then when I went to tell Mabel and Cornelius that Jake had died. He was huge and gentle, as sweet a man as I've ever met, massively strong and easily influenced. Another inmate named Eddie Walker had used him as his muscle to become powerful in the prison. Eugene had been torn between Jake's loving idealism and Eddie's scornful cynicism, and eventually he broke away from Eddie to follow Jake's way. But it was too late: by that time Eugene had killed Eddie's cousin Archie in the prison yard because he'd stolen a bottle of whiskey and some cigarettes from Eddie. His case had been tried and appealed and appealed again, and now he was scheduled to be executed in the gas chamber. Eugene had come to prison years before for his part in several murders resulting from a drug deal gone sour; in the eyes of blind justice, he was a repeat offender.

My friend Ward was on the Vestry at Holy Incarnation and was also the city attorney in West Branch. I asked him about capital punishment and the gas chamber. After making sure I wasn't going to preach about what seemed to him an issue crammed full of political potholes, he told me that the state of Mississippi used to have a movable electric chair, but they thought the gas chamber was more humane and more reliable. He also said there had been several legal complications that had resulted in nineteen years without an execution, but now there were some who wanted to catch up: the next execution was scheduled for September 2.

I did not want to go back to Parchman. The last time I'd been there, Eddie Walker had almost killed me. I actually did not know Eugene particularly well. It was out of my way, I was busy, there wasn't anything I could do to help him, and I was afraid to go to Death Row. I rummaged around in my head for some other reasons and excuses, but the truth was that I was afraid of failing to help this man whom Jake had tried so hard to help.

But I found that I couldn't *not* go. I tried, but it wasn't going to work. Ward said Death Row prisoners typically had visitors on Sundays only. I got a retired priest to cover for me that next Sunday, and on Saturday I put Jabbok into the Mercury Comet and drove west into the Mississippi Delta, flat as a basketball court for as far as you could see, which was miles and miles. I always feel like there's no place to hide in the Delta——no hills, no woods, no gullies, just soybeans and cotton and heavy farming machinery in vast, monotonously horizontal fields.

When we got to Riggsville, I went to Mabel's house, where I'd done her wedding before I was ordained. I took Jabbok around behind the house and found her mother, Dulsey, asleep under the back porch. It wasn't a touching mother and daughter reunion scene, but after a moment of becoming accustomed to each other, they seemed to be glad for the company.

As far as I knew, Mabel and Cornelius didn't have a telephone, so I hadn't called ahead to tell them I was coming. All I could do now was sit in an old rocking chair on their front porch and wait. The dogs came and nuzzled together, lying near my feet. It was late afternoon, sticky hot, bees buzzing and wasps menacing. It was humid too, but it was nice not to have anything to do or anywhere to go for a little bit . . . .

The thumping of two dogs' tails woke me up. Miss Mabel had finished at the parsonage and come home for a couple of hours before going back to prepare supper for the Reverend Swayze and his wife, Claire.

She was squinting, trying to see me more clearly. "Who's that up there on my porch? Who're you?"

I stood up to let her see me better, and to give her a hug after she did. She came up the steps onto the porch and, recognizing me, threw her arms wide. I stepped into her hug and felt like I'd come home.

"Preacher Buddy!"

"Yes ma'am."

"How long has it been since you been here, honey?"

"Too long, Miss Mabel—since your wedding, I think. How are you doing?"

"Oh, we're just fine, all of us. Cornelius is at the prison kitchen, of course, and Benjamin and Rosalee are living out in Texas, expecting our first grandbaby in a few months. Abraham is working in the business office out at the Parchman Farm. We were hoping he'd found the right girl, but she broke his heart and left him for a lawyer up in Memphis."

She paused then, sobered by remembering why I had come. "You're here to see Eugene?"

"Yes ma'am."

"He ain't doin' so good, Buddy. I took some of my Sunday school ladies out to see him this past Sunday evening. We have a service out there sometimes. He couldn't come to the service, but we went to see him out there on the Death Row."

She paused, waiting for me to say something, but I couldn't think of anything to say.

"Oh, honey, it's terrible in there. It's so hot, there's no air, like you can't catch a good breath. There's no hope in there, Buddy."

"Can you take me out there to see him?"

"I'll take you tomorrow, right after church. He'll be glad to see you, might help him rest a little easier. You ain't preachin' tomorrow?"

"No ma'am; tomorrow I'm visiting an old friend."

"Well, then you can come to our church."

My first instinct was to object, but I couldn't think of any reason I wouldn't go to church with her. She saw my hesitation and poked me with it: "You think somebody there at the Second Avenue Baptist Church might stab you? Or try to convert you?"

I caught myself and answered, "No ma'am. I'll be honored to go to your church tomorrow."

We caught up for a while, and I told her about my work in the parish and about special sessions at camp. "No, I'm not dating anyone right now," I said when she asked, reminded again that nature abhors a vacuum. Later in the afternoon, Mabel had to go back to the parsonage to cook the Saturday evening meal, so I sat and rocked on the porch with the dogs, whistling.

Cornelius finished his work in the prison kitchen and came home, surprised to see me, and we started all over again. The visit with Miss Mabel had filled the porch with words, questions, answers, and more questions. After a brief time of catching up, the visit with Cornelius was filled with smoke from his pipe and companionable silence, set against the backdrop of the ubiquitous symphony of cicadas and tree frogs, along with two sleeping dogs.

Mabel brought home three plates from the Swayzes' dinner: pork chops in gravy, fried okra, black-eyed peas, white rice, and cornbread that was slightly sweet. I had eaten her cooking years before when I'd come to visit my friend Jake in prison, and she still remembered that I don't eat okra, so she made a point of not putting any on my plate. I thanked her for the supper, and for leaving the okra off, and she shook her head saying, "I don't know what to think of a grown man who don't eat his vegetables." She smiled then, and we enjoyed the supper together. I helped her do the dishes, and Mabel and I talked and laughed long after Cornelius fell asleep in his comfortable chair.

The next morning, Cornelius was gone long before I woke up. Miss Mabel made scrambled eggs, grits, fried ham, and big flaky biscuits with white gravy, all served up with her strong black chicory-laced coffee. I told her that breakfast was worth the whole trip over here; she told me she cooked it up every Sunday morning and she'd be glad for me to come any time. I told her I worked most weekends now, and we both laughed.

Mabel's '67 Chevy Impala that had taken us out to Parchman my only other visit was gone now; it was hard to believe it had been nine years since I'd visited Jake there and first met Eugene. The Impala had been replaced by a muddy brown 1976 Volkswagen Rabbit, which was small and noisy and burned diesel fuel instead of gasoline. She'd bought it from someone at her church who'd convinced her the Rabbit was going to be the next big thing.

"You like your new car?" I asked, after I'd folded myself into it.

"Oh, Lord no."

I didn't know what to say to that, so I sat quietly as she started the engine. It sounded like something had come loose, clanking around in the cylinders. She continued, "But it was cheap, and it's so ugly it doesn't matter much if I run into something, and I ain't afraid of nobody stealing it."

We rattled along to the Second Avenue Baptist Church in Riggsville. I knew I wanted to wear my clerical shirt and collar to visit Eugene, and had asked Miss Mabel whether it would be okay to wear it to her church. She chuckled a little and said, "Honey, you goin' to stick out like a poodle in a yard full of hound dogs anyway, so go ahead and put it on. It don't really make no difference one way or the other."

In my experience in the Church, people always enjoy having something to complain about: the music, the temperature, the children, disregarding tradition or being bound by it. If a person wants to complain, there is always something to complain about in the Church. Most people agree about the sermon, though: the consensus seems to be that a sermon is something to be endured, something the clergyperson is paid to do to the members, like a dentist is paid to inflict pain on the patient. The people might tell you it was a good sermon, and it might even have been enjoyable, but it was always too long. I don't think I've ever heard anybody complain that a sermon was too short.

But the people at the Second Street Baptist Church in Riggsville were accustomed to enjoying the sermon, even though it was long, even though it was hot. They not only enjoyed it but also participated in it: encouraging the preacher, supporting him as he put them through their emotional paces from laughter to tears, from despair to hope.

The congregation at Second Street answered questions the preacher asked and bridged the brief breaks by encouraging him to keep going: "Well, well," "C'mon, now!" "Well, all right!" or "Tell it, Preacher!" They stood up, raised their hands, and each point made was celebrated with Amens and Hallelujahs. The more he preached, the hotter it got; he just mopped his brow and face with a white handkerchief and kept right on preaching.

I have no idea what he said or how long the sermon lasted, but I know I was physically tired at the end of it, just listening to it. It was followed by an energetic musical offering from the choir, during which the preacher came down to talk to me and Mabel, asking if I would mind speaking to the membership.

"You mean, just sort of introduce myself?"

"Well, no—I'll introduce you. You're a preacher, ain't you? Just give us a few words."

"You mean, preach?" I was petrified at the idea of standing before this crowd.

"Just a little something."

Miss Mabel was gratified by the prospect, and I thought it would be rude to refuse. I rummaged around in my head to find something to say that wouldn't be a complete waste of everybody's time. I had been preaching without notes for a while, but never without thinking about what I was going to say—that would come much later. The music ended and the preacher stepped back into the pulpit.

"Now, sisters and brothers, we have a special guest with us this morning. Y'all might already have noticed the Reverend Doctor Buddy Hinton, senior pastor at the Episcopalian church over in West Branch. He is a friend of Sister Mabel and Brother Cornelius Jones, and I understand he was a friend of Preacher Jake out at the prison. Y'all might remember how Preacher Buddy performed Cornelius and Mabel's wedding about two years ago."

That got some reaction from the congregation; I had a little credit built up from knowing Mabel, Cornelius, and Jake. Everybody in the place was looking at me, the only white face among all those shades of coffee and caramel. I stood up, not knowing what to expect, and the preacher boomed into the microphone, "Ah, here he comes! C'mon, preacher, and give us a little something to think about, why don't you please."

Some of the congregation murmured their encouragement, but without much conviction. They'd probably heard white preachers before and were not optimistic. Truthfully, neither was I.

Then I realized that I'd seen many of these people at Mabel and Cornelius's wedding, just two years before. They'd already heard me speak and knew it wouldn't be anything like what they were used to. I cleared my throat and said, "Good morning, friends."

I thanked them for their hospitality and told them that I was enjoying the service very much. I told them I was a priest in the Episcopal Church, and when it didn't seem like that registered I told them the Episcopal Church was the American branch of the Church of England, and that didn't help, either. I told them we were sort of like Roman Catholics, which they regarded with some wariness; Catholics they knew about, but apparently not with universally favorable reviews.

I told them that when I was growing up south of Vicksburg, I just sort of thought church was church, and that the church I grew up in was doing things the way they were supposed to be done, and that everybody else must be doing about the same thing. But when I went to seminary, one of the things I learned is that the Church is a lot bigger than that and very complicated, and that different congregations and denominations do things differently. I got an Amen from the back pews, and continued: "The church I serve is not so energetic as y'all are." A man in the choir said, "You got that right!" which got a big laugh.

As I was coming into the church, I'd noticed that there was only one stained glass window with an image. It was in the back of the church so that the preacher and choir were looking at it the whole time. It was a common likeness of Jesus holding a child with other children gathered around, the difference being that Jesus and the children were all black. I'd had some time to think about that, and time to consider that the historical Jesus probably looked fairly Jewish and probably not like the blue-eyed version with light brown hair who appears most white Anglo-Saxon Protestant stained glass windows, not at all pink like me. Now, standing in the pulpit, I was looking straight at it, and it caused me to wonder.

At the Church of the Holy Incarnation in West Branch, I had become accustomed to pausing between thoughts. Some of the people thought it was to give them time to digest what I'd just said, but most often it was to give me a moment to think about what I was going to say next.

Now, as I was contemplating the black Jesus with a lengthy pause, a sweet elderly woman wearing a purple hat cried out, "Help him, Lord!"

I pointed to the Jesus of the stained glass window and said, "That's my Jesus, too." There was an uncertain hush, and I continued. "Just as Jesus' Father in heaven is your father, he is my father, too. God our Father, Jesus our Brother—that makes us all sisters and brothers together, right?"

There was a tentative "Amen," probably just trying to help me out, and then I said, "I believe I came here to learn that today. We are different, not just our skin but how we talk, how we sing, how we preach." A lot of the people were nodding, and one woman said, "Yes, Lord!" before I continued, "But we are all children of one Father, and that makes us all brothers and sisters. Thank you very much for helping me learn that."

There were a lot of "Amens" at that, and I thought it would be a good time to sit back down. But before I did, and without thinking about it, I lifted my right hand up and made the sign of the Cross as I gave them the blessing I used every Sunday: "May the peace of God which passes all understanding keep your hearts and minds in the knowledge and love of God, and of his Son Jesus Christ our Lord; and the blessing of God Almighty, the Father, the Son, and the Holy Spirit, be among us, and remain with us always." Into the stunned silence I said "Amen" the way we say it in the Episcopal Church— "Ah-men." A moment or two later my African-American sisters and brothers responded: "A-men," with a long 'A'.

I sat back down next to Miss Mabel, and she reached over and patted my knee, whispering, "Thank you, Buddy. You did good." The rest of the service passed with more energy and lively music, and after it was over almost all of them came and shook my hand and welcomed me.

I still think about the woman with the purple hat sometimes, when I'm preaching and wondering what I'm going to say next, when the pause goes on a little too long: "Help him, Lord!"

9

NONE BUT OURSELVES
CAN FREE OUR MINDS

We rode out to the prison after church. Mabel said the visiting hours were from one to three, and it was already past one. The Reverend and Mrs. Swayze always went to the Country Club for Sunday lunch; Miss Mabel said she'd cook me something when we got back to her house. She took me to the gatehouse, where I saw the same pot-bellied guard who been there the last time I visited, sitting on the same stool. Back then, I was in college, and Mabel had told him I was writing a paper; this time, I was wearing a clerical collar and he didn't ask any questions.

Mabel drove to the Visitors' Center, where the air conditioner was amazingly effective. I put my car keys and wallet in a plastic bag and signed my name on a form, and another guard took me out a side door and led me to a pickup truck. Mabel waved as we drove off toward Unit 17; she would wait for me there in the Visitors' Center.

There were picnic tables and old chairs outside the Death Row camp, the unit for men waiting their turn in the gas chamber or to see if their cases would take them there. As we approached, I asked the driver if I would need to go inside the unit to visit Mr. Jefferson. He kept his eyes straight ahead as he answered, "You can if you want. It's hot as hell in there," and then he remembered who he was talking to and continued, "Sorry, Reverend. It's real hot in there. If you want, I can go get Big Eugene and bring him out to you. He ain't gonna hurt you, and there'll be guards all around."

I told him that would be fine, that I'd be glad to talk to him outside. As we bumped along to the building, he looked over at me and said, "Can I ask you somethin', Rev?"

"Sure."

"Well, 'scuse me for askin',' but are you some kind of liberal or somethin'?"

"A liberal?"

"Yeah, y'know, like one of them bleedin' heart preachers that visits inmates and tries to stop us from killin' 'em? It's just, I don't think I've ever seen a real liberal 'cept on TV, and I'd like to tell my wife if I gave one a ride."

"Why would you think I'm a liberal?"

"I don't know, I guess you just don't look like no preacher I ever seen before."

"Oh. No, I don't think I'm a liberal." And then, just because I couldn't resist, I asked, "How can you tell if somebody's a liberal or not?"

He paused and then asked, "You vote for Reagan?"

I hadn't, and I told him that I voted for Jimmy Carter instead. He looked a little disappointed and said, "Well, you seem like a nice enough guy, though." I decided I'd failed his test and didn't need to say anything else. He said almost to himself but clearly intended to be loud enough for me to hear, "Figures a liberal would come out here and visit a man sentenced to die for his crimes."

I couldn't resist and asked, "So a Reagan voter wouldn't visit somebody on Death Row?"

"Naw—no, sir. I guess a conservative ain't gonna waste his time on none of these ol' boys."

"Hm. So I guess Jesus must've been a liberal, huh?"

"What? Hell, no!"

"Oh. Well, in my Bible there's a story about Jesus telling the disciples that when the nations are judged, the ones who will be blessed by God are the ones that fed the hungry and gave them something to drink, welcomed strangers and visited them in prison. That's not in your Bible?"

He kept his eyes straight ahead and grunted his dissatisfaction. We rode in silence the rest of the way, and when he turned the truck off, he got his shotgun from the rifle rack in the back window and went into the unit without a word. I got out of the truck and sat on an old wooden chair under a big cottonwood tree to wait. I was grateful for the feeble breeze that moved the leaves overhead; it would have been unbearably hot without it. It was just barely bearable with it.

In a few minutes my conservative driver came back out with Eugene. The last time I'd seen him, he was large and strong. Now he was alarmingly well built, like an obsessive bodybuilder or a caricature of a comic book character. The muscles on his shoulders made it look as if he didn't have a neck, and his arms looked like they'd been chiseled from granite.

His high-top Adidas were unlaced, as if his feet had become too muscular to be contained. His ankles and wrists carried chains, and the chains attached to his wrists were connected to a heavy leather belt around his waist. Obviously the guards were impressed with all those muscles, too. His head was shaved, and he was wearing an old pair of overalls not buttoned on either side, with one strap unfastened and dangling, and no shirt. He kept his eyes on his feet as he shuffled over to where I stood waiting.

The guard said, "Stop. You got a visitor, Eugene."

Eugene still didn't look up as he said, "Yes sir."

I said, "Eugene, it's me."

He kept looking down at his feet, not like his shoes were interesting but like he was afraid to look up.

"It's Buddy Hinton."

Still no recognition. I persisted, "Preacher Jake's friend—Buddy."

Now he looked up, slowly, and looked me in the eye for less than a second. It was just a moment, but it was long enough for me to see the pain and fear buried deep inside. He was like an abused dog in a trap, ready to bite anything that got too close. I said, "I came to see my friend Eugene."

"Preacher Buddy?"

"Yes sir."

"You came to see me?"

"Yes sir."

"I didn't want nobody to see me up in here, like this."

"Well, I wanted to come, see how you're doing. I just wanted to check on you."

"You talk to Miss Mabel?"

"Yes sir."

"She tell you about . . . about they goin' to kill me?"

"Yes sir."

"I don't think you can't do nothin' 'bout that."

"No, Eugene—I can't. Unless the governor of Mississippi calls it off, you're going to be executed in a few weeks." There was a pause, and it didn't look like he was going to say anything else, so I said, "It sounds like your lawyer did everything he could."

"I guess so. It was a woman."

"Who was a woman?"

"The public 'fender. She was a woman, just out of the Ole Miss school."

"Oh. Was she good to you?"

"Seemed like she was real mad all the time. She said she wadn't mad at me, but I told her I was sorry anyway. She told me to don't keep sayin' that. I don't know why."

"But you are sorry?" His chin sagged down into his pectoral muscles. "Eugene?"

He whispered, "Yes sir. I's so sorry. I did not really want to hurt nobody."

"I know, Eugene. You just got caught up in some bad things, with some bad people."

"Yes sir. But I's a growed up man. It ain't nobody else's fault. I should not have let that fool Eddie do me that way."

"No, that's right."

"Lissen, Preacher Buddy—I know I ain't got no right . . . but can I ask you to do somethin' for me?"

"Sure, Eugene. If I can do it, I will."

"Tell my mama I's sorry. Tell her I's so sorry for everything."

I'd thought he was going to ask me to get him a pack of cigarettes or a candy bar or something. "Oh. Okay, I'll try." He gave me her name and the street she lived on in Pearl, Mississippi, a community southeast of Jackson. He couldn't remember the number of the house, but he described it to me as a white wooden house with a front porch.

I told him I'd try to find her, and asked, "When was the last time you saw her?"

"Oh now, I don't know that."

"Has she come to see you at Parchman?"

Too late I realized that I'd stumbled on a nerve and pinched it hard. There was ice and pain in his voice when he answered, "No sir."

"Oh, Eugene, I'm sorry."

"She . . . she 'shamed of me, Preacher. I don't blame her for none of this. I guess—well I guess I's 'shamed of myself, too. It'll be better . . . better for everybody after I's kilt. They goin' to kill me like I's some kind of mad dog, like I got the rabies."

"What about your father?"

He shook his big shaved head slowly and whispered, "I didn't never know nothin' 'bout my daddy at all."

One of the things Jake had taught me over and over was that shame will eat you up. Eugene was living proof—barely living, and not for much longer, but proof all the same. It was terrible to see a human being so broken and lost, and I wanted to do something to ease the deep pain that radiated out of him.

I said, "Eugene."

Still looking down, he murmured, "Yes sir."

"Look at me." He just shook his head, and I repeated, "Eugene, look at me."

He looked up briefly, daring a quick glance into my eyes before he put his head back down. I said, gently, "Eugene, you're a man. You can look me in the eye like a man." He kept his face down so that I couldn't see it; I thought he looked like a hound that had been beaten one time too many. I said, "You're not a dog, Eugene; you're a man."

He looked up then, wide-eyed. "That's jus' what you said, that other time."

"What other time?"

"The other time I seen you in the kitchen, that time when you was talkin' to Eddie. You 'member?"

It was not a day I will likely ever forget: I'd gone to the prison to tell Cornelius and Mabel that their friend Jake had died, and instead I'd met Eugene and Eddie Walker, an inmate who hated Jake and all he stood for. Eddie was like a gang lord in Parchman and had used Eugene's size and strength to build his influence in the prison. That day in the kitchen, Eddie had been convinced that I knew about a stash of money I didn't know Jake had hidden, and he'd held a kitchen knife to my throat as I tried desperately to appeal to Eugene's better nature. It was also the day that Eugene walked away from Eddie, after he'd wrestled the knife away from him.

I said, "I remember it very well. Where's Eddie now?" Surely Eddie wasn't in Unit 17.

"In hell, I b'lieve."

"He died?"

"Yes sir. Somebody kilt him with a homemade, jus' after all the lights was out."

"A homemade?"

"Yes, sir. You can make a blade out of almos' anythin' up in here."

"Somebody stabbed him?"

"Yes sir. It wadn't me, but I wadn't real broke up 'bout it, neither. Somebody did the world a favor, and sent ol' Eddie to hell."

I sat for a moment, trying to take this in, and Eugene said, "That day, in the kitchen, you tol' me I wadn't a dog, that I was a man. You 'member?"

"Yes sir. I remember that Eddie wanted you to be his big scary dog, so people would respect him."

"But I ain't no dog."

"No, Eugene. You are a man. You're a good man."

"I ain't no good man, Preacher. Not after all this."

"Eugene, you've done some bad things—some terrible things. But you're not a bad person." He looked skeptical about this, cutting his eyes at me in doubt. What I was saying didn't line up with what had been drilled into him his whole life, even before he'd come to prison. I said, "You remember what Preacher Jake used to say?"

He shook his head, and I told him, "Ain't nobody no better'n you, and you ain't no better'n nobody else."

He muttered, "Yeah, I 'member Preacher Jake tol' me that, too. But . . . ." His life had been formed and shaped by buts like that one, I thought; there's always a *but.*

"But what, Eugene?"

"But that ain't . . . that ain't 'bout me.

His head was back down now, and I watched a tear fall to land on his big leather shoe. He murmured, almost inaudibly, "Is there a place for the hopeless sinner?"

I was stunned. Eugene was quoting from "One Love," an old Bob Marley song that I knew and liked. Eugene was convinced that he had no hope, in this life or the next.

After Jake had been released from prison the first time, when I was just eight, I met him down in the woods behind my house, and we struck up a deep friendship. I was a young boy, and he was in recovery—from alcohol and from a career in preaching. When I went off to college, Jake contrived to get caught robbing a bank so he could go back to the prison, partly for the room and board but mostly because he said the men in the prison needed to have some hope. He had taken a special interest in Eugene. I couldn't stand the idea that Eugene would die in a few weeks thinking he was a hopeless sinner.

"Eugene," I said, "Preacher Jake taught me there's no such thing as hopeless, unless that's the way you want it to be."

"Ain't nothin' the way I want it to be. They ain't no hope up in here, no hope for me."

"Your hope is not in you, your hope—everybody's hope—is in the love and mercy of God. Your only hope is to believe that God loves you and forgives you."

"Yeah, well, that ain't the way it go up in here."

"Well, of course it is. If God is real and not just something we made up, it makes sense that God loves us. Why else would God put up with any of us?"

"That ain't what Preacher Jerry say."

"Who's Preacher Jerry, and what does he say?"

"He a preacher from over in Shelby who comes over here and visit us sometimes. He tol' me the Bible say I have to go to hell when I die, 'cause I done too many bad things. God can't make no 'ceptions, 'cause he done promised his word and all. I don't . . . I don't want to go to hell, Preacher Buddy."

"No, of course not. But listen—if God loves all his children, he loves you. Why would God want you to go to hell?"

"'Cause I kilt them mens! And Preacher Jerry say—"

"I don't care what Preacher Jerry says. What kind of man would drive all the way over here from Shelby just to tell Death Row prisoners they're going to hell when they're executed? Who does that help? Preacher Jerry? Eugene, I'm a preacher, too, and I want you to hear me say that there is nothing any of us can do that will ever make God give up on us, or make God stop loving us. Jesus died on the cross so we will know we are forgiven—all of us."

"Ain't no mercy for me. That's what the preacher say."

"Well, this preacher believes in mercy. And Preacher Jake believed it too: that God's mercy is deeper than the ocean and higher than the sky."

"I hope you right."

"If I'm wrong, God is a mean old man and we're all in more trouble than we can get out of." We sat there a moment, both of us wondering what to say next. I thought for a moment, trying to bring up Bible verses that would assure Eugene that Preacher Jerry was a cruel, stupid bastard. Then it occurred to me that I wasn't going to make any lasting progress with an argument about biblical interpretation: if I used Bible passages to prove my point about God's boundless mercy, Preacher Jerry from Shelby would come back and prove his point about God's eternal wrath, also using Bible verses.

Then I remembered some of the other Bob Marley song I knew. I'm not a big singer, but I thought a snatch of song might touch another part of Eugene's mind. I sang,

Old pirates, yes, they rob I,
Sold I to the merchant ships,

Minutes after they took I
From the bottomless pit.

I stopped when I saw how surprised Eugene was. "I didn't
'magine you'd know no Marley."

"A little. In that song, he says he has been sold into slavery. He's
in bad trouble, but he holds on to his hope."

"Why you say that?"

I sang the next verse.

But my hand was made strong
By the hand of the Almighty,
We forward in this generation triumphantly.
Won't you help to sing
These songs of freedom?
'Cause all I ever have:
Redemption songs,
Redemption songs.

"How I'm goin' to sing songs of freedom up here in Parchman?"

So I sang the next couple of lines, which turned out to be where
I was trying to go the whole time.

Emancipate yourself from mental slavery,
None but ourselves can free our minds.

"What do he mean 'bout 'mancipate your self?"

"It means 'free yourself.'"

"You mean bust out of here?"

"Well, no. I don't think that's possible. I mean you need to free
yourself of the idea that God is a big angry Boss who wants to punish
whoever he can."

"But that . . . that's what Preacher Jerry say God is like."

"Yeah, I know. I want you to free your mind, to consider another
idea: that God is a loving Father who wants all of us to accept his
love."

Eugene was quiet for a while; this required a little thought. Then, "So if I consider that, if that's the way it is . . ."

"Yeah?"

"Then they ain't no hell a'tall."

"No, I didn't say that. I don't think God is going to make people love him. If somebody would rather not be loved by God, if somebody wants to think the whole world is all about them, that other people are just things to be used, I believe God will let them be alone. I think heaven is when we choose to live with God, and hell is when we choose to live by ourselves."

"Hmm. All right, Preacher Buddy, I need to think on that. I'd like to hope that I ain't goin' to hell. I'd like to think that Jesus could forgive me."

"I swear Jesus will forgive you, or already has if you've told him how sorry you are."

He looked dubious, so I continued, "Eugene, Jesus died so you would be able to accept God's forgiveness. Preacher Jake told me it's just arrogant to hold on to something when God has forgiven you. Maybe that's what Bob Marley is talking about: free your mind from mental slavery."

He raised his head and looked up at the sky. "All right, all right. Redemption songs, I'll need to think about that. Try to 'mancipate myself from mental slavery. If you say it, and Marley say it, and Preacher Jake say it, they got to be somethin' to it."

I thought it was a good moment to leave, and started to stand up. He put his huge hand on my shoulder, gently. The guard was alarmed and pumped the action on his shotgun. I held up my hand to ask him to stay where he was, to let him know I was okay.

Eugene said, "Yeah, I s'pose they must be somethin' to all that. But you can't never be sure 'bout Mr. Marley."

"Well, I think he has a lot to say, especially about hope. Hope is a powerful thing."

"Yes sir. They's somethin' else I needs to ask you 'bout, though."

"Okay, what's that?"

"That day, when you was in the kitchen with me and Eddie."

"Yes sir?"

"You changed my life that day, you know that?"

"Oh. Well, thank you for saying that. You saved my life that day, as I recall—and I thank you for that."

"No sir. It's me should thank you. You was awful brave that day."

"I was scared to death!"

"Yes sir. But you wadn't scared of death. You see what I'm sayin'? You wadn't scared to die, that's what you said."

I remembered saying that. I was trying to convince Eugene to throw off Eddie's influence, to save my own skin but also to save Eugene. Eddie had a knife to my throat at the time, so I didn't really remember all the details.

He said, "Eddie looked like he was 'bout to kill you, and you said, 'They is worse things that could happen than dyin'.'"

"I remember."

"That's what I want to ask you 'bout. What is worse than dyin'?"

I was suddenly aware that I was talking to a man whose date with death was on the calendar of the Mississippi State Correctional Facility. This was not a philosophical, theological question. This was life. And death.

I put my hand on his massive forearm and leaned close to him. "It would be worse to live without hope. It would be worse to live in such a way that you did not accept the love of God. It would be worse to be all alone."

"Buddy, you know I'm goin' to die. My time's jus' 'bout up."

"Yes sir. Would you like me to be here for you?"

"No sir. They ain't no need for that. But I 'preciate you comin' and talkin' to me today."

The guard announced, "Time's up."

Eugene nodded and said to me, "Say me a prayer, Preacher Buddy." The guard nodded his approval.

I thought for a moment and prayed, "Lord, look down in love and mercy on your son Eugene and on his mother." Eugene took a deep, sharp breath, and I paused a moment before continuing: "Give him hope when he is weak or afraid, and help him to know and believe that you are with him and that you love him and forgive him as you do all your children. Give him courage to lean on your mercy,

in his life and in his death and in the life to come, through Jesus
Christ our Lord. Amen."

He shuddered out a sob, and when he stood up he had tears
running down his face. "Thank you, Preacher Buddy. Thank you."

Just after midnight on September 2, 1983, Jimmy Lee Gray, who'd
been convicted of raping and killing a three-year-old girl, was led into
the gas chamber at Parchman, where lethal gas was released. Later,
officials at the prison would say he died in about two minutes, but
witnesses including a reporter from the *New York Times* said that eight
minutes after the gas was released, Gray was still convulsing, banging
his head on the steel pole behind the chair he'd been strapped to, and
gasping for air. The prison officials cleared the observation room, but
the account of the brutal execution made the national news.

Eugene's execution was postponed, and by the time the prison
officials felt confident enough to resume executions, the guards and
supervisors had noticed a change in him, Miss Mabel wrote to tell
me. He wasn't likely ever to be released, she thought, but he had a
good chance of being released back into the general population of the
prison, once they decided he wasn't likely to be a danger to himself or
others. Over a year later he was removed from Unit 17 and put back
in his old camp.

But before Jimmy Lee Gray's execution, I did go to Pearl to find
Eugene's mother. It took a while to find the right white wooden house
on Davis Street in Pearl, Mississippi, and when I found her she told
me through a locked door that she didn't want to see me or have anything to do with Eugene, that she wasn't his mama anymore. I told
her that all he wanted was to tell her he was sorry, and she told me
she would be glad when he was dead, and closed the door in my face.

I got back in my car and sat there for a long time, wondering
how any of us could ever understand love if we'd never been loved.
Maybe it hadn't always been this way with Eugene's mother, maybe
she'd been pushed over an edge of some sort. Or maybe she was why
he was where he was. I will never know.

When I got home, I called my mom just to say hello, to tell her I love her, and to thank her. She said "For what, sweetheart?" and I said, "For . . . everything, Mom. Thanks for everything."

10

Salva Vida Men

Just after the new year, in January 1984, I got a call from Mrs. Downs, the bishop's secretary, telling me that the bishop wanted to offer me an opportunity. I'd been around long enough to know that when the bishop had an "opportunity" for you, it almost always meant extra work; I said, "Yes ma'am," which was a precursor of the "Yes sir" I would inevitably say to the bishop when he let me know what the opportunity was.

She said he wanted her to ask me to go with the diocesan medical mission team on a trip to Honduras, and informed me that the team was going to leave at the end of March, just over two months away. Apparently the priest who had originally agreed to go couldn't because his wife was having a medical procedure of some sort. Mrs. Downs told me that the Diocese would pay my way, and I told her I'd be glad to go. I remember thinking it was exciting when she told me I'd need to get a passport, a thing I'd only seen in James Bond movies. Then she wondered hopefully whether I spoke Spanish.

As it happens, I'd taken Spanish in high school, mostly because my brother and sister before me had taken French, and I took it again in college for the sole reason that I had to take six hours of a foreign language and it made sense to take a language I was familiar with, at least a little. I told Mrs. Downs I spoke a little Spanish, and she said the bishop would be glad to hear it and delighted that I could go.

It was the second year of the medical mission to the little village of Santa Maria de las Montañas, in the mountain-filled Honduran state of Santa Barbara. A doctor from one of the parishes on the coast had seen that ships would come into Gulfport, Mississippi, loaded down with bananas and coffee beans and teak wood, and then go back to Central America empty. He suggested that with a little effort, his parish could gather medicines and supplies and send them down to Honduras, one of the poorest countries in the Western Hemisphere. They did, and it didn't take them long to realize that the medicines weren't actually getting to the poor people, that someone would have to go with them. The doctor and his colleagues developed the idea that they would take the medicine themselves and dispense it. A few years later, the plan evolved from a parish mission to a Diocesan mission, working through the Diocese of Honduras, which directed the mission into Santa Maria de las Montañas.

I paid a little extra to get a passport quickly and talked to the other priest on the team, who happened to be my friend Ellis. He'd spoken with one of the priests who had been on the first mission the year before, and he found out that we would be staying in the church in the village, sleeping on the concrete floor. He said he'd been told to pack light, and said he was going to get a duffel bag from a military surplus store to pack all his stuff. The team leader wrote us all a letter suggesting we pack light sleeping bags and something to keep the mosquitoes at bay, and in a handwritten note he asked me to pack a bottle of Communion wine.

Ellis also told me that the priest who had been before said there were people in the village who didn't like us coming there. He said most of the local women were helpful, but the men stood at a distance watching suspiciously and didn't help at all. Apparently the other priest from the first mission, whose wife was going to have surgery, had not been well received, probably because he'd been condescending.

We gathered at the parish in Gulfport and had a big send-off dinner with some of the congregation. The next morning, we rode in a borrowed bus to the airport in New Orleans and flew to San Pedro

Sula, the industrial center in the northern part of Honduras, and spent the first night at a hotel in the big city.

We had a team dinner that evening, with introductions all around: four doctors; four nurses; two dentists; two dental assistants; some people to weigh the patients, keep the clinics running in an orderly fashion, clean the dental instruments, and distribute medications from the pharmacy; and two mostly bewildered priests.

Nobody really knew what the priests were supposed to do, including and especially the priests. Ellis had taken Greek in seminary, which he said was "remarkably unhelpful" when you needed Spanish. He had printed two copies of the Eucharist from the Spanish version of the Book of Common Prayer, and told me we'd have to conduct services in Spanish.

After the dinner, Ellis and I went to the hotel bar to practice our liturgical Spanish. The bartender spoke no English at all, or wouldn't admit to it—and so I had my first substantive exchange in a foreign language, trying to order a beer. I'd brought the handy Spanish-to-English dictionary I'd gotten in college; I fished it out of my book bag and put it on the bar. I already knew the words for "two" and "please"; all I needed was the word for beer: *cerveza*. I closed my dictionary and said, "*Dos cervezas, por favor*," quite proud that I'd overcome the language barrier.

The bartender looked at me in my smug simplicity and fired off a long sentence of words colliding with other words; I have no idea what he said, but it took a long time. I didn't even know how to tell him I didn't know what he was talking about. Ellis leaned over to me and suggested I could ask him if he spoke ancient Greek.

After a moment or two, in which the bartender undoubtedly realized that he might lose a couple of customers who had money and the potential to drink several *cervezas*, he brought out two bottles and displayed them on the counter. One was labeled *Nacional* and the other *Salva Vida*; he'd been asking us which brand of beer we wanted. I figured it didn't matter much and, thinking we could go patriotic, pointed to the Nacional—which I figured had to mean *National*.

The bartender gave me a look I couldn't interpret. It might have been a smirk, but it was hard to tell because of the way his moustache had overtaken his lips.

A few short minutes later it was time for another, and now I had a strategy. I pointed to the Nacional and asked "*¿Es bueno?*"—literally, "Is good?" He gave me another possible smirk and said with some distaste, "*Es para mujeres.*" I didn't know the word and was fumbling through my dictionary when the bartender put his hand on my arm and said in heavily accented English, "Woman beer." When I told Ellis we were two large pink *gringos* drinking woman beer in a macho country, he pointed to the other beer and asked "*¿Bueno?*" The bartender gave us a reassuring nod, and Ellis and I clinked our bottles together and pledged that we were *Salva Vida* men from then on.

We started working on the words of the Eucharist in Spanish, with the bartender looking on. After a while he joined the cause and worked with us to pronounce some of the more confounding words like *misericordia, reconciliarnos, santificalos,* and *agradecimiento.* By the time were finished, we judged that our Spanish skills had improved all the way from hopeless up to unlikely, which would have to be enough.

As we were leaving, I tried a little of my newfound vocabulary on the bartender, saying "*El Señor te bendiga*" ("The Lord bless you"). I was surprised that he came around the bar to kneel in front of me, then crossed himself, folded his hands over his chest, and bowed his head. Ellis, who'd gone to General Seminary in New York where they know about High Church, whispered for me to put my hand on his head and bless him, which I did, repeating the same words. He looked up with eyes full of tears and crossed himself again.

The next morning we crammed about twenty-five gringos, all our luggage, and more than a ton of medicines and medical supplies on an antique yellow school bus and started what we had been told would be a four-hour trip up into the mountains.

We had not gone far before some of my fellow gringos grew concerned that our bus was simply too large for the narrow mountain road we were traveling. That concern reached a crescendo when one of the stones in the rock face on the right side of the bus made a long screeching scrape all the way down the length of the vehicle, which was a great concern to the people on that side, while on the left-side folks were trying hard not to look down at the sheer drop off the mountain, which was a great concern for us. The trip was terrifying for all concerned.

At a hairpin turn, the driver had to put the bus in reverse, go back a few feet, then into a low gear to go forward a few feet, and then back and forward and back and forward six or seven times before we could resume. It was when some of the other team members were trying to figure out who could express our concerns to the driver that I realized nobody could speak Spanish any better than I could, and most couldn't speak it at all. We would have interpreters when we got to the village, but for right now, as the driver was grinding the gears to go up an unbelievably steep hill on our way to another tight hairpin turn, they had all apparently decided it was up to me to say something to him. I rounded up enough ninth-grade Spanish vocabulary to initiate the conversation.

I went up to the driver and said, "*Hola, señor.*" I was pretty sure that meant, "Hello, sir." He looked amused that I was trying to talk to him and said, "*Hola.*" Then I began to make my case: I said, "*El auto-bus es muy grande, sí?*" ("The bus is very large, yes?") He looked at me as if I'd said water is wet or rocks are hard, but, trying to be agreeable, he said, "*Sí.*" And then I came to my point: "*Y el camino es pequeño.*" ("And the road is small.") I believe at this point he understood my concern; he responded with several sentences, all in rapid-fire Spanish, accompanied by hand motions and facial expressions, none of which I understood. When he was done, he looked at me for a response but I had no idea whether he'd cheerfully said that he made this trip every week or that we are all sure to die, so the best I could do was look at him blankly. He took his eyes off the road, which did not diminish my concern, to look into mine, and he removed one of his hands from the wheel to pat me on my shoulder and say, "*Con-fía en mí*" in a meaningful way. I said, "*¿Como?*"—which, translated loosely is "Huh?"—and he said it again: "*Confía en mí.*"

Now, I knew that "*en mí*" is "in me." I knew that "con" is "with." I didn't know the word "*fía,*" but to my deeply Southern ears it sounded suspiciously like "fear." So literally, I interpreted, "With fear in me?" Was he telling us to be afraid with him? That didn't match the reassurance I hoped I'd seen in his face or the pat on my shoulder. I went back to my friends and told them I didn't understand what the driver said. Then I went to the back of the bus and dug through the small mountain of duffel bags to find my bag and the Spanish-to-English dictionary. It took a while, but finally I think I found the verb he'd been using: "*Confiarse*," to trust. What he was saying, all he could say, and what I really needed to hear was, "Trust me."

I decided we only had two choices. The first was to panic, get off the bus, and find our way back to the city and try to make it to the village another day. And the other was to trust our driver.

I told the team what I hoped: that we would be okay. I told them we were fine. And, of course, we were. Hope is powerful stuff.

At one point as our journey continued, the driver stopped the bus altogether and came back to talk to me. It took us a while again, but finally I realized that he needed us all to get out so that he could get the bus across a creek without the weight of twenty-five people making the bottom of the bus scrape the rocks. My friends grumbled about having to walk through the creek, and I told them, with all the assurance I could muster, "Trust him." It was the best we could do.

When the bus couldn't get us any closer to the village, the driver turned off the engine and explained to me that we would have to carry our things the rest of the way. I asked him, I think, how far it was, and he told me, I think, two or three kilometers, over the ridge. I didn't know the word for "mile" in Spanish and wasn't really sure how far a kilometer was, but I did catch "*dos o tres*," so I knew it was two or three something; all I could do was nod and thank him. Then he surprised me by grabbing a couple of duffel bags full of medicine and carrying them up into the village alongside me.

When we got to the village, after I'd caught my breath, I introduced myself and asked the driver his name. I don't remember all of his names—there were four or five altogether—but I do remember that one of the names, the one I latched onto and the one that we called him for the rest of the week, was Jesus. I did have to explain that even though it's spelled the same, in Spanish our Lord's name is pronounced *Hay-soos*, which was a little difficult for some of my friends. You can't imagine how many times I've preached about trusting Jesus the Bus Driver since 1984.

Since I had more or less successfully negotiated with the bus driver, since the people in the village were apparently expecting a Eucharist that night, and since the translators wouldn't arrive until the next morning, the medical mission team leader asked me to set up the service. I asked around and found out that the person I needed to work with was a small man named Rodolfo, who kept the keys to the church building.

Rodolfo had a large moustache, sad brown eyes, and a ring of keys as big as a grapefruit. I wouldn't have thought there were that many locks in the entire village. He spoke no English at all, so we had to go with my pitiful Spanish. He showed me the altar and on it the service book *en Español*. I opened the book, and to show him that I really was a priest I read the first thing I saw: "*Señor, ten piedad de nosotros*" ("Lord, have mercy on us"). He said it again, for me to repeat, hoping to help me pronounce the words correctly. I said them again, exactly the way he had, and he shook his head. I tried again, and he looked at me dubiously. I said, "Okay?"—the same in English and in Spanish. He nodded, not convinced but not willing to continue criticizing a priest.

I said, "*Gracias, señor. Necesito practicar mucho.*" ("Thank you, sir. I need to practice much.")

He said, affably and without any visible irony, "*Sí*."

So Ellis and I practiced some more, trying not to laugh at each other as we butchered the language. When we finally admitted that our slow Southern diction was so poorly suited to the staccato rhythm of *Español* that the service might take all night, I negotiated with Rodolfo that he should conduct the majority of the service so that Ellis and I would just need to read the parts that should only be read by priests: the Eucharistic prayer. I would also say a few words for a sermon. All three of us were greatly relieved.

The service itself went well, all things considered. So many people wanted to come in the church that we decided it would be better for us to have the service outside. We'd brought lots of Communion wafers—thin, round, white Styrofoam-looking things offered at Communion in many Eucharist-centered churches, but as the crowd gathered it became apparent that we wouldn't have enough. So I encouraged Rodolfo to ask around to see if we could get some local bread, and he brought us a short stack of corn tortillas made by his wife. These were desperately poor people, but when I offered to pay for the bread, he would not hear of it.

One of the local men played the guitar, and for the service he had an amplifier and speaker connected to a car battery that sat under the altar. The songs were all familiar to the Hondurans and a complete mystery to the visitors, so we joined together in clapping along: clap, clap, clap-clap-clap; clap, clap, clap-clap-clap.

From my position behind a rickety table we'd set up for an altar, I looked out at the congregation. Each member of the medical team was given a seat of honor, and even though it was a warm, still night, every gringo had at least one child holding both hands. All the pink members of the team were perspiring profusely, wondering how long it would last; all the Hondurans were tickled pink, proud of their church, excited that the medical team from Mississippi was there to visit and worship with them.

An opening hymn—clap, clap, clap-clap-clap—prayers, readings, and another hymn—clap, clap, clap-clap-clap—the reading from the Gospel, and then it was time for the sermon. Ellis and I had agreed that since I could speak a little Spanish, and since he'd taken ancient Greek and seemed better at words with five or more syllables, I would preach and he would do the Eucharistic prayer. Rodolfo, as promised, conducted the service, made the announcements, and generally ran the show.

The sermon was short. In fact, it was pithy and succinct, very nearly abrupt: a relief to my sweaty American friends and a little disappointing to our new Honduran friends. I'm not sure what I said exactly, but I hope I thanked the people for their help and told them that the medical team was there to bring doctors and medicine because of the love of Jesus. Or something like that, anyway.

After the sermon, there were long announcements as dogs roamed in and out of the congregation. I think Rodolfo and the leaders of the church welcomed us at some length and cajoled the people with fervor to help us set up and run the clinic. They took up a collection, and I was glad to see some US presidents in the baskets: that part we all recognized.

Ellis did admirably well with the Eucharistic prayer, and it was beginning to look like we were going to survive the whole thing without a liturgical scratch. But as the people came up to receive the bread and wine, I noticed a few things that soon converged with unlikely and unpleasant consequences.

The first thing I noticed was that, as Ellis gave each person the bread, he held it up for them to see and then made the sign of the Cross with the bread before giving it to them. It wasn't something I'd ever done, but I'd seen it done before—not unusual or troublesome, just a little High Church for me. The second thing I noticed was that while the gringos received the bread in their hands and dipped it into the wine as Ellis and I had suggested, the practice in the village was to wait until the priest dipped the bread into the wine so he could pop it into their mouths. I think the old idea is that the unordained are not worthy to touch the Body of Christ with their hands.

It was confusing at first, as neither Ellis nor I knew how our hosts wanted to receive Communion, but Rodolfo stepped in and after a little game of charades indicated what we should do. So Ellis established his pattern: he took a piece of bread, dipped it into the chalice I was holding, held it up for the person to see, made the sign of the Cross with it, and then put it into their waiting mouths.

But just as it was a different pattern for us, so was it different for the people of the village, and somehow holding the bread up for them to see and then making the sign of the Cross caused confusion, who followed the bread with their eyes as it went up, down, right, and left before coming toward their mouths.

The first time Ellis's moving hand missed someone's moving mouth, the bread fell onto her blouse. She felt unworthy to touch the bread, and neither Ellis nor I felt comfortable removing it from her breast, but Ellis gathered himself and retrieved the bread with some grace. The next time the bread-to-mouth connection failed, the bread fell to the ground.

The traditional Anglican sacramental theology is that we believe in the Real Presence of Christ in the Eucharist. The bread and wine of the Eucharist is understood to be the Body and Blood of Christ in that Christ is present in the sacrament, but not necessarily in the bread and wine itself. There's some room for disagreement about this; some Episcopalians believe that the bread and wine are simply symbols to bring us to an awareness of the Lord, while others, like my friend Ellis, are more likely to believe that the bread and wine somehow become sacred in themselves. I'm somewhere in the murky middle, I suppose, but like Ellis I had been trained to pick up a dropped host from the clean church wood, tile, or carpeted floor and consume it, invoking the unspoken sacramental five-second rule.

Still, I was horrified to see Ellis bend down in the darkness and pick something off the ground and eat it. This wasn't a nice, round, white Styrofoamish host—it was a piece of grayish-brown corn tortilla. And it wasn't a polished or waxed or vacuumed floor—it was grayish-brown dirt in a third-world country, where the pigs rooted for scraps and the dogs scratched for fleas.

I looked over at him in alarm and revulsion, and he murmured, "It's the sacrament, man." I appreciated his devotion, but I couldn't help questioning his judgment.

I also wondered if maybe the next time the Communion tortilla fell to the ground, he might be thinking that I should take my turn at rescuing it from the ignominy of resting among the dirt clods and pig droppings at our feet, as it surely would with his waving the Body and Blood of Christ in an intricate pattern and the Honduran worshipers following it with their open mouths.

In seminary somebody told me a story about a young Catholic priest who was in a monastery whose practice was for every priest to celebrate the Mass every day. This young priest became aware of an older priest who was waiting impatiently behind him for his turn at the altar, and the young priest wanted to do it just right, to impress his older colleague. After the bread and wine were consumed, he was picking the little morsels of bread from the altar cloth one by one when the older priest could stand it no longer, snatched the white square cloth up, and shook it into the air, little crumbs flying everywhere. As the young priest looked on in dismay, the older priest returned the cloth to the altar and said, "Young man, Jesus can take care of himself." It was a story that I'd been much impressed with, and happily I'd told it to Ellis, my High Church friend.

The next time the bread fell to the ground, Ellis watched as I reached out with my tennis shoe and stepped on it. He looked at me with horror and anger, no doubt questioning my judgment, and I quoted the older priest in the story: "Young man, Jesus can take care of himself."

Ellis was upset with the whole thing, and upset that I had not only stepped on the bread but also on his liturgical sensibilities. I said, "Switch with me," and handed him the chalice. He reluctantly gave me the paten, the plate holding the corn tortilla fragments, and I changed gears into somewhat lower church, so that I took the bread, dipped it in the wine, and then put it into the people's mouths, and we proceeded without any further difficulty.

I knew Ellis was upset with me, and I went to talk to him about it after the service. He said he understood, that he knew I was right, and that it wasn't a big deal, but I knew it was. Hoping to patch things up a little, I told him I'd buy him a beer when we got back to the city. He looked at me as if I'd lost my mind until I reminded him, "You and me, amigo—we're Salva Vida men," and we both laughed.

In the village, the women on the team were to sleep in the school, with the men setting up in the church. The service had taken so long that by the time we were laying out our sleeping bags on the mats some of the people in the village had provided for us, it was completely dark. I retrieved my sleeping bag from my duffel bag and was just about to lie down when I heard one of the other guys yell out, "Holy crap—look at that!"

Several flashlights followed his flashlight to illuminate the object of his alarm. It was a spider climbing up the wall. I've heard this story told many times since that night and told it a few times myself, and I can tell you that a nasty-looking spider never gets any smaller as its story is repeated. Without exaggeration, it was about four inches in hairy diameter, but its most arresting feature was its impressive mandibles, which were a fuzzy, lethal-looking red.

Jimbo, the man who'd first seen the spider, came over to me and asked me to talk to Rodolfo about the creature. I said, "What do you want to know?"

"Ask him if it will bite!"

I got my dictionary, brought it back to the circle of men watching the spider, and looked up the word for "bite." The spider, doubtless stunned by all the lights, remained still. Jimbo brought Rodolfo over to me, and all the men listened with intense interest as I asked him, "*¿Este araña—puede picar?*" ("This spider—can he bite?")

Rodolfo was amused by our concern and shrugged his nonchalance, saying, "*Sí.*"

One of the other guys said, "Ask him if it's dangerous!" The spider started crawling up the wall as I looked up the word for "dangerous." "*¿Es peligrosa?*" Again, Rodolfo seemed determined to display his lack of concern: "*Sí.*"

Wes was a member of the team, the kind of guy who thought he knew everything about flora and fauna and everything else in the whole wide world and wanted to tell you about it all the time, the kind of guy I naturally tried to stay away from. He proclaimed with dread in his voice, "It's a tarantula." But Rodolfo, hearing the Spanish word *tarantula*, said, "*No*," which, like tarantula, is the same in both languages. He then went on to tell us what kind of spider it was, and I suppose all about what would happen if it bit one of us, and maybe a story or two about people who were bitten by such a spider and how they died gruesome and painful deaths, but none of us could understand anything after he said, "No."

The men on the medical team looked at me to provide some translation, and I said, "It's not a tarantula." There was a long pause as the spider inched further up the wall, and Jimbo whispered, "Ask him if it could kill you."

I had already been looking up the word for "kill," and in a moment I asked Rodolfo, "*¿Puede matar?*" ("Can it kill?"), and he shrugged again before saying "*Sí.*" Just then Wes approached with a shoe in his hand and swatted the wall an inch or two to the right of the where the spider was. I saw the spider moving at great speed off to the left before the lights followed the men running in every direction, and the spider was gone. Or actually—and much worse—the spider was not gone but still there somewhere, in the dark, in the church with us, waiting for one of us to get too close to wherever it was. We looked and looked, each of us searching with our flashlights, hoping one of the other guys would find the damn thing, but we never saw it again. It made for a long, restless night.

11

There Is Still Magic in the World

The next day, we set up the clinic: the doctors and nurses in the church where the men had slept, the dentists and their helpers in the school. Wes told his wife and everyone else who would listen about the spider, which got larger, hairier, and more dangerous every time the story was told, and we all looked for it as we set up the pews into stations for the doctors, nurses, and translators.

The translators arrived before lunch; it turned out that none of them had ever been so far up into the mountains and weren't real happy about the prospect of encountering a deadly spider, either.

After lunch we opened the clinics. My first job was to get the patients' names and weigh them on an antiquated set of scales. The weighing was easy, but getting their names was much more complicated than I thought it would be. I would ask "¿*Como se llama?*" ("How are you called?"), and the person would answer with a long, complicated string of names. When I checked to see if I'd heard the first name correctly, he or she would tell me the second, third, fourth, and sometimes fifth name, so that I still didn't know if I'd gotten the first one right or not—frustrating for them and bewildering for me.

It was a struggle, and I felt like I was holding up the whole operation, stationed as I was at the entrance of the church. We didn't have enough translators, but I was just about to ask that one be assigned to me when the Lord sent an angel instead.

Her name was Suyapa, she was nine years old, and she lived in the village. After I weighed her, when I asked her name, she said "Suyapa." I'd never heard that name before, and I didn't want to misspell it with her looking on, so I handed her my pen and indicated where she should write it: Suyapa Gutiérrez. Then I asked her brother his name; he gave me five or six names, and she wrote Tomás Gutiérrez under her own name. Then she wrote down the names of every other member of her family, and the next family, and after Tomás had seen the doctor he came back and started putting people on the scales and telling his sister how much people weighed, and she wrote that down, too.

My job had been taken by children more skillful than I was.

The mission coordinator, an insurance salesman from Biloxi named Dave, came to check on me, and I told him I thought I'd worked my way out of my job. He said we needed somebody to wash the lice out of people's hair. I told him I'd be glad to do that, and a few minutes later he brought me a big blue plastic bowl with three or four bottles of lice shampoo and a box of rubber gloves. He told me I could go to the pump by the side of the church to set up shop, and that I shouldn't get the shampoo in my eyes. I looked up the word for "lice" in my dictionary, and the words for "wash" and "hair," and I was ready to go. Then I told Suyapa *gracias* and *adios*, and went off to find the pump.

After I tried to talk several reluctant customers into getting their hair washed with no success, Suyapa walked up again. Apparently, some of the women of the parish had taken her job. So I told her what I knew: "*Quiero lavar los cabellos con la medicina para los piojos*" ("I want to wash the hair with the medicine for the lice"), and she took it from there. She told the people gathered around what I was doing, got them lined up, convinced one of the village boys to work the pump, and in a few minutes we were winning the war on lice. By the time Dave the team leader came out to check on me, I'd just taken my gloves off: some of the women of the village had taken over the whole operation, and I was feeling useless again.

Dave said we needed to set up a station for deworming, showed me the liquid to squirt into people's mouths, and helped me work out a chart for how much medicine each patient should have according to weight. I set up a little table outside the church where I could keep my eye on both the weighing station and the de-lice station, and in another half an hour Suyapa came to my rescue. In a few minutes the locals had stepped in, treating their neighbors for worms, and I was useless again. I went and found the team leader and told him about it; he said, "Some people just can't hold a job."

He laughed, and after I knew he was kidding, so did I. Then he said maybe he could use me in the clinic. Apparently some of our translators were better than others, and two or three of them weren't much good at all. Dave said a couple of the guys were what they called "work averse" in his insurance office, and one of the young ladies was especially averse. He wanted me to see if I could be helpful somehow.

And so it came to pass that I became a medical translator. I borrowed a few sheets of paper from one of the translators and asked her how to say few questions I needed to ask, such as

"What is your main problem?"
"Show me with one finger where it hurts."
"Does it your urine burn?"
"Does your urine smell bad?"
"Are you pregnant?"
"Are you nursing your baby?"
"Do you have lice?"
"Do your children have worms?"

And I learned how to say a few things the doctors wanted me to tell our patients, like

"You have high blood pressure, and you need to eat less salt and rest in the shade in the heat of the day."
"We have medicine for that, and you can get it in the pharmacy." (We were dispensing medicines from the school building.)
"I'm sorry, but we have no medicine for that."

The Honduran translator assigned to Dr. Thompson, a pediatrician from Jackson, was Julianna: seventeen years old, cute, vivacious, aware of her appeal, and from a well-to-do family in San Pedro Sula. She was quite serious about flirting with the male translators but exhibited little or no interest in anything else. She answered my questions and laughed at me when I mispronounced something; eventually, it became so regular that she resorted to rolling her perfectly painted teenage eyes instead and then ignored me altogether.

In an hour or so, Suyapa found me again, and I felt like I could do all right with her sitting beside me. She didn't speak English, but she spoke Spanish with words I knew, and taught me some I needed to know. By the end of the afternoon, I had to go back and get more paper to write down what I was learning.

All that afternoon, we translated for Doctor Bob. After a while, Julianna got up and left and didn't come back. I was concerned, but Doctor Bob wasn't: "Let her go be useless somewhere else."

Most of the medical situations were routine: everybody got worm medicine except for women who were or might be pregnant, every child got vitamins no matter what, and most adults got something for achy knees and backs. I did have the opportunity to assist Doctor Bob when he removed a cyst from a woman's neck and when he cut out a lump containing spider eggs from a young man's armpit.

Finally, late in the afternoon, the last Honduran family of the day took the prescriptions I'd written to the pharmacy, and we were finished. Julianna was nowhere to be seen, but Dr. Thompson thanked me and Suyapa for our work. I thanked him for his patience, and we walked outside.

That was the first time I noticed something that was a major element in all the medical missions I ever went on: we were the biggest show in town. All the children crowded around me to hear me talk, to marvel at how tall I was and at the pinkness of my skin, or just to see what sort of goofy thing I was willing to do to make them laugh. When I could tug my focus away from the powerful draw of the dark eyes of the children and look over their heads, I saw that there were dozens of men loitering about, keeping their eyes on things. Most of the women were working, guiding their own families through the clinics, or helping other families, but the men just watched.

The kids all wanted me to pick them up, or to hang on my arms with their feet dangling, as if I was a movable tree. I sat down and tried to talk to them, but I soon realized that the only entertainment value for them was to listen to me butcher their language. Hoping to find an amusing distraction, I looked around to see what else we could do. There were lots of rocks, in all shapes and sizes, and when I noticed that some of them were somewhat round, I thought of an idea.

I'd learned to juggle a little while I was in seminary, under the absurd pretense of making an effort to explain the Doctrine of the Trinity. Children in the United States were usually marginally impressed, but they always wanted more: "Can you juggle four?" "Can you juggle behind your back?" "Can you juggle knives and fire and eggs and chainsaws and things that will hurt you or make a mess when you drop them?"

But when I found three tangerine-sized stones and started to juggle, it was as if I'd made a papaya tree disappear before these children's very eyes. And when I did a little trick, two rocks going up and down in one hand, some of them ran away, returning with other children or their mothers.

I juggled a while, dropping the rocks from time to time. One of the boys bent down faster than I could, grabbed the rock I'd dropped, and scurried off as if he had a great prize. When his mother brought him back to return the rock (under considerable duress and accompanied by the jeers and gibes of his *amigos*), I found three more rocks about the size of walnuts for his little hands, and on a whim I started to teach him how to juggle: first one back and forth, then exchanging one for another, then the other hand, then all three. It took a while, but the expression on his face when he finally juggled a few was worth the whole trip for me. There is still magic in the world, and it is within our reach.

The medical team ate in shifts in the pharmacy, and after spending a little more time with the children of the village the men went back to the church to look for spiders before going to bed for the night. Rodolfo came up to me with an air of great secrecy, holding out a large paper bag. He said, "*Hamaca.*" I didn't have to look it up in the ever-present Spanish-to-English dictionary; I looked in the bag and found that he'd brought me a hammock. Then he said, "*Para las arañas.*" That word I remembered from the night before: spiders. I thought he was giving me a hammock so I didn't have to sleep on the ground where the spiders could get me, and when I started to thank him he told me how much it would cost me. I didn't understand the whole business with exchange rates, and I didn't have much Honduran currency, but when I showed him a US twenty-dollar bill, he seemed satisfied. I'm sure I could have gotten it for less, but it was worth it that night, and for the rest of the mission, to at least make it more difficult for the spiders to find me.

Rodolfo helped me string up the hammock inside the church, and I was the envy of all the gringo men. It took some getting used to, but I enjoyed sleeping in a hammock, and not just for spider protection. The rocking back and forth was soothing. The next evening, Rodolfo and another enterprising guy whose name might have been Victor did a brisk business in hammock sales. I thought about telling them that they probably could get more than twenty dollars, but I decided my gringo friends wouldn't be happy about that.

Each morning the members of the medical team met and prayed, ate our breakfast in shifts, and opened the medical and dental clinics. We came together in the church for lunch, usually fruits and Gatorade, and closed the clinic in the late afternoon. It was exhausting and deeply gratifying work. Most of our patients had routine complaints and concerns, but a few of them had ailments we weren't equipped to address: epilepsy, dementia, and one especially heart-breaking moment when the mother of a child with Down Syndrome pleaded with me to heal her son, and all I could do was tell her that we have that infirmity in the United States, and there is nothing that can be done there, either.

For the next couple of days, Suyapa and I helped in the medical clinic. We mostly worked with Doctor Bob, but we also helped some of the others from time to time. Actually, Suyapa did most of the hard work of listening to our patients and asking the questions the doctor needed to be asked; I was just the flimsy linguistic bridge between Suyapa and the doctor.

It wasn't always easy, and it didn't always go smoothly, of course. Suyapa could only do so much. A woman came with several children; after a brief conversation we prescribed vitamins and worm medicine for her kids, but when the conversation turned to her, she started mumbling and looking down at the floor so that even Suyapa couldn't understand anything she said.

The doctor rightly identified that she was embarrassed and suggested that I ask her if she was pregnant. She wasn't, but we could tell by her reaction that we were getting closer to figuring out what the situation was. The doctor encouraged me to ask her if it burned when she urinated; it didn't. He wanted me to ask her if it smelled bad when she urinated; it did, but we figured no one's urine smells minty fresh. He told me to ask her if she had a vaginal discharge, and I had to look that one up. I went to the dictionary, and after a minute or two I worked it out to ask her if she had "*descargas en su vagina.*" She was horrified, and so was Suyapa. The woman assured me that she did not, and the doctor diagnosed (correctly) that she was having some sort of trouble in that area and that a broad-spectrum antibiotic would be helpful in any case.

It was later that night when I found out that a much better word in Spanish would have been *secreciones*, secretions, and that the word I'd chosen for discharge would have been appropriate if I'd been asking about discharging a weapon, or an electrical discharge. I've often wondered what they must have thought of us, especially thinking that some women in the United States go to the doctor to help them with explosions or shocks in their nether parts.

12

¡BUGIDAW!

Just before breakfast on the last day of the clinic, Rodolfo brought Dave the team leader to talk with me. It took a while, but I figured out that Rodolfo wanted me to go further up the mountain to another village, where his parents lived, to do the Eucharist there. Dave went to talk with Doctor Bob, who said they were anticipating a slow day and that we were running out of medicine anyway, so if I wanted to go, I could.

I didn't have to think about it for long—a chance to see more of this beautiful country and to bring the service to some people in another village. I told Rodolfo I'd be glad to go.

Ellis was working in the dental clinic, which seemed like a fresh definition of hell to me. I asked him if he wanted to come with us, but he told me they were expecting a big day there, and he would have piles of dental instruments to clean and sanitize.

So I ate a good Honduran breakfast—scrambled eggs, black beans, toast, and two cups of strong coffee—and went to pack for my road trip. I put a couple of bottles of water into my knapsack and made sure my trusty Spanish-English dictionary was in there, too. I rolled up my stole and cincture in my alb and stuffed them into the backpack, along with my copy of the Eucharistic prayer in Spanish, folded inside Ellis's Spanish Book of Common Prayer. Ellen, one of our nurses, insisted that I take her floppy, flowery cloth hat to keep the sun off my head and neck. She said I could just stuff into my pack and I'd have it if I needed it, that I didn't have to wear it, for which I was grateful: it's a macho culture, and I didn't think all those light orange and yellow flowers would do much for my masculine image. At the time, I thought I was humoring her when I agreed to take it.

Suyapa wanted to come along, and I knew she would be helpful, but her mother wasn't willing to let her go with us unchaperoned, so it was just Rodolfo and me.

I had assumed that the village was a short walk up the mountain, but it was much more involved than that. Rodolfo took us a little out of the village, where four large horses were tied to the barbed wire fence. The owner of the horses owed Rodolfo's family a favor and was willing for us to take one for me to ride.

I'd ridden a horse before, when I was a kid and when someone else was walking in front to guide the beast, but I felt completely unprepared to choose the horse that was be most likely to haul me up to San José and back. The owner of the horses was large, with a pistol tucked into the waistband of his jeans, just to the left of an impressive beer belly. He was looking at me with great apprehension, or at least that's the way it felt; his straw hat was crumpled down in front so I could hardly see his eyes. He was obviously not thrilled that one of his prized stock would have to suffer under an extra-large pink priest, and I had to wonder what he owed Rodolfo's family.

All four of the animals were large, all of them eyeing me cautiously. One stamped its hooves in a way that made me think it was impatient, and I assumed I would need a patient horse, so I decided against that one. Another was clearly and proudly a stallion, and I thought that could present problems if we came too close to a potential girlfriend, so he was out. That left two, one black and the other light brown. With nothing else to draw on, I chose the larger horse, the big black one. I patted the left side of his neck, and he seemed okay with me. Maybe this wouldn't be so bad.

Soon, and well before I was mentally prepared, it was time to go, and I put the strap of my knapsack over the horn of the saddle, slid my foot into the stirrup, and hoisted myself up, at considerable strain to both man and beast. I'm a large person, even in the United States;

this horse had never had a passenger nearly so large before. He tried to buck, and I was grateful that Rodolfo was there to hold the bridle until he settled down.

My mounting the horse caused something of a stir among the gathered Hondurans; they pointed and made comments I couldn't hear and probably wouldn't have understood anyway. I heard one word several times and decided to look it up: *gordo*. The dictionary said it meant "fat person." Suyapa told me later it was a compliment, but that was hard to believe.

Rodolfo had intended to walk, but I insisted he ride if I was riding, and so he wound up riding a mule that seemed to be putting some effort into looking completely bored by the whole thing.

We were followed by a couple of Honduran families who were apparently walking with us to San José, having visited the clinics in Santa Maria. I was proud to see a number of them holding rags against their mouths, a sure sign they'd been worked on by the dentists, and that they all had plastic bags full of vitamins and other medicines.

It took my horse and me a while to figure out who was in charge. Eventually we both decided it was inevitable that I had to be in charge, although we silently agreed that was probably not such a good idea.

We followed the trail out of the rear of the village, past the church building where all the men on the mission team slept, and onto a little shoulder at the side of a hill. I worried about the horse falling; the trail was narrow, and he kept tossing his head to the left. After a while, we both settled into it, although I thought he tended to steer us off to the right all the time. But soon we both decided that all we could do was trust each other, and we found a rhythm.

In a few minutes we passed the graveyard, which I had never seen before. I was surprised by the size of some of the headstones, given the poverty of the region. Apparently honoring the dead is something they're willing to splurge on, at least a little.

The hill we were skirting became a little steeper, and then a lot steeper. When we came out of the trees, I could see that we were actually on the side of a mountain. The horse stopped, as if he was more afraid out in the open. Actually, I was sort of on his side. Alarmingly, the trail we were clinging to was a boundary of some sort, and to our left, down the steep grade of the mountain, were the remnants of a fence in some places, old fence posts holding two and sometimes three strands of barbed wire. I started to imagine falling down the side of the mountain, rolling over and over with a large black horse, and then getting tangled up in barbed wire.

We rode for what seemed like hours. It was hot, and the sun was merciless. Finally I decided that I was man enough to put on the flowered hat, especially since there was no one around to see it. It was actually quite helpful; I felt cooler as soon as I put it on.

After a while we came over a little rise in the path, and I was comfortable enough on my horse to risk a look at the panoramic vista. I could see for miles and miles: ranges of hills and mountains all green and blue and purple, a river or creek meandering through the valley below, all sorts of trees and plants I didn't recognize—it was gorgeous. I stopped to admire the view and took out a bottle of water. Rodolfo stopped beside me, and then, thinking it was only hospitable, I decided to offer him the other bottle.

He drank a few swallows and handed the water bottle back. Then, with what might have been a little smirk, he said, "*Me gusta el sombrero. Esta muy . . . agradable*" ("I like your hat. It's very . . ."). I didn't know the word *agradable* then, and I asked him what it meant. He said, "*Esta . . . bonito.*" Bonito, I knew, means pretty. I couldn't tell if he was kidding or being sarcastic. I got out my Spanish-English dictionary and looked up *agradable*: agreeable, pleasant. Then, while I had the book out, I looked up "sarcasm." I said, "*¿Esta sarcasmo?*"

"*¿Como?*" ("Huh?")

"*Sarcasmo.*"

"*¿Esta una palabra en Inglés, o en Español?*" ("This is a word in English or in Spanish?")

"*Español.*" ("Spanish.") Then I wondered if I'd read the word from the dictionary correctly, so I looked it up again and saw the word for "sarcastic."

"*Sarcástico.*"

He looked at me helplessly; he had no idea what I was talking about, and I was beginning to lose the concept myself. The important thing, though, was what I said next: "*No es mi sombrero*" ("Is not my hat").

This he understood. He nodded, and then pointed into the sky and said several sentences much too quickly for me to understand them. I did pick out the word *sol* because he said it several times and because I happened to know that word from something the doctors wanted me to tell our high blood pressure patients about staying out of the sun, *el sol.* Rodolfo was making excuses for me to wear the hat.

He stopped talking, and I said, "*Gracias.*" We had an understanding. All the same, I took the damn hat off and put it back in the pack. Macho is macho, after all. He nodded again, and we continued our ride in companionable silence. I relaxed enough to look around, even down the steep hill. There was a creek at the bottom, and a narrow valley before the next mountain rose up across the way. I was surprised to see that there were cultivated fields on the side of the mountain facing us. I pointed at them and said, "*¿Cual es eso?*" ("What is that?")

Rodolfo shrugged and said, "*Una montaña.*" ("A mountain.") He thought I was asking the word for mountain. I looked up the word for crops in my Spanish dictionary and asked more specifically, "*¿Cosechas?*"

He shrugged again and said, "*Sí.*"

I asked, "*¿Cual tipo de cosechas?*" (What type of crops?")

He looked and said, "*Maíz.*" Another word I knew: corn. Now we were getting somewhere. This was an actual conversation!

I launched into an investigation of Honduran flora and fauna, asking about the flowers and what sorts of crops the people grow, what kinds of animals live in the mountains, are there any monkeys, do they grow coffee, are there snakes or deadly spiders? By the time we worked all that out, we were both laughing: at my poor Spanish, at his complete lack of English, and at my obvious distaste for spiders.

In the mountains, they plant corn and a root called yucca, and they grow trees to produce coffee, mangos, papayas, and avocados, as well as other things I wasn't familiar with. They also grow teak and balsam trees for the wood, much of which they sell to companies from the United States.

I asked about bananas and sugar cane, and Rodolfo told me that there were many of these crops, but not in the mountains. There were some monkeys and many other animals native to the region: small deer, beautiful birds of many colors, and a wide variety of snakes and spiders. And yes, he told me with some amusement, some of them were deadly.

After a while we came to a place where a creek made its way down the side of the mountain and across our narrow path before it meandered on. There was a little pool formed by four or five flat rocks strategically placed to give people a place to walk; the creek was constricted there, running through the gaps between these stones. It was beautiful, I was tired of sitting in the saddle, and I imagined that our mounts needed a break. I didn't know the word for "Stop," and I was afraid we'd miss the spot if I took the time to look it up. I said, "*Un momento, por favor*" ("A moment, please").

Rodolfo looked around and smiled, but didn't stop, so I tried a different tactic: "*Aquí, por favor*" ("Here, please"). He slowed but didn't quite stop, so I tried again: "*Agua para el caballo, aquí*" ("Water for the horse, here"). He started to tell me that the horse didn't need water, but I was already trying to get off, so he had to stop in order to help me before I fell and hurt myself.

With no discernible grace, I dismounted and was glad for my feet to be on the ground. Rodolfo led my horse and his mule over to the pool of water, where they drank noisily for at least a minute. Then they found some grass and munched contentedly.

In the pool, maybe fifteen feet long and ten feet wide, I saw a flash of red and looked more closely. It took me a minute or two, but then, beneath a rotting log, behind a rock, I saw it: the largest firemouth meeki I'd ever seen.

In college, I'd had a variety of part-time jobs, including working at an aquarium shop in a shopping center, between an ice cream parlor and a steak restaurant. I'd kept aquariums when I was a kid, and I knew enough about them and about tropical fish to get the job and keep most of the fish healthy most of the time. A couple of other college students worked there and seemed stoned much of the time, and I'm pretty sure they made me look more knowledgeable than I actually was.

One of my favorite fish, at the store and in my apartment aquarium in college, was the firemouth meeki. It was a cichlid, in the same family as Oscars, Jack Dempseys, angelfish, and bream; it was named firemouth for the bright reddish-orange color on its belly and under its mouth, especially when mating. I'd had a mated pair in college, almost four inches long, until a party guest decided to share his rum and Coke with the pretty fish, which killed everything in the tank. Now I was excited to see this fish, nearly six inches; in the wild it could grow much larger than in a tank. I wondered how much that fish would sell for at an aquarium shop in the States.

I pointed at the fish and said, "*¡Mire eso, Rodolfo!*" ("Look at that, Rodolfo!") Seeing my excitement, Rodolfo rushed over, hoping to find something extraordinary or valuable, and was disappointed to see that I was only pointing at a fish. He gave me that shrug I was getting used to and said, "*Solamente un pescado*" ("Only a fish").

"*¡No!*" said I. I couldn't stand for this beautiful fish to be dismissed as common. "*Es mas de solamente un pescado. Es un pescado muy bonita, and muy caro.*" ("No! Is more than only a fish. Is a fish very pretty, and very expensive.")

Rodolfo looked at me with a mixed expression, combining disbelief and concern. It was, after all, only a fish, just a common fish in a pool on the side of a mountain trail. I looked again and saw there were plenty of firemouths and some other colorful fish I didn't recognize.

Without being able to speak in past tense, my abilities are sorely limited, but I had to try. It took a long time, a great deal of it spent in my handy dictionary. I'm not sure what I said, but the best it could have been was something like, "In the years past, I work in a market which is selling pretty fish not to eat but to have. This fish is called Mouth of Fire. In the United States people buy a fish like this for much money." Both Rodolfo's skepticism and his concern increased, but he only said, "Okay," letting me know that whatever I was trying to say wasn't worth the time it took me to say it.

I was frustrated, in equal parts by his blasé disregard of the beauty of these fish and by my own inability to convey the wonder of it all. Another moment or two passed, and I realized I couldn't do any better than that, as pitiful as it was. I wrestled my way back onto my poor beast of burden, and we started again.

Five or ten minutes passed, and I was comfortable in the saddle again when I saw a bird about thirty yards away. I pointed and asked Rodolfo what it was, but he didn't see it. I didn't know the word for bird, so I said, "*¿Cual tipo de animal puede* [and here, not knowing the word for fly, either, I made a flapping motion with my arms] *en el aire?*" ("What type of animal can [flapping motion] in the air?")

With an overly patient attitude, explaining something a child should know, he said, "*Los pájaros*" ("The birds").

Undeterred by his exaggerated patience, I persisted. "*Sí, sí. ¿Y cual tipo de pájaros son rojo y azul?*" ("Yes, yes. And what type of birds are red and blue?")

"*No se*" (I don't know").

It was incredible to me that he would have lived in this beautiful country his whole life and not known what sort of birds were flying around sporting such extravagantly beautiful red and blue plumage. "*¿No sabe?*" ("You don't know?")

"*No.*"

"*¡Pero es un pájaro muy hermoso, es increíble!*" ("But the bird is very beautiful, is incredible!")

Again, the shrug I was coming to hate. "*Sí.*"

How could he take all this for granted? It was too much. "*Rodolfo, su pais es muy bonita. ¡Los montañas, los arboles, los pescados, los pájaros en el aire . . . no tenemos cosas como esos en mi pais!*" ("Rodolfo, your country is very pretty. The mountains, the trees, the fish, the birds in the air . . . we do not have things like those in my country.")

He looked back at me, like he was trying to figure out what was going on. He didn't disagree with anything I was saying; he just didn't understand why I was so agitated about it. The fish were pretty, the birds were pretty, the mountains were pretty, but they were also part of his life every day. He said, "*Sí.*"

Now we rode a while in disgruntled, frustrated silence, and then Rodolfo surprised me by initiating a conversation. As we started to make our way down a slight incline, he asked what seemed to be a fairly complicated question, which I didn't understand. Then he said, "*¿Donde vive?*" ("Where do you live?")

"*En Los Estados Unidos*" ("In the United States").

"*¿Sí, pero cual estado?*" ("Yes, but which state?")

"Mississippi."

Now, it's sort of an odd thing to tell people you're from Mississippi. I'm actually quite proud to be from my home state, but after a while you do develop a certain expectation that people will have connotations and assumptions that are not so pleasant. But I was not prepared for Rodolfo's reaction; he was downright excited about it.

"*¡Mississippi!*"

"*Sí.*"

"*¡El Rio Mississippi!*" ("The Mississippi River!")

I wanted to tell him that it wasn't all that much, that it had sort of become the nation's sewer, really, and that it looked more like a big long lake than one of the largest rivers in the world. But I didn't know how to say all that, and he seemed quite excited about it, so I just said, "*Sí.*"

"*¿Es muy grande, sí?*" ("It is very large, yes?")

"*Sí.*" I didn't say what I was thinking: *Really, you're making way too much out of this.*

"*¿Y muy fuerte, sí?*" ("And very strong, yes?")

"*Sí.*" Again, I was thinking, *Now calm down before you hurt yourself. It's just a big muddy river.*

He tried a few more sentences, but there were long, rapid words I didn't know. I think he had more to say about the Mississippi River, but he was learning to accept the limitations of my Spanish, and he also seemed frustrated by trying to say things in words he thought I'd know and probably by my lack of enthusiasm about something he'd read about, something that had been part of my everyday life.

A little too late, I realized I was doing the same to him that I'd been so frustrated with him doing to me. I guess most of us spend most of our lives blind to grace and beauty all around us by our constant contact with it, anesthetized by familiarity.

By the time I'd worked all that out, I looked at Rodolfo with fresh understanding. I wanted to tell him that it was all right, that the Mississippi River is huge and over a mile wide where I grew up, that I understand being complacent to my surroundings, but it was too much, well beyond my linguistic limitations. In Spanish or in English, for that matter.

The visit to San José de las Montañas was a wonderful experience. I met with the *padrones*, the leaders of the town and church, and cautiously ate a plate of chicken and rice that they promised would be safe for gringos—"*¡No microbios!*" ("No microbes!") After the lunch we had a service, with Rodolfo doing the majority of it except for the brief homily and the Eucharistic prayer, which I stumbled through, but I think they were pleased that I was trying.

After the people had taken Communion, Rodolfo came up and told me that a woman had a baby she wanted me to baptize. It was too late for me to say that we should have started the service with the liturgy for baptism; he said they could bring water, and I said that would be fine. There was some scurrying around and an extra song or two, no guitar powered by a car battery but the same essential rhythm—clap, clap, clap-clap-clap—and by the time they were ready to continue there were three pots of water on the altar and a large bucket on the ground beside it.

I got Ellis's Spanish prayer book and found the baptism service. I asked God in Spanish to bless the water, confident that he at least would be able to understand me. I took the baby girl from her mother and sprinkled her forehead with water in the name of *El Padre, El Hijo, y El Espíritu Santo*.

Then another woman came up with a young boy, probably two or three years old. Then a father brought four children up, and after I'd baptized them he leaned over the pot of water I'd been using and I baptized him, too. More came after that, children and adults, until I'd used up most of the water in the first pot and started working from the next.

It was a profoundly holy moment for me, and I wondered if this was what it was like in the early days of the Church.

Rodolfo and I got back to Santa Ana just after dark, as the celebration of our week in the village was getting tuned up. I'm not much of a dancer, but after a couple of Salva Vida beers I danced with Suyapa and her mother and some of the women in the village. The language barrier dissolved in the music, and we danced.

During the last dance of the night, I looked across the heads of a small sea of Hondurans to see my friend Ellis, a foot taller than anybody near him. He caught my eye with a big wide grin and yelled out to me, "Boogie down!" I yelled it back to him and we both had to laugh when Suyapa yelled it, too—but with her using a different set of vowels it came out more like, "*¡Bugidaw!*" with a long U, which others in the crowd picked up as well, excited to be speaking English.

The next day, we hauled our luggage back down the mountain to wait for the bus. There was no realistic expectation that it would be there on time, but we surely didn't want to miss it.

Less than a week before, when we'd brought our bags and medical supplies and dental equipment and all that medicine up the hill, we didn't have much help. The people of the village had been wary. Now, as we made our way back down the hill, we had lots and lots of help, and lots of little hands to hold. Rodolfo took my duffel bag; all the other bags were hauled by people from the village. The big black horse I'd ridden to San José was pressed into service carrying several pieces of luggage and equipment, as were the other three horses I'd chosen not to ride, and Rodolfo's mule as well.

When we were all settled at the place where we thought the bus would arrive, it was time to tell our Honduran sisters and brothers goodbye *hasta el año proximo*—until next year. I tried and failed to thank Suyapa enough for all her help, and after she left in tears I gave her mother my last twenty-dollar bill. I was afraid pride would keep her from taking it, but she was a pragmatic woman and she hugged and thanked me. On an impulse, I dug through my duffel bag until I found my hairbrush, and asked her if she could give that to Suyapa as well. She hugged and thanked me all over again.

Rodolfo was the last one to head back up the hill, and I was his last goodbye. We stood looking at one another at a 45-degree angle, until I sat on a large stone by the side of the road and we could see eye to eye. I had no words and neither did he, partly because words had only gotten in our way and mostly because we knew what the other wanted to say. Finally I said, "*Gracias, amigo*," and held out my hand. I was surprised when he ignored my hand and gave me a disproportionally large hug from such a small person. When he backed away, I had the idea that he wanted to say something but couldn't. I nodded, and he nodded, and then he turned and walked up the trail into the trees and was gone.

I sat there and wondered what his life must be like, what he would do for the rest of the day, what he had planned for the next day. I considered the things that made my life so different from his, the accidents of our births: where we were born, who are parents were, the sort of culture we both grew up in. None of our circumstances were anything either of us had chosen. It was not because of any choice on my part that I grew up in a white, middle-class family in the United States, nor had he chosen to grow up in the beauty and poverty of Honduras.

And yet . . . was my life any happier than his? For all the resources and opportunities I'd been given, for all the technologies and luxuries I enjoyed that he couldn't even imagine, was my life any better?

I wondered about that for years, and wonder about it still: how different our lives are, in what we experience, in what we expect, in what we hope, in what we fear. I wonder, too, if all of us take our blessings for granted to the point that we no longer see them, like Rodolfo riding blindly through the amazing beauty of his home country, or me growing up beside the Mississippi River.

13

Damn the Torpedoes

My life continued with a procession of successes and challenges that all seemed important in their day, a never-ending procession of sermons, Bible studies, Sunday school classes, youth events, vestry meetings, visits in hospitals and homes—always against the backdrop of a society that was increasingly apathetic to religion and church. The Episcopal Church was becoming thought of more and more as a "liberal" denomination, and North Mississippi was becoming more and more reactionary conservative.

Still, life in the parish was good, although it seemed like we never had enough volunteers to do everything we wanted to do, and some of the most faithful helpers were too old to do much anymore. The budget was always tight—the new families that were joining were young, with young children, which is great of course, but that also meant they were starting off in their careers or jobs, without much disposable income to pledge to the church.

In January of 1985, as I was going into the opening session of the annual Convention of the Diocese of Mississippi, I ran into my friend Allyn Dawkins, who told me that she wanted to ask a favor of me. I'd known and loved Allyn since we'd met at summer camp in 1973, when we were on the permanent staff together; back then we called her Allie. Now she wanted to reclaim her full name, Allyn, an old Celtic name which means "Bright." Actually, I'd always called her Al, a gentle poke that we still laughed about. Her father had been a priest and was apparently into Celtic spirituality. Now Allyn was a deacon, soon to be ordained a priest. She would be the first woman to be ordained a priest in the Diocese of Mississippi, at St. John's in Pascagoula.

When she said she needed some help, I figured she wanted me to help take her luggage to her room or move her car, something that would use my gifts and abilities to their fullest. So I said, "Anything for you, Al," and didn't think any more about it until later that evening, while we were enjoying some hospitality in somebody's hotel room. When she picked the conversation back up, she assured me that I could say no if I wanted, that it wouldn't hurt her feelings, and I realized we probably weren't going to be talking about how many suitcases should be delivered to which floor.

She said she wanted me to preach at her ordination, and I was stunned. I told her I'd have to think about it, because I think you're not supposed to appear to be too eager to do this kind of thing, but I knew I would accept. The more I thought about it, though, the more I realized why she was so nervous, almost hesitant, to ask me to do this. It's quite a chore to preach at an ordination, in front of family and the bishop and all the clergy. And . . . she would be the first woman ordained a priest in Mississippi.

I told her I'd be glad to, but suggested that she might get somebody more experienced or more important—somebody who knew what they were doing. She said, "No, I want you."

I took a deep breath and agreed to preach, and she said, "The bishop really doesn't want this to be about the ordination of women. He's ready for us to get past fighting about this, and he was very clear that he wants the sermon to be about the priesthood and the Gospel, and not about ordaining a woman."

The closer I got to the date in May, the more nervous I felt about the whole thing. Not only would I be preaching in front of the bishop and other clergy, but a lot of our old camp friends would be there, along with quite a few people I'd never met. Even if I didn't say anything about the first ordination of a female Episcopal priest in Mississippi, it would be very much in the minds of most people there.

If I didn't mention it at all, it would seem like I was trying to ignore the elephant in the room, a raging elephant that had been trampling us all for years.

By that time, it had been years since I'd written out a sermon, but I decided that in this case I'd probably better—can't be too careful when the bishop's in the house. I wrote and rewrote, fretted and fussed, and finally got it close to how I wanted it.

The night before the ordination, my friend Ellis and I drove down to Pascagoula, and I practiced my sermon over and over during the long drive. Ellis made a few suggestions, but mostly he reassured me that nobody was going to get mad and that I shouldn't chicken out and change the main idea—but I wasn't so sure.

That night the parish had a dinner for all the out-of-town guests, and it was great to see some of our old camp friends. I might have had a drink or two by the time the bishop came and sat beside me. He took off his glasses and rubbed the crest of his bald head as he said, "Now, Buddy, I understand you're a good preacher, even though I hear it seems like most of the time you're making it up as you go along." I wasn't sure if that was a compliment or a criticism, so I just said, "Yes sir." He continued, "I don't want the service or your sermon to be all about the ordination of women. We've got plenty of people on all sides hopping mad without you adding any fuel to anybody's fires, understand?"

"Yes sir."

We chatted for a bit, and he asked about my nonexistent love life, and other people came up to talk to him and left, and after a while he went back to sit with his wife. A few minutes later, Ellis sat beside me. "What did he say?"

"He said he didn't want me to talk about the ordination of women."

"Yeah, well, you already knew that."

"Aw, man—I don't know about this. Maybe I should just skip that part."

"No, Buddy. It's perfect. Stay with it. Just stay with it."

Ellis and I shared a room at the Ramada Inn, where I spent the night thinking about the possible dire consequences of my sermon the next morning. It took my mind off listening to Ellis snore.

We had coffee and muffins in the lobby and went to the church for the run-through. I carried my sermon with me, all printed out, and told Ellis one last time that I thought I ought to play it safe. He grinned and told me it was one of those "Damn the torpedoes" moments, and that I would regret it forever if I backed out now.

Finally, the time came for the sermon. I don't think I've ever been so nervous. I started by thanking Allyn for inviting me to preach, and then wondered why she should pick me, since there were clearly many more qualified folks in attendance.

I still have the sermon in my computer files. I said, "It's difficult to think of myself as someone who has something worthwhile to say to you, Allyn, as to how to go about this priesthood business we've gotten ourselves into. It seems like you'd have gotten somebody with some expertise in the field, like the bishop or somebody ol— somebody more experienced and learned." There was some nervous laughter, with people not quite sure whether it was okay to have a chuckle at the bishop's expense.

"But the real difficulty, of course, is something more serious. It's a difficult sermon to preach, because of who Allyn is and what we're doing. On a purely physical level, there is quite a difference between this ordination to the priesthood and mine, only three years ago. All ordinations are different to some extent, but this is an obvious difference, one that will be all too evident for all to see when Allyn stands up later in this sermon.

"In my more idealistic moments, I see that there is really no reason to bring this up at all—Allyn's call to the priesthood has nothing to do with her body but with her essential self, who she is. But in my more realistic moments, I know that some people, some good people, are distressed and discomforted, not questioning Allyn as a person but questioning whether that call can overcome the circumstances of biology that put her in her body."

At about this point, I happened to look down to where the bishop was sitting at the top of the steps into the chancel, below me and to my left. He was not looking at me, but straight ahead. The top of his bald head was about the color of a ripe plum, which I could only interpret as being, as he might say, "hopping mad." But all I could do now was to stay with it, and damn the torpedoes.

"Psalm 139, which we read tonight, is, I think, well-chosen and very appropriate to the issue. Listen again to the psalmist praising his Creator for the particulars of his own creation; listen again to the words with which we praise God in our own turn:

> Darkness is not dark to you;
> The night is as bright as the day;
>> Darkness and light to you are both alike.
> For you yourself created my inmost parts;
>> You knit me together in my mother's womb.
> I will thank you because I am marvelously made;
>> Your works are wonderful, and I know it well.

"Our Church, our little part of the one, holy, catholic and apostolic Church, has determined, with great deliberation and consideration, by the power of the Holy Spirit, that we will this night ordain into the priesthood Allyn Leigh Dawkins, to be a priest among us in the Episcopal Diocese of Mississippi. Allyn, the particulars of your physical being are not only not your fault, or something that you can't help, but something for which you ought to praise God, as each of us ought to praise God: 'I will thank you because I am marvelously made; Your works are wonderful, and I know it well.'"

I paused, long enough for people to be a little concerned, and then I brought it home:

"So what if she's . . . short?" The whole congregation exploded into relieved laughter, and it was a few moments before I could continue. "Being 5-foot-1 is nothing to be ashamed of, and it shouldn't be any reason to keep her from serving as a priest. So what if she has to stand on a milk carton so she can see over the pulpit? So what if the entire youth group is taller than she is? So what if she has to buy her vestments from the children's section of the liturgical catalogue? With the support of this congregation, her friends and family, and by the power of the Holy Spirit of God Almighty, all of this can and will be overcome. God has not called her little body, but her whole self into his service. It is indeed what's inside that counts."

Now the bishop turned to look at me with a big grin on his face, and I knew I was going to be okay. I kept going.

"I hope I haven't dealt with this serious subject too lightly. And I hope you will agree that a person's height is no more or less important in responding to God's call to the priesthood than the color of the person's hair or eyes, whether the person is a man or a woman, or whether the person is right- or left-handed. God has made each of us marvelously, and calls each of us to our vocations: clergy and layperson, man and woman, short and tall. And none of us would be here tonight if we weren't absolutely sure that Allyn will be a fine priest.

"It is an honor and a privilege to be asked to preach at your ordination, Al, and I thank you very much. As to why you asked me, I guess I have to be honest enough with myself to admit that it's not because of my theological prowess or oratorical skill, but because we have been dear friends for a long time. And that is by far the greater honor, and a greater privilege."

14

Among the Ringers and Leaners

As the months grew into years, I became more and more involved in the community and in the diocese. I went back to Honduras each spring and directed a camp session every summer. I settled into the life of a priest in the Episcopal Church. Then, in the summer of 1986, my life changed forever.

It was my fourth year to direct the special session, and I was beginning to be comfortable with my role and the adult staff I'd gathered around me. A few of the people I'd done special sessions with in the past had gone into the field, teaching special education or working in centers for people with disabilities, and some of them had allowed themselves to be coaxed into coming back to camp.

My friend Charlotte had been a counselor with me back in the early 1970s; now she worked at a state center for people with disabilities south of Jackson and had brought several campers and two members of her staff to camp for the last two years. When I called Charlotte just after Easter in 1986, she said she had somebody coming to camp whom she thought would be fun: Beulah Bayer. I was trying to remember who Beulah was in the Bible, when Charlotte said, "She's a lot of fun."

I said, "Well, surely somebody named Beulah's gotta be fun, right?" Charlotte said, "Oh, you'll love her." She was right: I did. I still do.

Later Beulah told me she'd been named after her two grand-mothers: Beulah Brown and Grace Bayer. The name *Beulah* came from Isaiah 62: "You shall no more be termed Forsaken, and your land shall no more be termed Desolate; but you shall be called My Delight Is in Her, and your land Married; for the LORD delights in you, and your land shall be married." She laughed at my failure to understand and explained that *Beulah* is the Hebrew word for *married* in that verse. I supposed I looked concerned because she continued, "It could have been worse: I could have been named *My Delight Is in Her*, which in Hebrew is *Hephzibah*. "Hephzibah Bayer, can you imagine?" I told her I couldn't.

In early August, the staff for the Special Session arrived to begin the training session before the campers came. There would be two days of trying to form a community out of fifteen or twenty adults and thirty young people, most of them in high school. The training session's lofty goal was to help the staff build the knowledge, empathy, and trust that would prepare them to serve the campers and one another. There were plans to make, schedules to post, anxieties to relieve—and it helped if we could find some fun to be had in the process.

Many of the counselors knew each other from earlier camp sessions or diocesan youth events; it was an energetic reunion for them. They were all excited about being at camp, about coming to special session for the second or third time. For others, there for the first time, it was as frightening as it had been for me when I was fifteen.

As people were arriving, I went to unpack my suitcase. When I came out of my cabin, I saw Charlotte walking toward me with a young woman I'd never seen before. She was wearing a red and white cotton sweater and a pair of white shorts, and she was laughing. From the first moment I saw her, I was mesmerized by her eyes, which seemed to shine as she laughed; when she stopped laughing, they twinkled. Now, sometimes, when I'm away from her I still see her in that moment—filled with joy and much too pretty to be interested in somebody like me.

Charlotte saw me as I approached and stopped. She said, "Buddy, this is my friend Beulah Bayer." Beulah looked up at me through those beautiful, captivating eyes; I just wanted to stand there and look at her for a while, but I realized I was going to have to say something.

Just then, I became painfully aware of my appearance: raggedy cut-off jeans and an old blue pullover shirt with holes around the collar. I hadn't shaved, and I was hot and sweaty already. I might have been "camp chic," but Beulah Bayer was altogether chic; I was overmatched from the very start. I managed to say, "Hi, I'm happy, or . . . glad to meet you. Thanks . . . thank you for doing this."

She looked at me with what I imagined was a faint hint of disappointment and said, "Well, I had to come and see what Charlotte is always talking about. She says you're . . . a preacher?" She looked at Charlotte to see if that could be true, and Charlotte said, "Beulah, I'd like you to meet the Rev. Buddy Hinton, director of the session."

I said, "Usually when I'm . . . being ministerial, I'm more dressed up."

She said, "Bad as I hate it." And then they walked away toward their cabin, leaving me to wonder what she meant and what had just happened.

By this time I was thirty years old. I'd been ordained for more than five years. I'd always been shy, but I'd long since accepted that I live in an extrovert's world. I thought I could talk to anybody about anything. It had been years since the last time I'd been so dumbfounded by anyone, and usually in the past I hadn't liked it. But this time, with this young woman, I found myself looking forward to having another chance.

There was work I needed to do, plans to make, people to settle into their cabins, but I couldn't get Beulah Bayer out of my mind.

After supper, we all gathered in the chapel and began the training session with a worship service. In a week, we'd end the session with a service for all the campers that always involved lots of tears, so we would wrap the entire week in worship. We started with an energetic version of "I'll Fly Away," which had become a camp favorite, mostly because of the young people's enthusiasm during the chorus, in which they would run around with arms outstretched, as if they were birds or airplanes, when we sang, "I'll fly away, O Glory, I'll fly away. When I die, Hallelujah, by and by, I'll fly away." Their joy and energy raced on, beyond uninhibited and getting close to unbridled rambunctiousness.

As I stood there, out of the way of flying counselors, I noticed that Beulah was standing with Charlotte, looking slightly distressed. I could tell this wasn't what she was expecting. But then the song ended and the service started, and I had other things to deal with.

The previous year, someone had suggested that we use a service of foot washing during the training session as a way of embodying servant ministry. I wasn't immediately sold on the idea, but it is a liturgy of the Episcopal Church; I allowed myself to be talked into it, and it had proven very effective. So, at the appropriate moment in the opening service of this special session training, I explained what we were going to do and why we were doing it and how it was going to work. I have to admit that I was looking forward to being close to Miss Beulah Bayer, even in this unconventional way. But when I looked up as the last of the counselors and staff came up to have their feet washed, I didn't see her. I didn't see Charlotte, either.

The service continued and ended; the training session continued and went on and on. It wasn't until breakfast the next day that I knew we had a problem.

Charlotte met me at the coffee pot and said, "Buddy, you need to talk to Beulah."

"Okay . . . why?"

"Well, she's talking about going home."

I was devastated. "Why? She just got here!"

"Well, I think she just wasn't ready for all of this."

Now I was defensive. "All of what?"

"Well, I think she was expecting something more . . . churchy. She doesn't feel included. She's not used to us."

"You think she will get used to us?"

"I don't know, Buddy. She said she called her mother last night. She told her she thought she might have fallen into some kind of cult."

Well, that sounded pretty serious.

At the end of breakfast, I stood up and told everybody that we would gather in the chapel at nine o'clock. During the confusion and bustle of cleaning the tables and going to the cabins to primp for the morning session, I found Beulah and said, "Are you okay?"

"Sure, why?"

"Well, Charlotte said you—"

"No, I'm fine."

"I know it's a lot to take in, but—"

"I'm fine, thank you."

Clearly I was trying to open a door that she was determined to keep closed, so I left it there. I told Charlotte I wasn't hopeful that she was going to stay.

"Did you tell her we're not a cult?"

"Well, no, I didn't get a chance to tell her much of anything."

After the morning session, and after lunch, we had about an hour of free time. One of the guys on the adult staff, an energetically contrary young man named Kyle who'd worked at camp for several years and was now teaching school and trying to get into seminary, asked me if I wanted to play horseshoes. He knew I love to play horseshoes, and the place we played was one of the few relatively cool, shady spots at camp, under some pine trees by the arts and crafts shack where there was almost always a breeze. I said I'd be glad to, and then he told me we were going to play doubles and that he'd already asked Susan, an adult returning from last year's session, to be on his team.

I thought, "Well, all right—what could it hurt?" I looked for Beulah but found Charlotte instead, who told me she was back in the cabin. So I went and knocked on the door of her cabin. She called out, "Yes?"

I said, "Beulah?"

She repeated, "Yes?"

I said, "Come play horseshoes with me."

Looking back on it, I might have realized that she was already thinking I was a little peculiar, and that an invitation to play horseshoes in the middle of a hot August day in Mississippi would just confirm her assumptions. But, happily unaware, I sailed on in blissful ignorance.

She came to the screen door and looked at me as if I'd suggested that we swing naked from the trees. She was polite, though, in an "I suppose I have to tolerate you" sort of way. When she spoke, it was with admirable patience and restraint: "What?"

"A few of us are going to play horseshoes, and I thought it would be a good way for you to get to know some people."

"I've never played horseshoes."

"That's okay. It's not hard, and you don't have to be good."

"Well, we'll see. Maybe I'll play later."

"But—"

"But? Sew your butt up!"

I realized she was playing, so even though I didn't understand the game, I tried to play along: "Whatsamatter—you chicken?"

She smiled slyly and said, "Chicken ain't nothin' but a bird."

I guess I must have looked lost; I know I was speechless, because I remember really wanting to have something clever to say, just to keep the game going. But I didn't, so I stood there until she said, "Oh, all right, I'll play—just 'til I get hot." Neither of us could have known it at the time, but it was a decision that would change our lives.

So we played, and she stayed, long after we got hot. She was very witty, very quick, and we laughed a lot. And she was so totally different from me or anyone I'd ever met. She would say things I didn't expect, and sometimes didn't understand, so I felt off balance whenever I was around her. Really and truly, I've been off balance ever since.

After a while, we talked, and I found out that she'd grown up in Leland, a small Mississippi Delta town near Greenville, that she'd graduated from Delta State with a degree in special education, and that she was living in Jackson and working with Charlotte. I also learned that she'd grown up in the Southern Baptist Church, but that she hadn't been to church for years, despite her mother's best efforts. She said she vaguely remembered a high school friend who she thought was an Episcopalian and had always thought she was a little on the strange side, "in a Birkenstock sort of way."

By this time in my ministry, I'd accepted some parts of being a priest that I'd never learned in seminary: that people in the church are going to defer to you, that all sorts of people will give you more respect than you could ever deserve, that people watch what they say around you—all because you're a priest. Beulah did none of that. She spoke her mind whether anybody else liked it or not. She wasn't afraid of me or anybody else. If the emperor had no clothes, Beulah was the kid who was going to tell him.

At supper that night, Charlotte told me Beulah was staying, and I was surprised how strongly relieved I felt—as if I'd been holding my breath and could now breathe again. Beulah was adding something to my life I hadn't known was missing. One night in the middle of the session, she and I walked around after lights out, checking on the campers (and the counselors). There was a muddy patch between two of the cabins on the boys' side; after I took her hand to make sure she didn't fall, I didn't let go, and neither did she.

In that moment, well before I could analyze it or understand what was going on, I realized I was interested in her, and it seemed, much to my surprise, that she might be interested in me, too. Somewhere under the pine trees among the ringers and leaners, we had fallen in love. She is cute and sweet and tough, and has a great sense of humor; she is honest, stubborn, and outspoken, and can be quite challenging; she became the love of my life.

The session itself went very well, I think, although to be honest I wasn't paying as much attention as I normally did. We played horseshoes almost every day, and we laughed a lot. I asked if I could call her after the session ended, and she laughed with her eyes shining and said, "Why wouldn't you?"

It was funny, at least at first, that I was the preacher and that she knew the Bible so much better than I did. She knew it well because her church had an interesting educational practice for young people called Bible Sword Drills. I'd never heard of such a thing, so she explained that a Sword Drill was a competition. Every kid would bring a Bible. A Sunday school class would sit in chairs facing their parents and the preacher and other adults, holding their Bibles. When the teacher yelled, "Sheathe your swords!" the students would tuck the Bibles under their arms; when the teacher yelled, "Draw your swords!" they would hold them out in front of them. Then the teacher would call out a verse—"First Corinthians 15:88!"—and the students would repeat it. When the teacher yelled, "Charge!" they all raced to find that verse. The first one to find it would stand up and then be asked to read the verse. Somebody kept score, and apparently it was a big deal. Beulah said she only lost once, to an older girl, and she hated it so much she never lost again.

I said, "So you really love the Bible."

She said, "I really don't like to lose."

From then on, if I needed to remember where something was in the Bible, I asked her first. She's not as good with the Old Testament, but she's deadly accurate with the Epistles.

Beulah struck up a special friendship with Bobbo and JoJo McCain. She thought Bobbo was a lot of fun to be around, and from the first time they met, she had a special kinship with JoJo. One night as we were waiting for the staff meeting to begin, she told me she wished JoJo could be tested again, that she was convinced his IQ wasn't really as low as his records indicated. "I don't think he has any intellectual deficiency at all, other than being treated like he's stupid his whole life." She thought people just lumped JoJo in with Bobbo, but that JoJo was smarter than he wanted people to think. Beulah said, "I think he just wants to take care of Bobbo."

I remembered the first night we'd given Bobbo a placebo to help him sleep, how JoJo had seen through the nurse's ruse from the start. I told Beulah she might be right.

"If people treat you like you're not intelligent your whole life, it's pretty easy to live down to their expectations," she said.

Most of the campers came every year and were well known to the staff. But most years we would have two or three new campers, and that year was the first year that Patricia came. She was a short, heavy woman with a round face who loved to laugh and sing. Her left arm had atrophied so that her hand stayed curled up at the wrist, and she would clap her good hand against the back of that hand at the end of almost every song we sang and say in her funny voice: "Oh, that's so purty!" She was an instant hit.

We figured out the day after the campers came that one of Patricia's favorite games was a peculiar version of hide and seek: every morning she would wake up before anyone else and go somewhere and hide. She was amazingly good at hiding. It sounds more fun now in the writing than it did in the finding, but we began every day that session looking for Patricia. It took us a couple of years to figure out that if we didn't go seek, she wouldn't go hide, and that in any event she was not going to miss breakfast. But it was fun while it lasted, for Patricia anyway. That first year, Patricia happened to be in the cabin in which Beulah was the cabin adult, and I have to admit that made it a lot more fun for me.

At the end of that session, I invited Beulah to come to West Branch and go to church with me the next morning. Yeah, boy: I was a real Romeo.

15

Do You Believe All This Crap or Not?

For a while there was a lot of going back and forth between West Branch and Jackson. She met my parents, and I met hers; no one seemed particularly alarmed, though her mother had some internal difficulty with her daughter dating a priest: she'd grown up Roman Catholic, and even though she was very Baptist now, it was still unsettling deep inside her. Some of Beulah's friends had a lot of fun with the idea that she was dating a preacher, too, but nobody really objected. Most weekends Beulah would come to West Branch and stay with the Millers, a family in the parish. For a while there I think I was the talk of the town, at least in church circles—"Did you hear the young Episcopal minister is seeing someone?" Then the rumors shifted to the Methodist youth minister who'd apparently had an affair with the organist, and I was sort of sad that our time in the spotlight was over.

Beulah and I continued to see each other, continued to have fun, and started to make plans. I tried to explain the Episcopal Church to her, and she tried to explain the Baptist Church to me, both of us with somewhat limited success. The Eucharist service was an obstacle for a while, until it became clear that it wasn't about sacramental theology or Catholic tradition. She had two separate concerns. The first was that we celebrated the Eucharist for pretty much every service. "Every Sunday? You say the same thing every single Sunday?"

The other concern was with the communion bread. The wine she was okay with although it's not generally something you'd serve with a meal. But the bread we used there was a thin white wafer, more like Styrofoam than bread, really. She said, "I can imagine the wine being the blood of Jesus, I guess. I just have a hard time imagining that little wafer is really bread." I told her that some more progressive parishes used real bread, but that I couldn't imagine us making that sort of change. She didn't say anything at the time, but pursed her lips together. As the years passed and I became more fluent in reading her facial expressions, I would recognize her "We'll just see about that" face.

After a while we both began to talk about what it would be like for us to be married. She worried about playing the role of the priest's wife, and I told her I wanted her to do whatever she wanted to do in the parish, and assured her that she didn't have to do anything she didn't want to do. I don't think she's ever had her feet washed to this day.

I had dated a few girls here and there, but none of them had ever found a place in my soul the way Beulah did; after a few months I couldn't imagine living my life without her in it. It's hard for me to explain because I'm not sure I understand it myself, but part of my life had become transient, so that I never felt like I was at home. Until Beulah came. In her I found my roots again. Now, still, nearly thirty years later, wherever Beulah is, is home.

Not that it's always been easy or pleasant, even from the first. Both of us can be difficult to live with, especially me. (She'd say especially her, but she'd be wrong, and she's going to have to write her own book to ever see that in print.) There was never any thought for either of us that it would be best to walk away. When we met it was like we'd both found a piece that had been missing.

At special session the next summer, Beulah and I showed Kyle and Susan her engagement ring. It wasn't overwhelmingly large or impressive, but we both thought it was perfect.

A week or so before that special session was to start, I received a letter from a man in Jackson whose daughter had been a counselor a few years before. I opened it, expecting it to be a complaint, and was surprised and relieved to see that it was a long thank-you letter, with a $500 check enclosed. It seemed that the man's daughter had been deeply touched by her time at special session and that even though she was not able to return, the man wanted to support our work.

The man wrote that he wanted the money to be used for an activity for all the campers. I have to admit I didn't have any idea what to do. You might say that the special sessions at Camp Bratton-Green had been run on a shoestring, but there had been times when we didn't have a shoestring, either. We'd done wonderful things with butcher paper and tempera paint; we'd created magic with refrigerator boxes and mimeographed songbooks. I didn't know what to do with a little money. We had gotten so used to running lean that I didn't have a clue what to do with a little extra.

I called my friend Ellis, who by then was serving a little parish in nearby Columbus. He'd been on the adult staff of the special session for the last couple of years. I told him what was going on. "What should I do?"

"First, write him a real nice thank-you letter."

"Yeah, okay." I'd already thought of that; my mother would be so proud.

"Well, then, we need to figure out a way to spend all that money." We thought for a moment, and then he said, "You know what we could do: we could take the whole session to see the Mets." The Mets were a minor league baseball team in Jackson, about forty miles from camp. Ellis said, "Call 'em and see if they're in town that week."

I got the number and called and spoke to an enthusiastically friendly young woman in the front office. I asked her if the Mets were in town that week. She said that the team would open a home set with the Birmingham Barons on Friday, August 14, our last full day of the camp session; the next day we would all be on our way home, happy and exhausted, with stories to tell. I couldn't have anticipated the stories that I would take away from the week.

I told her who I was and what I was trying to do, that we wanted to bring about sixty people with mental and physical disabilities to a baseball game, hoping I could get a deal. I asked her how much tickets might cost and again suggested that I was hoping to catch a break on the price, as I was working with a limited budget.

She put me on hold, I listened to some elevator music, and when she came back I was startled to hear her tell me that they would love for us to come as their guests, at no charge. I told her I'd still need to get tickets for the staff. She asked how many people were on staff, and I told her about fifty.

She put me on hold again, I listened to more cheesy music, and then she came back and told me that the staff's tickets would be free, too! And not only that, but she told me that some of the cast from *One Life to Live* would be there that night, and that they would put the name of the camp on the scoreboard during the seventh inning stretch.

I asked her who I could write a thank-you letter to, and she gave me the business manager's name and an address, my mother surely getting prouder by the moment. I called Ellis back. After I'd told him the good news, and after he'd explained to me that *One Life to Live* was a soap opera, we were basking in our good fortune when he said, "So what are we going to do with five hundred dollars?" We thought for a moment, and then Ellis said, "Hey—we could go to the zoo!" The Jackson Zoo is in the same part of town as the baseball park, and Ellis suggested we could take everybody to the zoo, have a picnic dinner outside the stadium, and then go in to see the game. He said I should call the Jackson Zoo and see if we could get a deal.

So I called the Jackson Zoo and talked to a enthusiastically perky young woman in sales, telling her who I was and what I was trying to do, and she put me on hold and I listened to some truly cheesy music with tape distortion, and she came back and told me that they would love for us to come and be their guests, campers and staff—for free! I thanked the young woman and asked who I could write a thank-you note to, then called Ellis back. This time I knew better than to bask in the glory of it for too long, and I reminded him that we still had five hundred dollars to spend.

He said a friend of his from college worked for the Jackson Bus Company and that he could call and see if we could get a couple of buses to come get us and then take us back to camp for the trip. I waited as he made the call, imagined Ellis talking to an enthusiastically chipper young woman who would inevitably answer the phone, and him listening to the dreadful music when she put him on hold. In a few minutes he called me back to say that we had two buses with two drivers who would come and get us and take us back, all compliments of his friend and the Jackson Bus Company. I got the friend's name and address, and we wondered what we were going to do with the money.

Finally, we decided to buy each camper a baseball cap, with "Camp Bratton-Green" written on the front and a space to write the camper's name on it in magic marker. Even then we got a good deal and had enough money left to give each camper a brand new five-dollar bill to spend however they wanted, at the zoo or at the baseball game. Most of our campers never get to hold their own money and never have the opportunity to decide how they will spend it; that summer at camp, they'd have five bucks to blow however they wanted.

I'd hoped all of this would be a big surprise for everybody, but my friend Ward, an attorney, suggested that we needed to have release forms signed by the legal guardians of all campers and counselors, allowing us to take their campers to another site. So I sent letters to parents and guardians, asking them to return the release forms.

At the training session, I told the staff about the Big Trip, and we talked a lot about how this would be a big treat for a lot of our campers, most of whom had never had this sort of opportunity before. I told them we would have to be extra careful when we went into Jackson, that we'd need to stay together and make sure everybody was safe and accounted for at all times.

There was no keeping such a secret, and by the end of the week the campers were buzzing with excitement about our trip to the zoo and the baseball game. Patricia was especially excited that she might to get to meet Robert Woods, who played Bo Buchanan on *One Life to Live.* I remember that because she must have told me at least three times every day.

On the last full day of the session, the buses arrived right after lunch, bringing the excitement of the campers and staff to a fevered pitch. On our trip to the zoo, I mentioned to Beulah that I thought Patricia might be a little sweet on Robert Woods, but she explained to me that Patricia felt like it was her duty to tell Robert that Delilah was not really Bo's sister after all, and that he could be in danger. I told her it was a whole new complicated world that I knew nothing about whatsoever, and Beulah said, "Oh, you'd love it—it's just stories."

We got to the Jackson Zoo and ushered all the campers inside, wearing their caps with their names on them, each person with a crisp new five-dollar bill. A few minutes later, I saw many of them with cotton candy, peanuts, or the first thing they saw that they could buy. A few of them, however, were guarding their money very closely, waiting for just the right thing.

Bobbo was following along this difficult path, holding on to his five-dollar bill and trying with some passion to convince the other campers that they were wasting their money, that they needed to buy things that would last so they would have something to look at and remember.

When we walked through the reptile house, another camper named Curtis became loudly disconcerted when he saw two iguanas mating. At some point in the clamor, Bobbo, wanting to appear worldly and sophisticated and in the know about reptile sex, was impatient with Curtis's outburst and told him to shut the hell up. Curtis, who tended to become more upset when people told him to calm down, got so agitated that he took a swing at Bobbo, hitting a glancing blow on his ear. JoJo stepped in and pulled Bobbo away before he could try to return the punch. One of the counselors heard JoJo telling Bobbo he "shouldn't never get in a fight he know he ain't got no chance to win."

Bobbo's counselor that year was a sweet young man from Greenwood named Foster. After we discovered the wonder of placebos, Bobbo had become a camper who trained first-year counselors, as he was now considered one of the easier and more enjoyable campers.

Foster really wanted to do the right thing, but he was completely flustered by the Iguana Incident, and in the aftermath of the punch he tried to be more forceful with Bobbo than either of them were accustomed to. Bobbo stormed off, and I suggested that Foster keep him in his sight but give him some space. "He's just being dramatic," I said, "but if you don't provide an audience, he'll let it go pretty soon."

As it turned out, Bobbo found a different audience in some of the campers, including a female camper named Mayvelle whom Ellis had said was a little too uninhibited. "Everybody needs some inhibition," he said, "for the sake of society." Mayvelle and Curtis lived in the same center, and apparently they had a history together, including a regrettable season of romance that both of them were now loudly trying to forget. Sometimes it might be better to have *not* loved and lost, especially if it leaves you with an adversary as venomous as Mayvelle Wilson. She was only too glad to be presented with an opportunity to strike out at Curtis, using Bobbo's anger and frustration as her weapon.

Apparently, Mayvelle's counselor hadn't spent much time with her charge other than telling her what to do. It turned out to be a dangerous combination of sentiments. When Bobbo found that Mayvelle was in full support of his wounded indignation, she was happy to share not only her hatred for Curtis but also her resentment at having a young counselor telling her what to do all the time. By the time we were leaving the zoo, Bobbo was all worked up. I looked for JoJo to see if he could calm his brother, but saw that he was hanging out with some of the counselors from previous years and didn't want to disturb him.

We left the zoo and walked a couple of blocks to a field outside the baseball park, where the cooks from camp served us hot dogs, chips, soft drinks, and cold slices of watermelon from the back of a pickup truck. When we were just about to round everybody up and send them in for the first pitch, Foster ran up to me, out of breath.

"Bobbo's run off!"

I admit that I didn't take it as seriously as I later wished I had. Bobbo was high drama but not one to forsake his audience. Foster said that he'd walked up the hill, told him he wasn't coming back. I told Foster to run after him but not to crowd him or try to force him to return. Then I went and found my old friend Harry, who was on staff again, and told him what was going on.

Harry went to get Bobbo back, and I got everybody organized and going into the baseball stadium. When it looked like we were as organized as we were going to be, I went to check on Bobbo. When I caught up with Harry, he and Foster were watching Bobbo going up the hill toward a building that looked like it had two arms coming toward us, like an upside-down U. Bobbo was going right into the U, and I relaxed. All he could do was come back out toward us.

After a few minutes Harry went to talk to him and yelled back to us, "It's three buildings!"

Foster and I ran up the hill, and I shouted, "What?"

Harry waited for us to see for ourselves, and then he put the terrible reality into words. "He's gone."

The building I'd thought was one U-shaped structure was actually three separate buildings; looking up at them from down the hill made it seem as if it was one building, but it wasn't. There was no sign of Bobbo. I told Foster to go to the stadium and join his other campers watching the game, that Harry and I would find Bobbo— surely he couldn't have gone far. But just in case, I asked Foster to send Charlotte, Beulah, and Susan to help us look, and to tell Ellis that he was in charge until I got back.

We scoured the area, yelling for Bobbo. Harry suggested that we stop yelling: if Bobbo were hiding from us, the noise would just alert him to our location. So we searched in silence for a while, but that didn't work, either. Beulah and Susan came to help and told us that Charlotte said she thought she needed to stay at the game. We fanned out, looked and yelled and looked some more.

After more than an hour, Beulah told me that she thought we needed to call the police. I knew she was right, but I didn't want her to be: I did not want to involve the police. She found a pay phone while I kept looking and yelling.

Two squad cars arrived; I was thankful they didn't have their lights flashing. The senior officer, a short, pudgy man who looked as if one more Twinkie would pop half the buttons on his uniform, came up to me. "Are you in charge?"

"Yes sir."

"Dispatch said you've got a missing retard."

"I'm running a summer camp session for people with mental and physical disabilities, and just as we were about to go into the stadium, one of our campers got upset and walked away."

The officer seemed completely bored with the whole thing. "Describe the perpetrator."

"He's not a perpetrator," I said, "He's a missing person." I explained that he was a black male, about forty years old, and indicated how tall he was. I told the officer he was wearing a white baseball cap with the words "Camp Bratton-Green" printed on it, and his name, "Bobbo," written in magic marker. How hard could it be to find him?

Susan suggested that we should let the police handle it, go into the stadium and watch the game, but even as she said it she knew we couldn't. I'd been underwhelmed by the policeman's apathy.

Harry said he'd brought his car, and that we could ride around and look for Bobbo too. It was a Nissan Sentra, with barely enough room for two, especially if one of them was me, so Susan and Beulah went back to the game, and I contemplated squeezing into a car that was clearly not built for anybody over six feet tall, especially such a well-rounded individual as myself.

Ellis came up and asked if we'd found Bobbo. I told him we hadn't, but that we'd called the police and that Harry and I were about to ride around and keep looking. When I asked him why he'd left the game, he motioned me away from the others and said, "The bishop is here, with his grandsons, watching the game. He's sitting in the next section, and he's asking me where you are."

The gravity of the situation hit me like a slap in the face. I was the director of the session, I'd set a camper with limited mental and emotional capacity loose in downtown Jackson, I'd given him five dollars to do whatever he wanted with, and the bishop was there, asking for me. I was concerned about Bobbo, of course, but I was also thinking this could be the end of my career in the church, or at least at camp.

I thought about telling the bishop what was going on; it's what I should have done if I were playing by the book. But that particular book was still being written. And I thought, "Surely we don't need to burden the bishop with every little thing."

I asked Ellis to tell the bishop that I was dealing with a camper problem, and that I would be happy to see him as soon as I could. Harry and I could listen to the game on the radio and check back with Ellis after it was over, just to see if Bobbo had returned. Harry and I wedged ourselves into the Nissan and drove on.

As we rode around I saw several places that sold alcohol, and I spotted a couple of women whose virtue might be for rent. I wondered where the hell Bobbo was and how far five bucks might go in this part of town.

The game ended, and Ellis got everybody back on the buses to head back to camp. Harry and I watched everybody leave, and then we kept looking.

At about 2:30 a.m., Harry said it was time for us to go back to camp too. He said the police would find Bobbo, and it wasn't doing anybody any good for us to keep riding around in circles looking at the same liquor stores and hookers over and over. It was hard for me to give up, hard to admit to myself that I could be in real trouble. Harry saw that I was in distress and tried to be comforting, but it's not really his strong suit. When he realized that I was not going to accept any reassurance, he got a little impatient. "Look, Father Buddy," he said (I'd known Harry since I was fifteen, he'd never called me Father before), "you've been talking about trusting God and hope and faith ever since you got out of seminary. Do you believe all this crap or not?"

Now, you might not know this, but most preachers don't really like to be preached to, especially when somebody points out the log in our own eyes. But Harry was preaching, and he was right. We went back to camp.

A little after 6:00 a.m., Harry knocked on my door and told me he'd been sleeping in the infirmary in case the police called, and that he'd just spoken to someone from the Greyhound Bus station in Jackson. They said they had a man there who was trying to get a ticket to

Mayersville with a five-dollar bill, and that it didn't look like he was going to take no for an answer. They asked him who they could call, and he told them his brother was at the camp whose name was on his hat. They found the number for Camp Bratton-Green and called. Harry went back into Jackson to get Bobbo, and I went to sleep. I felt like the bulldozer that had been on my shoulders had rolled off.

At breakfast, Bobbo and Mayvelle were sitting together, regaling their tablemates with their version of the evening's amusements. Bobbo had what he always wanted: an audience. And Mayvelle had what she always wanted, too: a man under her influence, a tool for her vengeance. She smirked at me.

It was going-home day. Families and vans from centers were coming to get the campers; we invited all of them to join us for the closing service. It was usually very emotional for campers and staff alike, with lots of tears all around: the community we'd built was being broken apart, and all we could say was, "See you next year!"

The theme for our chapel services that year was "We Are Family," from the 1979 disco hit by Sister Sledge. We'd talked a lot about brotherhood and sisterhood in the morning and evening services. The plan for final service was for Ellis to conduct the service and celebrate the Eucharist, and for me to preach. I had already worked out what I was going to say, the big, boffo conclusion to our theme and our week. I decided I wouldn't mention the night before, not wanting to end the week on a sour note.

The campers started crying before the opening song was even going, and I knew we were in for some weepy worship. We kept the music upbeat—"Do Lord," "All God's Critters Got a Place in the Choir," "I'll Fly Away"—but we couldn't stop the tears. In the sermon I tried to lighten the mood a little as I talked about being brothers and sisters.

I expounded, "We are family—the family of God! Who are you going to kick out of the family of God? Should we kick Patricia out?" Patricia's game of early morning hide and seek had caused us no end of anxiety, but it was sort of fun, too. Everybody called out, "No!" Patricia stood up and put her good hand on her hip and boomed, "You better hope not!" Everybody laughed.

I orated, "Well, what about Big Ross?" Big Ross was a really nice guy, but he'd gotten a little carried away with his Elvis impersonation during the talent show and taken his shirt off. Some people can get away with that sort of thing, but Big Ross was not one of them. Everybody cheered as Big Ross stood up and gave us his signature Elvis gyration, but some of us were still recovering from the intensity of the moment. I said, "Can we kick Big Ross out of the family of God?" and everybody yelled, "No!"

I preached, "Well, what about Lanny?" Lanny was a second-year counselor I'd hoped in vain would improve, but he was just as indolent and condescending as he'd been the year before. Okay, so my words were a little shot at a lazy counselor. He sat in his chair and waved feebly, not sure what might happen next. "Can we throw Lanny out of the family of God?" Some of the counselors said, "Yeah!" but the campers knew what I was talking about: "No!"

And then, just as I was about to bring the sermon to its stirring conclusion, one of the campers called out, "What about Bobbo?"

What *about* Bobbo? I hadn't seen a single pitch of the baseball game, never even made it into the stadium. I didn't get to see some of the cast of *One Life to Live*, or witness our name on the scoreboard during the seventh inning stretch. And I knew I was going to have an uncomfortable conversation with the bishop in the next few weeks. What about Bobbo? Could I kick Bobbo out of the family of God?

I hate it when people preach to me.

I said, with my conviction drowning out a little regret, "No, we can't throw Bobbo out of the family of God, either. If any of us are children of God, then we're all children of God. This camp, the church, is our home; when we come together, at camp or at church, we are brothers and sisters coming home. We are, all of us, the children of God forever—no matter what, no matter what."

By that time I was crying, too, so I thought that would be a good place to stop. Bobbo and JoJo came up for Communion, and before JoJo took the bread he hugged me, hard. He said Bobbo was very sorry, and I told him it was okay.

After the service, JoJo told me that Mayvelle had tricked Bobbo; apparently it was her idea that he walk away. As JoJo and I talked,

I saw her watching us, still smirking. Right then I was just glad the campers hadn't asked me, "What about Mayvelle?"

16

Miraculous and Wonderful

A few weeks after that camp session, the bishop and I had the uncomfortable conversation about letting a camper loose in downtown Jackson, and I assured him I would be more careful in the future. He also told me that it was a great game, and it was fun to see the special session campers interacting with some people from a television show. He asked about one of the campers, describing Patricia quite accurately, said that she was clearly infatuated with one of the actors and that, after the game, she wanted the bishop to go and tell the actor that somebody wasn't really his sister at all, and that he needed to watch out for her. "I told her I couldn't get involved, that he would need to work that out for himself."

Also in that conversation, I shared with the bishop that I was planning to get married, and told him all about Beulah Bayer. He said that his wife, Miss Nora, would be pleased and a little relieved, and asked me if we'd set a date. I told him we were looking at October 3, 1987, and he glanced at his little pocket calendar and told me that he couldn't officiate—he and his wife were going to visit family in North Carolina, and there was no way he could get out of it.

I hadn't realized that I was supposed get his permission to marry, or that I was supposed to ask him to do the wedding; I didn't tell him that we'd already asked my friend Craig, a priest in Jackson, to do the service. So it all worked out just about right.

Beulah and I had talked about having the wedding at her parents'
church in Leland, but she said she wasn't feeling particularly Baptist,
that she didn't really know anybody at that church, and that she'd
rather have the service at Holy Incarnation, where I was the priest and
where she'd come to love some of the members. I was glad to think
she might be starting to feel at home there. My friend Craig was the
priest at St. Philip's in Jackson, where Beulah had been confirmed at
the Easter Vigil.

It was a beautiful, sweet wedding. A special session counselor
played the flute, both of our mothers cried, and Beulah and I were
more worried about giggling during the vows. The Baptists sat on
the bride's side, the Episcopalians on the groom's, all of them keeping
their denominational spirit in check. The Episcopalians came up for
Communion, but the word was out that we were drinking wine in
church, and the bride's side stayed glued to their pews.

We had the reception at Cedar Point, the one and only nice
restaurant in West Branch. Before the reception was over, Beulah
and I left for our honeymoon, a trip to Disney World; we had a
long drive. I'm still hearing about how I made her leave our wedding
reception too early; it's a story our children remind us of now, even
though it's obviously filtered through their mother's point of view.

And I'm also still reminded that we came back from our two-
week honeymoon trip about a week early, because a member of the
Vestry died and I felt like I had to come back to do the funeral. I've
thought about that for years and years now, and while I'm grateful
for my sense of duty and responsibility to the Lord and the Church,
sometimes I wonder if I let it get out of balance with the rest of
my life.

We look back at the pictures from time to time, marveling at how
dark my hair was or how thin I looked. There's a picture of Beulah
with Minnie Mouse, another with me and Mickey; there's a photo
of me standing in front of Space Mountain, which she rode alone
because she couldn't entice or shame me into going with her, and
another of her looking in wonder at one of the huge aquariums in the
Living Sea. We were young and silly a long time ago, so full of energy
and dreams, and so deeply in love. Now we're still silly, but without

needing to waste as much energy about it. My hair is still there, but the gray is being replaced by white. And I am still very much in love with Beulah Bayer Hinton, now more than ever.

Our son was born in January 1989, a beautiful boy we named Judah Benjamin Hinton, correcting my name, which is Judah Bennie. I worried about bringing another PK into the world, but it doesn't seem like Jude has ever let being a Priest's Kid get in his way much.

A few months after the baby was born we wondered what we'd ever thought or talked about before his birth; a few months after that we wondered what it would be like to be able to just go somewhere without having to pack the stroller, diaper bag, toys, and teething rings that had completed taken over our new reality.

On the day that Jude was baptized, Beulah had a gift for me. The baptism itself was glorious and wonderful, Jude squirming and burbling and trying to kick his way out of the long white baptismal gown that had him trapped. It wasn't until I removed the burse and veil on the altar that I saw the bread on top of the paten, a beautiful round loaf of whole wheat bread, about five inches in diameter and two inches thick in the middle, with a cross creased on top.

I looked up to find Beulah, who stood with Jude on her left hip and right hand on the other. She had her "What are you going to do about it?" face on—that one I'd already learned. I looked over at the chair of the Altar Guild, realizing as I did so that she would either be in on the surprise or furious that something had changed. Happily she nodded her approval, and the service continued in peace and harmony.

After the service, people told me that they enjoyed the sermon, that Jude was a beautiful baby, and that they loved the bread. The next Sunday, when we went back to the wafers we'd used forever, some people were disappointed. We talked about it at the next Vestry meeting, and they voted to give it a try—if Beulah was willing to make the bread. By the end of the year it was generally regarded as The Way We've Always Done It.

So life went on, greatly improved. I was working for a wonderful parish in a nice, small town, recently married with a newborn son;

Mr. Rockwell could have come and painted our happy life. It was an enchanted time for us, filled with love and hope.

Jabbok, the good hound dog Cornelius and Mabel had given me as a present at their wedding, had been more comfortable living outside. She had a pen and a doghouse that I had built, and loved to sit in the shade of the pecan trees in our backyard and watch the birds and squirrels. When we brought Jude home from the hospital, the dog's maternal instincts kicked in and she needed to be inside to help raise him, even if it meant she had to have regular baths: Jude was her puppy, too.

At the Church of the Holy Incarnation, Jude was everybody's grandson or nephew. He didn't seem to mind being passed from matron to matron, all of them cooing and oohing and celebrating his little fingers and toes, rejoicing over each tooth as it came in with much chewing and slobbering.

For a while there, life was about bassinets and car seats, feeding schedules and diaper after diaper after diaper. Jude took his first steps, said his first words—all of it fairly routine in the larger scheme of things, all of it miraculous and wonderful for us. At every developmental stage of his life, I felt a little impatient that he move on to the next, and every time he did I missed the stage we'd left behind.

I was elected to the Diocesan Executive Committee, something like a board of managers for the Diocese of Mississippi, and it was a real education for me. There were lots and lots of spreadsheets with numbers in columns. I was the new guy, and it was a lot of spreadsheets and budgets; I mostly kept quiet.

Among many other things, the executive committee was the group that reviewed plans being made by people from parishes who wanted to build or expand and needed to borrow money, either from the Diocese or from a local bank. Either way, the committee had to vote to approve, and I was amazed at how often we didn't, and at the reasons we gave.

After the third or fourth parish was told they'd have to go back to the drawing board, to trim back their vision and make smaller drawings of more modest naves or parish halls or education buildings,

I said, "Do we ever just say yes?" Nobody said anything, so I continued, "I mean, I know there are financial consequences and we have to operate with sound business practices and all that, but these are people's dreams we're shooting down here!"

The wise old priest across the table from me was impervious to my idealism and said, "This is where the Dream meets the Budget, kiddo."

I said, though not loud enough for him to hear, "But does the Dream ever win?"

At my first Clergy Conference in the spring of 1981, I had been intimidated, the new boy in a well-established fraternity. I'd wandered around lost after the evening program was over, not wanting to insert myself into a group that had already been formed. An older priest named Phil, whom I'd known for years at camp, invited me to play poker. I reminded him that he'd taught me to play poker in 1971, and that I still wasn't very good, and he told me that was just fine; they would be glad to teach me and take my money. It was only nickels, dimes, and quarters, but they did pretty well the first night, both with teaching me and with taking my money. The second night, I recovered what I'd lost, plus a little bit more, and I found a place in a circle of friends, not as the kid from camp but as a peer.

Now I was one of the main players, at home among the priests of the Diocese. At the clergy conference poker table in the spring of 1989, the rector of the parish in Oxford gave me a heads-up that I was going to be invited to preach at Daniel Rodgers's ordination. Some of the other guys at the table started telling stories about ordination sermons they'd heard, most of them academic and boring, most of them delivered by dignitaries and stuffed shirts.

I reminded them that I'd already preached at an ordination, when Allyn Dawkins became a priest. They said they hadn't been there because it was a long drive to Pascagoula, and, if the truth were to be told, because it was the ordination of a woman, which had been quite controversial at the time. And besides, they hadn't known me as well then, so that one didn't count as far as they were concerned. One of them, the rector of the church in Laurel, said, "So you're gonna preach an ordination? No offense, Buddy, but I'd like to see that!"

The rector of St. Peter's said, "May 20th, 7 p.m., God willing and the people consenting. Red stoles."

17

I Never Saw This Coming

Daniel was a kid I'd known at camp, both when he was a counselor at special session and when he was on the permanent staff; now he'd grown up some and was set to be ordained a priest at St. Peter's in Oxford, where he was serving as chaplain at Ole Miss. I'd gone to his ordination to the diaconate at his home parish in Greenwood, and I was honored that he'd asked me to preach his ordination to the priesthood.

I was also intimidated and nervous. His church history professor had bored us at some length at Daniel's diaconal ordination, displaying great wit apparently understood only by himself, although some people had chuckled along out of politeness.

So I exegeted the Scripture passages that Daniel chose and made notes; I started to write it all out, because that's how I'd prepared for Allyn's ordination, and also so I would be assured that I had something to say. But Beulah said, "Don't do that! Nobody wants to be read to—just say what you want to say." I protested, "But the bishop is going to be there, and the guys from the poker table said they're all coming . . . I can't just stand up there and wing it!"

"Are the bishop and those other priests that much more important than the people you preach to every week?"

"Well, no. Of course not. But this is an ordination."

So I typed my words into my computer and added and deleted and rearranged it so much that I wasn't actually sure what it said anymore, but I printed it out and took it to the ordination in a manila folder. It was comforting to have it in my hand; I didn't especially like the sermon, but it made me feel safe somehow to hold on to it.

When I got there, I saw some of the guys from the poker table and a lot of the priests I knew from around the Diocese, including a very old priest we called Father Tup. The Rev. Tupper Stuart Emerson had been a camp director back in the seventies when I was a counselor and then on the permanent staff hired to work at all the sessions. I hadn't seen him since I'd gone to seminary, and assumed he must have died, but he was living in a retirement home there in Oxford.

When he saw me he loudly exclaimed, "Ah, the preacher!" The people around us laughed; it's traditional for priests to rib the preacher at these things, but Father Tup continued, "I tell you the truth: I never saw this coming, that I'd be sitting in the congregation listening to you preach! You've come a long way since the Canton, Mississippi, jail, boy." There was a hushed silence, and then the old priest winked at me and said, "Well, we'll just have to hope God knows what he's doing."

The people listening didn't know how to react, and I wasn't in a position to help them. I'd forgotten the story of the spook house and the Canton, Mississippi, jail until he reminded me of it, or maybe I'd repressed it. Either way, I knew I'd found my sermon; I threw the manila folder in the trash.

In the summer of 1975, I told the congregation, I was working at camp for my third year on the permanent staff. For the last night of some of the sessions, the session director asked the permanent staff to put on a Spook House in the big house up the road from where we stayed. It was sort of a scary house all by itself; all we had to do was help it a little.

That summer, we really had the Spook House down: Celia played the role of the green-faced witch who conducted the campers up the winding steps and through the twisted hallway upstairs; my old friend Clif rigged a harness to hold him up from a beam in the attic so that he looked like a hanged man until they got too close and he'd lurch at them, arms and legs flailing; Deena made up her face to look like the little girl in *The Exorcist* and robed herself in a white bedsheet, never making a sound but coming up and standing silently too close to a camper; I wore a pair of jeans I'd ripped and torn off below the knees and a bloody T-shirt, with stitches carefully painted on my face with mascara, and carried a big, dull axe. I looked like a monster who'd been put together by a committee. My job was to chase the campers out, down the back steps at the end of the hall. The trick was for them to be scared but not so scared that they'd fall down the steps.

The Rev. Tupper Emerson was the director of the second session for campers who'd finished the fifth and sixth grades that year, and we knew from previous years that he loved a good Spook House. We all loved Tup but were tired of him telling us how much better the Spook Houses were in Years Gone By, so we decided to really do it up right.

When our friend Miles, who'd been on the special session staff for the last few years and who played tight end for the Mississippi State Bulldogs, called to say he had a free weekend off and wondered if it would be okay for him to come and party with us, I was glad to ask him to come down early enough to be part of the Spook House.

We all had our costumes and makeup, and the roles we played were well established. The campers, especially those who'd come to camp before, were eager to identify us: pointing to the witch, they'd say, "That's Celia!" or to the guy hanged by the neck, "That's just Clif!" Or they'd point out Deena, or me, or the other people playing their roles—it was disheartening. "But," as Deena pointed out with devious delight, "they don't know Miles!"

I was large but soft; Miles was even larger and hard as a rock. He was also stunningly handsome; Deena and Celia started planning his costume and makeup two days before he got to camp.

Miles arrived the afternoon of the Spook House, and we told him the plan. Celia and Deena said they would do his makeup, a lot of black around his eyes and red coming from his mouth; he would be a manic vampire, dressed only in jeans. When I said, "Doesn't he need a shirt?" they assured me that he did not, mumbling something about abs and pecs that I didn't understand.

After supper, the permanent staff left, telling some of the campers that we had to go to Jackson. They didn't believe us. It was the same tired lie we'd told them the year before. We took a plate for Miles, since we didn't want anybody to see him before coming up the Spook House stairs. When we got back to the house, he wondered, "We are having a party, right?"

In the excitement about the Spook House, we'd forgotten about the party. "Imagine," I said in Daniel's ordination sermon as I told the story, "seven college kids with no adults anywhere in sight, and they forget they're having a party! So I told Miles we'd go into town after we took off our makeup and costumes from the Spook House, to get our party supplies." Then, remembering that I was preaching a sermon to the bishop and a bunch of clergy and a lot of people I'd never met, I added, "You know, party supplies: bean dip and chips! You can't have a party without bean dip and chips." I assumed they all knew that I was talking about alcohol, but I was content to leave it to their imagination.

So we put on our costumes and makeup, and Celia and Deena rubbed black and red grease paint over Miles's pecs and abs with oddly distracted expressions on their faces. When the campers came, Celia brought them up the front stairs, and they quickly identified her, Clif, Deena, me, and some of the others, but when they saw the huge man painted in black and red jumping around with maniacal abandon, they didn't know who it was or what to say. Every group of six or eight campers ran down the back steps with no prompting required from me.

After the Spook House was over, before we'd even finished congratulating each other and telling the stories of how scared the campers were, Father Tup came up the steps and with great energy told us that we had scared the campers way too much. He said we'd have to come down to the camp and go to each and every cabin to assure them that we were people they knew, and that they were okay. He ended his tirade by saying, "Leave all your get-up on so they can see you in the light," and then, pointing at Miles the vampire, he spat, "And bring that guy!"

"By the time we'd gone to all eight cabins," I preached, "we were concerned that the store that sold bean dip and chips might be about to close. So somebody suggested—I think it was somebody else who suggested—that we could just go into town like we were, without removing our Spook House costumes or our makeup. If anybody asked, we could tell them about the Spook House; everything would be perfectly understandable.

"Five of us piled in Deena's Volkswagen Beetle Bug, and one was me, and one was Miles. We drove into Canton and arrived at the bean dip and chips store just as the owner turned out the lights; we watched him lock the doors and walk to his car.

"Then somebody suggested—I really hope it was somebody else who suggested—that there was another store on the other side of town, across the tracks, that also sold party supplies, that probably stayed open a little later, and we could get our bean dip and chips there."

I paused and looked at the congregation before saying, "It was 1975, and five white kids decided we would go across the tracks, to the other side of town, the side of town where we never went. But still, you can't have a party without bean dip and chips . . . .

"We got to the party supply store, they were still open after midnight on a Friday night, and the five of us piled out of Deena's Beetle Bug like clowns from a clown car. We would probably have attracted a crowd anyway, even if Deena hadn't taken three oranges from a bag in the front of her car and started to juggle, but when she did, it removed any chance that this would be a routine trip to the store.

"Miles and I went in and bought the bean dip and chips—two cases of ice cold bean dip and chips, I seem to recall—and as we were coming out of the store and marveling at the size of the crowd that had gathered, a squad car pulled up with lights flashing. Most of the people seemed to evaporate at that point, but the five of us were not overly concerned since we were all over eighteen—the legal age for purchasing bean dip and chips in Mississippi in 1975. We were not concerned until the sincere young officer stepped out of the squad car and asked for our license and registration.

"That's when we learned that this was not actually Deena's Volkswagen Beetle Bug, but that she was pretty sure her brother knew where it was the entire time, and then, after that, we learned that Deena didn't actually have a driver's license . . . anymore. And that's when the sincere young officer decided it would be best to take us down to the station.

"The other four had a quick caucus without any words exchanged, and decided that I should be the one to explain to the officer who we were and what we were doing, so I stepped toward him and held out my hand, which he ignored. I ventured, 'Hi. My name is Buddy Hinton. I know this looks bad, but I can explain.' It might have worked, but my next words were 'We work for a church camp,' and it all fell apart.

"On the way to the Canton police station, those same four people reached another agreement that I should be the one to call the director of the camp session to come and get us. I called camp and woke up the session nurse, who went to wake Father Tupper Emerson. He came to get us, and he didn't say a word for the eleven miles between Canton and camp, but when he let us out at the big house where the permanent staff stayed, he said, 'We will talk about this in the morning.'

"And we did—well, he did. We mostly listened. And that's why, a few minutes ago, when the Reverend Tupper Emerson saw me coming in the door and knew it was me who was preaching Daniel's ordination, he said, 'Well, I never saw this coming!'"

The congregation broke out in laughter, led by Tupper Emerson and joined by the bishop. I waited, and then I said, "Well, you know what, Father Tup? Neither did I." There was more laughter—the congregation was having a grand time.

I continued, "When I was a kid, when I was a counselor at Camp Bratton-Green, Father Tup was one of the priests who gave some of his time to work at camp. He was one of those guys who came looking for us when we snuck out after curfew, and almost caught me twice!" The congregation laughed another comfortable laugh, filled with love and memories, and I said, "When I was a kid at camp, people like Father Tup told us that we ought to offer the gifts we've been given into the love and service of God, and I believed them. I believed *him*." I pointed at Father Tup on the front row. "And I offered myself to God in love and service, and just look at what happened! I never saw it coming, but it's what happened to me. It's what happened to Tup, too—right?"

Tup proudly said, "That's right."

"And now it's happening to Daniel, who will be ordained into the service of God in this part of God's Church—not because he's perfect, not because he's worthy, but because he has chosen to offer the gifts God gave him, offering himself to love, offering himself to service."

Tup gave me a thumb's up, the bishop nodded, and Beulah had tears running down her face.

I looked out at the congregation and continued, "What if all this stuff is true? What if God gives us gifts and calls us to use them to love the children of God? What if God calls all of us, not just deacons, priests, and bishops? What if God calls you? What could happen to you? What if you hoisted your sails in the breeze of the Holy Spirit and picked up your anchor? Where would you be five years from now, or ten, or thirty?"

There was a little ripple of uncertainty in the congregation now; they had been comfortable enough with me talking about myself, or Daniel, or even old Tup being called to serve God, but now I was getting all up in their business. Still, I'd come too far to let it go.

"I expect some of you are lining up your excuses. Why, the preacher must surely be talking to somebody else: 'I'm too old, I'm too young, I'm not educated enough,' or, when that doesn't seem to be enough, you can try to hide behind the illusion that God wouldn't want to call you because of that terrible thing you did that one time. I know I'm a little too close to you now, but that's none of my business, really. What I'm telling you is that God gives all of us gifts and calls all of us to love and serve. What if you really believed that? What would happen to you?

"I'll tell you"—I looked around to let the suspense catch a little bit—"I don't know. But if God can take a nineteen-year-old kid who looked like he'd been put together by a committee out of the Canton,

Mississippi, jail and make me into the preacher for tonight's ordination service, there is no limit to what God can do with you."

18

All God's Critters Got a Place in the Choir

Baby Jude grew, bringing us joy and love and frustration one little handful at a time. Beulah taught special education in West Branch Elementary School, putting up with the petty rivalries and grudges of the faculty until she got a better offer as a social worker. She has some heart-breaking stories to tell, but she liked the people she worked with. I probably worked too much, but I loved it. I was appointed or elected to several diocesan involvements and activities—more responsibility for the same pay. Somewhere in there, as we were watching, little Jude stopped being a baby and started being a little person: everyday magic.

Peter Tomasi was the principal of the local high school and had started coming to the parish with his wife and three daughters; I was delighted when Peter joined the choir and his wife, Elisa, became part of the Altar Guild. They were glad to be members of the parish, and we were excited by what they had to bring into our community. Then one Thursday night our phone rang, and Sally the organist and choir director told me that Peter had been arrested in Columbus for soliciting an undercover policewoman posing as a prostitute.

I went to visit him the next day in the county jail, and he assured me that it was just a case of being in the wrong place at the wrong time. He said he had no intentions of picking up a hooker, that he had just been trying to be nice. I told him I didn't have any reason to think he was lying to me, but I was concerned for Elisa and the girls, because the Columbus, Mississippi, police department didn't seem to believe him at all.

He was released that afternoon, but the scandal of the high school principal being arrested for solicitation was the talk of the town. Sally the organist called me Friday night to find out what we should do. I asked her what she meant, and she said some of the choir members were saying that maybe Peter shouldn't sing in the choir that Sunday.

"Isn't he innocent until proven guilty?" I asked.

"But what if he did it?" she countered. "Then we'd have a felon singing tenor in the Holy Incarnation choir!"

Well, I have to admit that worried me, and I had to think for a minute before I said, "But if he didn't do it, then we'd have kicked an innocent man out of the choir." Then Sally had to think for a minute, and I decided, "It doesn't matter. I'm not telling him he can't sing in the choir, whether he did it or not." Sally wasn't convinced, and I reminded her of a special session song I'd been trying to get her to teach to the children's choir. The chorus is all you need to know:

> All God's critters got a place in the choir:
> some sing low, some sing higher,
> some sing out loud on a telephone wire,
> and some just clap their hands, or paws,
> or anything they got now.

The police never proved that Peter had been trying to hire a hooker, but they never completely cleared him, either. The high school had to let him go, and Elisa took the girls back to Baltimore to live with her parents and filed for divorce. A few months later, Peter landed a job teaching chemistry in an independent high school in Missouri. Before he left, he made it a point to thank me for letting him stay in the choir. He said, "Do you believe me, that I wasn't trying to solicit a prostitute?"

I looked into his eyes and saw a man who really wanted to be believed. There was no way for me to be sure what had happened in

Columbus that night, but I didn't think he would be asking me to believe him so earnestly if he were lying. I said, "I believe you."

The worst thing, I figured, was for me not to believe him if he was telling the truth. For me to believe him if he was lying just meant I'd been fooled, and I could live with that.

But for better or worse, Peter's controversy continued to follow me. That fall, I agree to serve as the chair of the local Habitat for Humanity organization, which was just getting started. I told them I wasn't their best choice, especially since the job involved organization and administration, and they thought I was being humble and coy. The truth is that I'm not much good at that, or not much interested, but I was very interested in this new effort for the churches in West Point to cooperate for affordable housing, and that seemed to be enough.

At the next meeting of the Holy Incarnation vestry, I explained that I had been honored to be asked to lead the Habitat for Humanity ministry in West Branch, thinking they would be proud that their minister was well thought of and trusted by others in the community. I had not anticipated my announcement triggering a political dispute.

I was surprised when two of the people on the vestry described Habitat as a "liberal" program, and aghast when Chuck Wallace, a prominent attorney, a former mayor of the town, and up until now a fairly decent sort of guy, said, "Well, we all know who you're trying to help. We can't stop you from doing this, but it's not what we're paying you for."

I probably should have kept quiet; maybe I should have let the moment pass. But I was taken off guard and hurt that, far from being proud of this honor for me, it was as if they were being mistreated by it. I knew better than to have an adversarial conversation with an attorney, but I said, "Who do you think I'm trying to help, Chuck?"

He squirmed a little; that was the reaction I'd been hoping for, I suppose. He looked around to see who was on his side, and I did, too. Everybody else was looking down at their papers, as if the financial reports were suddenly the most interesting thing of the moment, all except for Kate Johnston, who looked at me and said, "Well, we think it's all right that you're more progressive most of the time, but this is business." I couldn't believe what was going on and couldn't think of anything to say, which seemed to encourage her to continue to argue her case: "This is how things are in the real world."

As calmly as I could, I said, "Yes ma'am, this is how the real world is. This is about race. This is about politics."

She looked at me as if I was a stupid child who had forgotten something I'd learned before. "Those people are going to have to learn to help themselves," she insisted. I suppose my face betrayed me. She went on, "Oh, we know you're a Democrat, Buddy—it's cute most of the time. You'll vote Republican when you grow up. This is about the reputation of our parish, which has already been tarnished enough with that criminal singing in the choir. This is not about silly idealism; this is real."

I'm not actually sure what happened after that. I don't think I said much, except for the closing prayer, and I don't think anybody else did, either. Chuck and Kate had had their say, and nobody disagreed with them. Nor had I put up much of a fight.

When I got home, Beulah took one look at me and asked, "What's wrong with you?" I told her, without naming names, but she figured it out quickly enough. She said, "Why didn't you stand up to them?"

I didn't have an answer for her then; I don't think I have an answer still. Some of it had to do with JoJo's advice to Bobbo: that I shouldn't never get in a fight I know I ain't got no chance to win. Some of it was that I was just so stunned that the conversation took such a turn. But some of it was the simple fact that I dislike confrontation, always have, and I didn't want those people to be angry with me. I'm not proud of that, but it's true.

The next time I was in Jackson for a meeting, I got on the bishop's calendar and told him it might be time for me to start looking around for a new parish to serve. I explained about Habitat and Chuck and Kate, and he understood. "But no matter where you go," he said, "you're going to have people like that."

It got a little bit better and a little bit worse two or three Wednesdays later, at the 10:00 a.m. Bible study. There were ten or twelve regulars in the class, and the occasional visitor. All of them were women, most of them with children now grown and out of the house. On this day we were studying the First Book of Samuel, and we were happy to welcome Joan Reynolds, a friend of Kate Johnston's. Kate introduced her, and she told us all that she and her husband went to the Presbyterian Church of America. I said that we were glad to have her with us.

We had gotten to the thirteenth chapter when we hit a snag. It had been our practice that each of the women could bring different versions of the Bible so we could compare, and we went around the circle taking turns reading the passages we were going to discuss. Miss Elizabeth always read from her ancient and venerated King James Version, and I asked her to start the thirteenth chapter for us.

"Saul reigned one year," she began, "and when he had reigned two years over Israel, Saul chose him three thousand men of Israel; whereof two thousand were with Saul in Michmash and in Mount Bethel, and a thousand were with Jonathan in Gibeah of Benjamin . . ." She stopped, aware that she had created a little bit of a stir. Everybody was suddenly looking at their Bibles more closely, and some were looking at the Bibles of the women next to them. I said, "Miss Elizabeth, would you read that part again, please, starting with verse 1?"

She picked up her Bible because she couldn't always trust her bifocals, held it close, and read, "Saul reigned one year; and when he had reigned two years over Israel . . . ." She paused, and I said, "Thank you. Miss Frances, would you read that same verse from your Bible?" Frances Schwedering always brought her Good News Bible, which she argued was the Ungarbled Word of God because it made the most sense to her.

"Saul picked three thousand men, keeping two thousand of them with him in Michmash and in the hill country of Bethel and sending one thousand with his son Jonathan to Gibeah, in the territory of the tribe of Benjamin. . . ."

Elizabeth said, "What about Saul reigned for *one year*, and when he had reigned *two years* over Israel?" Francis looked again, and said, "That's not in the Ungarbled Word."

Karen, one of the younger members of the group whose son was still in high school, raised her hand as she always did; she didn't feel quite comfortable in this gathering of matrons, and they'd never done much to put her more at ease. I called on her and she said, "Verse 1 in the New International Version is, 'Saul was [thirty] years old when he became king, and he reigned over Israel [forty-] two years.' The thirty and the forty are in brackets."

I heard Elizabeth muttering about that Bible being Garbled, but I didn't take the bait.

Miss Katherine was a sweet soul who peed on herself if she laughed too hard, a useful fact we'd learned in several memorably funny moments. Now we generally tried not to be too funny, just to save her the embarrassment. She said, "Mine's more like that, but it says Saul was forty, and that he reigned for forty years. I don't have any brackets." And Miss Edna, who hardly ever spoke at all, said, "I just have dots."

I said, "Ma'am?"

She repeated, "I just have dots. Three little dots."

I said, "So how does it read in the Revised Standard Bible?"

"It says 'Saul was dot dot dot years old when he began to reign; and he reigned dot dot dot and two years over Israel.'"

Miss Frances said, "Well, all right. I guess we need the preacher to ungarble this for us."

I was using the Interpreters' Bible, which has both the King James and the Revised Standard versions, extensive footnotes, and a running commentary for every passage. The footnote for the first verse of 1 Samuel 13 read, "Hebrew obscure," which was not as helpful as I'd hoped it would be. I said, "Apparently the Hebrew in the oldest and most reliable texts that we have don't agree or can't be deciphered. The fact is that we just don't know."

I would have moved on, but Miss Frances, not willing to let it go, said, "So why do some of them have thirty, or forty, or one or two? Couldn't they just say they don't know?"

It was one of those a-ha moments you hear about, for me and for women of the Church of the Holy Incarnation 10:00 a.m. Bible study. "No," I said. "I guess they'd rather be wrong than to admit they don't know."

Miss Elizabeth, an excessively proper woman who'd been a member of that parish for all of her eighty-two years, who'd been chair of the Altar Guild for years and taught Sunday school for decades, and who'd taken several turns as parish treasurer, was scandalized. Her indignation straightened her until she sat up completely vertically, her hands folded on the Bible before her as primly as any duchess would do. "Do you mean to say that the Word of God is unclear?"

"Well, yes ma'am, I suppose that's what we're saying. I guess if one Bible says it was one or two years, and another says it was thirty or forty, and another just has dots, that's pretty unclear, don't you think?"

"No sir. In the King James Bible, it is not unclear. It says clearly that Saul reigned for one year; and when he had reigned two years over Israel, he chose three thousand men—"

It was young Karen who dared to speak, without even raising her hand. "So did he reign for one year, or two?"

Miss Elizabeth read again: "Saul reigned one year; and when he had reigned two years over Israel, Saul chose him three thousand men of Israel . . . ."

We were uncharacteristically quiet for a long moment, as I watched a new realization spread through the room.

Kate, always willing to point out my faults and shortcomings, had been quietly listening to the discussion. She broke the silence to say, "Buddy, are you telling us that the Holy Bible has errors in it?" It was unabashedly and shamelessly a trap. Whatever I said next was guaranteed to upset somebody.

"I'm telling you that the Bible is a collection of writings by people over hundreds of years, much of it taken from oral tradition much older than that, which has been copied and recopied by hand for centuries. The oldest manuscripts we have do not all agree. It's up to us to understand it as best we can, and find the meaning of it for our lives in the twentieth century. That's why Bible studies are important; that's why we're here."

Kate was not willing to surrender what had seemed like an advantage and an opportunity to share her concerns about this young priest. She said, "But surely you believe it's inspired, the infallible Word of God!"

"I believe the Bible is inspired," I said. "I also believe Beethoven was inspired from time to time, and Emily Dickinson, and Mark Twain. But that doesn't mean everything they ever said was the unadulterated Truth. Surely some parts and passages of the Bible seem to be more inspired than others."

They were quiet for another moment, wondering what this meant for their understanding of the Bible. I continued, "Have you ever been inspired? With a good idea, by knowing exactly what spice to add to a casserole or what color to paint a room? Have you ever had that moment when you didn't know what you were going to say in a difficult situation and the words just came to you? Sometimes I think I am inspired when I'm preaching, when it seems to me I'm listening along without even wondering what I'm going to say next."

Kate's friend Joan long since realized she was in a different kind of group, not like anything she'd ever experienced or imagined. Apparently we'd come to the moment that she couldn't stand it any longer. "Surely you're going to say whatever you've written for the sermon that morning!"

The other women in the circle looked at each other and smiled a little, knowing that I didn't ever write down a sermon. Kate said, "No, Father Buddy doesn't ever write his sermons out like your preacher, or like most other preachers. I guess he doesn't have the time to waste on writing a sermon.

The ever-proper Miss Elizabeth turned on her in withering indignation. "Father Buddy loves and cares for his flock, and preaches the best sermons I've ever heard. We all know you don't agree with him about politics, we've all heard about that until we're sick of it, but it doesn't give you any right to piss in our punchbowl!"

Everybody was stunned and looked at her, not quite believing she'd said that. She glanced around the circle and said, "I heard that on cable TV. Was that a bad thing to say?"

I think it was the Ungarbled Miss Francis who laughed first, just a snicker that she tried to contain, but it broke the ice, and soon everybody but Kate and Joan were consumed with uncontrolled laughter, the kind of guffaws that start in your belly and don't let go of you until they're done. The fact that Kate and Joan weren't laughing but just sitting there stone-faced made it even funnier; I knew I shouldn't be laughing at Kate's expense, but I couldn't stop. It was like giggling at a funeral.

After the initial wave had passed and we were catching our breath, Miss Katherine very quietly said, "Oh my—I think I'm going to need a towel," and that started the laughter all over again.

19

Jus' Brothers and Sisters Comin' Home

One Saturday morning the following spring we were having a cleanup day at the church, people working in the yard and polishing the pews, taking all the brass into the sacristy for a good cleaning—getting ready for Easter, which was late that year.

I was outside, talking with some of the men about digging up a dying boxwood bush so we could plant a new one. Kristen, one of the high school kids, came running up and panted, "Father Buddy, you better come."

"Why, what's going on?"

"There's a man here to see you."

"Can you send him back here?"

There was a hesitation I didn't understand, and then, "Well, Miss Elizabeth said to tell you, you better come 'round front."

I went around to the front yard to see Miss Elizabeth and Bobbo's brother JoJo McCain standing together, both of them looking awkward. Neither seemed able to find anything to say; it was hard to tell which was the most uncomfortable with the other. I looked around and realized something was wrong: you hardly ever saw JoJo without Bobbo.

Every summer JoJo was glad to see me at camp, all grins and crushing hugs. This reunion was not so happy. When I asked him what was wrong, he just shook his head; when I asked him where Bobbo was, he lowered his chin to his chest and shook his head more slowly. He looked like he was very tired, and when I hugged him I could smell that it had been a while since he'd had a bath or a change of clothes.

A group of ten or twelve people gathered around, drawn by curiosity and tired of working in the church yard on a hot day. I said, as naturally as I could, "Hey, y'all—this is JoJo McCain, a friend of mine from camp."

JoJo was unpleasantly surprised to be the center of so much attention. He was more accustomed to being ignored altogether. Bobbo was the star, JoJo his supporting cast. He mumbled, "Glad to meet y'all," to no one in particular, and everybody turned to me to find out what would happen next. Something was clearly wrong, but I wasn't going to find out what it was in a crowd. I said to the members of the parish, "Y'all excuse us, please," and took JoJo by the arm.

As we walked toward my office, JoJo whispered, "Who was them folks?"

"Parishioners." I could see that word meant nothing to him, so I said, "Members of the church I work for."

"Oh. They go to your church."

We went to the kitchen to get a cup of coffee. Chuck and Kate were there; I imagined they were conspiring. I introduced them to JoJo as a friend of mine, and they looked at each other meaningfully, although I couldn't be sure I knew which meaning it might be, and left. I got both of us a cup of coffee—black for him, cream and sugar for me—and as JoJo and I went toward my office at the other end of the building, JoJo said, "They friends of yours?"

I said, "Well, maybe not. But they're members of the parish, too."

He said, "I guess you got to be nice to ever'body, huh?"

"Yeah, something like that."

We sat in my office for a while, me trying with little success to get him to tell me why he'd come. After five or ten minutes there was a knock on the door, and when I opened it I was glad to see Beulah, who wanted to know if she could help. She went over and hugged JoJo, whose shuddering sobs shook them both. When she sat down, he started to tell his story, with a little help from time to time. The following is a reasonably accurate recounting of our conversation.

JoJo said, "Bobbo, he got killed in a car crash. He and Momma and our Aunt Trudy was goin' into town to get somethin' for the garden. I didn't go 'cause *Family Feud* was about to come on, and I love me some *Family Feud*. 'Sides, I knew when they got back I'd be doing most of the work. So I jus' stayed home."

There a long pause full of pain, and Beulah said, "What happened?"

JoJo took a deep breath and said, "One of them big log trucks must've been in front of 'em. I guess them logs got loose and come crashin' down on 'em. They didn't never find the driver or what truck it was, just Bobbo and Momma and Aunt Trudy, under the water in that ditch, all smushed in they car, with all them logs on top of 'em."

I said, "Oh, JoJo, I'm so sorry. When did this happen?"

"I don't know. I ain't been payin' no 'tention to that."

"In the last couple of weeks?"

"Yes sir, not much more than that, I don't s'pose."

Beulah asked, "So do you have other family? Where are you staying?"

"Well, my Aunt Trudy's boy Roberto—that ain't his real name, his real name's Robbie but he wants ever'body to call him Roberto now 'cause he saw it in a movie and he thinks that makes him sound all big and tough—he moved into the house where me and Bobbo and Momma lived. He said he goin' to take care of me now, but I told him don't need no takin' care of. But him and his friends jus' stay up in there all the time playin' they noisy music too loud, smokin' and drinkin' and playin' cards and all. They got womens up in there, too—they smokin' and drinkin' and I don't know what all else they doin'. In my momma's house!"

Beulah put her hand on his arm and loved him a little before she said, "So what did you do?"

"Well, I tol' Robbie I was leavin'. He said he didn't give a damn. So I left."

I said, "Where did you go?"

He paused, and after a minute he said, "Preacher, you 'member what you said the next day after the baseball game?"

It had been a while, so I said, "What baseball game?"

Beulah said, "When we all went to see the baseball game in Jackson?"

"Yes ma'am. That next mornin', in the church service, you 'member what you said?"

Well, I remembered that one of the campers had said, "What about Bobbo?" I remembered thinking I couldn't kick Bobbo out of the family of God. But I was struggling to remember much else until Beulah said, "He told us that when we come together, we are coming home."

JoJo said, "You told us when we come to church, we all jus' brothers and sisters comin' home." JoJo sat up on the edge of his seat: this was important. He said, "Is that really true, Preacher?"

"Well, yes, that's true." JoJo sat back, clearly relieved. I continued, "What does this have to do with—"

"But it ain't true ever'where, is it?"

"It is true, everywhere."

"It ain't true at the First Baptist Church of Mayersville."

"It's not?"

"No, it sure ain't."

Beulah said, "What happened at First Baptist?"

JoJo said, "They wouldn't even let me sit down, jus' wanted to give me some money so I'd go 'way." And while I was taking this in, he went on to say, "It ain't true at the Methodist church, neither."

Beulah said, "What happened there?"

"They didn't even let me come in they buildin.' They didn't have no money to give me, neither. I couldn't even get a glass of water at the Methodist church."

Beulah said, "Oh, JoJo, I'm so sorry."

JoJo nodded. "So I thought maybe Preacher Buddy was just wrong 'bout that, and I jumped a freight over here to ask him."

I was slower on the uptake that Beulah, and clearly confused. I said, "Ask me what?"

She said, "He doesn't have anywhere else to go, Buddy."

"What?"

"He doesn't have anywhere else to go. He hitched a ride on a train to come here. He has no family except for Roberto, and he doesn't want to stay there."

I turned to Beulah in complete confusion. "What do you want us to do? Do you want him to stay here? With us?"

She had a playful but slightly dangerous twinkle in her eye as she said, "Well, maybe he could stay with us until we find him a place to live. And a job." She looked at JoJo and said, "Would you like that, JoJo?"

He brushed away the tears in his eyes and said, "I just want to be home."

He went to the bathroom sometime after that, and I said to Beulah, "Are you sure about this?"

"Sure. What else are we going to do, throw him out on the street like those other churches? Do you believe what you say or not? This is a church, right? We're supposed to welcome people. 'Which one of you, having a hundred sheep and losing one of them, does not leave the ninety-nine in the wilderness and go after the one that is lost until he finds it? When he has found it, he lays it on his shoulders and rejoices.'"

I looked at her in surprise, and she said, "Luke 15:3-5." Sword drills.

Beulah said she would find the name of his caseworker in Mayersville and call her Monday morning. Until we figured out what to do, she informed me, JoJo would stay in our guest room. While I was straining to catch up with what was going on, JoJo came back into my office and said, "What are y'all doin' 'round here today?"

When I told him it was a workday and that I had been working in the yard, he said he wanted to help. I told him he didn't have to do that, but he said he liked yard work. So Beulah took Jude to the house to get ready for our guest, and JoJo and I went to the backyard, where I showed him the boxwood. I handed him a shovel and said, "We're digging up this bush."

"Why?"

"Because it's dying. Just put your shovel in right about—"

"Well, hold up a minute here. It ain't dying. You just need to put some peat in there, you waterin' it too much."

"What?

"I been takin' care of some yards in Mayersville. Mr. John, he knows all about yard bushes. Peoples think you have to water them boxwoods, but this one has taken too much."

"Who's Mr. John?"

"I don't know the rest of his name. He pays me to help him sometimes. He the gardener for that rich white woman who husband died. She have lots of boxwoods in her yard. They live 'bout forever—boxwoods, not rich white folks. Don't dig this one up," he said, pointing at my intended victim with his shovel. "Jus' let me shovel in some peat, and it'll be fine."

Later that day, when we got home, he took a shower. While he was in there, Beulah took all of his clothes to our laundry room and laid out some new socks and underwear, a pair of jeans, and a shirt that she'd gotten from Walmart. She got him a new pair of tennis shoes, too, but he'd never worn tennis shoes and didn't like them. He told her, "I don't never even play no tennis." So after supper they went back to Walmart and got him a pair of shoes he liked, along with some more clothes so he could come to church with us. He sat right up front with the rector's wife and son, which caused no small amount of surreptitious pointing and inaudible murmurs that JoJo was oblivious to, and which Beulah tried without success to ignore.

On Monday morning, Beulah used her social work connections to talk to JoJo's caseworker in Issaquena County, who verified JoJo's account of the accident and the situation with his cousin Robbie. Then she used some other connections to get JoJo a job as a bag boy at the Piggly Wiggly grocery store, which Beulah and I called The Pig. By the time I got home on Monday afternoon, she was looking for an apartment. By Tuesday afternoon, I was helping assemble a bed frame and used mattresses that a friend's mother wanted to donate. By the next Sunday, JoJo was asking about joining the church choir.

Sally the organist asked me if JoJo could read music; I told her I didn't think he could read anything. But it turned out that JoJo had an ear for music and a big, rich bass voice. He didn't always know what he was singing, especially when the choir went into Latin or French, but he always sang it beautifully.

And so JoJo McCain came home.

20

Unique and Peculiar Vagabonds

JoJo was great with Jude, who called him "Uncle Joe." Jude would climb all over him, and JoJo would throw him into the air so high it took our breath away. At first JoJo was afraid of our dog Jabbok, but she was as sweet to him as she was to everybody else and they soon became great friends. Whenever she saw him, she would go over to him and lean against his leg if he was standing, or lie down on his feet if he was sitting. It seemed important to both of them.

And JoJo was quickly loved by most of the parish, especially the members of the choir. He was the first African-American member of this fairly conservative Episcopal congregation in Mississippi. It was 1992, and you would think we were done with all of that, but we weren't. I think some of the members had come to accept the idea in principle, assuming this was the sort of thing done in New York or San Francisco, and maybe even in Atlanta. But it was not in principle anymore, it was in reality, and it was hard for some of the members to snuggle up with. But even those who had issues with having a black member of the church really liked JoJo.

After JoJo started to accept the fact that he was accepted, by most if not all of the congregation, he began to assume that the people of the Church of the Holy Incarnation must be the same sort of people he'd met at camp, which was, of course, not completely the case. He thought they would love and accept him without any limits, that they would value anything he had to say, that the love of God was a part of their everyday lives—which was, of course, not always true. I thought about having a talk with him, to tell him that these were not camp people, but I didn't want to make him think they were unloving or unfaithful. Most of them were very good people whom I loved, but they weren't all camp folks. They were just regular people doing their best to live their lives and pay their bills, and if the Church or their faith entered into it, that would be just fine.

So when JoJo started hugging people at church, like we do at camp, there was an immediate and varied response. Some of the members of the parish liked it, others tried to avoid it, and a few thought it was somewhere in the neighborhood of scandalous that a large African-American man was going around hugging people all the time.

It seemed especially difficult for Chuck and Kate, the two adversarial vestry members. They didn't say anything, at least to me, but they made sure they were never within hugging range, or in a situation that they had to speak to JoJo or even acknowledge that he was there.

The boxwood I'd almost dug up grew new leaves and was strong and healthy. Beulah said, "'Sir, let it alone for one more year, until I dig around it and put manure on it. If it bears fruit next year, well and good; but if not, you can cut it down.' Luke 13:8-9."

JoJo started cutting a few yards and doing some yard work in addition to his job at the Pig. I gave him my lawnmower for his business, and he cut our yard for free. By the end of the summer, he had a bank account with money in it.

On Christmas Eve, the biggest service of the year, the soloist singing "O Holy Night" as the introit was listed in the order of worship as Mr. JoJo McCain, and his voice filled the nave and sanctuary with evident love and genuine good will. As he sang the last note, the people in the pews clapped. I was never sure what upset Chuck and Kate more, the fact that an African-American man with alleged mental limitations sang a solo, or that there was applause in the Episcopal Church of the Holy Incarnation.

Beulah set JoJo up in a literacy program and worked with him after hours for months at our kitchen table. He was proud to be learning to read, and put great effort into it. He told us he wanted to read so that he could have a driver's license and buy a pickup truck for his lawn-mowing business, and Beulah told him there was no reason in the whole wide world that he couldn't do that. I smiled at the perfection of it—both of them doing exactly what they were supposed to do.

That spring I was invited to do a wedding for the daughter of a longtime member. The bride had moved away to Colorado before I'd come to the parish, and she was coming home to get married. She'd always wanted a big church wedding, but her groom was Jewish—not a practicing Jew, but from a Jewish family in Brooklyn—so things were a little complicated. I offered for the wedding to be in the church, but they thought it would make the groom's family uncomfortable. They compromised on having an Episcopal priest doing the wedding ("Could you just tone down the Jesus part?" she asked) by the side of the swimming pool in her parents' backyard.

Most of the parish was there, including Kate and Chuck, who I always felt were trying to find something to be upset about. I was careful to use the service just as it is written in the Book of Common Prayer, but the sermon was based on a passage from the Song of Solomon 8:6—"Set me as a seal upon your heart, as a seal upon your arm; for love is strong as death, passion fierce as the grave."

Maybe I was a little rattled by toning down Jesus in the homily, or maybe I was thrown off watching Kate and Chuck exchange what seemed to me to be meaningful but inscrutable glances. Maybe I was distracted at the tension of the separation between the Episcopalians on the bride's side and the Jews on the groom's. Or maybe I'm just goofy sometimes. Whatever the cause, it became one of those liturgical moments that I've laughed about ever since.

At the rehearsal, we'd carefully practiced the groom taking the bride's right hand in his, and repeating after me: "In the Name of God (In the Name of God), I, Harold, take you, Anne (I, Harold, take you, Anne), to be my wife (to be my wife), to have and to hold (to have and to hold) from this day forward (from this day forward), for better for worse (for better for worse), for richer for poorer (for richer for poorer), in sickness and in health (in sickness and in health), to love and to cherish (to love and to cherish), until we are parted by death (until we are parted by death). This is my solemn vow (this is my solemn vow)." The idea is that I would say it very softly, and then Harold would say it loudly enough for the people to hear. Then Anne would say her vows, again repeating after me.

Remembering the names in weddings, funerals, and baptisms can be somewhat challenging in an unhappy way, so I'd made it a practice for years to write the names on little sticky notes and stick them in my prayer book. So we were all a little surprised during the wedding the next day when I said, "In the Name of God, (In the Name of God) I, Harold, take you, Helen—"

Harold didn't know what to do, and stood there helplessly; I didn't know what had gone wrong. After a long pause, Anne whispered, "Anne."

I said, "What?"

She hissed, "My name is Anne."

I said, "I know."

She accused, "You said 'Helen.'"

I said, "No, I didn't."

Harold affirmed, "You did. You said 'Helen.'"

The sticky note read "Harold and Helen," for no reason that I could imagine.

By this time, everybody in the congregation was beside themselves with laughter, everybody but Chuck and Kate. There was nothing I could do but admit I'd made a mistake; everybody knew it already anyway.

I looked up at the congregation united in laughing at my blunder and proclaimed, "Y'all, I'm sorry. I messed up. Let's try that again."

I worried that I'd ruined their beautiful wedding for a minute or two, until we came to the exchanging of the rings, when Harold was slipping the ring onto the appropriate finger and repeating after me,

"Anne, I give you this ring . . . ," and she said to Harold, in a stage whisper loud enough for everyone to hear, "Who's Helen?"

Then we all laughed, even me. For years after that, I got a Christmas or Hanukkah card from Harold and Helen.

The Church of the Holy Incarnation is a couple of blocks away from the railroad tracks and down the road from the bus station. We didn't have a lot of people traveling through town who came and asked for money, but it wasn't unusual for us to be visited by vagabonds, either. I kept an envelope for twenty-dollar bills in my desk drawer; a few members of the parish made sure to keep me stocked.

A few months after I'd started at the church, a man came into the office and told me he was from Chicago, his mother had died in Sarasota, Florida, his car had broken down somewhere in Kentucky, and all he needed was twenty dollars for a bus ticket. He seemed sincere. When he smiled as I handed him a twenty, I noticed that one of his front teeth was crossed in front of the other, and that above the intersection of teeth was a significant collection of greenish gunk that looked like it had been there a while. He took the money and left, promising to pay me back as soon as he could.

Years later, a man came into the office and told me he was from Baltimore, his mother had died in Houston, Texas, his car had broken down somewhere in Tennessee, and all he needed was twenty dollars for a bus ticket. He looked familiar, but I couldn't quite place him until he asked me if we had a bathroom. He smiled when I told him where it was, and I recognized the tooth gunk. When he got back, I said, "Sir, the last time you were in this office your mother had died in Florida." He looked at me and calculated whether it would be worth it to try to deny it, and said, "I'm sorry." I didn't say anything, and he stood there a moment before walking out without saying another word.

Every minister in every church has similar stories, and I imagine that we all build up our defenses as the years roll along. Still, I was not prepared for the day when a man stepped out of the Bible and into my office.

It was in October 1992, just a few months after JoJo had come home. I'd been the priest at Holy Incarnation for almost nine years and was starting to feel like it was time to consider other options, maybe move to a different parish in another town. I'd had several parishes send me letters asking if I was interested in being part of their process, but the only ones I was interested in were in other states, and I wasn't ready to leave Mississippi.

One unusually crisp Monday morning when I got to the office, there was a man sitting on the front steps of the church. Six or seven steps led up to a covered porch we called the vestibule, which sheltered the red double doors leading into the nave. The man was sitting on the steps, gazing up into the huge old oak trees in the church's front yard.

He was striking in his appearance, medium height and built, with long, wildly tangled, mostly black hair with some white, especially at the temples and in streaks in his beard, which was untrimmed and untamed. It was the contrast of black and white that struck me, almost as if he'd planned it, as if he were a character in a comic book. He was wearing a faded old pair of jeans, a ragged military surplus jacket, and a brand new pair of excessively white tennis shoes. I thought of Kris Kristofferson's "The Pilgrim, Chapter 33":

> See him wasted on the sidewalk in his jacket and his jeans,
> Wearin' yesterday's misfortunes like a smile.
> Once he had a future full of money, love, and dreams,
> Which he spent like they was goin' outta style.
> And he keeps right on a'changin' for the better or the worse,
> Searchin' for a shrine he's never found.
> Never knowin' if believin' is a blessin' or a curse,
> Or if the goin' up was worth the comin' down.

I walked over to where he was sitting but he didn't look at me; he seemed intent on looking up at something in the trees. When I sat on the steps a few respectful feet away he said, "Mornin,' Cap," and turned his head so that his eyes connected with mine.

From a distance it was his hair that caught your attention, but up close it was the intensity of his eyes that held me so tight I wanted to escape, or at least back away a little.

I said, "Good morning. How are you?"

He said, "You ever sit out here, Cap? You ever just sit here and watch the squirrels? It's real peaceful and all."

In that moment I remembered sitting on an old, fallen sweet gum tree in the woods behind the house I grew up in, talking with my friend Jake and watching the squirrels playing and fussing in the trees. I wondered how I had allowed my life to come to the point that I didn't have time, or didn't make time, to watch the squirrels anymore. I was sad to hear myself say, "No, I don't."

He said, "That's too bad, man. They's about five or six of 'em out here, I reckon—just a-chasin' and a-flirtin' with one another and all."

I said, "Yeah—they do love to flirt."

He looked at me appraisingly, and wondered, "You a married man, Cap?"

Most people are not Episcopalians, and those who've heard of us confuse us with the Roman Catholics, so they're not sure whether Episcopal priests can marry. I said, "Yes sir. I've been married for five years, and we have a son who'll be four in January."

He didn't move or make a sound, but it seemed like I could feel a wave of grief radiating from him in that moment—the distinct sadness of something missing. I felt like I was stepping out on a shaky limb as I asked, "What about you? You have a family?"

There was a long, heavy pause, so long that I thought he wasn't going to answer. Then he whispered, "No sir. Not anymore."

I didn't know what to say, and I've learned that usually it's better if I don't try to blunder my way through a conversational muddle just to replace the silence with clumsy words. I watched the squirrels with him, content to wait for him to talk if he wanted to or to leave it alone if he'd prefer that, and after a while it was looking like that's how it was going to go. Still, I couldn't just sit on the steps all day; I did have some work to do, so I started planning my exit strategy. I said, "Well, I'm glad to meet you. My name's Buddy."

He smiled and took my hand and said, "It's nice to meet you, Buddy."

It didn't seem like he was going to say anything else, so I said, "Tell me your name."

He answered, "John."

I said, "It's nice to meet you, John."

He said, "John the Baptist."

21

The Calling of the Lord and All

Sometimes you don't really know if you heard what you thought you heard. Surely, I thought, the man hadn't said what I thought I heard him say. I said, "You're a Baptist?"

And he looked at me without any obvious insanity in his eyes and answered, "I am *the* Baptist. *John* the Baptist."

What do you say when somebody tells you he's John the Baptist? I said, "Oh," and wondered if he would be a fun nut or a dangerous nut. Sometimes it's hard to tell the difference.

Sometimes it's hard to tell the difference between a saint and a psychopath.

I didn't want our brief conversation to end abruptly on that peculiar note, but I didn't want to pursue it, either, and I couldn't think of anything else to say. So I stood up to leave, thinking I'd look out a window in an hour or two to see if John the Baptist was still sitting on the steps of the church. I was thinking I'd say something like, "Well, see ya," when I realized he was standing up, too. He said, "Y'all drink coffee in this church?"

I told him we did, and that I could make some. When I stopped at the office door to unlock it, he looked at me as if he was searching for something in my eyes. I don't know if he found it or not; I do know it was unsettling for me. As we walked back to the kitchen, he said, "You sure got a fine church here, Cap." I thanked him, and as I fumbled with the filters and found the can of coffee in a cabinet, he said, "I sure would like to preach here."

"Are you a preacher?"

"Oh, yeah. Well, no, not a preacher—a prophet. Ever since I was called to make straight the path for the Second Coming of Jesus Christ and all." I noticed that when he talked as John the Baptist his voice was pitched a little higher, and that his hands fluttered like butterflies being chased by a blue jay. I remember wondering if he was in control of his hands, and then wondering who would be if he wasn't.

"Have you . . . done a lot of prophecy?"

"Well, no. I'm just getting my start and all. I was thinkin' this could be where I start my public ministry. It sure is a beautiful church and all."

It turns out that John the Baptist prefers his coffee black, or at least this one did. Later I wished I'd asked him if he wanted honey in his coffee, but I wasn't quick enough in the moment. I wasn't sure how much to explore his claim, or whether I should try to steer the conversation back into a more believable slice of reality. I asked, "Where are you from?"

Now, I'm not sure how this sounds to people not from the Deep South, but where I'm from, it is a significant and profound question. Where you're from is more than geography or history; it explains part of who you are and why you're that way; it explains some of why you talk the way you talk and why you think what you think. It's more than "Where are you from?" It's also "Who are you, and who are your people?"

He said, "I was born in Egypt, but I've been all around, all over the whole wide world and all."

He didn't look even faintly Middle Eastern; I assumed it was part of his delusion. I was trying to remember what I'd ever learned or read about John the Baptist in seminary or since, and whether he had any Egyptian connections, when my new friend said, "My mama still lives in Egypt, and I try to get there often as I can and all."

I asked, "How do you get there?"

"Usually I hitch a ride. It ain't more than twenty miles." He watched me with his piercing eyes as I struggled to figure this out, and in a little bit he decided to have mercy on me. "You know they's a town up the road called Egypt, don'tcha? Egypt, Mississippi, I'm talking about. Egypt, Mississippi, just up the road and all."

"Oh, okay."

"You thought I was tellin' you I was born in way over there Egypt on the other side of the world, 'cause I told you I'm John the Baptist? No, I ain't John the Baptist 'cause I was born over there. I was born in Egypt, Mississippi. My mama still lives there and all, but it's been a time and a time since I seen her last. I'm John the Baptist because God called me to prepare the way for the Lord and all."

Thinking he was heading toward asking me for money so he could go and see his dying mother or something, I decided I'd abandon the John the Baptist angle and try to get him to the point. "How can I help you, John?"

"Well, Cap—the Lord is comin' back. 'And now also the axe is laid unto the root of the trees: therefore every tree which bringeth not forth good fruit is hewn down, and cast into the fire.'" At this his hands flew through the air, as if they had taken on a life of their own—butterflies trying to escape.

I never can think of Bible verses fast enough to hold up my end of this sort of conversation, but I remembered when Beulah quoted me the one about the boxwood tree, something about giving the tree one more chance; I liked that part. And indeed, that particular boxwood was doing quite well. I was thinking it might register with John that Jesus also talked about second chances, but before I could arrange all that into some sensible wording, he continued.

"He that cometh after me is mightier than I, whose shoes I am not worthy to bear: he shall baptize you with the Holy Ghost, and with fire: Whose fan is in his hand, and he will thoroughly purge his floor, and gather his wheat into the garner; but he will burn up the chaff with unquenchable fire." Now I was afraid his hands might break away from his control altogether, and scooted away from him a bit more.

I recognized the words of John the Baptist prophesying the coming of Jesus the Messiah. I knew I couldn't go verse for verse with this guy, so I thought I ought to figure out what he wanted. I repeated, "How can I help you?"

"Well, Cap, since I've gotten the calling of the Lord and all, and since I am the one crying in the wilderness, Prepare ye the way of the Lord, I'm gonna need a place to preach. Can I see the church part, where you preach?"

"Well, sure." I took him into the nave, and he went around to all the stained-glass windows, and behind the altar, and finally up into the pulpit. "Oh, yes sir—this is it! This sure is beautiful! I could do some powerful preachin' here!"

"Here?"

"Yes sir, right here. I believe it is the will of God that I preach and baptize here, this Sunday."

I thought about telling him Episcopalians weren't accustomed to "powerful preaching," but all I could come up with was "This Sunday?"

"That's right, Cap. Since it's the will of the Lord and all."

He was just so matter-of-fact about it, as if he was a mechanic telling me the flat would have to be fixed. His tone of voice and affect seemed to indicate that he believed what he was saying and couldn't imagine that somebody else might have any difficulty with it. It was just the way it was going to have to be. And all.

I said "Well, see, that's where we're going to have a problem. John the Baptist lived and died a long time ago, two thousand years ago. He's the one who prepared the way of the Lord."

"Well, sure. I understand that. I read all about it when I was over there in the Vietnam. But now, see, Jesus is comin' back. History just goes round and round like a wheel, see? Jesus is comin' back, and he's gonna need a new messenger before his face, to prepare a way before him and all."

He went on to tell me, in his strange, rapid-fire, rambling way of speaking, that he was a Baptist, just like John the Baptist was, that his name was John too, and that he'd read enough of the holy word of God to know that Jesus was coming back real soon and that Jesus would be needing someone to be "the voice of one crying in the wilderness, Make straight the way of the Lord, as said the prophet

Esaias." I realized I was having a hard time listening to what he was saying because I was so mesmerized by all his hand motions; I tried to focus.

Most of the Bible reading or studying I've ever done has been in the Revised Standard Version, or more recently the New Revised Standard Version. I've never been that familiar with the King James Version, which spells Isaiah as Esaias, and Noah as Noe. So I when legitimately asked him who the prophet Esaias was, because I really didn't know, he said, "Hell, I dunno, Cap—you're the preacher here, ain't cha?"

When I asked him why he called me Cap, he told me he thought maybe I'd been in the Vietnam with him, that I was the Captain. I thought about telling him I'd never been in Vietnam, or that I'm not the Captain, but I decided against it, just in case I ever needed to pull rank on him.

He talked for a long time, with great energy and conviction. Some people talk with their hands, and the motions have something to do with what they're saying; when John the Baptist spoke, his hands moved in a dazzling array of motions and gestures that didn't seem obviously connected to what he was saying, as if they happened on their own. It was distracting and frustrating, like trying to watch all three rings of a circus at the same time.

I started to wonder if he would ever stop talking, so when he paused to inhale, I interrupted to tell him he couldn't preach at the Church of the Holy Incarnation, because we had strict rules about who could preach in the Episcopal Church; he would have to be licensed by the bishop in Jackson, and that would take months if not years. I started to walk back toward my office and was relieved that he followed me out of the nave. We sat in the chairs that faced my desk.

He seemed to accept that he couldn't preach at the Holy Incarnation that Sunday with some disappointment, and then he asked me where I thought he could preach. He said, "Christmas is comin' up—the people need to know that Jesus is comin' back real soon and that they need to repent, bein' a generation of vipers and all."

I told him he might have a hard time finding a church that would let him preach, and he decided he'd have to let the Holy Ghost guide him with that. So I asked him a third time, "How can I help you, John?"

"Well, have you got twenty bucks?"

I did, though I knew in that moment I wouldn't have it for long. I asked him what he needed twenty dollars for, and he said the Lord had also told him that he was to build a model railroad set in his home, for the children to come and see. Once again I was caught completely off guard: "Why a train set?"

With passion and enthusiasm, he told me about the train set he'd already started, how it sat on three sheets of 8x4 plywood three quarters of an inch thick, and how there were three separate lines of track, and how one of the locomotives was a diesel but the other two were steam engines, both with coal cars. The two steam engines were Lionel train sets, and he told me what the other was but I'd never heard the name before and forgot it. He had it all drawn out, on two old pieces of typewriter paper. Some of it he'd already put together, but some of it he needed to buy at the store up in Memphis. He said there were railroad crossings with gates that came down and bells that rang, and that one of the steam engines had a whistle and all.

I felt like I was working on two or three jigsaw puzzles at the same time with the pieces all jumbled together, and was getting desperate to find a corner piece. "Does the Lord want you to build a train set because you're John the Baptist?"

Well, that was the most ridiculous thing I could possibly have said. "No, Cap! The Lord told me to build a train set for the children!"

"Which children?"

This seemed to touch a deep place in him, and his voice came from a little farther away when he answered, "The children of the town."

I got a twenty out of my desk, and as I handed it to him I said, "Now, don't spend this on booze, all right?" It was something I'd said to several other recipients, but he seemed genuinely offended, and quoted, "He shall be great in the sight of the Lord, and shall drink neither wine nor strong drink; and he shall be filled with the Holy Ghost, even from his mother's womb. And many of the children of Israel shall he turn to the Lord their God. And he shall go before him in the spirit and power of Elias, to turn the hearts of the fathers to the children, and the disobedient to the wisdom of the just; to make ready a people prepared for the Lord."

I didn't have a response to any of that, and after a while he left, more of a mystery than when I'd met him, and I thought I would probably never see him again. About that, as with so many other things, I was wrong.

22

Partly Truth and Partly Fiction

I told Beulah all about my visit from John the Baptist, and she said she'd love to meet him. I thought it was sort of funny, for the most part, but she cautioned me: "You never can tell with crazy people, and you can never be too careful. He could be dangerous." I told her I didn't think so, that he was just a lonely man with a sad story that he couldn't make himself tell, but he didn't seem the type to hurt anyone. She waited for me to look into her eyes and repeated with all seriousness, "You never can tell with crazy people."

A few days later I was walking out of the West Branch Hospital where I had been visiting an older parishioner recuperating from pneumonia, and I saw JoJo sitting on one of the benches under the trees in the hospital yard. It was a hot day; I could see that JoJo had been cutting grass. He was wiping his face with a blue bandanna and drinking from his water jug, and as I looked more closely, I could see that he was listening to somebody talk to him. Then I recognized the pattern of energetic hand motions and saw the black tangle of hair highlighted in white, and knew that JoJo was hearing the prophecy of John the Baptist.

I walked over and sat by JoJo. John the Baptist was talking about the days of Noe, the days that were before the flood when they were eating and drinking, marrying and giving in marriage, until the day that Noe entered into the ark; he didn't seem to notice that I'd joined the conversation. I listened and watched for a minute or two, and then I leaned over and whispered to JoJo, "You all right?"

"Yeah, I think so. Who's this guy?"

"He says he's John the Baptist."

JoJo's eyes went wide. "You think he really is?"

"No. I think he's a nut."

"You think he need to take a pill?"

I chuckled, "Yeah, maybe so."

"Maybe a placebo?"

"He might need something stronger than that."

By this time John was talking about trees and fruits: "'Even so every good tree bringeth forth good fruit; but a corrupt tree bringeth forth evil fruit. A good tree cannot bring forth evil fruit, neither can a corrupt tree bring forth good fruit.'"

JoJo whispered to me, "What's an evil fruit?"

"Well, it's complicated, but I think it means that people are like trees, and you can't expect a peach tree to have pecans on it, that sort of thing."

"Because pecans are evil?"

"Ah . . . no," I whispered, and then said, speaking loudly, "I think he means that good people do good things, and evil people do evil things. Is that right, John?"

He stopped, almost bewildered to notice the world around us, and said, "What?"

"Is that what you're saying, that good people do good things, and evil people do evil things?"

JoJo said, "Or is evil people evil because they do evil things, and good people is good because they do good things?" I looked over at him, and he gave me a little wink.

Whereupon John the Baptist, called by the Lord God to prepare the way for the coming of Christ to rural Mississippi, didst lay his hand upon JoJo McCain, and declared unto him: "Thou art Peter, and upon this rock I will build my church; and the gates of hell shall not prevail against it. And I will give unto thee the keys of the kingdom of heaven: and whatsoever thou shalt bind on earth shall be bound in heaven: and whatsoever thou shalt loose on earth shall be loosed in heaven."

JoJo and I were stunned, and it was a moment or two before JoJo said, "But I don't want to be Peter." He turned to me in genuine fear. "Can't I just be who I already am?"

I put my hand on his sweaty shoulder and squeezed it softly. "Of course you can," I whispered. "No matter what anybody says, you're just exactly who you're supposed to be."

JoJo was relieved, but John the Baptist wasn't through. "Verily I say unto you, There be some standing here, which shall not taste of death, till they see the Son of man coming in his kingdom."

That seemed all right to JoJo, but then John continued, in his matter-of-fact, inescapable truth tone of voice, "No, you're Peter, called by God just like me. They ain't nothin' you can do about it now, since you've been ordained to be an apostle and all."

It was only recently, and with considerable pain and struggle, that JoJo had learned it was okay to be who he was and how he was, and he was not going to be forced to be somebody else now. He stood up, towering over the wild-haired, wild-eyed Baptist, and declared right back at him, "I ain't. I ain't Peter. I ain't nobody but JoJo McCain, and ain't you or nobody else gonna make me be nobody else."

John the Baptist didn't look like he was changing his mind, but he also didn't look like he wanted to say anything that might result in his being knocked down by a large, angry man. And then JoJo said, "And you ain't no John the Baptist."

Now I stood up, too, hoping to calm JoJo and diffuse the situation. But John the Baptist could not bear the challenge to his rickety identity. His voice was a little shrill as he retreated into Scripture: "Get thee behind me, Satan: thou art an offence unto me: for thou savourest not the things that be of God, but those that be of men."

JoJo turned to me. "What did he say?"

I said, "Don't worry about it, JoJo."

"What did he call me? Did he call me Satan?"

"It's what Jesus said one time, when Peter said he didn't want him to be crucified."

"He usin' the Bible on me?"

I was afraid one of them was going to do something that we would all regret, so I took JoJo's arm, turned him around, and led him away. "JoJo, listen—he's a little crazy, all right? You don't have to listen to anything he says. He's not John the Baptist, and you're not Peter. You're okay, just like you are. The guy's got some problems, that's all."

JoJo was still angry, but cooling off some. "He sure do have some problems, if he thinks I'm Satan. I ain't got nuthin' to do with Satan, you know that."

"I know that."

"I think that feller is a fruit off a evil tree, is what I think."

"Well, I think maybe it might be some kind of nut tree."

JoJo smiled at that, and we continued to walk away. I looked back to see John the Baptist talking to nobody, his hands gesturing wildly in the air.

Then JoJo said, "Peter who?"

I'd met John the Baptist on a Monday morning; the following Monday morning I got a call from Beulah, asking if I'd ever met a man named John Earl Cahill. I told her I didn't think so, and she said that a man had been arrested the day before for trespassing and disturbing the peace, and she wondered if it might be the John the Baptist I'd told her about. She said that apparently this man had stormed down the aisle of the First Baptist Church of West Branch, despite the best efforts of the ushers and most of the deacons, in a full rant about "the voice of one crying in the wilderness, Prepare ye the way of the Lord, make his paths straight!" and telling the surprised members of the congregation that they were all vipers who needed to flee the wrath to come.

I told her that did sound an awful lot like my friend John, and she said I could find him in the county jail.

When I came into the cell John and six or seven other guys were sharing, I noticed the others were gathered together off to the left, and that John was sitting by himself to the right. He saw me and brightened up: "Cap!" He shook my hand like we were old friends, and I sat on the concrete bench with him, three feet away.

I had decided, with some helpful convincing from Beulah, that it was time to puncture the veil of illusion and invite John to live in this world. I said, "Look, John—I was never in Vietnam, all right? I'm not the Captain. You're not John the Baptist, and you can't just walk into a church and start preaching."

He wrestled with what I'd said, and I think part of him wanted to hear it, but in a few seconds he rejected it. Maybe it was the only reality that made any sense to him.

"But I'm a Baptist, just like John the Baptist was, and now I been thrown in jail for telling the truth about God and Jesus and all, just like he was. It was like a test, Cap, me bein' thrown in jail and all."

He believed it with every fiber of his body and soul, from his hirsute head to his shiny white tennis shoes. He was John the Baptist because he'd been called by God and all, and it didn't seem as if there were anything I or anyone else could do or say that might convince him otherwise.

I wondered if maybe JoJo was right, and there was some medicine John was supposed to be on. "Are they treating you all right in here, John?"

"Yeah, pretty good. Them boys is scared of me and all. I think they might be a generation of vipers and all, you think?"

"Could be, John, I don't know. I think I'd stay away from them as much as I could if I was in here."

"Yeah, I guess some people just don't take to preachin.'"

"I think that's true. Hey John, can I get you anything?"

"No, thanks. I'm just gonna be in here for about three more days. I'm all right."

"Do you take any medicine I could get for you?"

"No. I don't need no medicine. It makes me feel stupid."

"Does the doctor say you ought to be taking medicine?"

"Yeah, 'course he does. Every time you go to the doctor they tell you some other medicine you have to be on. But look at me—I ain't takin' none of it, and I'm doin' just fine."

"John, you probably need to be on some of that medicine, just to feel a little calmer, maybe see things a little more clearly."

"I ain't takin' no medicine. Makes me stupid."

I wasn't getting anywhere with that, and John was starting to shut me out. So I said, "John, tell me about your family."

I watched him struggle with the question, with whether he should trust me with this dark part of his story. He nodded, coming to a decision and agreeing with it, and said, "We was married for near twenty years when she . . . when they stole her away."

"Your wife?"

"Yes sir."

"Tell me about her."

"She is . . . my wife is the Queen of the South"—I could almost hear the capitalization in his voice as he said it—"and she will . . . the Queen of the South shall rise up in judgment with this generation, for she came from the uttermost parts of the earth."

He spoke these lines as if he was reciting something memorized, but it was nothing I thought I'd ever heard before. I asked, "Where is she from?"

"From the uttermost parts of the earth," he repeated, as if it was something I should already know.

"Where's that?"

Then it was like he was uncertain, knocked out of a familiar script, and no longer sure of his lines. The spell he'd been under had broken, and he faltered: "She is from . . . my wife grew up in Louisiana, way down there where the land runs out, from the uttermost parts of the earth, the Queen of the South."

"Where is she now?" I asked, half dreading the answer.

"They took her away. They took her where I can't go, because after our little, because after . . . after that and all, they took her away. They didn't want her to rise up in judgment and all, so they . . . and that's when, that's why I had to start preaching, when the Lord called me to prepare the way and preach repentance to the hypocrites and the generation of vipers and all."

"What is your wife's name?"

The sadness in his eyes made me want to look away, but I held his gaze for an intense few seconds until he let his head roll back on his shoulders and looked up at the ceiling of the cell. He took a deep breath and said her name so quietly I could barely hear: "Suellen."

"And you loved her. But she left you."

There was a scary flash of violence in his eyes when he turned to look at me, but I don't think he was seeing the same day I was. Then the ferocity faded, and he said with resignation, "She didn't leave me, Cap. They took her away."

"Who? Who took her?"

His answer came from another time and place: "The scribes and the Pharisees plotted to silence her. They took her, far beyond the horizon, took her where I could not follow."

The chorus of that Kris Kristofferson song goes like this:

He's a poet, he's a picker
He's a prophet, he's a pusher
He's a pilgrim and a preacher, and a problem when he's stoned
He's a walkin' contradiction, partly truth and partly fiction,
Takin' ev'ry wrong direction on his lonely way back home.

That pretty well summed him up; the man was a mix of pain and prophecy, of the difficulties of the present day and a long-remembered Bible story. Some of what he said was matter-of-fact, and some of it was just crazy.

I wondered how I could be helpful to him, and if he'd ever had anybody to talk to about whatever had happened. Dreading the answer, I asked, "Is Suellen still alive?"

And then he talked for a long time, so fast and much of it so garbled that I couldn't keep up, his hands completely out of his control. His wife was alive because they couldn't kill her, and if they had killed her she would come back even stronger as in the days of Noah before the flood when they were eating and drinking, marrying and giving in marriage, when two will be in the field and one will be taken and one will be left, and if the owner of the house had known in what part of the night the thief was coming, he would have stayed a while and would not have let his house be broken into.

This biblical stream-of-consciousness rant went on for several minutes, outlasting my efforts to tag along by identifying the different passages from the King James Version that he was stringing together. It was as if his speech was on autopilot, not connected to his mind or our surroundings in any way. A couple of times, I tried to interrupt or ask a question, but he just talked louder and faster, his voice getting higher and higher, his hands moving faster and faster.

He rattled on for a while, until he mentioned that Jesus had not only been raised from the dead but had also raised others. He was a little less sure of himself about that, though, and paused a moment, looking up at me and asking, "Right?"

Glad to be on more familiar ground, I said, "That's right. He raised Lazarus, and the daughter of . . . ."

I hesitated at the name, but he supplied it: "Jairus. Jesus raised the daughter of Jairus. Some said it was too late, and some laughed at Jesus. But Jesus took her hand and told her to get up and she began to walk about. She was twelve years old, just like . . . just like—"

Then John turned away from a moment of tenderness and was agitated and animated again. "They laughed at Jesus," he spat, "and said it was too late—a generation of hypocrites who claimed to believe in the power of Jesus, but they turned away to trust only themselves." He took a deep breath and continued, "They laughed at me, Cap, just like they laughed at Jesus. They told me it was too late to save her. And then—"

And then the pain of the memory was too strong, and some stories can't be told.

He was hunched over, with his head resting on his knee, sobbing quietly. I said, "I'm so sorry, John. I'm so sorry." He just nodded, all out of words.

We sat there for a while, him sobbing over his knee and me with my hand on his shoulder. It occurred to me that if I was ever going to be of any real help to this guy, I would need to find my way around or through the barriers he was maintaining to wall off whatever terrible thing had happened, to help him face it so he could start healing. I said, as gently as I could, "Then what, John? What happened then, when they laughed you and said it was too late?"

"Then they took her away." He retreated into the established narrative, where he was safe. "They took away the Queen of the South, and took her where I could not follow, beyond the horizon."

I tried a couple more times, but he'd regained his defenses and I hit the same wall each time. We went around and around, but I never did completely understand what we were talking about. The best I could piece together was that it might have had something to do with his wife, who was the Queen of the South, who had been taken from him after something terrible happened, and that either his wife's abduction or the other terrible thing had signaled the coming of the end of the world, which he'd been sent to warn the rest of us about.

After a while we talked some more, not about his call to prophecy but about his present predicament. John the Baptist Cahill was content to serve out his five days in jail, and I was content to let him. He did ask that I bring him a King James Bible, which I was glad to do, and a carton of Marlboro Red cigarettes, which I was not so happy about. But still, he was out of the weather and out of trouble, for which I was grateful.

I didn't offer to post his bail, and it never seemed to occur to him to ask. As he saw it, he was doing time for preparing the way of the Lord before a generation of vipers who just didn't take to preachin'.

23

HOLD YOUR COURSE

The Foster family was one of the primary families in the parish, and in fact they were pretty primary to the town as well. Mr. Foster had served in the Air Force for thirty years, starting back when, as he said, "It was new and shiny," in the years after World War I, and he had instructed new pilots for World War II. His name was Cletus, but everybody in the church and in the town called him Pops. He was married to Elizabeth, whom he called Betsy and who was known to all as Meemaw, and their only child was Cletus, Jr., who was called . . . no kidding . . . Sonny. Sonny and his wife, Louise (she was just called Louise), were very active in the parish, and their daughter Bet, or Little Bet because of her resemblance to her grandmother, joined us for worship on Christmas and Easter out of obligation. However, they were clearly not comfortable in church. They had a son, too, named Curtis.

Pops and Meemaw didn't get out much by the time I came to Holy Incarnation, but I always enjoyed visiting with them. The first time I went to visit, Mr. Foster offered me hot tea because that's what Meemaw thought he ought to offer the visiting priest. Happily, he noticed my lack of enthusiasm and brought out a couple of cups of coffee instead. He asked me if I'd ever served in our nation's military—Meemaw whispered, "*Cletus!*"—and I said I had not, that I was too young for Vietnam and had different ideas for a career.

There was a tense moment as he considered, and then he said, "Well, I s'pose that's just fine. We used to call the Air Force chaplains Sky Pilots, and tell 'em they were flyin' higher than any of our planes."

One day he told me a story about an Air Force chaplain who'd had to jump out of a plane at 10,000 feet in order to secure a promotion. He said the chaplain had told him he wasn't worried, that he put his trust in the Lord, and that he seemed as "calm as a grazing cow on a sunny day." He said the chaplain jumped out of the plane and deployed his parachute "smooth as silk," and that when Mr. Foster ran out to congratulate him, the chaplain seemed self-conscious and ill at ease, and wasn't "jumpin' around like all the other fellas."

Mr. Foster said he went over to the chaplain to ask if he was okay, and "that Sky Pilot told me he'd shit and pissed himself all the way down." He said, "I had my own jeep, so I took him back to the base so he could wash out his jumpsuit without anybody else around." Judging by the relish with which he told it, it was a favorite story for him to tell, and it ended with, "That right there was courage, though, bein' scared to death and doin' what you had to do anyway. That was true courage." And then he looked at me and added, "And true faith."

I went to visit the Fosters about once a month or so, and loved to hear Mr. Foster's stories, especially the ones he told mostly to embarrass his wife. After a while he started telling me stories I'd heard before, and they were even better the second time around, since I could focus on the telling of the story rather than the plot—like reading a good book again. He shared stories about his time in the Air Force, flying and teaching others to fly over England and France. When I told him he'd had an adventurous life, he beamed.

A week or so after I met John the Baptist on the steps of the church, Mr. Foster had a heart attack. Sonny's wife, Louise, called me and said that the whole family was at the hospital and wanted me to come. I went to see him, and hugged Sonny in the hall outside the room. He teared up when he saw me, as if the situation had all of a sudden become a little more real.

Sonny said, "It's bad, Buddy. I just talked to the doctor—a woman young enough to be my granddaughter—and she said she didn't know if he was going to make it. He's so weak, like all the strength just leaked out of him."

I knocked on the door, and Meemaw told me to come in. Pops was lying in the hospital bed, his white hair thinner than I remembered from our visit two weeks before, a tube looped around his ears feeding oxygen into his nose. His skin was grayish, and his breathing was shallow, as if each breath could be his last. His eyes were closed until Meemaw said, "Cletus, Father Buddy is here."

He opened his eyes slowly and worked to get them into focus, then looked at me and smiled. "Ah, Sky Pilot," he rasped, "good to see you."

"It's good to see you, Pops. I understand you're having an adventure with the doctors and nurses."

"They're having all the fun." He paused to catch a breath, and went on. "Ain't been all that much fun for me."

"Yes sir, I know that's right. Can I do anything for you?"

"Just say a prayer or two."

I took his hand, paper-thin skin sagging from the old bones, and we said a prayer, asking God to look down in love and mercy on Cletus, to keep him from pain, to give him patience and hope and trust in the resurrection of our Lord Jesus Christ.

Pops said, "You ain't praying for me . . . to get well?"

"Yes sir, I am. I'm praying for you to be whole again."

"Oh," he said. We sat there for a minute, and he said, "You afraid to die, Buddy?"

I remembered that moment in the kitchen at Parchman prison, when Eddie held a knife to my neck and death was a distinct and real possibility. I'd told Eugene, "I'm not afraid, Eugene. I'm not afraid to die." I remembered when I'd gone to see Eugene on Death Row, and him reminding me that I'd said there are worse things than dying. I'd said all that, and meant all that when I'd said it—always the central question, for me and for any person of faith, is whether we really believe what we claim to believe.

Am I afraid to die? I'm not afraid of what will come after I die, but I am afraid of the process of dying, afraid of what it will do to the people I'll be leaving behind. I guess we all are. Maybe the prospect of death is part of what makes life precious, so that when life ends we all feel a loss. We don't like to be reminded of death, but we hold on to the hope that life in faith is eternal.

But Pops wasn't looking for a sermon or a cliché, some sort of Band-Aid theology to cover up the boo-boo. He was facing death nose to nose and didn't want to be facing it all alone. The doctors and most of the nurses wear white to work every day and talk about healing and recovery, but the priest wears black and walks alongside a person facing death. Their family and friends want to encourage them and talk about coming home and watching football and who's coming to Thanksgiving dinner, but Cletus Foster just wanted permission to let go.

"Well, I'm not worried about being dead," I told him, "but I think we're all scared to die. That day will surely come for all of us; there's nothing we can do about that. And when it does, when it comes for me, I'm glad to think I'll have faith in Jesus, and that faith will give me courage. 'Life is changed, not ended,' that's what we say in our funerals."

We all sat for a moment, none of us knowing what to say next, so I added, "I guess maybe I'm like that Sky Pilot you told me about, not afraid to jump from ten thousand feet, but then he needed to change his jumpsuit after he landed. That's true courage, you told me: true faith."

He smiled to remember one of his favorite stories, and then he whispered, "I think I'm gonna die."

Meemaw had been sitting in the chair next to his bed; I'd pulled up a little stool of some sort so that I faced her, with Pops between us. She reached out and took his hand, and was about to say something reassuringly and optimistically false, but I spoke first: "Yes sir. You've had a life full of adventures, and now the next adventure is straight ahead. You're flying right into it—hold your course. We believe in God, and we believe in Jesus, and we believe you're going Home."

Meemaw looked at me sharply, as if I'd said something rude or inappropriate, but then she nodded and put her forehead down on their clasped hands. I reached over Pops and put my big hand on her little shoulder in time to feel her sobbing.

Then, uncharacteristically impromptu, I quoted the 23rd Psalm: "Yea, though I walk through the valley of death, I shall fear no evil, for thy rod and thy staff, they comfort me."

I stayed for a while after that, and when I leaned down to kiss Pops on the forehead he murmured, "Take care of 'em, Buddy." I said, "Yes sir."

He died that night in his sleep with his beloved Betsy sleeping in the chair beside him. I went to the hospital room and said the prayers to be used at the time of death, which end with these words: "Almighty God, our Father in heaven, before whom live all who die in the Lord: Receive our brother Cletus into the courts of your heavenly dwelling place. Let his heart and soul now ring out in joy to you, O Lord, the living God, and the God of those who live. This we ask through Christ our Lord. *Amen.*"

The visitation was set for three to five the afternoon before the funeral, at Dobbs Funeral Home right there on Main Street, just half a block up from Holy Incarnation. I got there around four, signed the guest book, and waited in line to greet first Meemaw, then Sonny, then his wife, Louise, and then their daughter, Bet. Their son Curtis was coming later that evening, according to Louise.

There were hugs and tears and a smile or two, and then I hung around for a few minutes, wondering how or if I might be helpful, when Bet got out of the line to talk to me. I was surprised; she'd never sought out a conversation with me before. She started with, "Meemaw said you're not full of crap."

"Well, sometimes I am, but usually I try not to be."

She thought about that for a bit and nodded. "You think Pops is okay?"

"Yes ma'am, I do. I think the part of us that makes us who we are is spiritual, not physical, and I think the spirit lives forever. He just wore out his body, and it was time to go."

"Death is a door."

"Yeah—I like that. Where'd that come from?"

"I said it."

"Ah." We stood watching the people in the funeral home receiving line, and then she said, "You wouldn't believe some of the stupid stuff these people say."

"Like what?"

"Like, 'The good Lord only gives us so many days on earth,' or 'It's all part of God's plan.' You think God planned Pops's death?"

"I think Pops had a heart attack because his heart had been pumping for ninety-four years. I think God didn't design us to last much longer than that."

"But you don't think that God had it all worked out so that Cletus Foster was destined his whole life to die on October 2, 1992, like God planned it that way since before he was born?"

"No, I think God gave Cletus Foster his life, and that he had a heart attack which brought him to the door of death, into the next life."

"You mean reincarnation?"

"No, I don't think so. I mean eternal life in love and in harmony with God."

"You think I'll see him again?"

"I do."

She took a sharp breath, reassured for the moment, and then said, "You see that lady over there, talking to the tall, skinny guy?"

I saw her: a short, plump woman wearing a bright magenta jacket and skirt with a matching pillbox hat, holding a large black Bible to her chest like a shield. "Yeah?"

"She told me it was a shame that Pops wasn't saved when he died."

"You're kidding!"

"Who would kid about something like that?"

"Why does she think he wasn't saved?"

"She asked me if Pops had been born again, and I told her I didn't think so. He never said he was, anyway. She said if he'd been born again he'd have been talkin' about it *all* the time. I told her I guessed he wasn't, and she said it was a shame because you have to be born again to go to heaven. She had Bible verses and everything."

"That's a terrible thing to say! Did she know your grandfather?"

"I don't think so. She called him Cletus, and you know everybody who really knew him called him Pops, except Meemaw."

"What did you say?"

"I told her thank you for coming. I didn't know what else to say. I don't have any defense against these people, with all their cruel ideas and empty slogans."

"Yeah, me neither."

She was trying so hard to be polite, but it was an effort. We stood there for a few seconds, and I had an odd idea, which I shared with her: "You need a squirt gun."

"What?"

"If you had a little squirt gun in your purse, you could just whip it out and squirt somebody in the face when they say something cruel or stupid."

We laughed, a good, solid laugh—a little too much for the funeral home, but it was an important moment. She hugged me around the waist and thanked me.

About two weeks later Meemaw died. It happens like that sometimes, when one partner goes and the other doesn't really have any reason to stay. Sonny said she'd told him she was tired, took a nap, and just never woke up.

The same people gathered in the same line at the same funeral home, but this time I snuck in a little squirt gun for Bet to put in her purse. It wasn't loaded; I couldn't trust her not to call my bluff, but it was a good chuckle. I stood with Bet for the visitation, and her brother Curtis, who'd also been a victim of the Magenta Lady, came and stood with us.

This time when the Magenta Lady came up, I stepped up and asked her very politely who she was and whether she was a friend of the family. She told me she didn't actually know the family, but that it was her ministry to visit in times of bereavement and offer counsel and comfort to the grieving. Her husband was the pastor at a congregation outside of town, she said, and this was part of her ministry.

I told her that a lot of the people there were from the parish I served, and that we had enough counsel and comfort, but thank you just the same. She looked like she'd suffered an affront, but she got the message and left. I whispered to Bet and Curtis, "I'm glad that worked, or I would've had to squirt that smug look off her face!"

Then, in the middle of November, Sonny died too, apparently from a stroke. His wife, Louise, told me, "I woke up and kissed him good morning. He told me he was going to rest a little, and when I got back with a cup of coffee I was talking to him but he didn't answer me. He was just gone, all of a sudden."

Again, the whole congregation came together, for the visitation and for the funeral; again, the whole town came to pay their respects. We were all sick at heart. This time, I brought Bet and Curtis both a squirt gun, both of them loaded. We didn't see the Magenta Lady again, but it's always nice to be prepared.

24

YARDBOYS AND HALFWITS

After serving five days for disturbing the peace, John the Baptist Cahill was released from jail and I gave him twenty more dollars, presumably so he could build a model railroad set. I didn't know what else I could do for him, and I suppose I hoped that building a train set might help him find a little bit of sanity and stability, or at least keep him from invading any more pulpits.

There were those few weeks filled with deaths and funerals and squirt guns, and I didn't see John the Baptist for a while or hear anything about him. Then one day he came into the office and asked me what I knew about Martin Luther. I told him what I knew: that Martin Luther was a priest in the Church in the 1500s, that he was not satisfied with several things about the Church, especially the sale of indulgences, and when he talked to his bishop about it he was not satisfied with the response, so he tacked a list of ninety-five theses to the door of the chapel in the little town in Germany where he was a college professor. That resulted in an ugly church fight, in which either he was kicked out of the church or he quit in a huff, depending on who's telling the story, and that's what started the Reformation.

John asked me what the ninety-five theses were, and I told him they were topics on which Martin Luther was inviting debate. He asked me about the Reformation, and I explained that it changed the Church forever. Then I started to tell him about the English

Reformation, which is the limb of the tree the Episcopal Church sits on, but he didn't seem interested in that at all.

I asked him why he wanted to know about Martin Luther, and he told me that some of the men in the jail had been talking about how Martin Luther had fought for their rights until he was shot and killed in Memphis, and that they needed to keep fighting. I told him they were talking about Martin Luther King, Jr., but now he was more interested in Martin Luther.

As it happened, there were some books high up on the shelves in my office that had been left by previous occupants, and I knew that one of them was about Martin Luther. Hoping to divert his attention away from his calling to be John the Baptist, I took it down, dusted it off, and handed it to him. He told me he'd bring it back in good shape, but I said he could have it, which pleased him greatly.

The next morning, JoJo came to see me. He didn't usually just stop by for a chat, so I was already wondering what was going on; he seemed unusually fidgety and uncomfortable, which was also not normal. I had to try to coax his news out of him over a cup of coffee. Finally, he allowed himself to be brought to the point of his visit: "Buddy, I'm just worried about this John the Baptist feller."

"What's worrying you?"

"I'm afraid he might be gonna hurt somebody. I'm afraid he might hurt you."

"Oh, I don't think so. I think he's a nut, but I don't think he wants to hurt anybody."

"I don't know, Buddy—he just scares me."

It was odd to think that JoJo would be scared of anybody, and that aroused my concern. I had come to trust JoJo and his intuition; if he was hearing alarm bells, I ought to pay some attention.

"What is it about John the Baptist that scares you?"

"He ain't no John the Baptist, to start off with. John the Baptist lived and died a long time ago in the Bible times. A man who don't know who he is is scary. You don't never know what he's gonna do next, 'cause he don't know neither."

"Do you really think he might hurt somebody?"

"No, I don't know that for sure. I just want you to be careful, is all. And don't let him get nowhere near Miss Beulah or little Jude. That man ain't right, Buddy. He just ain't right."

I smiled and said, "Some folks might say you and me ain't right, either."

He looked me dead in the eye and answered, "And they might be right about you." We both laughed, and the moment passed. I had to go set out some tables and chairs for the women's bridge club that afternoon, and JoJo came to help. After that it was time for lunch, so I offered to buy him a barbeque sandwich at the Little Fat Pig restaurant a few miles north of town. He hesitated, reluctant for me to pay for his lunch, but I told him I wasn't going to pay him for helping me with the tables and chairs, so he agreed.

That afternoon Chuck Wallace came into my office and closed the door behind him. I always left it open unless I was anticipating a serious and confidential conversation, partly because I like the idea of having an open door, and partly because it got stuffy in there when the door was closed.

He was agitated, and it seemed to me that he was ready for a fight. I said, "Hi, Chuck. What can I do for you?"

"I hear you went to the Little Fat Pig for lunch today."

I was afraid I knew what this was about. "Yes sir," I answered. "I took JoJo McCain there for lunch; we had a couple of sandwiches. Is there a problem?"

"Well, Father Buddy, you know how people talk. It's all over town that you took that . . . Afro-American yardboy to lunch, as if he was a friend of yours."

"He is a friend of mine."

"Father Buddy, you just can't do that."

"What, I can't take a friend to lunch?"

"Did the church pay for it?"

"No, I paid for it."

"I heard you charged it to the parish."

"That's crazy! I wouldn't even know how to charge it to the parish."

"Did you write a check from our discretionary fund?"

"I paid for our lunch with money out of my pocket. My money."

"Money that we pay you."

And there it was. I had stepped outside of the lines that Chuck and whoever he'd talked to had imagined, like your neighbor's dog coming into your yard to do her business. We were just a few steps away from the idea that the parish owned me and that I had somehow misbehaved. I was thinking of Chuck as a member of the church, and he was thinking of himself as an owner.

I said, "It was my money. Money I earned."

Chuck had not become a prominent attorney or the mayor of the town by backing down. He repeated, "Money we pay you."

I was putting together a sentence or two in which I was going to tell him that I'd already had conversations with the bishop about leaving, that I'd been at the Church of the Holy Incarnation long enough, but before I could start saying it he continued, "And what's this about the halfwit who tried to preach at the Baptist church? Is he a friend of yours, too?"

"No, not a friend. But he is somebody who deserves our compassion. Something terrible happened to him, something he can't face or talk about. He—"

"Have you given him money, too?"

"Yes."

"For what?"

I didn't know what to say. I didn't want to tell Chuck that I'd given a man I thought was a nut twenty dollars to help him build a model train set for the children of the town, hoping he could grab hold of some scrap of his unraveling sanity. I really didn't want to tell him that the man was claiming to be John the Baptist.

I said, "I don't think he has any money at all."

"How long is he going to be here? Are you planning on giving him more money? How long will this go on?"

"I don't know, Chuck. A man asked me for help, and I helped him. That's all."

"We don't have unlimited funds, you know."

"I understand. I'm not trying to bankrupt the parish. I'm just trying to do what we say Jesus wants us to do, and help a man in need."

"Ah," said Chuck, as if some suspicion had been confirmed. "That idealism you're so well known for."

"Yeah, I guess so." Then, remembering what Kate had said in the vestry meeting when we were talking about Habitat for Humanity, I added, "That silly idealism."

He stood up and moved toward the door, doubtless as frustrated with me as I was with him. With his hand on the doorknob, he turned and said, "You represent the rest of us in this community, Buddy. I'll ask you to have some respect for that."

"Yes sir," I said. "And I hope you'll respect that I also represent our Lord, who told his followers to love our neighbors. And feed the poor. And treat people with dignity—even yardboys and halfwits."

He glared at me for a moment and then concluded, "Well, I guess it's a good thing you're a priest, because you could never make it as anything else." He opened the door and left before I could respond. And that was a good thing, because the only thing I could think to say was that it was a good thing he was an attorney and a politician, because . . . he was a selfish jerk.

On November 22, 1992, a few days after Sonny Foster's funeral, I came to the church early to unlock the doors and make coffee. It was the Sunday before Thanksgiving, and we were going to have a community Thanksgiving service that evening at the big Methodist church, so I was anticipating that our morning crowd might be a little light—Episcopalians don't normally want to go to church twice in one day.

As I walked up to the building, I saw that there were papers thumbtacked to the red doors under the vestibule. When I saw the heading of the first page, my breath caught in my throat: "95 Theses for a New Reformation, by John the Baptist."

They were all numbered and precisely printed out by hand. He had taken a lot of time doing this. I read the first several and decided I needed to take them down—fast:

1. I am touched by the Spirit of God, called to be John the Baptist, the voice of one crying in the wilderness, Prepare ye the way of the Lord, make his paths straight.

2. Therefore say I Repent ye: for the kingdom of heaven is at hand.

3. O generation of vipers, I am given vision and voice to warn you to flee from the wrath to come.

4. I am come to bear witness of the Light, that all men through Jesus Christ might believe.

5. In the Name of Christ, I demand to speak to the preacher Cap Buddy, who is my friend and not a stranger, that I may begin my ministry by preaching the Word of God unto the people of this church.

As I was trying to figure out how to get the tacks out without further damaging the door, I heard the grating voice of my recurring nemesis Chuck as he came up the sidewalk and demanded to know what had been pinned to the door of his church.

I turned toward him and tried to block his view of the pages and said as casually as I could, "Good morning, Chuck. How are you?"

"What the Hell is all that nailed to the door of the church?" He was already reading despite my best subtle efforts to be in his way; there was no trying to sugarcoat anything.

"Well, you know we talked about this man who has some mental problems, and . . . "

"He's says he's armed!"

"What?"

"Look: right there in number seven—crazy bastard says he's armed and dangerous!"

I turned around to look, and there it was.

6. I will not suffer myself to be returned unto jail, as that generation of vipers have rejected the Truth and have listened to me not.

7. To be sure I am not ignored, I have armed myself, so that I am a danger unto ye all.

John the Baptist armed? Surely not! Crazy, maybe, but not armed and dangerous. I said, "Chuck, he's not dangerous. He's not going to hurt anybody."

But Chuck wasn't listening—despite his insistence that John was dangerous, he continued reading. So I took a minute to give the 95 Theses of John the Baptist Cahill a closer look.

It took a few seconds for me to realize that the first twenty were original, and then he'd filled out the rest with Bible verses. It took me years to realize that he was really talking about the Emergent Church, well before anybody else was.

9. For the people of God are not being served by the preachers and pastors, who demand that we serve them.

10. We are not led by the preachers and pastors, blind guides who serve only themselves, and make for themselves a fine living while the poor suffer and the people hunger for the Word of God.

11. We are not served by preachers who talk about Jesus and the Bible like it was all make-believe, or only long ago and far away, making the rest of us as blind as they are.

12. We are not served by preachers who make the people suffer long boring sermons that wander around looking for a place to stop: surely they should not expect the people to listen, nor should they expect them to come back.

13. We are not served by choirs who sing every song like they are at a funeral: surely they can't expect that God is listening to all their sad dull songs.

14. We are not served by preachers who quote writers that nobody has ever heard of, or talk in Latin or Greek because they know that nobody else can understand those languages: surely they are just proclaiming themselves and not Christ the Lord.

15. I say unto ye: preachers and pastors who do not listen to anybody else might be missing the voice of God in their lives.

16. As Martin Luther King tacked 95 thesises to the college door in Germany, so now I tack these thesises to the door of the Church of the Holy Incarnation in West Branch, to start a new Reformation of the Church.

17. The new Reformation will come, yea even to the ends of the earth, to bring God's holy Church back to serving all of the people of God, even those who don't have homes, or jobs, or families: even those the fine people in their soft rainment don't want to sit next to.

18. The new Reformation will come, yea even here, to deliver the Church from all of its silly fighting about things that don't matter to anybody except maybe the professors, the preachers and the pastors.

19. The new Reformation will come, yea to all who have ears to hear, to make the Church a place that will offer help and hope and a reckoning to families whose little girls die for no reason at all.

20. The new Reformation will indeed come, to offer salvation to the lost before the days of the great tribulation, which is coming soon and very soon.

A few days later, after the danger had passed, I had time to sit down and read all ninety-five. Twenty-one through ninety-five are verses about John the Baptist from the King James Bible, sometimes slightly altered to fit his peculiar understanding of reality. One thesis was John the Baptist's words from Matthew 3:9, updated to our day and situation:

24. And think not to say within yourselves, We are members of fine congregations and respectable denominations: for I say unto you, that God is able of the mud to raise up children unto Abraham.

In Mississippi we don't have much stone, as the original John the Baptist would have been familiar with, but we've got lots and lots of mud. And from the ease of my office, I had to chuckle at his rewriting of Matthew 11:21:

49. Woe unto thee, Tupelo! woe unto thee, Starkville! for if the mighty works, which were done in you, had been done in Tyre and Sidon, they would have repented long ago in sackcloth and ashes.

The mysterious Queen of the South is featured in Theses 55 and 56, from Matthew 12:42 and Luke 11:31:

> 55. The Queen of the South shall rise up in the judgment with this generation, and shall condemn it: for she came from the uttermost parts of the earth to hear the wisdom of Solomon; and, behold, a greater than Solomon is here.

> 56. Yea, verily: the Queen of the South shall rise indeed, and come again among us to judge the wickedness of this generation.

John Cahill concluded with Matthew 24:40-42, as Jesus gives a dire warning for his followers to be watchful.

> 93. Then shall two be in the field; the one shall be taken, and the other left.

> 94. Two women shall be grinding at the mill; the one shall be taken, and the other left.

> 95. Watch therefore: for ye know not what hour your Lord doth come.

25

Ain't the Kind of Thing You Want Your Mama to Find Out on TV

"He's got a bomb!"

"What? It doesn't say that!"

"Look right here, number seven: 'To be sure I am not ignored, I have armed myself, so that I am a danger unto ye all.' He's got a bomb, or a gun—he's armed!"

"I don't think he would—"

"This is no time for your ridiculous idealism, Hinton. He's armed! He's dangerous! I'm going to get the police!"

Chuck hurried down the steps, got back in his car, and drove away. The police station was just a few blocks away; it wouldn't be long before they rolled up with their lights flashing. I had two or three minutes to do something. Or to do nothing. I didn't think John Cahill would hurt anybody. But Beulah had made a point of saying, "You never can tell with crazy people." And JoJo had warned, "A man who don't know who he is is scary. You don't never know what he's gonna do next, 'cause he don't know either."

Surely the best thing would be to wait for the police to come and let them deal with it. But what if John was armed? Would he set off a bomb in the church with me standing at a safe distance, watching? Or what if he had a shotgun or something? Would I stand by and watch him shoot it out with the West Branch police? What if they killed him? What if he killed one of them? What if I could do something to prevent any of that and instead I stood there playing it safe because I was too scared?

I unlocked the door, went to my office, and called Beulah, telling her what was happening. I explained that I was going to talk to John, to see if I could head the situation off before anything bad happened. "I don't want anything bad to happen to you!" she said.

"I don't think he will hurt me, honey."

"Buddy, if he hurts you, I'm going to be so mad at you." There was a long pause and she continued, "If he kills you, I'm going to be furious!"

"He won't. I promise. Look, I've got to go before the police get here. I'll call you later."

When we were dating, Beulah and I had lengthy, lingering, long-distance telephone goodbyes, each of us waiting for the other to hang up first. We weren't teenagers; we were just behaving like teenagers. Somehow that had evolved into ending every phone conversation with both of us saying, "I love you bye." I told her I'd call her later, then said, "I love you bye." She hesitated, and said, "I love you, Buddy. Be careful."

I hung up the phone, more nervous now that our agreed-upon protocol had been broken; it didn't feel right, like I was going into a sword fight without my shield. Not for the first time, or the last, I recognized how much I depend on my sweet, spirited, strong-willed wife.

I went into the nave, where I knew John would be. He was sitting on the steps that led up to the altar. He nodded as I walked up the center aisle. I didn't see any bombs or guns, but I knew that didn't necessarily mean there weren't any.

I said, "Good morning, John. How are you?"

"You ever sit in here, Cap?" he said. "You ever just sit here and watch the light move through the windows? It's real peaceful and all."

It was a replay of the day we'd met, on the steps outside, watching the squirrels. I said, as if I was reciting the lines someone else had written, "No, I don't."

There was a long pause, and then I said, "Look, John, we just have a few minutes. The police will be here pretty soon."

"The police? What for?"

"Because your note said you were armed and dangerous."

He was indignant. "Well, that's no reason to call the police on somebody."

I was indignant right back. "I think that's a perfectly good reason to call the police, if somebody says they're armed and dangerous."

"Well, it's not like I'm going to hurt somebody."

"I don't think you would, John. Somebody else went to get the police when they saw your note."

"It ain't a note; it's ninety-five thesises, like Martin Luther King did. I nailed 'em up on your door to start a new reformation and all. I read in that book where it got Martin Luther King a lot of attention, and I figured that's what I needed to do, too."

As I was agreeing that it would surely get him a lot attention, we heard the police siren crank up at the police station, get louder as the cruiser got closer to the church, and then switch off when the car stopped on the street outside. A moment later we heard a man's voice over the bullhorn: "John Earl Cahill, this is the police. Come out with your hands behind your head!"

He turned to me in a complete panic, completely surprised by this outcome and scared out of his wits. "What am I gonna do, Cap? I ain't going back to jail, I just ain't! I ain't done nuthin'! They're all hypocrites and generations of vipers in there! I ain't done nuthin' wrong!"

"John, listen to me. Look at my eyes and listen to me. You wrote in your ninety-five theses that you are armed and that you are dangerous. Give me your bomb, or gun, or whatever it is, and I can take it to the police and get you out of here."

"I ain't got no bomb, Cap—I swear it. I ain't got no gun, neither. You gotta believe me, Cap—I swear!"

"But you said you were armed and dangerous!"

"I am armed with the Word of God, and dangerous to those who don't believe, as the furnace of fire is to the wicked and unjust, when there shall be weeping and wailing and gnashing of teeth and all. I ain't got no bomb, Cap—you have to believe me!"

"John Cahill," came the voice over the bullhorn, "come out now, with your hands behind your head!"

All the windows in the church were stained glass, but there was a place just to the right of the door going out to the street where a small panel of an angel's wing had been replaced by a piece of clear glass. I walked down the center aisle and looked through the glass to survey the situation outside. Most of the congregation and much of the town had gathered, and all three squad cars of West Branch's finest were there, with blue lights flashing. Policemen were hunched down behind their cars with rifles and shotguns pointed at the church.

In the few seconds I watched, a news crew from the Columbus, Mississippi, CBS affiliate set up a camera tripod, the local anchor spoke to Chuck Wallace, who looked eager to tell his story. It was becoming an event out there.

I turned around and walked back toward the altar. John the Baptist Cahill was pacing in front of the altar rail in great agitation. He was talking to himself, with a full range of hand motions and exaggerated gestures. His black and white hair seemed to stream behind him whichever way he was aimed, a little comet tail following him with every step.

"John, there's a lot of people out there—police, church members, reporters—"

"Reporters!" This seemed to upset him the most. "What kind of reporters?"

"Well, they've set up a TV camera across the street . . ."

"Oh, no! No, no, no! Cap, you gotta help me! I don't want to be on TV! What if my mama's watching? I ain't told her I'm John the Baptist yet, see? That ain't the kind of thing you want your mama to find out on TV!"

"Well, no, I don't guess it is."

I felt sorry for him: all he wanted to do was start a reformation of the Church; he'd never meant for his mama to find out that he was John the Baptist.

"Look, John"—I pointed to a choir pew—"sit down, and let's think about this."

He sat down quickly, desperately compliant for the moment. I continued as gently as I could. "Okay. Now. I have to be sure about this part, John. You have to tell me the truth. Do you have a bomb?"

"No!"

"Can you swear you're telling me the truth?"

"I'll swear it on the Holy Bible!" He looked at the books in the pew racks around him, only to find hymnals and prayer books. There was a huge, heavy, ancient King James Version Bible at the lectern, but it was frail and in danger of coming apart; I figured I would probably be in enough trouble without contributing to the demise of the holy book of the parish. John said, "Bring me a Bible, and I'll swear on it."

I had Bibles in my office, of course, but I didn't want to leave him alone right then, and I wasn't sure if he'd recognize anything but the King James Version. I thought I could probably find one but didn't know exactly where it might be. I certainly didn't want to be rooting around for one while pressure from the police continued to mount. I said, "John, swear it on your wife. Swear to me on the love of your wife that you don't have a bomb in here."

He said, "I swear it on the Queen of the South, who shall rise in judgment with this generation—"

I interrupted him brutally; this was no time to slip into a recitation of biblical passages. "Can you swear to me on your honor as John the Baptist that you do not have a gun in here?"

He answered, "I swear it on my honor as John the Baptist, called to make straight the crooked places for—"

"Okay. I'm going to go out there and talk to the chief of police, and see if we can defuse the situation a little."

"I told you I don't have a bomb!"

"I know. I believe you. I meant I'm going to go see if I can get you out of here without going to jail or going on TV. Just sit right here, and I'll be back, okay?"

When I opened the door to the porch vestibule, the first person I saw was JoJo, who was under the porch roof, so that a lot of the crowd could see that the door had opened but couldn't tell if anybody had come out, or who it was. He grabbed me in a big bear hug, and some of the people behind him must have thought there was a struggle of some sort, judging by the reaction of the gathering crowd.

"You okay, Buddy?"

"Yeah, I'm fine—thanks, JoJo. I've got to talk to the police."

"You want me to go in and bring the crazy man out?"

I said, "No. But would you stand right here and make sure nobody else tries to get in?"

JoJo agreed to do that, and I went down the steps and across the street, looking for Lester Busby, chief of the West Branch Police Department.

I'd met Chief Busby a few years earlier, after I'd addressed the local Kiwanis Club prayer breakfast. He'd pointed out that I hadn't mentioned sin in my little speech, and went on to tell me that the reason our country was in such a terrible mess was because of liberal politicians and preachers who were afraid to talk about crime and sin. The conversation hadn't gone much further; it hadn't needed to. We'd both sized the other up fairly quickly and accurately, and both had decided neither of us needed to trouble the other any further.

Now it seemed the chief was the only one who could help me.

I saw him as I was crossing the street and headed for him, ignoring the various expressions of concern and curiosity and trying to avoid the television camera I was walking straight toward. I hoped Beulah would be in the crowd, but I didn't see her.

"Good morning, Chief." We shook hands, me cringing inwardly as he squeezed my hand with unnecessary manly vigor.

"Morning, Preacher. What kind of bomb does he have in there?"

"He doesn't have a bomb. He doesn't have a gun."

"But Mayor Wallace said—"

"The man inside the church is John Cahill. He has some mental issues, but I don't think he's dangerous. He wrote on those pieces of paper, on the church door there, that he is armed, but what he meant was that he is armed with the Word of God. He wrote that he is dangerous, but he was talking about being a danger to those who reject the coming of Christ."

The chief seemed disappointed but not quite ready to give up the drama of the moment. "What kind of danger?"

"Look, Chief—he's not a danger to anybody. He's just . . . sort of a nut. Sort of a religious nut."

"Who's that big black fella up there on the porch?"

"JoJo McCain. He's a member of the church, and a friend."

"A friend of the crazy man?"

"No, a friend of mine."

"A member of your church?"

"Yes sir. Sings in the choir."

"Your church choir?"

"Yes sir."

"I hear he's some kind of retard."

"No sir. He was raised like he had some kind of developmental disabilities, but he's probably just about as smart as either one of us."

"Watch it, son."

"Well, at least as smart as I am, anyway—maybe smarter."

"What's he doing over there?"

"Just making sure nobody tries to go in there."

"Why? You think this Cahill might hurt somebody?"

"No sir. I just think John is really agitated and needs to calm down. He's afraid of the police, afraid to go back to jail. And he doesn't want to be on television. I don't think anybody ought to go in there and try to force him to come out."

"Well, what do you want to do, then? Sweet-talk him out? Have a little singsong with him? Or are you just going to leave him in there?"

"I don't know. But this crowd's making it worse. Could you make them all go home?"

"No, we can keep them back, but this is a public street; they have every right to be here."

"Okay, I understand. I think yelling at him through the bullhorn really upsets him, too. Could you hold off on that a little?"

The chief looked at me for a moment, assessing me again. After a while, he nodded and said, "All right. We'll lay off the bullhorn."

"Thanks, Chief." I was doing a little reassessing, too. "Look, I'm going to go back in, see if I can—"

"Preacher, I can't let you go back in there. I don't know much about Mr. Cahill, but I know you ain't going back in that church until he is under restraint."

We argued about that for a while, without me getting anywhere. I assured him that I appreciated what he was trying to do, and that I wasn't trying to make his position more difficult. I assured him again that John Cahill was not armed, but I had to stop short of telling him that he'd sworn on the Queen of the South that he didn't have a bomb, and on his honor as John the Baptist that he didn't have a gun.

Our one-sided argument ended when Beulah took my arm and pulled me away. I resisted, but she reminded me of the wisdom of JoJo McCain: "You ought to know better than to get in a fight you know you ain't got no chance to win." As that sank in, she continued, "Look, Buddy—I've been to my office, and I have some information about John that you need to know."

She led me away from the crowd and the camera, and when we were alone, she pulled a piece of paper out of her jeans and began telling me the heartbreaking tale of John Earl Cahill.

"I looked in the state social work network records and found John Earl Cahill." She looked at her paper and continued, "He was born in 1948 in Egypt, Mississippi, the son of Earl and Elwina Cahill. He dropped out of high school to join the army, went through basic training—blah-blah-blah." She sorted through her printed material in search of pertinent information. "He went to Vietnam in 1968. He served as a helicopter mechanic for four years—blah-blah-blah— never got into any trouble—blah-blah-blah—and was honorably discharged in 1972.

"He came back to Chickasaw County and went to work for the Kansas City Southern Railway as a mechanic. He met and married Suellen Melinda Smithart at the First Baptist Church of Okolona,

Mississippi, in 1977—blah-blah—and they had their only child, Caroline, in 1979."

Somewhere about here, JoJo walked up and joined us. I said, "Hey. What's going on?"

JoJo said, "The police chief sent a man to get me off the vestibule, said it wasn't safe. I told him Preacher Buddy told me to stay right there, and he said he was telling me to leave, and that I'd either walk away now or I'd walk away in handcuffs. So I left and come over here."

"Okay, thanks. I don't think the police are going to let anybody in there anyway. Thanks, JoJo. You did good. Beulah's done some research and is filling me in on our friend John the Baptist."

JoJo growled, "He ain't no John the Baptist, that's his whole problem."

Beulah and I both nodded, and she went on. "According to the Chickasaw County file, he became a deacon in the church and taught Sunday school—blah-blah-blah. When Caroline was twelve she developed septicemia, which apparently started as a urinary tract infection and turned into sepsis. She was dead within a week. Gruesome details about fever, vomiting, confusion, elevated respiration—oh, Buddy! The hospital workers had to pry the child's body from her mother's arms—oh my Lord—and after the child was taken, the mother became belligerent and violent. The hospital staff was unable to get her under control, and the police were called in. They sedated her with injections—John Cahill was trying to defend his wife and struck an officer with a folding chair before being subdued by other officers on the scene."

"Did he just sort of . . . nudge the officer with a folding chair?"

"Well, no, he sort of . . . broke the officer's jaw and collarbone with a folding chair."

"Oh."

"Yeah. Both John and Suellen Cahill were referred for psych evaluations, and medication was recommended for her, which apparently she didn't like taking. The next entry for her has to do with breaking into the doctor's office with an aluminum softball bat and threatening the receptionist and several patients in the waiting room. Then—oh, y'all—she was taken to the Burnett Center in Hattiesburg, Mississippi, with a diagnosis and treatment for psychological and emotional trauma.

"It says here that John Cahill would not accept the agency's offer for him to go down to Hattiesburg with her, that he would not accept any money from—and this is a quote from his file—'this generation of vipers.'"

I said, "Oh, man. This explains a lot. The reality he saw was not what he wanted to see, so he transferred all that prophetic language in the Bible onto himself and became John the Baptist; his wife became the Queen of the South. It's mentioned by Jesus in an odd passage in Matthew somewhere. The only thing—"

"Aw, c'mon, Buddy—"

"No, wait, the only thing that could make it all right in John's mind was for Jesus to come back and sort out the wicked from the righteous, and so John Cahill became John the Baptist, to prepare the way. This is the deep, deep pain that he can never talk about, never understand, and never get past. 'They took her away, to where he could not follow, and she shall rise again in judgment with this generation.' Poor guy."

"Yeah, well," Beulah said, "right now that poor guy is occupying your church, and half of West Branch is wondering if this whole thing is going to come to a violent end." We stood there wondering the same thing for a few seconds, and then she said, "Buddy, you've got to do something."

"Chief Busby won't let me go back in there. I told John I'd be right back, but I can't."

JoJo said, "I can get you in."

Beulah and I were dumbfounded. "JoJo, the police aren't letting anybody in. Chief Busby told me—"

"Listen, Buddy, you know I cut Mrs. Caruthers's yard next door, she's real nice to me, brings me sweet tea on hot days."

"Yeah?"

"Well, one afternoon I got there and it was getting all cloudy. I had just started to cut her grass and it looked like it was about to come down in buckets. Mrs. Caruthers said I could put my mower in her little shed there and come back the next day. So I thanked her and put the mower up in there, and then it was like God had turned on the shower, comin' down in sheets, you know how the wind blows the rain like that sometimes?"

Beulah said, "Raining really hard."

"Really hard. So I was looking for something to sit down on in her little shed there, and found that there was a door out the back of the shed. Well, I was just a little snoopy for a minute there, not wantin' to get all up in her business but just wonderin' why a shed would have a back door, so I opened it, and what I found was another door."

He paused, waiting for us to make some response. Beulah said, "Another door?"

"That's right. So I opened it, too, and then I was lookin' into some kind of old room all full of old chairs and stuff. I was in that old storage closet off that old parish hall that we don't ever use anymore."

I asked, "In the church?"

"You know, in that old part of the church you said we must've outgrew forty or fifty years ago."

The parish had an old wing that was hardly ever used anymore, except by two Alcoholics Anonymous groups. For some reason, when they build a new, larger parish hall they had left the old one standing, even though they had no use for it; I guessed it would have cost money to demolish it. I knew that Mrs. Caruthers's house next door had been the church rectory at some point. Her lot and the church's lot had been one parcel of property. The shed had apparently been built so that its back wall was the wall of the church building, and somebody had thought it would be a good idea to have another way in and out of the parish hall. I hardly ever went into the old parish hall; we never used it for any of our events and it always smelled like cigarettes. The two AA groups who met there were well attended because we still let them smoke in the building.

Beulah was putting the pieces together faster than I could. "So we could get into the old parish hall through Mrs. Caruthers's shed."

"No," I said. "I could get in there. You can stay out here."

It has for many years been an undisputed fact of our relationship that I have never ever been able to tell Beulah Bayer Hinton what she can or can't do. The number of times I've tried it you could count on one hand; the number of times she's listened you could count with no fingers. So all three of us were surprised that I would even try it in this moment. She gave me a look just to acknowledge that I was being ridiculous, but otherwise ignored the attempt altogether and said, "JoJo, you better come with us, to show us how to get in." JoJo smiled and said, "Yes ma'am." At least as smart as I am. Maybe smarter.

26

A Hand Full of Spider

JoJo walked away. The crowd seemed to part for him to pass through. They were not so willing to let either Beulah or me leave, with everybody wanting to ask us what was going on. It took us a while to get far enough away from the gathering to be of no notice to anyone. Once we were sure nobody was looking at us anymore, we circled our way around towards Mrs. Caruthers's old shed.

JoJo was already inside, standing as sturdy and solid as a rock, just as he always was. Beulah squeezed my hand as she held it, supportive and challenging. I thought then how grateful I was for her love, her support, and her dedication to me, and for JoJo's unflagging steadiness in my life. Where would any of us be without the people who love us?

John Cahill had lost his daughter and his wife in a confused blur of grief and confusion, and the world could not remain the same for him.

Beulah and I ducked into the shed, and JoJo said, "This way, y'all." He opened the ancient, dilapidated wooden door to reveal another old wooden door on the other side. His big hand swept away some of the cobwebs and spider egg sacs before he opened the second door for Beulah to go through, and I followed.

The doorway opened into a small, crowded closet filled with old metal folding chairs, cardboard boxes of Sunday school materials from the sixties, bits and pieces of artificial Christmas trees, and other assorted flotsam and jetsam of a small parish that never wants to throw anything away because that might offend whoever made it or gave it, or their children, or their grandchildren.

JoJo made his way through that closet to open the door into the old parish hall, the musty, old-smelling air of the closet mixing and being replaced by air thick with stale cigarettes and countless cups of coffee in Styrofoam cups. Beulah said, "Y'all need to get this carpet cleaned, get some of this smell out of here." I thought about objecting, but I knew she was right: "Yes ma'am."

When we came into the nave, we saw John the Baptist Cahill up by the altar rail, consumed by his own agitation. He was pacing at full speed up and down between the altar and the choir pews, talking to himself with hand motions so vigorous and energetic and that I had to wrestle down the image of a plucked bird trying to take flight. It occurred to me that maybe his frail structure of biblical identity reassignment was colliding with the harsh reality of police and television cameras on the street outside.

Beulah whispered, "He's really worked up. Is he supposed to be on some sort of medication?"

I answered, "Yeah. He doesn't take it because it makes him feel stupid."

JoJo moaned, "Aw, man! He's really hurtin.'" Then, almost a whisper, "He's hurtin.'" Maybe he saw a familiar pattern of agitation, fear, and energy that brought his late brother Bobbo to mind. Beulah and I could see that John's pain was causing JoJo pain, and we watched in slow-motion horror as JoJo walked over to him, arms spread wide to engulf him in one of his locally famous overwhelming embraces.

I looked away from JoJo to glance over at John the Baptist Cahill, wondering what he thought as he saw what was approaching him like a large dark thunderstorm, and recognized terror in his eyes—the kind of panic you might see in a wild animal cornered or caged. JoJo, six inches taller and easily a hundred pounds heavier, advanced with all the inevitability of nightfall, and John was looking around wildly to see where he could run.

But there was no escape. As JoJo opened his arms to hug him, John tried to push him away. In the case of a resistible force meeting an immovable object, the outcome can only be predictable: John was pushed further back into the corner, trapped against the altar rail, and he became even more desperate. JoJo stepped closer, and John, ever more terrified, slapped him, hard. JoJo was stunned, John was frantic, and Beulah and I could only watch in a mix of helplessness, fascination, and dread for what might happen next.

JoJo lifted his hand to rub his left cheek, which was surely burning and stinging from the righteous slap of John the Baptist Cahill, and then leaned down a little, turning his big head to the left, and offered his right cheek. As I watched, I saw him close his eyes tight, fully expecting to be slapped again.

But John was not so lost that he didn't see and understand. When the expected slap did not come, JoJo opened his eyes to see John Cahill standing, eyes lifted to heaven, arms extended as a priest at the altar, evidently deep in prayer. Then John the Baptist said, "Behold the Lamb of God, which taketh away the sin of the world."

And he stepped into JoJo's open arms, felt himself fully embraced by the love of God, and wept like a small child.

Beulah breathed, "Wow," which was one word more than I could have come up with right then. I found her hand again, and we stood there taking in the moment together for a long time. I didn't know I was crying until she took my bandanna out of my back pocket to wipe the tears running down my face.

I said to her, "Okay. I'll go out and tell Chief Busby that John Cahill is ready to surrender."

She was instantly and diametrically opposed to the idea. "What? Why?"

"Well, I guess because that's what they're out there trying to do. Isn't that right? They need to arrest him."

"For what?"

"What?"

"I said, 'For what?' Has he broken the law somehow?"

"Aw, c'mon, Beulah—they think he's armed and dangerous!"

"We can't let him be arrested because of what they think!"

"What do you want me to do, tell Busby to just go away?"

"Would that do any good?"

"It wouldn't do any good at all!"

It was one of those moments when my wife and I agreed, and I still knew I was wrong. I took a step back, and in a moment I found something sensible to say: "What would you suggest?"

"You and JoJo stay here with John, and I'll go explain things to Chief Busby."

"Right. Okay."

She started to go back the way we'd come in, and I called after her: "Where are you going?"

"What—you want me to walk out the front door so everybody can wonder how we got into the church?"

"Well . . ."

Beulah walked back to me so she could explain without John Cahill hearing her. "Buddy, I'm going out through Mrs. Caruthers's shed; I'll come up behind Chief Busby and tell him what I found out. I'll make sure he understands that he doesn't want to arrest a crazy but completely innocent man on television, a man who's a grieving father and a Vietnam veteran, who's come to the church for sanctuary. I'll just have to keep explaining it until he understands how bad it looks, and remind him that he has an election coming up."

"When's the election?"

"Who knows? But these guys always have an election coming up." I leaned down to receive her kiss on my cheek, and she said, "Stay here. I'll try to bring Busby in through the garage."

I watched her leave, and then turned to see that JoJo and John were still standing there, rocking gently in their embrace. The sound of the door creaking closed broke the spell of the moment, at least enough for JoJo to look over at me, hoping I would do something to pry him out of the clutch of the small, crazy man clinging to him as if his life and sanity depended on it. And maybe, I thought, it did.

JoJo was clearly uncomfortable in his current predicament, beseeching me with his eyes to rescue him. I walked over and tapped John on the shoulder. He ignored me completely; his only response was to tighten his grasp on JoJo.

Now it was JoJo who was starting to feel trapped. I put my hand on John's shoulder and gently said, "John." There was no response, so I repeated, a little more loudly and a little less gently, "John."

His face was buried in JoJo's shirt, his nose pressed against the big man right around his collarbone. So his voice was muffled, but I heard him say, "What?"

I said, "John, let's sit down and talk a little. Let go of JoJo, and let's all go sit down."

Reluctantly, John patted JoJo's back, put his hands down by his side, and allowed me to lead him over to the choir stall. He sat on the old dark pew, and looked at me vaguely from what seemed like a great distance, measuring spiritually. I wondered where and when he was, and whether I could or should bring him closer to here and now. Before I could get a good start on working my way through all of that, JoJo said, "You okay, man?"

It seemed to me that John didn't want to speak or listen, but he recognized the voice of the Lamb of God and could not keep his silence. He murmured, "Yes." And then, when I thought he'd said all he was going to say, he continued, "I'm okay." JoJo and I were standing facing John; JoJo looked to me and nodded, putting the conversation in my hands. Then he brought two of the chairs the acolytes normally sit in so we wouldn't be looking down on John. JoJo was always sensitive to that sort of thing. We sat with John, not knowing what to say or how we could help.

I probed a little, carefully, knowing that I was near the deep source of his pain and hoping I could ease it some by naming it. "John, tell us about your daughter."

He sagged into himself, as if I'd taken the air out of his lungs and the strength from his bones. Then he took a deep breath, recovered as much as he could, and said, "Her name was Caroline. We called her Callie. She was . . . she was . . ."

A couple of the puzzle pieces fit together, and I said, "She was twelve, right? Like the daughter of Jairus."

"She was just twelve years old, just twelve. And she never did nothin' wrong, never hurt nobody. She didn't . . . ." He couldn't continue.

I said, "John, how did Callie die?" He took another deep, shuddering breath, and then said with surprising lucidity, "She came down with septicemia, a bacterial infection in the blood."

I realized that he was reciting lines he'd heard repeated, but this time, instead of selected verses from the King James Version, he was recounting words he'd hated to hear, from medical professionals in white coats and scrubs, words they had to repeat several times because he'd never wanted to hear them at all.

JoJo said, "Did it hurt?"

John closed his eyes, trying and failing to shut out the memory. "Yes. She was burnin' up with fever, and cried all night. Me and my . . . we stayed with her all night, but there wasn't really anything the doctors and nurses could do . . . nothin' me and . . . nothin' we could do but pray."

JoJo said, "Oh, man—I'm so sorry."

John turned to face me. "We couldn't do nothin' but pray, so that's what we did. We prayed all night, Cap, and in the mornin' she was . . . she was . . ."

He didn't want to say it, and I didn't want to force him, but I thought it had to be said, so I said it for him: "She was dead."

I stood up and sat beside John on the pew in the choir stall, thinking I could put my arm around him or try to comfort him somehow, but right then he wasn't interested in being comforted.

"We prayed all night! She never done nothin' to nobody! She was just a little girl, just twelve years old!" The agony of it came smoldering up from his soul, unearthed after having been hastily buried in hysterical, uncomprehending grief. "Why did she have to die, Cap? Just tell me that: why did God have to let her die?"

By this time I'd been ordained for eleven years. I'd sat with the dying, and told grieving families their loved ones had died. I'd comforted friends whose doctors had told them they only had a short amount of time to live. I'd gone to offer support and help pick through rubble to rescue photos and stuffed animals after two fires and a tornado had destroyed the homes of people I knew, and people I didn't know. I'd sat with old people ready to die who couldn't, and I'd done the funeral of an eight-year-girl named Nicole.

John's question was there in all those moments: "Why did God allow this terrible thing to happen?" I'd been looking for the answer It's a question that haunts us all, I suppose, if we're willing to ask it, a question about the nature of God and the world we live in, a question about life and death and fairness, and who we are to question God, and what all this is about anyway.

The honest answer is that I don't know.

The real answer is that this is a great mystery.

These answers are not adequate, and I couldn't bring myself to disappoint John Cahill, whose debilitating grief had finally been laid bare, by trying to answer in theological obscurities. Not for the first time, and not for the last, I didn't know what to say.

It is the anxiety of every preacher that she or he will stand in front of a group of people and not have anything to say; often we make up for it by saying two or three times as much as we need to. But now, when just a few words were really needed, I didn't have them. The thought tramped through my head as I tried to defend myself from my own inadequacy, *At least I had my sermon all planned out. If this wasn't happening, I'd have been ready. I would have known what to say if the situation was different.* And I suppose my mind took some comfort in that.

The sermon I'd intended to preach was about the thief who repented, the one who said, "Jesus, remember me when you come into your kingdom." It was part of the story from the Gospel of Luke appointed in the prayer book lectionary for Christ the King Sunday, and I had planned to talk about how Jesus on the cross was not our favorite vision of the kingship of Jesus. We'd rather talk about the miracles, about the raising of Lazarus or the feeding of thousands with a little bread and a few dried fish. We want to think about Jesus in terms of strength and success, not weak and certainly not dying.

As I sat there silently unwilling to admit that I didn't know why John's daughter Callie had died, as I was desperately thinking of something to say that was both honest and helpful, I imagined the soldiers mocking Jesus as he hung on the cross, as they came up to offer him sour wine and say, "If you are the king of the Jews, save yourself!" Save yourself, they said.

What kind of king is this, anyway? Why didn't Jesus save himself? Why did he suffer? Why do children die, why are there earthquakes and hurricanes, why are some people so damn mean all the damn time?

While I was chasing that ancient and elusive questing beast, JoJo saved us all. He said, "You know, I used to think about this all the time. I think Momma believed my brother Bobbo was . . . the way he was 'cause of somethin' she done, like God was punishing her for somethin', I never knew what. I s'pose God could punish us all if he had a mind to. But it don't make no sense for God to punish some of us for some things and not all of us like how we deserve. And your baby girl Callie"—he spoke with incredible tenderness—"she never done nothin' to deserve to die."

John moaned, "No, she didn't. But we prayed, and God didn't listen."

JoJo looked over at me and asked, "Is that right, Preacher Buddy?"

I said, "What?"

JoJo said, "You think God didn't listen?"

God didn't listen? "If you are the king of the Jews, save yourself." God wouldn't even save his own Son . . .

JoJo was asking for a little help, and reminding me who I am. I jumped in before I had all my thoughts in line, which is not usually a good idea.

I said, "No, I believe God is listening. Just because he doesn't fix everything doesn't mean he doesn't love us. If I know anything at all, I know that God loves us, all the time, no matter what."

"So why didn't he save my little Callie?"

It was the moment I dreaded, the moment I was most inadequate, the inevitable moment when I had to admit the terrible truth that I don't know.

John's head sagged onto his chest, his bleak despair palpable and radiating out from him into the choir stall around us. It stained the entire sanctuary, darkened the pulpit, and threatened to lap up against the altar. The altar, not just a table to remember a Last Supper so long ago but also a place of sacrifice, where blood was shed, a Body broken and offered. The altar, where Sunday after Sunday I stood proclaiming a faith I don't fully understand, inviting people to come and join in the mystery of faith . . . the mystery of faith—how did that part go again?

In the Book of Common Prayer, on page 363, the priest says, "Therefore we proclaim the mystery of faith," and then the priest and the people say together, "Christ has died. Christ is risen. Christ will come again."

There's a whole lot of theology in those three sentences, a whole lot to wonder about, a whole lot to argue about if you enjoy that sort of thing. Why did Jesus have to die? How is it possible that someone who'd died could come back to life? And what do we mean when we say Jesus will come back? The mystery of faith has been proclaimed but not fully understood for centuries. But Jesus at the Last Supper with his friends and disciples said he was giving his life for them and for us, and that we are to do this in remembrance, that we are to remember, and celebrate, and give thanks. We can't understand a mystery, or it's not a mystery anymore. We can't understand what can't be understood, any more than we can count or measure eternity; we just can't do what just can't be done.

I suppose I got a little lost in all of this for a moment; JoJo must have thought I'd fallen asleep. He said, "Buddy?"

"I don't know why Callie died," I told them. "I don't know that much about medicine or bacterial infections. Every living thing must die, and sometimes it seems like life is too short. Other times it seems like death doesn't come quickly enough. But we're not in charge. We just take what we are given and try to be faithful and thankful."

"You want me to be thankful that God let Callie die?"

"No. Of course not. But I do want you to be faithful enough to trust that God loves Callie, and you, and your wife, no matter what."

John the Baptist Cahill put his head on his knees, with his hands clasped behind it, trying to make the pain in his soul go away. I was failing him—doing the best I could, but still failing. I said, "Look, John. I don't understand all this stuff. Nobody does. It's a mystery, just as it has to be."

Just then the Lord appointed a spider to sit down beside us.

I do not like spiders; even though I recognize that they are important cogs in the larger machine, I think they're creepy. This one wasn't especially large and didn't look particularly threatening. It was a brown spider, unremarkable except for its timing. In the moment I was ready to launch into an explanation of why mysteries can't be explained, this spider came rappelling down from the chancel light that hung from the ceiling, lowering itself on its thin silken line, and it looked like it would have gotten all the way to the top of John's head until JoJo intercepted it, trying to catch it on the order of worship from the previous week.

The spider scrambled away, scurrying for its life, and leaped off the paper in JoJo's hand to land on John's leg. I started to hit it with a prayer book but didn't want to assault John with the Book of Common Prayer, and JoJo said, "Don't kill it!" Then he reached down and caught it in his hand. As I watched him, shuddering at the thought of holding an icky spider in my bare hand, JoJo stood and said, "I'll just put this little guy outside."

He walked down the aisle and opened the door before I could think what that might mean, and when he did there were flashbulbs and people shouting questions. JoJo gave them an awkward little wave with a hand full of spider, and I saw him open his fingers to toss it aside. He closed the door and came back up the aisle and sat in the chair facing us as if nothing had happened.

I looked at John and JoJo with a newfound smile on my face. I said, "Look, John—I don't understand why Callie died so young. I don't understand a lot of the things we say in church. I don't understand why God loves us the way he does. I really do believe that God loves us, you and me and JoJo—all of us, all the time—and that's about the best I can do. I believe that God hurts when we hurt, and that he is here with us every single day, every single moment.

"But we don't understand. We can't understand God. We keep thinking that God is like us, only bigger and older and more powerful. He's not. He's not even a he, really.

"A few minutes ago JoJo caught that spider so he could let it go. It was a kind and beautiful thing for JoJo to do. But the spider didn't know that. I don't really know what a spider knows, or how a spider thinks, but you could see that it was trying to get away. It didn't know JoJo was trying to help—how could a spider know that? All it saw was a big hand coming for it, so it ran as fast as it could. But the hand was coming to help, see?

"Us trying to understand God is like that spider trying to understand JoJo. But for us, people like us created in the image of God, we have the ability to trust God if we choose to. We can't understand, but we can trust. And if we can trust God, we can have faith, and hope—hope for ourselves and those we love. Or, if we choose not to trust, we live in fear and darkness and despair."

My dear friend JoJo said, "What in the world are you talking about?"

I almost laughed with the clarity of it all. "We can't understand God any more than that spider could understand you, JoJo. All you were trying to do was to help, but it thought you were trying to kill it."

"You was gonna kill it."

"Yes. I know. But you had mercy, even on a spider. God is more like you than me, I think. God has mercy, even on people like you and me."

John the Baptist Cahill had looked up at some point during this line of conversation. "So did God take our little Callie because he needed another precious blossom in his heavenly garden?"

JoJo and I looked at each other before saying together, "What?"

"That's what the preacher said. That's what Brother Jimmy said, up at the First Baptist Church of Okolona. That's where we used to go to church and all."

JoJo said, "Tell him that one about how old Saul was."

"What?"

"You know," JoJo persisted, "in the Bible study when Miss Katherine peed on herself. 'Bout how Saul was thirty or forty years old and was king for some amount of time."

I guess he was zigging while I was trying to zag; I couldn't bring to mind what he was talking about. So he told John himself. "Look, back in the Old Testament, they was tellin' a story 'bout ol' King Saul—I don't know 'bout chapters and verses—and one Bible said he was thirty years old, and another said he was forty, and another just left it blank 'cause they don't really know.

"It don't much matter 'bout ol' Saul, really, but the thing I want you to know is that a lot of times we'd just say somethin' to have somethin' to say, even if it's wrong. It's like Preacher Buddy says, a lot of folks would ruther be wrong than to say they don't know. Like that preacher up in Okolona saying all that baloney 'bout God needin' another flower up in heaven, just sayin' somethin' to have somethin' to say. He just wanted to have somethin' to say so he didn't have to say he don't know."

I was amazed that JoJo remembered this. I suppose he must have heard me telling Beulah about it. "John," I said, "I don't have all the answers. There's a lot that I don't understand. But I'm not going to say something just because I'm afraid to say I don't know. We can't understand God, any more than that spider could understood JoJo. All we can do is trust that God is doing what's best for us. When Callie died, you have to know it was a wonderful moment for her, an end to her suffering. It was a terrible time for you and your wife, but it was a glorious thing for her to leave all the pain behind and be welcomed into heaven."

We sat there in silence for a long moment, until John said, "Yeah, it didn't really make much sense to think God needed another flower and all."

Then, just when I was thinking we might be finding our way out of the mental logjam we'd been tangled in, John was shaken by a sob he must have felt down to his toes, and he whispered, "But I need to know." JoJo and I looked at each other helplessly, and John turned his eyes toward me and moaned, "Cap, I need to know."

I was about to launch into a long diatribe about how needing to know is really about needing to be in control, but JoJo said, "It ain't faith if you know. Faith is when you can't know."

There was a long, still moment while we all thought about that, and then we heard the door open, and my sweet Beulah walked in, followed by Chief of Police Lester Busby.

TIME FOR CHURCH!

Beulah and the chief had worked it all out. Or perhaps it would be more accurate to say that Beulah had it worked out and Chief Busby was smart enough to know when to agree. Actually, as it turns out, Beulah had by some coincidence—if you believe in that sort of thing—played bunko with a group of friends from the courthouse where the social work office was, and become good friends with the chief's daughter Julie Anne, who worked in the Circuit Court judge's office. Julie Anne was standing in the crowd to see what was going to happen, and when Beulah explained the whole thing to her, the two of them went and explained it to the chief in a way that he could not fail to understand.

Beulah and the chief came in, and when John saw the uniform, he began to back away in fear. JoJo stepped in front of him to protect him, eclipsing him from view altogether, which made the chief a little more cautious. He put his hand on his gun, and I moved toward him. "Chief Busby," I said, "welcome to the Church of the Holy Incarnation. I want you to meet a couple of friends of mine: this is JoJo McCain, and behind him is John the Baptist Cahill." JoJo turned aside so John could see the chief, and I stepped aside to let Busby see John—it was like introducing cats to each other, both of them leery and suspicious and ready to fight or run.

"John, this is Chief Busby of the West Branch Police Department. My wife, Beulah, has explained to him what's going on here, that you're not going to hurt anybody. We're going to see if we can get us all out of this without anybody getting hurt or going to jail." With this last part, I looked past Chief Busby to Beulah to see if I was telling John the truth, and she nodded her reassurance.

Then she said, "John, Chief Busby is a Christian man— a Baptist, like you are. His job is to serve and protect the people of West Branch, including you and me and Buddy and JoJo. I told him about Caroline and Suellen, about how hard that's been on you. I told him you're a good man, just trying to do what God wants you to do. The chief and I talked about it for a while, and agreed that this is not where you need to be." John let his head droop down on his chest, and Beulah continued.

"You need to be with your wife, down in Hattiesburg." His head came up sharply then. "John, Suellen needs you. She needs her husband. I've talked with the people down there, and they would be glad for you to come and stay there, with her." John looked at JoJo and then at me, with the beginnings of hope in his eyes.

"Chief Busby talked to Sheriff Avant," Beulah continued, "and he said he's got somebody who can take you down there. We can take you out the back way, like I just came in. You won't be arrested, you won't be on television, and all those people out there won't even know you've left until you're gone."

There was a lengthy pause, as a very confused man tried to sort through the whispers in his mind: whispers of doubt, fear, anger, duty, and the unlikely possibility of escaping the impossible moment in which he found himself. After a long while, after Beulah and I had both started to say something and decided not to, he said, "Okay. I'll go to Hattiesburg."

Everybody exhaled their relief, and then John looked at me and said, "I'll go beyond the horizon, if you'll come with me." My first thought was that I should be cautious about this, but all I had to do was look at Beulah, who nodded, before I answered, "I'll be glad to."

We all agreed that John would go with Beulah, JoJo, and the chief through Mrs. Caruthers's shed to Sheriff Avant's office. Busby said it would be a while before the sheriff's deputy would be ready to go, and I asked him what time it was—11:05 am. We'd missed the early service altogether, but if I hurried I could manage to be just a little late for the 11:00 service. As it happened, there was a big congregation waiting outside just across the street. I told John he was going to be okay, that I would see him in a little while, and then I went to my office to put on my vestments.

As I tied the knots on my cincture, I noticed that my hands were shaking. I felt like I should sit down for a minute, but we were already late starting the service, and I was afraid that if I sat, it might be a while before I got back up. I almost opened the door near my office out to the street but realized it would be a much more theatrical entrance if I came through the front doors of the church that everybody was already looking at, so I went back into the nave, took a deep breath, and swung both doors open.

Everybody wanted to know what was happening, where the crazy dangerous man was, if there was a bomb, was I okay, had anyone been hurt, did he really think he was John the Baptist—everybody asked all their questions at the same time so I couldn't possibly have heard or answered all of them. I opened my arms wide, and the crowd fell completely silent.

I could have told everybody what had happened, but I was concerned that the cameras and some of the people would chase the story to the sheriff's office. And, to be honest, I wanted as many people as I could get to come inside and worship with us. So I opened my arms, waited for everybody to be quiet, and projected as loudly as I could: "Friends and neighbors, it's time for church!" It was on the evening news: Episcopal priest invites city of West Branch to worship after bomb scare.

The Episcopalians started moving without hesitation toward the steps where I stood, but other folks from other churches didn't really know what to do. I left them deciding between curiosity and denominational loyalty and went to the sacristy to start setting up the altar for our larger service. Sally, my friend and our organist, found me there and hugged me, asking, "Buddy, are you all right?"

I assured her that I was, and she asked if everything would be normal in the service. I knew that right then, normal was an absurd thought. But for the purposes of playing the organ, nothing had changed, so I said, "Yes ma'am. I'm hoping we might have a few visitors, though."

One of the reporters came and started asking me what happened. I told her I would talk to her after the service, and that she and her camera operator were welcome to join us without their camera. "No photos, no filming during the service." She rolled her eyes and started to protest, but I told her this was not negotiable, and if she couldn't go along with my wishes she'd have to wait until after the service. She didn't like it, but she went to talk to the camera guy, who must've put the camera back in their van; at least he didn't have it when he came up for Communion.

The choir came together, the acolytes showed up, the ushers asked people to share bulletins until we ran out altogether. The Church of the Holy Incarnation was completely overrun by people who'd never been inside the building. Everybody did the best they could to find a place to sit; the ushers asked for help to bring in more chairs down the center aisle and along the two aisles on the sides, until we ran out of chairs too, and people had to stand.

My friend Ward said, "We're stuffed in here like Vienna sausages in a can—I hope you've got a hell of a sermon this morning."

Oh, yeah. The sermon. I tried to remember what I'd been planning to say, and vaguely wondered if any of that still applied. I answered, "Me, too."

Sally ended the prelude and started the first hymn. I was just trying to make it up the aisle without wobbling.

> Though with a scornful wonder men see her sore oppressed,
> by schisms rent asunder, by heresies distressed,
> yet saints their watch are keeping; their cry goes up, "How long?"
> and soon the night of weeping shall be the morn of song.

When the choir and everybody in the procession was pretty much settled, I welcomed the congregation and told them our service was found in the Book of Common Prayer, the red book in the pews, and that we would start on page 355. Some people picked up a book but many didn't. I said again, "Page 355," like I really meant it, and a few more people found a prayer book and went to that page. The service was fairly close to normal for a minute or two, until we came to the psalm appointed for that day—Psalm 46, which we read responsively, by half verse:

> God is our refuge and strength,
>   a very present help in trouble.
> Therefore we will not fear, though the earth be moved,
>   and though the mountains be toppled
>   into the depths of the sea.
> Though its waters rage and foam,
>   and though the mountains tremble at its tumult
> The LORD of hosts is with us;
>   the God of Jacob is our stronghold.

It wasn't the psalm that was unusual, or the way we read it. What was unusual was how appropriate it felt to the moment, and how it seemed like most of the people gathered there were paying attention to what we were saying as it we'd never seen it before: "Therefore we will not fear, though the earth be moved . . . . The LORD of hosts is with us."

I read the Gospel passage appointed for that day, Luke's account of Jesus being crucified between two thieves. It always strikes me as an odd statement for the Church to make, reading that story on the day when we are celebrating Christ the King on the last Sunday of the church year, just before we begin the season of Advent and start the whole cycle all over again. Jesus is King not because of strength or power but in humility and vulnerability.

As I stood in the middle of the biggest crowd that church has ever had and read the Gospel passage, I heard it like I'd never heard it before: Jesus being nailed to the cross between two criminals, praying for those who drove in the nails, the leaders of the synagogue jeering, the Roman soldiers bringing him sour wine, one of the criminals pleading that he save them all.

The reading ended, and the congregation sat and waited for me to start the sermon. I looked at them and wished I had a sermon prepared for a moment like that, but of course that was impossible. Who could ever have been ready to come to work one Sunday morning and find that John the Baptist had tacked ninety-five theses to the front door of the parish, so that the police and the media would be alerted and half the town would be part of the experience, even coming to church and waiting for the priest to say something intelligent and appropriate to that moment?

I started the sermon like I'd started every sermon, by crossing myself and saying, "In the Name of God: Father, Son and Holy Spirit, Amen. Please be seated."

They sat, and I preached. More on that later.

After the sermon we continued with the service just like we did every week: the Creed, the Prayers, the Confession and Absolution, and the Peace. I remember inviting the people to come to Communion and telling them how we do it; I remember telling them it's real wine, not grape juice; I remember telling them that they were all welcome but that none of them had to come up. And I remember thinking that it was taking a long time to give the people the bread and wine; it seemed like everybody there was coming up for Communion. After the service ended, it seemed like it took an extraordinarily long time for the people to leave the nave.

I was tired and ready to get to the sheriff's office, so I wasn't paying as much attention as I should have, but I remember people saying nice things to me, complimenting me on my sermon.

I saw Kate and Chuck talking together, and watched as they left through the sacristy door without saying anything to me at all.

Finally, the last person left, leaving only my friend Ward, who often stayed behind to help me lock the doors and turn off all the lights. Usually he had something to discuss that came from the sermon or one of the Bible readings. Some months before, we'd both thought the other had turned off the coffee pot, which had continued to cook the last little bit at the bottom until I found it the next morning—the hardened paste looked like something you could use to patch a roof. Since then, almost every Sunday we'd met outside the office, both of us saying, "You check the coffee pot?" and then both of us nodding that we had.

After we had observed that last ritual of the day, I said, thinking to head off the weekly theological discussion that we both enjoyed, "Thanks, Ward. I've gotta go to the sheriff's office and ride down to Hattiesburg with John the Baptist."

"Right now?"

"Yeah boy."

"You've gotta be exhausted!"

"Well, yeah—I'm tired. But I'm not driving. I'm just riding along."

"They couldn't wait until tomorrow?"

"No, it's part of the deal we made with John, that we'd take him to be with his wife in Hattiesburg."

"Aw, man—that stinks for you, huh?"

"Yeah. But it'll be good to get him back with his wife."

I locked up the parish, Ward and I walked to the sheriff's department, just a couple of streets over. We walked in and saw Beulah and JoJo sitting in the waiting area in little plastic stackable chairs, Beulah looking like she was in command of the situation and JoJo sitting as lightly as he could, probably worried that the little chair holding him up was going to break apart at any moment.

Beulah stood and gave me a much-needed hug, then asked the same question she always asked when she wasn't there to hear the sermon: "Did you preach it good?"

Usually I'd tell her what I thought: that it had gone well, that it sagged a little in the middle, that I wandered around a little before figuring out what I was trying to say, or sometimes, rarely, that it had been magical. But right then, I had to admit to her that I didn't know. It was an odd thing, but I couldn't remember what I'd said just an hour before. I said, "I hope so. I think I talked about John the Baptist."

Ward said, "Aw, Beulah—you should've been there. He nailed it. You should've seen the people in there. They'd never heard anything like that. He preached the hell out of it!"

Beulah looked at me, wondering what was going on, before murmuring, "I'm sorry I missed it."

I was uncomfortable with this line of conversation and with not being able to remember what I'd said, so I asked where John was, and Beulah informed me that Sheriff Avant's policy was that a prisoner being transported in a Sheriff's Department vehicle first had to take a shower and be dressed in clean clothing. There had apparently been some difficulty about what John would be re-clothed in, as he was not at all willing to be dressed in an orange jumpsuit, and the people in the sheriff's office were apparently not interested in washing his dirty jeans or in waiting for them to dry.

It was looking for all the world to be a impasse until Beulah offered to go to Walmart to buy him another pair of jeans, some underwear, and a T-shirt, which seemed to placate everybody.

So in a few minutes, John the Baptist Cahill came out to join us, resplendent in his brand-new duds and freshly shaved and scrubbed, carrying a black garbage bag of his dirty clothes. He seemed happier than I'd ever seen him, on his way to be reunited with his wife, going to see the Queen of the South.

I told John he looked good, and he didn't know what to do with that. Beulah was telling him that Suellen would be so glad to see him when the deputy came in, motioning us to come with her.

She was a young African-American woman and clearly wanted us all to know that she was not happy to being the one who had to take John to Hattiesburg. She didn't look at any of us, but led us down a hallway to the dusty brown Ford Crown Victoria squad car, opened the door into the back seat, got in, and started the engine without a word. I got the distinct feeling that she had drawn the short straw or lost a bet or had the least seniority; whatever the reason, she was displeased about pulling this particular duty.

John knew what to do; he got in the back seat. But I wasn't sure where I was supposed to sit. I decided I'd probably be most useful if I sat in the back with John, but as I walked around the car and reached for the door handle I heard the locks click closed. When I opened the front door the officer told me, not looking at me but straight ahead, that it was against policy for anyone to sit in the back with the prisoner. I told her he wasn't a prisoner, but she said, "It don't matter. It's policy. You got to sit up here with me."

So I opened the door to sit up there with her, and hugged Beulah. JoJo put something in the pocket of my clergy shirt, saying, "Give this to John when you get down there." Then, all I could do was wave to Beulah and JoJo as we started the journey to Hattiesburg, beyond the horizon.

28

The Queen of the South

Sometimes you sit with friends or loved ones and the silence is comfortable, so that nobody feels the need to speak. This was not one of those times. John was fidgety in the back seat, and with the black nylon wire mesh separating him from the deputy and me, I imagined that he must have felt like he was in a cage.

I said, "You okay back there, John?"

He was excited and ready to go; he had slipped back into full John the Baptist mode. His hands were flailing as he muttered to himself, "I indeed baptize you with water unto repentance: but he that cometh after me is mightier than I, whose shoes I am not worthy to bear: he shall baptize you with the Holy Ghost, and with fire . . . ."

I looked at our unspeaking driver to gauge her reaction: she wasn't surprised. I guessed she'd heard from the sheriff that her passenger was a religious nut of some sort. I thought about trying to explain some of this to her, but she didn't seem interested, and I wasn't sure I had enough time, figuring we only had about two hundred miles to go. So, hoping to change the subject and to remind John that he had something to look forward to, I said, "We're on our way now, John—on our way to see the Queen of the South."

The deputy glanced at me, probably wondering if I was a religious nut, too.

John quoted, "The Queen of the South shall rise up in the judgment with the men of this generation, and condemn them: for she came from the utmost parts of the earth to hear the wisdom of Solomon; and, behold, a greater than Solomon is here."

At this I noticed our driver look back in her rearview mirror, and when she risked another quick glance at me, I said, as naturally and normally as I could, trying to get us all on the same page: "It's all right. This is John the Baptist Cahill, and his wife, Suellen, is the Queen of the South. She's in Hattiesburg, so we're taking John there, because she needs him."

The officer was trying to be inscrutable, but she had an expressive face and I have an active imagination: I watched her working through the mix of sacred and secular, and tried to imagine what she knew about John the Baptist from the Bible. Maybe she'd read one of the passages about the Queen of the South in the Gospel of Matthew or Luke.

I said, "John, make yourself as comfortable as you can back there—we've got about three and a half hours to go."

Whereupon he did reply, "Behold, I send my messenger before thy face, which shall prepare thy way before thee. The voice of one crying in the wilderness, Prepare ye the way of the Lord, make his paths straight."

I said, "Yes sir, we've got some wilderness to go through. So make yourself comfortable."

We rode for a while, and I watched the miles go by: south to Egypt, then through West Point, and past Mayhew Junction—the Crossroads where students from Mississippi State had for many years come to share a pitcher of beer or two, and maybe meet a girl from Mississippi State College for Women in Columbus. (I'd taken a date to one of the bars there when I was in college; she'd been scandalized that there were condom machines in the women's bathroom. It was a high-class place.)

John was still muttering to himself, his hands flapping in gestures with no meaning to anyone but himself. The more we bumped along south, the more animated he got. I remembered Beulah asking about medications when he was so agitated in the church and realized we could be in some real trouble if he kept getting more anxious and nervous. All I could do from the front seat was talk to him, and listen.

I said, "John, tell me about your wife."

"The Queen of the South shall rise up in the judgment with the men of this generation, and condemn them: for she came from the utmost parts of the earth to hear the wisdom of Solomon; and, behold, a greater than Solomon is here."

"Tell me her name."

There was a pause, and then he continued in a more subdued voice, "The men of Nineve shall rise up in the judgment with this generation, and shall condemn it: for they repented at the preaching of Jonas; and, behold, a greater than Jonas is here."

I thought this wasn't getting us anywhere, but our driver said, almost to herself, "No man, when he hath lighted a candle, putteth it in a secret place, neither under a bushel, but on a candlestick, that they which come in may see the light."

Now I was the one who was lost, and I looked over to her for some explanation. She kept her eyes on the road but said, "That's the next verse. Luke eleven, starting around verse thirty-two."

I said, "Thanks."

She said, "I thought you were a preacher."

"I am. I just don't know the Bible all that well."

Now she frowned at me. I shrugged.

John picked it up from there: "The light of the body is the eye: therefore when thine eye is single, thy whole body also is full of light; but when thine eye is evil, thy body also is full of darkness. Take heed therefore that the light which is in thee be not darkness."

"John," I said, "tell me about Suellen."

"The Queen of the South shall rise up in the judgment—"

I interrupted him, thinking it would be better to talk about things more immediate. "Where is she from?"

"She came from the utmost parts of the earth to hear the wisdom of Solomon; and, behold—"

"Was she born in Mississippi?"

"No, Houma."

I said, "Houma, Louisiana?"

"Yeah, Houma—the utmost parts of the earth."

Actually, I'd gone close by Houma, Louisiana, a few times when I was a kid, when the family went to my great-uncle's fishing house on Grand Isle, a couple of hours south of New Orleans, deep in Cajun country. It always seemed like the utmost part of the earth getting there, but it was like a piece of heaven when we were fishing in the Gulf.

I said, "My family used to go to Grand Isle—my uncle had a place down there."

John said, in a voice that signaled the storm had passed, "Good fishin' down there, mackerel and speckled trout and all." I noticed he put his hands in his lap.

I told him that my Uncle Bennie used to take us out into the Gulf and tie up on an oil rig to fish for speckled trout. John seemed somewhat soothed to be talking about something else, so I told him how one time my brother Lee had hooked something big—Uncle Bennie said it might have been a grouper or a drum—but the line had snapped before we ever saw it. I told him about the time I'd caught some sort of fish Uncle Bennie said was worthless, and that he'd gutted it with his knife and thrown it overboard, "just to let 'em know there's something to eat up here," and how my brother claimed he saw a shark fin slicing through the water. He was always telling me he'd seen things I didn't see, so I didn't believe him, but it made a good story, and I was just trying to keep talking, just to keep John calm.

I told him about catching crabs in a trap and how Uncle Bennie's wife, Delia, cooked them in a big pot out behind their house because the spices were so strong you could hardly breathe if you were anywhere close, and about trying to learn how to play bridge in the evening because there was nothing else to do.

I told him about the time Uncle Bennie had gotten a friend of his to take Lee and me out on his shrimp boat, and made sure that we were standing barefoot on the deck when the net released the catch: thousands of squirming, flapping shrimp, some squid, an octopus or two, a few unlucky fish, and assorted bits of debris from the bottom of the Gulf of Mexico. That night it had taken some convincing to talk me into eating boiled shrimp—some convincing and Aunt Delia agreeing to make special cocktail sauce just for me without so much horseradish and Tabasco. The punch line to the story, which I decided it would be best to leave out as we rolled down Highway 45, is Uncle Bennie complaining about the mild sauce, "That damn hot sauce is why God gives us beer!" to my brother and me, both of us well below the legal drinking age, even in Louisiana.

I asked John if he liked shrimp, and he said, "Fried." I looked at the deputy, who subtly shook her head—either she didn't like shrimp or she didn't want to be part of the conversation.

I think I was talking about the time we fished near a small, sandy island and my cousin Joe caught a nurse shark when the deputy pulled us into a little gas station. She got out without a word and closed the door. I said, "Hold on, John. I'll be right back."

To the deputy I said, "Is everything all right?"

"Yeah, just need some gas." Then, as I was thinking how to say what I wanted to say, she said, "You gonna talk all the way down to Hattiesburg?"

"I'm trying to keep him calm. He gets all riled up pretty easy."

For the first time, it looked like I had said something she was interested in. "Does he ever get violent?"

I told her I didn't know, but I didn't think so. Then I told her about John going down the aisle at First Baptist, being restrained by ushers and deacons until the police arrived. She asked, "Why'd he wanna do that?"

"He really believes . . . sometimes he thinks he is John the Baptist from the Bible. He was preparing the way of the Lord."

"Oh. Is he crazy or something?"

"Yeah, you know, I wonder about that, too. And I wonder what we would have said if we were there when John the Baptist came out of the wilderness. Was he crazy?"

"No! He was . . . he was doing the will of the Lord."

"He was eating bugs and wild honey. He was wearing stinky animal skins for his clothes. That seems kinda crazy, doesn't it?"

"Well, that's different."

"Why? Because that was then and this is now?"

She almost said something but decided not to. The pump clicked off, and she had to go into the station to pay. She said, "Stay with the . . . stay with the passenger."

She walked into the store and I asked John if he wanted anything to eat or drink. He said he'd take a Co-Cola and some Nabs, a package of crackers with cheese or peanut butter. I waited for the deputy to come back to the squad car and told her I was going to get John something, and asked if I could get anything for her. She said, "The sheriff's office ain't payin' for any of this, you know." I told her that I was paying; she considered that for a moment, and then said she be glad to have a Dr. Pepper and some peanuts.

We rode in silence for a while after that, enjoying our goodies and letting the miles slide by: through Brooksville, past Shuqualak and Scooba, and through Electric Mills. Somewhere around Lauderdale, I woke up and realized that John had fallen sleep, too.

I whispered, "Where are we?"

"Gettin' close to Meridian, where we'll pick up the interstate right into Hattiesburg." It was midafternoon by now, the sun making its way to the horizon off to our right. Sensitive to her concern that I might talk all the way to Hattiesburg, I rode in silence. I took my clerical collar off and put it on the dashboard.

After a while, she said, "Where do you preach?"

"The Episcopal Church of the Holy Incarnation."

"Is that a Christian church?"

"Yes ma'am." Another mile or two passed by, and I said, "It's the church where our friend John back there was . . . where he was this morning, when people thought he was armed and dangerous."

"Was he?"

"No. He was just . . . well, I guess he was just trying to do what he thought God wanted him to do, in his own mixed-up way."

"I heard he had a bomb in there."

"No, no bomb. No guns. Just a lot of pain."

"Whose pain?"

So I told her, as quietly as I could, about their little girl who'd died, and how they'd prayed; how his wife lost her sanity and had to be institutionalized, and how he'd been lost in grief and sadness and betrayal and loneliness so that he decided it had to be time for Jesus to come back and make it all right, and that he was called to be the voice crying in the wilderness. I told her about the model train set, and how that didn't make any sense to me at all, and that I didn't understand what the Queen of the South had to do with any of it.

"Well," she said, "maybe if he was somebody from the Bible he figured she'd have to be someone from the Bible, too." And that's about all the sense I ever did make out of it.

I must've fallen asleep again; the deputy woke me when we were coming into the hospital parking lot. We all got out, John carrying his garbage bag, me putting my collar back on, and went in. The security guard by the front desk was waiting for us. There were some papers for the deputy to sign, and then we headed back to the ward where Suellen Cahill was waiting, unaware. John was docile, intimidated by the sterile institution.

We came to some locked double doors with the words, "No Unauthorized Personnel beyond this Point," and the security guard stopped the deputy and me, saying, "End of the line." Then he pressed the automatic switch, and the door swung open slowly. The guard took John by the arm and would have led him away, but I remembered that JoJo had given me something for him. I mustered up all the authority I could imagine myself having, and said, "Wait a minute." They stopped, and I stepped in front of John, pulled out a twenty-dollar bill, and gave it to him. "This is from JoJo, all right?"

He took it gravely, and said, "Thank the Lord." Before I could even wonder what he meant, I put my hand around the back of his neck and said, "The Lord bless you and keep you, and make his face shine upon you." The automatic door started to close, and there was a pause as we all wondered what was supposed to happen next. I said, "Go in peace, to love and serve the Lord."

The guard said, "Amen," and pressed the switch to open the door again. I stood watching through the doorway as he led John into a large room with eight beds, four on each wall. The second bed on the left was occupied by a woman who was sitting up and looking straight ahead without apparently knowing or noticing anything; John went right to her and sat in a chair beside the bed, and took her hand.

As the door closed I saw him talking to her quietly, his hands moving, but much more slowly. Just before the door came completely shut, I think she turned to him, with just a hint of a smile starting to blossom on her face. It might have been my imagination, or what I really wanted and needed to see, but I believe she smiled.

If I'd known I was living a novel, I would have had an engagingly deep theological conversation with the deputy all the way home. But real life is disappointing sometimes; I slept most of the way, except when we stopped at a Western Sizzlin' outside of Meridian for supper.

It was an all-you-can-eat buffet-style restaurant; I hadn't realized how hungry I was until we came in and I smelled the enticing aroma of all the goodies. All I'd had that day was two grape Pop Tarts and a cup of coffee before coming to the church that morning, and then a Mountain Dew and a pack of Nabs on the way down to Hattiesburg. The deputy and I got our plates and started grazing on the buffet line. I wound up with several pieces of fried chicken, black-eyed peas, and turnip greens.

We sat down and I was about to start eating when I realized the deputy was looking at me expectantly. I put my fork down and said a brief blessing, then looked up to see her nod her approval.

After a while she said, "You really a preacher?"

"Yes ma'am."

"But you weren't gonna say a blessing?"

"Well, I—thank you for reminding me. Even preachers need reminding sometimes."

"I've never seen no preacher like you before."

"Is that a good thing?"

"I ain't sure."

I asked how long she'd been with the Sheriff's Department, and she told me she'd been there for about eighteen months. She said she'd moved to Detroit to live with an aunt to finish high school up there, and had been in the police academy when her mama got sick, so she'd moved back home and gotten a job with the sheriff's department.

"You like it?"

"Most of the time. Sometimes it's boring, waiting around for something to happen; sometimes it's like, crazy—drunks and rednecks shootin' at each other in bars, husbands and wives fightin' and cussin', and we're all up in the middle of all of it trying to keep the peace between people who ain't interested in bein' peaceful." She thought about it for a few seconds and concluded, "It goes between boring and scary."

"Which is better?"

"Scary."

We ate in silence for a minute, and then I asked, "How's your mama?"

She didn't look up. "She passed, about three months ago. I tucked her into bed, and when I woke up next mornin', she was gone."

I said, "I'm sorry." Then I added, "Still, that's not a bad way to go, you know? Tucked in at night by somebody you love and you just don't ever wake up. None of us get to call our own shot, but that wouldn't be such bad way to go."

"No, it could have been worse."

I was thinking the peach cobbler on the buffet looked inviting and was about to ask the deputy if she might like some, when she said, "Do you believe in heaven?"

"I do."

"You think my mama—"

"I do."

"But she was . . . she was a hard person. She lived a hard life, made some terrible hard choices."

I waited for her to say more, but she didn't, so I said, "Tell me your name."

She looked up at that, surprised. "What you need my name for?"

"Because we're talking about something important and personal, and I don't even know your name."

"It's Wanda. Wanda Cherice Stovall, but people call me Wanda. What's yours?"

"Buddy. Well, it's Judah Bennie Hinton, but people call me Buddy. It's nice to meet you, Wanda."

"It's nice to meet you, too, Reverend."

"You can just call me Buddy."

"All right."

We chewed a little, and when the waitress came to ask if we needed anything I asked my new friend Wanda if we had time for a cup of coffee. She said we did, and when the waitress left to get it I got us both some cobbler.

I said, "Wanda, did your mother love you?"

She was indignant that I could ask such a question. "Of course she did!"

I interrupted her indignation to ask, "Where did she get that love from?"

"What?"

"Where did that love come from? Where does any love come from?"

"It's . . . it's just the way we're made, I guess."

"Yes, it is. We're too mean and selfish to love somebody else unless it's part of how we're made. You go out and get all in the middle of the mean part of people, the fighting and fussing and cussing. If that's all there was to people, we'd have killed each other off thousands of years ago. But there's more. There's love. That's why I believe in God, I think: because there's love, even in the meanest of us, even in the craziest of us, even in the hardest of us. God made us to love, and God loves all of us forever, no matter what."

"You serious?"

"I'm absolutely serious."

"What about sin?"

"What about it?"

"Well, I mean—I've heard other preachers, most other preachers, you know, like the ones who remember to say the blessing, they talk about sin all the time. It's all about sin, and judgment, and repentance, and salvation. If you sin too much, and if you don't repent, God ain't gonna let you into heaven. And my mama . . . Mama was a hard woman, Reverend."

"But she loved you. She loved."

"But she didn't repent! She wasn't ever saved!"

She said this a little too loudly, so that some of the other diners looked over at us. I said, "It's God that saves us, not us. God loves your mama whether she repented or not. It's not a limited time offer; God will always love your mother and will always want her to love him, even after she passed."

"So you're sayin'—you're sayin' . . . what are you sayin'?"

"I'm saying that Jesus came to save us all—all the saints, all the sinners. We are all saved by God's grace in Jesus Christ, whether we deserve it or not."

There was a long pause as she thought about all of this, and I had a sip of coffee that was well on its way toward a career in roof repair. I waited, and at last she said, "I've never heard no preacher say nothin' like this before. You sure about it?"

"I believe it. I'm betting my life on it."

She was clearly thinking about it, wondering if it could be true, entertaining the idea that Christianity might be about love and grace and not about judgment and condemnation. I thought about one of my favorite books, C. S. Lewis's *The Great Divorce*, and considered telling her about it, but then I thought that the bus from hell to heaven, with the people deciding they'd rather get back on the bus and go to hell rather than accept grace, might be a fatal distraction.

I decided I'd just steal the line I wanted, hoping it would be a forgivable conversational plagiarism: "There are only two kinds of people in the end: those who say to God, 'Thy will be done,' and those to whom God says, in the end, 'Thy will be done.' All that are in hell, choose it."

"Who would choose hell?"

"Those who don't want to choose love. People who think having power, or being filled with hate, or being in control, or wallowing in bigotry, or being wealthy, is more important than loving and being loved."

We sat there for a minute or two until she said it was time to go. We got up, I paid the bill, and we left. A few miles down the road, I asked, "So what do you think?"

She replied, "I don't know."

"Don't know what?"

"I don't know if you're a nut or if you're some kind of holy man."

"Yeah, well—I guess sometimes it's hard to tell."

We rode a while, and I slept most of the way home. When we were coming into West Branch, Wanda woke me and asked where she should drop me off. I told her my car was at the church, and she asked me where it was. "It's on Main Street, down by Dobbs Funeral Home. It's the second-oldest church in town."

"That big Baptist church?"

"Right across the street from it."

"There's a church there?"

"Yes ma'am. It's been there your whole life."

So she dropped me by the church. As I got out of the squad car I said, "Thank you, Wanda. I enjoyed meeting you."

She said, "Thank you, Reverend—Buddy. I'll . . . see you soon."

And as good as her word, she was in church the next Sunday, and the Sunday after that, and somewhere along the line she caught the eye of a fine young man named JoJo McCain, but that's another story.

The Sermon

The capture and arrest of John the Baptist Cahill, dangerous fugitive, was the talk of the town for a week or two, until it was supplanted by the anticipation of the Christmas season. I tried to tell a couple of people that he was never captured or arrested, and that he wasn't in any way dangerous, but it didn't fit into the story they wanted to hear, so they kept getting their information from sources less reliable but more entertaining.

In mid-December, I was surprised when Beulah and Ward came into my office with a wrapped present. They told me they had an early Christmas present for me, and that I should open it right then and there. I did and found a cassette tape labeled "The Sermon."

It seems that the television cameraman was a little miffed that I had forbidden his bringing the big television camera into church the morning after we'd snuck John the Baptist out through Mrs. Caruthers's shed and had slipped some sort of tape recorder into his pocket to record the service anyway. "Mostly a passive-aggressive rebellion against authority," said Ward, who'd apparently been reading a little psychology.

"So when Ward heard about it," continued Beulah, "we got the guy at the TV station to make us a copy, and then Wanda at the sheriff's department converted it to this cassette." She looked at me as if she'd given me something of great value, and was disappointed that I wasn't as excited as she was.

I tried to fake some excitement of my own and said, "Hey, great—thanks!" I couldn't imagine anything more boring than listening to me preaching.

She went on, "It's really good."

"I'm glad."

"I want you to listen to it." I knew I would have to. I argued a little more, just for the form of it, but all three of us knew I'd wind up listening to the recording. And when I did, I thought it was pretty good. Even recorded, even listening to my own voice, I could hear the magic.

I've cleaned it up a little, and left out some fumbling around and a couple of times when I stumbled over the words I was trying to say, but this is the sermon from that day, pretty nearly word for word.

In the Name of God: Father, Son and Holy Spirit, Amen. Please be seated.

"God is our refuge and strength, a very present help in trouble. Therefore we will not fear, though the earth be moved, and though the mountains be toppled into the depths of the sea. Though its waters rage and foam, and though the mountains tremble at its tumult, the LORD of hosts is with us; the God of Jacob is our stronghold."

Well, it's been an exciting morning around here, with the police and the reporters all gathered around to see what was going to happen when John the Baptist tried to prepare the way of the Lord in West Branch, Mississippi. And you think he was crazy, right? Some kind of religious nut. You heard he was dangerous, that he had a bomb, that he pulled a gun on Father Buddy. You heard he was dirty, and that he smelled bad, that he talked funny, that he'd been in Vietnam and there's no telling what might have happened to him over there!

We love a good story, don't we? We love a story about somebody hurting and desperate to make sense out of things, a story about somebody on the edge of sanity, just barely holding on. Look at the TV programs we watch, about murder and greed and lust, programs with impossibly beautiful people we love to hate. We love to hate. We love to be afraid. We love to look down on people we think are not as good as we are. And here comes a man into our hometown claiming to be John the Baptist, straight out of the Bible—has to be some kind of nut. Of course we're going to find reasons to hate him, to fear him, to look down on him. It's what we love to do.

Yeah, I wonder what we would have thought about John the Baptist two thousand years ago, wearing garments made out of camel skin, eating locusts and wild honey. Have you ever been around a camel? They're nasty, stinky animals. I can't imagine walking around in camel skins. And you know locusts are bugs, right? Like grasshoppers—the guy was eating grasshoppers! I wonder what stories we would have told about him. "He's crazy, some kind of religious nut. I heard he was dirty, and that he smelled bad—like camels—that he talked funny, that he's from the other side of the Jordan, and there's no telling what might have happened to him over there."

So what if John the Baptist came in and sat down with you, maybe invited you to watch the squirrels playing in your front yard. What would you do? Tell him to go away? Call the police? You think we'd find reasons to hate him, to be afraid of him, to look down on him? Yeah, I'm pretty sure we would.

What if Jesus the Savior walked in that door right back there and wanted to sit in here with us? You know Jesus didn't talk like we do, either. He probably didn't take a shower every day, probably never went to the dentist. I don't think they had dental floss back then, did they? You think if Jesus came back we could find some reason to hate, to be afraid, to look down on him? Yeah, I'm pretty sure we would.

Or maybe we would just try to ignore him. We do that pretty easily, too.

What if Jesus was more like that poor man who we all tried so hard to ignore, that John Cahill who served his country in Vietnam, who lost his precious little daughter to a terrible disease that took her away when she was only twelve years old? What if Jesus was somebody like that? Would we ignore him, too?

You think we could? You think we could ignore Jesus if we wanted to? Yeah, I think we could. I think we do. If we can't get Jesus to fit into the little boxes we have reserved for him, I think we ignore him all the time. I think we feel better about Jesus when we can put him in little boxes.

Jesus, meek and mild—check.

Baby Jesus, laid in a manger—check.

Jesus at the right hand of the Father—check.

Jesus with cute little children all around him—check.

Jesus ascending into heaven—check.

Jesus holding a sweet white lamb—check.

We like that Jesus. He makes us feel better about ourselves. But there are other boxes, too—boxes we don't like to think about.

Jesus so angry he turned over the tables in the temple—uh, no thanks. I'd rather not think about that.

Jesus telling Peter to get behind him, out of his way, for thinking as people think and not as God wants us to think—uh, no.

Jesus writhing in pain on the cross—no thank you. I really don't want to think about that.

Jesus telling the religious leaders of the day that they were hypocrites and blind guides, leading their people astray—no thanks.

Jesus saying we should forgive our enemies, that we should pray for those who persecute us, that we need to turn the other cheek; Jesus telling us we will need to take up our own cross to follow him, that the first will be last, that we must lose our lives to gain them—no.

Yeah, I think we do a pretty good job of ignoring Jesus, even in our churches. We have reduced all of Christianity to a system of "thou shalts" and "thou shalt nots," so much that we lose the central idea that Jesus came to bring, that it's all about the grace and love of God. We make it all about being good little girls and boys, so that we earn the love of God, so that we don't burn in hell, so that the preachers—blind guides—can keep us in line, keep us coming to church and putting money in the plate. We ignore Jesus so we can make it about us, and not about the love of God.

Because if it's about the love of God, and if the love of God is truly unconditional and without limits, we'll have to let go of the pitiful illusion that we are in charge, that we're in control, and then we'd have to trust God instead of trusting ourselves. And that would be scary, wouldn't it? We'd have to trust God, even if we don't understand everything he does, even if we can't prove it or make it make sense.

And when a tornado strikes, and when there are wars, and when a little girl dies, we'd have to put our trust not in our feeble ability to make sense out of the whole infinite universe, but in a God we cannot see or touch or count or prove—we would have to have faith.

Right about now, I'm thinking that some of you who go to other fine churches here in town might be wondering if this is how Episcopalians think and talk, and it may be a relief to you and some of your Episcopal friends for me to tell you that it's not, for most of us. I think I'm a little off-script this morning. You might be thinking that you already have faith, thank you very much, and that you do trust God. I hope you do. I hope I do, too.

I hope you have faith in God, and that you trust Jesus, so that you love your enemies, so that you turn the other cheek, so that you give to all who beg from you, so that you do not judge lest you also are judged, just like Jesus told his followers to do. I'm not sure I have that much faith, at least not all the time, but I hope you do.

I hope you expect God to forgive you as much as you forgive others, like we say in the Lord's Prayer. I hope you live your lives rejoicing that God loves all of his children, no more and no less than God loves you—even the Jews and the Muslims and the Hindus and the Buddhists and the atheists; even the Ole Miss fans; even the people who voted for the candidates you voted against; even the people who don't look like you, talk like you, believe like you, act like you, smell like you, think like you; even the people who don't like you. I'd like to have that much faith, and I hope you would, too.

I hope you have faith enough to know that every other person is your sister or your brother, that, as an old friend of mine used to say, "Ain't nobody no better than you, and you ain't no better than anybody else." I hope you have the faith to hear me say that and know it to be true: you are no better than anyone else.

I wonder what our churches would be like if we actually had the faith we claim to have. You think we'd spend so much time worrying about money if we really trusted God? You think we'd fuss and fight about whether somebody has to be dunked all the way under the water to be baptized, or whether the Blood of Christ has to be wine or grape juice, if we really believed all this stuff? You think we would care who's a Baptist and who's a Methodist or a Presbyterian or a Roman Catholic or an Episcopalian if we really trusted God?

You think God really gives a rip about any of that stuff?

I wonder what it would be like if we came on Sunday mornings, not out of obligation or fear or guilt or duty or habit, but in the joy of the Lord, coming together to celebrate the love of God and bring other people into that celebration. Can you imagine that? At the end of the service, asking the organist to play another one, just because we enjoyed singing together so much? Or at the end of the sermon, being disappointed that it's over? Can you just hear somebody in the pews yelling out "Keep preaching!" when the sermon ends? Does that happen at your church? It's never happened here, as far as I know.

Well, I don't know if we'll ever do that, but how different would our worship be if we came together not because we're afraid, or guilty, or trying to get our ticket to heaven punched, but to celebrate the love of God, to celebrate being the beloved of God, the redeemed of Christ, the children of the King of heaven and earth?

There was a long pause; apparently I was taking a moment or two to figure out what I was going to say next. Maybe I was thinking I shouldn't have said some of what I'd just said.

A few weeks ago I saw a man sitting on the steps of this church, and he asked me to sit and watch the squirrels playing in those big trees out front. After a while he told me he was John the Baptist, and you know, I thought he was a nut. Of course I did! But we talked, and I listened, and I learned a little bit about him. His name is John Cahill. His wife's name is Suellen, and their young daughter Callie died from an infection in her blood that got terribly out of control.

He wanted me to tell him why God let his little girl die.

He wanted me to make sense out of the worst day of his life.

He wanted me to help him understand, and I couldn't, because I don't understand, either.

He wanted Jesus to come back, to make it right, to make it better.

He was the voice of one crying in the wilderness.

He got a little confused about Martin Luther, the sixteenth-century German reformer, and Martin Luther King Jr., the twentieth-century civil rights leader, and wrote out ninety-five theses and tacked them to the door of this church. I think the ninety-five Theses of John Cahill are like the man who wrote them—a mix of brilliance and baloney. I guess that's like you and me, too, you think? Maybe that's the best we can do—a mix of brilliance and baloney.

But he never had a gun or a bomb; he never wanted to hurt anybody. He just wanted somebody to listen to him. I wish I'd listened to him more. I think John was trying to do what we should all do: prepare the way for Jesus to come into the world. He was mixed up about that, too, but he was trying to do the right thing, which is more than I can say about me most of the time. He was a voice crying in the wilderness, "Make straight the way for the Lord."

Lord, please help us believe what we say we believe. Give us faith to trust you with our lives, even when we don't understand what's going on—especially when we don't understand what's going on. Help us to look for you within ourselves, in our families and friends, and in those who might seem least likely. Give us grace to prepare a place for you in our hearts and in our lives.

We've come together this morning for a lot of different reasons, but one of those reasons, at least for some of us, is to find out what happened. I'll tell you: I snuck John Cahill out a back way so that he didn't have to come through a big bunch of people who thought he was just a religious nut to look down on, as if he wasn't a person, too. He's on his way down to south Mississippi, to be reunited with his wife. The only crime he could be charged with is defacing the front door of this church, and we're not pressing charges.

So some of us came to hear the end of the story, just for the curiosity of it. But now you're here, and I hope you'll stay as we celebrate the mystery, the mystery of being faithful, in the mystery of our Lord's death and resurrection in the Lord's Supper, the

Eucharist. I hope you'll join us in offering yourselves into the mystery of God, and into the love and service of Jesus Christ our Lord.
Thanks be to God. Amen.

I did remember the next part when I heard it on tape, and I had to laugh along with the congregation when I heard my friend Ward call out, "Keep preaching!"

Postlude

Early in the new year, I came home late after a long and trying committee meeting and tiptoed into our room to find Jude cuddled up with Beulah, both of them sound asleep. Jabbok was snoring on the floor on her side of the bed; she always slept in the same room as her puppy Jude. I tried to get into bed as quietly as possible, but Beulah woke up anyway. She asked me if I was okay, and I stretched the truth a little and told her I was fine. Actually, I was frustrated and impatient and more than a little insecure. Usually she sees right through me, but she let it pass this time, and reached for something on her bedside table. "This came for you today."

It was an envelope from St. Thomas Episcopal Church in Greene, Alabama. She said "They're looking for a new rector; your friend Rusty put your name in." Rusty was a seminary classmate who had several times through the years tried to get me to move to Alabama, where he was a priest at a large church in Birmingham.

It was starting to feel like maybe I ought to consider moving to a new parish—not because of the conflict I suppose is inevitable at any parish, but because for the most part things were just too comfortable, bordering on stale. A few churches had inquired whether I might be interested, but so far there hadn't been anything I'd wanted to pursue. It was unusual that Beulah had taken an interest in this one, and I asked her about it. "Did you read their information?"

"Yep. A college friend lives in Greene, so I called her this afternoon and we had a good chat. She's a Methodist, but she's heard that St. Thomas is a great church. They do a lot in the community. It's bigger than Holy Incarnation, maybe twice as big."

"Jeez, I don't know—that's probably even more committee meetings, wouldn't you think?"

"It would probably be a raise, too. That might come in handy around here pretty soon."

"What's that mean?" I'm not always the first one to pick up a hint.

"Well, I'm not sure, but I think we might be adding another family member here soon."

"A baby?"

"Yes!" She was excited. I was trying on the idea, letting it become real a little bit at a time.

"Another one?"

"Yes." She was determined to be patient with me. "We're going to have a baby. Another one."

And then the excitement hit me in a torrent—I was going to have two children and I was in love with my wife and life would never ever be the same.

After a while, after that first wave of excitement lifted us and carried us to a new place, Beulah asked whether I would consider the church in Alabama. I told her I'd think about it, but that I wasn't sure about leaving Mississippi.

"Why?"

"Because it's home. Because I love Mississippi, and the Diocese of Mississippi. Because I'm known in the diocese, I'm a summer camp director, I'm on the Standing Committee." Then, a little more honestly, "Because it's all I've ever known."

"It would be an adventure to go to a new diocese, wouldn't it?"

"Yeah, I guess. But Beulah—"

"Yes, my precious?"

"Why would they want me? I mean, I can tell a story, but . . . ."

"I think it's like you said in that sermon, you know, the one they recorded that day after the John the Baptist Incident—you really believe all this stuff."

I was still thinking about that when she added, "Or maybe it's because you have such a fabulous wife."

"Yeah, that's probably it."

And I really do.

Made in the USA
Coppell, TX
25 March 2022

75492637R00174